THE LOST GIRLS

KATE HAMER

THE
LOST
GIRLS

faber

First published in the UK in 2023
by Faber & Faber Ltd
Bloomsbury House
74–77 Great Russell Street
London wc1b 3da

Typeset by Faber & Faber Ltd
Printed and bound by CPI Group (UK) Ltd, Croydon cr0 4yy

'Three Kinds of Pleasure' from *Silence in the Snowy Fields* © 1962 by Robert Bly.
Published by Wesleyan University Press. Used by permission

The New England Cookbook by Staff Home Economists. Published by
the Culinary Arts Institute, Chicago, Illinois 60616
Copyright © 1965, 1956 by Processing and Books, Inc.

A CIP record for this book
is available from the British Library

isbn 978–0–571–33671–5

MIX
Paper | Supporting
responsible forestry
FSC® C171272

Printed and bound in the UK on FSC paper in line with our continuing
commitment to ethical business practices, sustainability and the environment.
For further information see faber.co.uk/environmental–policy

2 4 6 8 10 9 7 5 3 1

THE LOST GIRLS

No one ever knew what happened to Mercy Roberts.

Although after she left her Appalachian home and had been gone a good while she still sometimes drifted through people's thoughts like a trail of smoke from a bonfire.

Sheila from The Cherry on the Cake bakery store would insert her tongue delicately but precisely in the mauve buttercream of one of her own blueberry cupcakes, making a perfect triangular groove. She would look out through the window onto their single main street as the sweet gloop dissolved in her mouth and remember how Mercy was also particularly partial to blueberry cupcakes.

Tony, a man now, thought of her as he threaded bait on his fishing line because he'd shown her how to do the exact same thing down at the pond. The image of her thin little arms as she threw the line and it wicking across the surface of the water was a stamp in his memory. She'd turned to him, beaming, because she'd done it perfect first time.

Bob, in the grocery store, would occasionally shift on his feet uncomfortably as he stood behind the counter, and remember her high five, her funny little eyebrows like window arches rising up as she performed it. He should've paid closer attention, he rebuked himself. He shouldn't have been so worried about interfering. But his wife had been sick with cancer at the time and although she'd now made a full recovery, he'd been too distracted to pay much attention. Besides, the town had changed so much. New people had come, old people had gone, everything shifting into fresh patterns so the place that Mercy had filled became smaller and smaller, less significant.

Miss Forbouys, with her rows of little ones in the classroom, would sometimes think of Mercy when she carried out her customary practice of putting some music on the old-fashioned record player at the end of each day when she was tired to the bone. She remembered how Mercy always did love the devotional music in particular, even though Miss Forbouys wasn't sure if she was really allowed to play it in school. But heck, music was music and her children should be introduced to all the good things in the world, wherever they sprang from. How Mercy had loved it, her little feet in their shoes with cut-off toes tapping away under her desk in time to the rhythm.

Miss Forbouys would at this point give a shake of her head. At least she'd had nothing to do with it all, she told herself. Something had stopped her becoming part of the whole enterprise and she was glad of it now. *That* she couldn't have lived with.

Mercy

1999, West Virginia

The day Mercy was saved she stood on the front porch and hollered in through the broken window of the bedroom.

'Ma, Father. I've been saved!'

Silence. The hole in the glass was pretty much where her mouth was so she knew her voice must've sounded in the room good and loud.

'Lazy asses,' she muttered. They were probably still asleep even though it was well gone noon. Inside would be shuttered up and dark, the malfunctioning microwave light blinking on and off in the kitchen-diner. Either they were asleep, or they were inside and ignoring the good news, probably because it highlighted the fact that they were no more likely to be saved than the spider weaving its fine, tiny web in the corner of the front door. It occurred to Mercy that perhaps they were even afraid and sorrowful a mere eight-year-old girl like herself would fly like a bird into heaven's kingdom and they would never get to see the shining gates, not even a gleam of them. In truth that made her somewhat sorrowful too.

She turned away from the wooden shack with its rickety porch and set off down the dirt path that led to the river where she had a hope of meeting Tony, her friend, and telling him the good news. She knew for sure he'd want to hear all about it.

As she walked along the road the joy she'd felt earlier returned, only now it had taken on a kind of shimmering quality that was outside and inside her at the same time – whereas before it was only contained inside. Now it had become beautiful to both feel and behold.

The mountain trees either side of the road seemed lit with a perfect kind of light. She looked down at her yellow cotton skirt and her skinny legs and the blue shoes, which, despite the fact they were opened up at the toe with a knife because they had grown too small, were still comfortable to walk in and in which she could get along pretty well. Though if she went *too* fast the ends of her toes tapped painfully on the dusty road so that fact gave her a problem on occasion.

Then she heard the noise of a car engine behind her and as it came closer she realised it was slowing down. Sure enough, a red truck came up alongside and the engine idled down to a steady beat as it stopped. She could only see the reflections of the trees on the window so it was impossible to see who was inside. Slowly, the window wound down and first off, all she could see was a battered suede hat with a leather thong around the crown, and then it got wound down further so it was completely open and she could see the face.

She felt her own face practically splitting in two in a grin. 'Bob,' she said, joy in her voice.

He cut off the engine and grinned back.

Bob owned his own store, The Full Cart, down in the tiny town on the outskirts of the mountain forest. It was where Mercy got pretty much everything they needed. She went with her two big plastic shopping bags with diamond patterns on the side and writing that shouted, 'Happy Shopping!' She'd used them for so long the handles had got cracked and crispy. After Bob filled them with groceries, he always seemed to find a way to put a little something extra in, a Peanut Butter Cup or more rarely – as Bob said they were hard to come by – a Whistling Pop that played real music, both of which Mercy was unsure if they were really included in the scope of food stamps.

He'd wink at her when he dropped these items in and she'd grin back and say, 'Happy Shopping!'

Then he always asked, 'You wanna wait and let me run you home?' as she picked up the bags to leave. 'Those bags are near bigger than you.'

But she'd always wave at him no.

'Don't you worry about me. My muscles are pretty strong.' She didn't think Ma and Pa would like seeing her get down from his truck outside the house, bringing people to their door.

Besides, she always liked the walk back through the quiet forest way, the dirt path that smelled so sweet, and the birds that sang their tiny heads off as if she wasn't there. If she had to stop and rest every once in a while because the bags were heavy and her arms were tired, what did it matter? There was no place she had to be and she could suck on the Whistling Pop in peace. First off, she made it sing away to the birds for half an hour until it got filled up with spit and stopped working. Only then she'd lick on the sweetness for another hour until just a soggy white stick was left and her lips and tongue were stained bright red or purple or orange.

Now when she saw Bob's truck it gave her the chance to tell someone else about the thing that had just happened and she knew he'd surely be pleased.

'Bob,' she said. 'I've been saved!'

He nodded up and down. 'Uh, huh, is that the case?'

'It is, Bob. You know, it's wonderful.'

She felt the need to convince him because he wasn't seeming happy enough about it.

'Uh, huh,' he said again. 'You been down to the tent revival then?'

'I sure have. You should go too, Bob. It's wonderful.'

'It's been there for a while now.'

'Yep, but they're saving for a real church now, made of stones that'll be around forever.'

'Uh, huh.'

This seemed about the only thing he was capable of saying and truth be told she started to get a little restless. She wanted to get down to the river so she could tell Tony and she thought he might be a little more enthusiastic than Bob was being. She felt like she might explode with joy if she just carried on standing there. She upended her foot and dragged her toes up and down the gravelly dirt of the road for the pain to take her mind off exploding.

'Well,' he said finally, when she thought she couldn't wait in that silence with only the birds singing round them a minute longer. 'I guess it don't do no harm, maybe.'

She was aghast at his statement. 'No harm? Bob, I told you, it's wonderful, like being filled up with honey.'

Something in his face went soft then. 'Sure. I'm sure it is. Plus, I like you went to church with that dirty face.'

He started laughing then, a deep chuckling laugh, but she didn't think what he'd just said was funny, not funny at all.

She put her hands up. 'I have a dirty face?'

He stopped laughing. 'Oh, come now. It doesn't matter. It's a pretty little face and no amount of dirt can alter that fact.'

'But I went to church with a dirty face?' She felt like she might start crying.

'Now then, no one in the circumstances would worry about the condition of your face, not one bit. Tell you what, next time you come by the shop I'll drop a couple of those packs of towelettes in the Happy Shopping! bags. How about that? Then you can clean that pretty little face whenever you like.'

That wasn't the point. The point was she'd gone to church looking like a bad and unspeakable person. She felt a tear come loose out of her eye and run down that dirt on her cheek. It got stuck at her chin and hung there.

Bob looked distressed. 'Oh, Lord. There's no need for that. Look, I gotta pack of tissues somewhere here.'

He ducked down to look for them in his glove box and while he wasn't looking at her something occurred to Mercy that calmed her so quick it was like she'd just floated back down to earth with a bump.

'Hey, Bob, it's OK.' She dashed the tear off her chin.

He was holding the pack of tissues out through the open window and she took them anyway 'cos when you refuse to take something someone is so gladly offering it can be a mean thing.

'It is?' he asked, looking relieved.

'Sure it is. 'Cos, something has just come to me, and it feels like the truth right in here.' She thumped herself lightly on the chest.

'What's that then, Delia?'

She realised then that she hadn't told him about not being called Delia anymore but the other thing had to come first. She'd tell him another time.

'It's when you are filled up with God's love it really don't matter about a bit of old dirt. God sees my face as all shiny and new like it's just been made. He don't care one speck about the dirt.'

She grinned and like God, she really didn't care about the dirt either anymore.

Bob's blue eyes went all soft then. For a funny moment she thought *he* was going to cry.

'Bob, you OK?'

'Sure, sure I am.'

'You wanna get yourself down that tent some time, Bob. I think you'll like it.'

'Maybe I even will, Delia.' He smiled and she was relieved he was back to being Bob again. 'The only thing being,' he went on slowly, 'well, you be careful now, won't you?'

'Careful?'

'Yep, some of those visiting preachers can be real snake oil salesmen.'

She puzzled over this for a moment. She was familiar with the local snakes – the black ratsnake, the hognose and the poisonous copperhead – but as far as she knew none of them produced oil. Perhaps that's what happened if you squeezed them, like the grease coming out of a pork chop if you pressed the back of your fork into it. Mercy hadn't had a pork chop in a long while and just the thought of it made her mouth water and her stomach growl so she shook her head so she wouldn't think of it anymore.

'Well, gotta go,' she said, putting the tissues in the pocket of her skirt.

He started up the engine. 'OK, bye, Delia. Remember what I said though.'

She started walking off but lifted her arm up so he could see her waving from behind. 'Bye, Bob.'

'Hey, Delia,' he called after her.

She turned. 'Yah?'

'Don't forget about those towelettes, will you. You remind me next time you come to the store. My memory ain't what it used to be.'

'Sure thing, Bob.'

She waved as he drove past, then his truck was gone and it was just the smoke from it left on the road. She played with it for a while, walking through it, parting it with her body till that went too and she remembered about setting off to the river and looking for Tony.

The path through the woods was steep. Going downhill made the flapping front of her shoes dig into the soft earth and the soil got in and felt gritty underneath her feet. She made a decision not to empty them out till she got to the river though because they were only going to get filled up over and over again. She longed to put her gritty feet in the water and feel the balm of it reaching right up to the roots of her hair.

She scrambled down the rest of the path, anticipating that moment, until below her she could see the river that ran alongside the river bed and the big green pool it fed and ran out of, so it always reminded her of a skinny worm that had eaten something huge that was stuck in its belly. Everything was bathed in a shaft of sweet golden light that drenched the scene. Her breath stopped, being in the presence of such beauty, then she spotted Tony, standing by the side of the water with his fishing line and she forgot about being quiet.

'Hey, Tony,' she yelled, waving. 'Over here.'

He squinted up into the trees. 'Tony, Tony. I'm here.' She could tell he still couldn't see her so she crashed down and exploded out of the trees at the bottom.

'Delia.' He smiled and took one hand away from his fishing line to wave.

'Hey, Tony. I'm glad to see you.'

'Yeah?' He turned back to his fishing. He was always real calm, Tony. Sometimes she wondered if it was all the fishing he did or if he was just born like that. He was eleven years old and much bigger than her but he didn't seem to mind being her friend. He spent a lot of time on his own down here. He was a bit fat round the middle, so his stripy T-shirt was raised up and showed his belly button. He generally looked hot, even if there was a chill in the air. Today his plump cheeks were bright red and the hair on his temples was wet with sweat. He readjusted himself around his fishing line.

'You been somewhere, Delia?'

She hopped on the rock next to him to take off her shoes. He often seemed to be able to tell things about her.

'Sure. How did you know?'

'I'm not sure. You look a little different.'

She opened her arms wide. 'Is there light coming out of me all around?'

He smiled. 'Well, I'm not sure I'd say exactly that, but kind of.'

She unbuckled her shoes and set them next to her.

'Your feet are near black, Delia. Stick them in the water to wash.'

'Yep, that's what I was about to do.' She dangled them over the edge into the green water and a feeling of sheer pleasure at the cool slipperiness of it engulfed her.

'So you going to tell me what's going on?' asked Tony.

'Sure, I've been saved by the blood of Lord Jesus Christ this very morning.'

He cocked one eye up at her. 'You been to the tent?'

'Uh, huh.'

'And you been saved?'

'Yep.'

'What was it like?'

She went quiet for a little, remembering. 'They called people up front. They said, anyone here who wishes to be saved can do so, right now, for free. All we had to do was walk right up, have people pray over us and put their hands on our heads.'

'Who was with you?'

'No one.'

'Then who were the others you went up with?'

'Just other folk there. I kind of tagged on to them.'

'Then what happened?'

It was hard to describe what happened next. 'Tony, you

know like this water is all lit up by the sun coming down from the sky?'

'Yep.'

'You see how it makes it sparkle like it's dancing?'

'Sure.'

'Well, that's what happened to me. I still can feel it and that feeling is never going away.'

'How d'you know?'

'I just know.'

It was Tony's turn to go quiet then, mulling over what she'd just told him. 'You tell your parents?'

'I tried but they weren't listening.'

'They might not like it.'

'They won't care.'

'No, I guess not. They still taking the needle?'

'Yep.'

'Maybe one day they'll stop,' he said kindly.

'Mmm. Don't think so. Think they like it too much.'

She splashed her feet up and down in the green water and sure enough the dirt began to melt away and the skin came up all pink and new like a baby.

She remembered something else then. She could hardly believe she'd forgotten it!

'Hey, Tony.'

'Uh, huh.'

'Don't call me Delia no more?'

'I like that name.'

'No, you mustn't. I've remembered now. The lady with the preacher asked me my full name and I told her, Mercy Roberts—'

'Your real name is Mercy?'

'Yep, and—'

'I never knew that fact.'

'Yep, it is; no one but school calls me that but it's my real honest to goodness name Ma and Pa gave me when I was born. Delia's my mom's name and they used to call me "little Delia" 'cos when I was little I looked just like her and acted like her and Pa said I even tried to speak like her. I followed her everywhere two steps behind and that name just got stuck. But when I told the lady in church about really being Mercy she said, "That's a real godly, beautiful name," and she said maybe I should think about calling myself that from now on instead of Delia which is somewhat heathen. So from now on in I'm back to being Mercy with everyone, even you and Ma and Pa.'

'I hear they often give people new names. Must be kind of hard to remember who you are,' he said softly.

But she wasn't listening. She'd pulled her feet out of the water and was inspecting them. 'Hey look, Tony, all clean.'

He smiled. 'Good as new.'

She let her toes dry in the sun for a bit before putting her shoes back on.

'Your feet are just gonna get dirty again with those holes in front,' he said.

'But I'm going *uphill* on the way back so it won't get into the holes in the same way.'

'I never thought about that. I guess coming downhill they act a bit like shovels.'

'You're right.' She liked that about Tony. He often came up with things that were kind of scientific.

13

She jumped off the rock and set off back up the path, giving her characteristic wave that was always seen from behind because she was so set on the next place to be.

'Bye, Tony.'

There was quiet for a moment, then he said, 'Bye, *Mercy*.'

She looked over her shoulder and gave him a huge, happy grin.

Carmel

2013, London

The lost girls; sometimes I feel like their representative on earth.

Often, I long to gather them up like chicks and watch over them in a brood. Other times, they're too much. I can feel their little feet running all over me. Their beaks in my mouth, my eyes, and I want to shake them off, violently.

I used to cut out and keep their pictures from the papers. I would study their faces for any trace they could tell what was going to happen to them. They could be standing in front of a bike, grinning, a scab on one knee; or in the back seat of a car, two fingers hooked into the corners of their mouth to stretch the grin; or more often a simple school head-and-shoulders shot – but whatever the scenario I never did find anything, no clues at all. They were innocent of their fate. Then one day I realised it was an unhealthy hobby and threw the cuttings all away. Mercy Roberts I knew was a lost girl too but I never had a newspaper cutting for her, so in a way she was easier not to think about.

There was a photograph of me that was used by the news programmes and the papers while I was *gone*. The picture was taken in a park. I'm seated on a bench in my red coat and looking a little to the right, dreamy as always. It is only now I think it, that perhaps there's something in *my* face – the gaze into the long distance, as if I was looking at my future and already had a stirring of what it might be? I was one of the lucky ones; I got unlost and returned like a parcel that spent five long years at the wrong address. My return was supposed to involve hugs and kisses and rainbows exploding into multicoloured droplets and big, fat pink hearts. But one thing I've learned is being *unlost* is not the same as being found.

In a film there is always an act towards the end where the story has reached its climax, the most dangerous point. Afterwards there's the final scene where all is resolved. They are all healed, the story goes! Then the characters turn into sunlight, vanish into their futures and there is a breathless pause as the screen turns dark.

That's where I live now, in the darkness of the cinema, the blank screen, that moment.

There is no ending.

The night after I turn twenty-one finds me lying in bed listening to something moving inside the wall.

When I was a kidnapped kid living in the back of a truck, I often used to be cold at night and I developed a method of piling up my bed with layers of anything to hand – my jumper, a cushion, a religious tract – and making a nest for warmth. I've never lost that habit, so when I hear the *scribble, scrabble* from in my bedroom wall I have to move the folded newspaper from my ear to listen properly.

'Who are you?' I mouth.

It starts again, like it wants to send messages. There's

a clawing inside the wall, then turning, something stuck inside a small space. I turn over and look at the ceiling and the paraphernalia on my bed shifts like tectonic plates. Before we moved to London I gathered injured things – birds with broken wings, cats found at the side of the road that had been hit by a car – and looked after them before I sent them on their way, and I wonder if the scrabbler might be in need of help like that.

In the morning I go downstairs and Mum's back from her nursing shift. She must've been smoking and chucked her rollie out of the window when she heard me coming down because the space above the sink is fogged with smoke. We smile at each other, though neither of us say, *We both know we can't carry on like this. It's killing us.* We are too tender and careful with each other for that.

The scrabbling starts again at midnight.

I sit up in bed and stare at the wall. 'Who are you?' I whisper again.

The noise stops for a moment like it's heard me.

'We need to meet,' I say.

There's an old-fashioned hardware store two streets away and in the morning I go to look at the mousetraps. I find them under a jumble of drain cleaner and plungers for unplugging sinks. I pick up and examine each one. Many of them have a little chopper designed to break necks and bash tiny brains out. I buy them all so the killing ones can't be used. The one I'll use is humane. It's like a tiny cage with a sprung trap on one end. I take the pile of traps to pay.

'Got some little visitors?' asks the man, looking at all the traps over his counter.

'Yes,' I say, and pay him and he drops the traps one by one in a large brown paper bag, then I bin them all except the humane one on my way to work.

In the café I keep thinking of the trap ready and waiting in my duffel bag as I'm rolling knives and forks in red paper napkins and with a damp cloth wiping tears of ketchup where they've stuck onto the necks of plastic bottles. I help Doris count out the money from her purse to pay for her egg and chips because she can't see well enough to know which coin is which. Then I cash up and take the money to the bank on the way home and the guy behind the counter tries to flirt with me, but I'm not interested so I turn my eyes to stones and he stops.

In the house Mum is already at it, ironing her nurse's uniform for her night shift though I don't know why; it's made of some kind of drip-dry material and doesn't really need ironing.

She puts the iron down before I have a chance to get my coat off.

'Carmel, you would tell me if something was wrong?' she asks. There are tiny rainbows caught inside her glass earrings.

We're both quiet for a moment. 'I can't think of anything specific,' I say finally.

'OK,' she smiles. 'But you would tell me if there was, wouldn't you? You can tell me anything, you know.'

What I really want to do is throw my arms around her and hug on to her, but I can't. I couldn't. I might end up squeezing the life out of her.

That night I bait the trap with a lump of chocolate and switch off the light and lie in bed. The London glow that never goes away reflects on my shelves and makes all the objects I've gathered out of the river gleam – bottles, keys, rocks, bones. They look different, as if their secret selves are coming alive. The roof groans. There's the gentle mewling of night traffic outside but the little visitor is silent tonight.

I go into a thin sleep. These thin sleeps often bring memories, forgotten in the morning, like faded watercolour paintings but with moving parts. My bedroom wall dissolves and there's a truck threading across a mountain road, canyons in the distance. I know I'm inside that truck being bounced up and down, my legs dangling over the edge of my bunk bed. The memories fold, merge into each other or turn to dust. They're not chronological but snatched from different times, different ages: I could be nine, eight, nine again, then twelve. There's my baptism in deep water, a near drowning. 'You shall henceforth be known as Mercy Roberts,' they say as I choke on river water. Afterwards I scratch my real name, Carmel Summer Wakeford, onto stones so I will never forget it.

There's a man whose eye looks like it's made of clear jelly. There's the lights of a city blinking in the distance. 'It's a godless place,' says a voice. 'We won't be going there.' I'm curling up on my hard bunk bed, the truck has just stopped and I can feel the vibrations of the engine still pulsing through the walls; I pull the crochet blanket over my head and try to still my breath, pretending I'm not there. West Virginia, the mountains, cool forests and twittering birds. Pennsylvania. Our truck crossing state lines and recrossing them like a scribble on a map. The faithful wait for us gathered under the white canvas roof of a tent. Then, like I'm dropped into it from above, a crowd of people, a sea of hands, reaching for me. 'I can't,' I tell them but they're gone already and I'm walking down a single street; there's the smell of hot dogs and frying onions in the air and my stomach growls.

The preacher rears up, dressed in faded black like he always was. I knew he'd come tonight. I'm looking up at him and he's outlined against a blue, blue sky – he has one arm raised above the crowd in front; he's sweating, smiling, declaiming, and his blue eyes burn so brightly they make the sky look pale. A bundle travels over the heads of the crowds, passing from one hand to another until it reaches him and it's lifted up into his waiting hands. A flap of white blanket falls down. It's a baby. He looks down at me. 'Heal her,' he says.

I must've tossed and turned because a book falls with a thump on the floor and I sit upright, wide-eyed and awake. The trap is still empty.

By morning two eyes, drops of brown ink, are staring up at me.

'Oh, little one,' I say. Its delicate sides are puffing in and out. 'I'll look after you.'

I dig out the hamster cage I know is in the garden shed. It

belonged to Mum when she was little and she told me that she had three hamsters in a row that all died quickly one after the other. She called each one Flossie and by the last Flossie she couldn't stand the idea of history repeating itself with Flossie number four.

For my creature I want to give it a proper man name. In the end I decide on Alan.

'Your new home, Alan,' I say, pointing to the larger cage.

I spend time making it comfortable, tearing up a cardboard box to put in the bottom, filling up the water bottle.

'Go on, Alan,' I say, but he's panicking. I'm trying to ease him out bottom first but his claws are clinging on to the floor of the trap and his tail gets caught in the door mechanism and slashes back and forth and I start to panic because I think he may be hurting himself. When he finally drops into the cage with a thump, I slam the trapdoor on the top of the cage shut and flip the catch. We stare at each other for long moments, both trying to calm down.

By night-time he's got used to his new home. He moves about in it, chewing on the food, scuffling about, only occasionally gnawing at the bars, attacking them as if he knows he's been caged.

As I'm lying in bed listening to him, my brain does one of those shifts.

Did I know? I think.

Something that's plagued me from time to time and that I used to talk about with the therapist, is how did I not realise, all those years, that I'd been kidnapped. Did I really deep down know but also, on some level, decide to *go along with it?*

But the new shift that comes in is like a flash of lightning and nearly tilts me out of my bed and I sit bolt upright and grab on to the sheet with both fists.

Maybe, maybe *this* is the captivity, this room, this woman I call Mum. How would I know? It's like me pointing at the cage to Alan and saying, go on, it's OK to get in there, it's not really a cage, it's more like a home. I wrap my arms around myself, panicking, breathing hoarsely.

'Alan,' I whisper into the dark. 'Everything's OK.' But of course, really, I'm talking to myself.

The next morning it's all over. I come back from the bathroom, barefoot and sleepy and there's Mum standing next to my bed.

'What are you doing in here?' I yell, but not as loudly as I might because I don't want to upset Alan.

'Carmel, that's not the issue,' she says quietly, although her face is red. 'The issue is you're keeping a fucking rat in your room.'

Before I turned twenty-one I'd forgotten many things. They returned to me in those thin sleep moments and by morning became lost in the sea of long ago.

But being twenty-one this year activated something long buried. The preacher once told me that at twenty-one I would come of age and if I chose to I could strike out on my own. At the time I think he only said it because he sensed I was growing restless, defiant. He didn't know how

I smuggled that idea into my heart and held on to it like a talisman. Whatever the cause, on my birthday the black cinema screen where I'd been dwelling up till then started sprouting rapidly multiplying pinpricks and the light behind began flooding through.

There were certain things I knew before that date, of course. I hadn't forgotten that at the age of eight I was taken by that preacher man who claimed to be my grandfather and that he told me my mother was dead. That was too big a thing to forget. Because of this lie he liked me to call him Gramps, others in the congregation called him 'Pastor', but his favourite way of being addressed by far was 'Father Patron'. I decided after I got back that I would ever after know him simply as 'the preacher' because it made him seem less real. Too big to forget as well, I remembered I was returned to Mum in my thirteenth year from where I'd been in the United States, only to find that she'd been alive all that time. My mother told me they were a religious nutjob cult though this was a description I didn't recognise. Other things sometimes would come back to me unexpectedly because I was reminded of them. I'd forgotten completely about the preacher's limp, his injured hip, until I saw someone on the street near Marylebone Station walking with a similar strange and jerking gait.

I also knew my kidnappers tried to make me take on another name, but this was vaguer. When I thought about it, which wasn't often because remembering was a painful business, I knew the name was Mercy Roberts and that was the name on the passport they used to take me there. But no one in those years told me what had happened to her.

What I hadn't remembered until turning twenty-one were the details, the things like how when I finger-painted when I was *gone* I'd pretend the blue thumbprint next to the yellow pinkie finger was hers. That sometimes in bed I'd think of her as my invisible sister hovering above me like a little apparition as if we were sleeping in twin bunks. How I was certain she must like strawberry jelly. I knew, because I'd seen a photo of her, that she had curly hair much like mine and I was sure she too would insert a finger into a spiral of it for the purposes of twirling. These were things that started flooding back. Up until that point I'd tried not to remember them at all.

But the tide had turned and I found I could not stop thinking about her, whether she was alive or dead or was in a lonely place somewhere, in need of rescue. A chain began to form that bound me to her. Days after that birthday, I blinked, shook my head, tapped my forehead because I realised that in fact the chain had been there all along, it's only that I hadn't been able to see its glimmer.

Then I found that her name was forever inside my mouth, and now I have the constant urge for my lips to form the shape required to say *Mercy*.

Beth

Jesus. A rat! Every time I think things are getting better with Carmel something like this happens. I know she was furious with me for going into her room without permission, but the urge this morning was just too strong. I ached to know she was really here, that the sound of the person showering in the bathroom wasn't some sort of horrible aural hallucination conjured by the trauma of losing her. Your mind plays tricks on you when you've had a missing child.

I saw the empty bed through the crack in the door and I just needed to smell her presence, sleep-warmed, yeasty like bread though actually it smelled of the Thames in there because of all of her river finds. I should have thought to use the excuse of taking some clean socks in or something because we were supposed to have settled on boundaries.

And 'Alan', for God's sake. I'll probably laugh about it later but for now I can't wait to get the thing out of the house. It took ages to persuade her. I eventually latched on to the idea of arguing about the notion of confinement and said, 'Wouldn't he want to be free?' and that seemed to work. Of course, I knew what I was doing. After her own experience it was bound to be the thing that made her reassess keeping a creature against its will. She suggested the garden but I'm not having that. He'll only want to come in again after the welcome he's had the first time.

'Come on, what about taking him to the river?' I said.

She nodded slowly in agreement and I could see she was coming round to the idea. 'Maybe.'

'Yes, he can be with all his little ratty friends.' It was out before I could stop myself.

'You really don't care, do you?' she yelled and that put everything back by several hours.

Leave it, leave her, I told myself, sitting at the kitchen table. I stayed put and drank my tea with shaking hands, but I couldn't help keep thinking, it's a *rat*.

Finally, she comes downstairs wearing her long, baggy mac and with Alan in an old hamster cage that she's cleaned up.

'Can I come with you?' I ask, surprising myself.

'I guess,' she says slowly. 'If you want. I'm taking him to Bankside.'

'I could do with a bit of fresh air, and I haven't been down there for ages. I could drive you so you don't have to take him on the Tube.' I nod at Alan who's looking up at me meanly from the cage. I guess I'm trying to make amends with her.

'There's a sort of pier there so he'll be safe from birds and things.'

Lovely, I want to say, *that'll be lovely for him*, but I don't, I suck my mouth to stop the words getting out that I know will be tinged with sarcasm and I probably look like I'm sucking on a lemon. Carmel doesn't realise how challenging this is for me and to be honest I don't want her to know.

On the drive there's silence between us. Alan's cage is in a huge hessian shopping bag and the top covered with a towel. I park up near the Tate Modern and we carry him out and I can't help thinking about everyone in ignorance as to what's in the hessian bag – a kind of rat handbag – and I turn my face away so Carmel can't see the smile plucking up the corners of my mouth. I have such an urge to laugh I have to gulp. She wouldn't get it, or would misinterpret it and we'd be back to square one.

I have to sprint after her as she heads to the river; she's capable of going really, really fast when she's annoyed.

On the embankment there's a cold little wind blowing and she zips up her red mac and puts her hood up and draws the string tight so she looks like she's looking out of a port-hole, eyes blinking at the world outside. When I was her age, I'd rather freeze than wear anything I thought looked odd or unflattering and it strikes me that in contrast she either doesn't know or really doesn't care when she looks odd.

The sky's a pale, pearly grey and the slab of the chilly surface of the Thames is grey also, but a different shade – darker and more like metal. A wind whips up from it and into my face. I close my eyes, breathe it in. I miss living next to the sea, and I don't know if it's my imagination when I get a taste of sea air off the water. It is, after all, a tidal river. Sometimes whales have become lost and swum right into central London and got beached on the encrusted shoreline so it's possible that I really can smell salt. I open my eyes. I often forget there's something magical about this river.

There's something so powerful about it too, brutal. I was terrified when Carmel discovered the shoreline. We lived in our old house in Norfolk at first when she got back, the home of her childhood, but she didn't like being inside and roved around the countryside, returning dripping wet from the rain. She often picked half-dead creatures up off the road and she always seemed to be able to nurse them back to health and send them hopping on their way. But the house was a problem, even after we removed the plaque inscribed with 'There's No Place Like Home' that she said had haunted her when she was gone. She couldn't settle. When I inherited Mum and Dad's house in West Hampstead it seemed an opportunity for a fresh start and she seemed interested in being somewhere else. I hoped she might start studying, go to college, but she was uncomfortable in this huge city, on edge, until she discovered the river and the foreshore and it became her place, and I'm grateful to the river for that and try not to think about tidal pinch points and mud you can drown in and the loneliness of it down there.

'Ready?' I ask.

Carmel toes the pavement with her tatty Converse and I melt. She often seems so hopelessly childlike. I peer over the wall.

'What's the best way down?'

'There's a gate there.'

She unlatches a forbidding iron gate that looked locked and holds it open for me.

'I'd no idea you could just go down there so easily.' Despite myself I'm intrigued.

She shrugs and I follow her and any enchantment is

quickly blasted away at the sight of the flight of stone steps covered in green slime. I grab on to a diagonal metal pole by my side.

'Hold on, Carmel, there's no rail.'

She stops in the middle of the steps, the cage dangling from her hand, and looks up at me quizzically.

'It's best to do it without thinking.'

She carries the cage to what looks like an ancient cobbled jetty at the bottom, broken and shining with water. I take a deep breath and lunge after her, trying to banish the image of lying at the bottom with broken limbs. It's a relief to hear the crunch beneath my feet of the foreshore. At least it feels stable.

She's parked Alan next to the jetty and is now on her hands and knees, her head hidden deep in the red hood of her coat and the image of that – almost a prophetic figure – against the steely water gives my stomach a painful twist because she somehow looks too strange to be my daughter.

I think I see her putting something in her pocket before she straightens up to standing.

'Come on,' she says, smiling at my mincing across the stones. 'It's not far.' Being next to the river seems to have softened her mood.

Further along water sloshes round the ancient wooden beams of the pier. Frills of green slime hang from the vertical struts. Other ancient wooden masts rise from the ground, the tide having turned them into jagged points. This is just about the last place I want to be. It actually makes me shudder. There's a rime of debris on the stony beach and I wish I'd worn thicker shoes. The mud always seems to have a peculiar consistency on the banks of the Thames. It's like human mud, as if fat and fingernails and ground-up teeth and the dirty water from ancient kitchens – centuries of filth – medieval, Tudor, further back than that, prehistoric even – have formed into a kind of fleshy silt. Today it gleams wetly in the odd shaft of fitful sunshine that's trying to come through the grey.

She's got her hand in her pocket like she's holding something.

'Find anything?' I ask.

She shakes her head.

'Hey, it's Eric,' Carmel says suddenly.

I look along the shore to see a group of three men examining the ground intently, one with a metal detector that he passes over the ground in sweeps.

'They look busy,' I say hopefully, thinking we might be done and gone by the time he looks up. Carmel seems to have even forgotten about Alan, who's been liberated from his hessian bag and is dangling in his cage from her hand and appears stock-still petrified, looking out at the enormity around him.

'Hey, Eric,' she yells. 'Over here!'

He's quite a way off but looks up and switches off his machine and peels away from the rest of them and starts walking towards us.

'Ahoy there,' he says, waving his metal detector around.

'Eric advised me about the rules for collecting finds down here,' she explains. 'He's really helped me.'

He leans his metal detector against his leg and puts his

hands in his pockets; his eyes are glassy and blank behind his huge plastic-framed glasses and he has pads strapped to his knees. 'Happy in helping anyone to harvest the treasures of the river.'

He nods in my direction as if he's just noticed me. *Treasures?* I think. *God knows* what could be sunk in these waters, getting dragged in and out by the tides.

'Have you found anything?' Carmel seems excited. She tugs at the cords of her hood, pulling it off so her curly hair explodes around her head and my heart throbs with tenderness for her.

'I have indeed.' Eric dips his hand into a leather bag hanging from his shoulder and scoops out brown fragments that could be bone, or not, in fact they could be pretty much anything. He holds one out to her and she takes it and turns it over in her fingers.

'What is it?' I ask.

'Pieces of clay pipe. The river's full of them; London must have been overrun with smokers,' he chuckles. 'Not that interesting really. My best find recently is a whole cow's leg bone.'

Carmel is impressed. 'That's really cool,' she says. I guess the vision of filth and mired secrets is all mine.

She drops the piece in his palm and he puts them back in the leather bag and she lifts up the cage so he can see Alan. 'We've come to rehome him,' she says.

'Excellent choice of venue,' he says, completely unfazed by Alan's presence. He sticks a finger between the bars of the cage and waggles it about making chucking noises. 'Hello, boy.'

He dips his hand in his pocket and – dear God – takes out a tinfoil package that he unwraps and takes a sandwich from. He holds the package out to us, 'Cheese, want one?'

'Cheers,' says Carmel, and I have to restrain myself from dashing the sandwich from her hand. Your hands, the muck, I want to wail, but they both stand, munching on the sandwiches and looking as healthy as anything, as if all the rats and river germs in the world have merely bolstered their immune systems into peak condition. Carmel puts the cage down on the ground and drops little pieces of bread and cheese down to Alan.

A young man about the same age as Carmel appears behind Eric wandering along the edge of the water, kicking at stones with his trainer. At the sound of stones clinking, Eric turns.

'Found anything?' he asks, then without waiting for an answer turns back to us. 'My nephew Ron, he thought he might be interested in coming with me today.'

Ron must be in hearing distance because he says, 'Did I ever get that wrong. It's dire down here. Can't wait to get home and have a good shower.'

I can't say I'm not sympathetic to his point of view but his uncle just smiles and shrugs. 'Yeah well, not for everybody.'

Ron's come alongside Eric now, and he's noticed us properly because he's staring at Carmel and a curious, knowing look creeps over his face. He nudges his uncle.

Carmel is hooding up again, pulling the drawstring even tighter so only her nose and her big hazel eyes are showing.

I say quickly. 'OK, let's get this rat gone and we can pick up something to eat on the way back.'

We open the cage which Alan really doesn't want to leave and I fight the urge to tip it up and shake it so he's dumped hard on the ground so we can just get out of there. Eventually, through an agonising series of manoeuvres where the cage is tilted and Alan is slowly and carefully slid down to the exit in increments, he is gently lowered onto the ground. He stays, frozen on the muddy stones for a minute, looking up at us as if he expected something more, something better from us, before he turns and lopes away, his thick, scaly tail whipping side to side.

'Let's go. Bye,' Carmel turns abruptly and starts crunching quickly across the shore towards the steps with the empty cage in one hand and the door flapping open and closed. She points. 'We'll go to the steps further down. It'll be easier for you.'

'Yes, bye,' I say and hurry after her. I'm panting by the time I reach her at the top of the steps and have to catch my breath.

'Maybe that boy fancied you,' I say.

'I thought perhaps he recognised me,' she says.

'Ahhh.'

She's against a sinister-looking pink and yellow sky, and the tower blocks with the dome of St Paul's Cathedral on the opposite bank. The river has turned two shades darker since we arrived. Down below, Eric is on his hands and knees. I've never been with her before. I'm surprised how visceral it felt down there.

She leans over the wall. 'Goodbye, Alan,' she calls, her voice muffled by the hood.

There's something suddenly different about you today.

You seem more awake, like something's happened. What's going on with you, daughter? Something's changed.

'Still hungry?' I ask.

'Starving.'

'There's an ancient pub somewhere down there that looks over the water. They used to do a nice curry.'

She smiles. 'Sounds good.' She leans back over the wall and calls again, 'Goodbye, Alan.'

I do the same, and add, 'I hope you have a good life.' I notice Eric is busy digging now while the other two watch on. The wind veers, turns and blows my hair out to one side like a cartoon. The salt smell has got stronger; it brings the scent of far-off places, of high seas, right into the heart of this city. I look to where Carmel's upright figure now walks ahead. Take that taste of adventure off your tongue, I tell myself sternly. It's not possible for you right now. I put my hands in my pockets and follow her towards the pub.

I am drawn to the heart. As a nurse I hope one day to specialise in it and at work I listen to its throbbing sounds, like distant machinery in my ears. I try to interpret the mystery of its various rhythms. I love the organ in a way, although I know that sounds strange.

And hearts know things we don't. My own heart might be physically healthy but in another sense it is a flawed and damaged thing. It's become a tightly wound bobbin, something tied up with strong threads. Not much else penetrates it, yet when Carmel called out that goodbye, for about the thirty-sixth time that day, just like on all days, I have the urge to gasp because it's as if a very slender knife has just entered my heart and penetrated it to the core.

It's the kind of knife only a daughter can wield.

Mercy

1999

'Mom, Pa, dinner!'

Mercy pounded her fist on their bedroom door inside their wooden shack and hollered for what must've been the third time in a row but there was still a great, fat silence inside.

She didn't want to dwell for a tiny minute on the possibility they might've died in there. She knew she wouldn't be able to stand the sight of them both lying lifeless in bed like two gigantic dolls. The thought of it alone was enough to crack her in two and she knew there was a good likelihood of it being the case.

There was another concern. She worried that the racoon would be after the food she'd laid out in the kitchen-diner. That racoon could smell everything and already she'd heard a scratching on the porch outside that could've been him. Ma said Mercy should never have started feeding him and Mercy guessed she was right but she loved to peep out of the window and see him gobbling up the Graham crackers she'd smashed up for him. He was kind of like a friend despite the fact he'd turned into a bit of a darn nuisance and roved round the shack looking for ways in.

Truth be told there were plenty of ways in. The wooden house was a honeycomb of them. Mercy left off hammering on the bedroom door and went through the house checking the racoon hadn't been successful in his incursion. In the hallway there was a big old hole in the floor that her ma was always falling in. It's like she would never learn or remember it was there and it drove Mercy crazy. She'd lost count of the number of times she'd heard her ma wailing and run to find her with her foot stuck down that hole past the ankle.

'Not again,' she'd scold before getting down on her hands and knees to pull it out.

Her pa was more alert to the danger and always remembered to skip to the side. Mercy wouldn't have said he was more intelligent than her ma. She guessed he just had a better memory.

Mercy decided to drag the rug from the living room out into the hallway to block the hole up. She always thought it would be a pretty rug if it was not so dirty. You could see that there were lovely colours behind the dirt; there was a red lozenge midpoint in the rug that reminded her of a ruby and she harboured ambitions to clean it up one day.

In the kitchen-diner that was also the living room she wiped the window so she could see the porch better but she had to do it carefully because the glass moved when you touched it. Where the glass went in at the bottom the wood had gone soft and there was a row of mushrooms that looked like a brown frill on the hem of a dress except they were hard and stiff to the touch. She looked at them for ages sometimes because they seemed so beautiful and unusual. It was like the house was getting eaten up. That idea, of the house being eaten, was scary but it was also kind of exciting. One day she came down and it near took her breath away because the frill had been joined – overnight, like a miracle – by a patch of miniature orange toadstools with white spots, each one a hundred per cent perfect.

She couldn't believe how quickly they'd grown there and she thought it must be like something out of a fairy tale that Miss Pauley would read out loud at school. Miss Forbouys used to do the same thing when Mercy was in her class when she was little, and would also play them music. Miss Pauley didn't play music but Mercy was always so keen to hear the tales she told that when they were finished she often realised she must've stood up and draped herself over her desk and propped her head in her hands and she'd done all this without even knowing. She guessed it was because of trying to get nearer the better to hear. But Miss Pauley never paid any mind and she would close the book and give Mercy a smile that was vague but so sweet it was like the perfect end to the story she'd just told.

Those orange mushrooms were a wonder and she checked every day to see if something new and magnificent had joined them on the window frame. Who knew what astonishing form it might take?

Mercy couldn't see the racoon through the glass so she sat back down at the table where she'd laid out three paper plates with peanut butter sandwiches and a side order on each plate of Wavy Lay's potato chips. Then she heard her parents stirring about in their room and relief surged through her. She grinned.

'Hey, Racoony, not going to be your lucky day,' she sang out.

Ma and Pa took forever getting out of bed and getting

ready, as always. By the time she heard their bedroom door open her eyes had got blurry from sitting so still and looking at the same thing but she managed to remember about the rug and call out to warn them, realising at the last moment it might indeed make matters worse as the hole was no longer visible.

She must've called out just in time because Ma came into the living room and she hadn't fallen down the hole.

'What did you put that rug there for?' she asked.

Mercy tapped the side of her nose. 'Racoon protection.'

'Well, ain't that clever,' her Ma said and smiled.

Pa came in behind Ma and put his arm round her waist. 'Look here. Look at the spread Delia has put on for us.'

'Hey, it's Mercy now. I told you.'

'Sure. Sorry, Mercy, I kind of forgot.'

'Well try not to forget again.'

'I'll sure try real hard but I can't guarantee that. I might slip up.'

They sat down opposite and looked at their plates.

'Well, everyone slips up now and again,' Mercy said, trying to be generous. 'I know that. All you can do is try.'

Ma took one of her sandwiches and nibbled at the corner. She always dressed nice, even though it was nearly evening now and she probably wouldn't be going anywhere. She had a red bandana tied round her hair and had put on Mercy's favourite bib dress of hers. She'd even put on some crimson lipstick that matched the bandana, that's how much effort she'd made. Mercy loved it when she wore lipstick.

'You look real pretty today, Ma.'

Her pa nodded and took one of his wife's hands in his.

'She always does, pumpkin. She always does.'

Mercy had a sneaking suspicion that he'd called her pumpkin because he'd forgotten what her new name was already but she let it pass. She loved it when he looked at her ma like that, a calm joy on his face. It made Mercy feel they were three links in a chain held together by sheer love. That feeling always made her throat go tight so she took a drink of water which actually didn't taste too good because the glass had been sitting there for so long it had bits in it.

Mercy set about eating her dinner and she emptied the plate quicker than she thought possible. Then she wetted her finger to pick up any stray crumbs.

But when she looked up Ma and Pa's plates were still full. She'd been concentrating so hard on eating she hadn't noticed what they were doing. Ma had only nibbled the corner off of a sandwich and all Pa had done was stirred his chips around so they were scattered round his plate on the table. This made Mercy so mad she could feel her mouth sucking itself up into a thin line.

'Hey, eat your goddam dinner,' she said.

She purposely made her eyes hard and glowered at them, at the same time sucking up all the chewed-up potato chips left on her teeth.

'Now then . . .' Pa started, but Ma interrupted him.

'Listen, honey. We think we'll take our plates into our room and eat in there. It's a whole lot more comfortable; it'll be kind of like a picnic.'

She beamed at her daughter hopefully. But Mercy was having none of it. They'd fooled her once too many times like this and she'd found the food shoved under the bed, dried out and nibbled by creatures. She slammed the table with her palm so hard the pain jolted up her arm. They both looked up, alarmed.

'Pumpkin . . .' her pa began, but Mercy hit the table again, this time with her fist, making the potato chips jump on her parents' plates.

'You're not listening. I said, eat your goddam fucking dinner.'

Then they picked up their peanut butter sandwiches and very slowly, in tiny bites, ate them all, even the crusts, and then nibbled on some potato chips, leaving only a little pile uneaten before they crept off back to their room.

Mercy had learned her cussing off of her parents who always did it discreetly, behind their hands. Mercy might not have been discreet but she kept her cussing for extreme circumstances and when she did cuss everyone knew she meant business.

It was her custom to take a breath of air out in the porch before she climbed the ladder to her bedroom. She loved the time of day when dusk began to colour the air and the whippoorwills began their evening song from which they were named that continued through the night. Tonight, dusk hadn't yet fallen and the whippoorwills had yet to start singing but there was already a daytime-white crescent moon floating high above the trees.

Mercy felt a great attachment to the moon in all its various faces and stages. She didn't remember this but her parents had told her how when she was little they would wrap her in a blanket and bring her out onto this very porch to moon bathe when it was full and the night was clear. Then they made the mistake to bring her out the night of a crescent moon and she was distraught, sobbing inconsolably and saying how the moon had broke. Of course, she wouldn't think such a dumbass thing now; she was happy with the moon in all its phases, whether it was waxing gibbous, or waning, or when it wore a lustrous halo. But it was after that her pa, back in the days when he was still doing things like that, made a tile out of Sculpey to hang next to the front door. He said he wanted to make her feel better about crescent moons and that the name she'd given it was real pretty. Mercy made the moon for the piece, which actually looked a little more like a wibbly banana than a crescent moon and pushed it into the clay before it was baked in the oven. The tile was still there now, a survivor, hanging on a nail in the hole her pa had made with a drinking straw. He'd fashioned the words out of the same yellow clay as the moon and they laboriously spelled out in looping letters the name for their shack: 'Broke Moon House'.

As spring came into its deep, full flush, the leaves turned the canopy outside into a floating green cloud and the sun warmed the last vestiges of winter out of Broke Moon House. The corners of the house dried out and the boards of the roof narrowed and shrank. Everything across the tree-topped mountain was active, on the move, like a vast workshop. Millions of spiders were weaving webs and dropping from trees on their fine silks like stealth soldiers.

Much of the industry was silent though; if the spiders alone could be heard in the way of a workshop fashioning tin or copper, the noise now would have been deafening. The only sound the snakes made was the crisping of last year's leaves as they wound through them and all the cacophony was left to the birds.

Around that time Mercy had begun living for Sunday when she could go back to the tent.

She was anxious about missing it because time often got kind of hazy. She used to know the time from the lit-up clock on the microwave. Her pa had taught her the twenty-four-hour clock by it and said she was real smart to learn it so quickly and easily. But then he unplugged it to plug in the electric meat-carving knife because the loaf had got so hard it broke the blade of the real bread knife right off from its handle. Since then, that stupid light on the microwave had been blinking on and off and driving Mercy crazy and she didn't have a clue how to fix it or make time real again. She kept forgetting to ask her pa to reprogramme it, probably because deep down she knew he'd never get around to it.

She'd had to learn new ways of doing things and began with tracking the sun. She saw it rise every day more or less from the same place, shining like hope and glory through the trees, and learned which point it was at when she needed to leave for school. She realised they were heading into summer and things would change on account of that so she began to take notice of other things too: the shiver of evening cold in the air, the point when the frogs stopped croaking. The crows were spectacularly helpful as every

43

evening before dusk they took to the air and swooped and called and hollered until they settled in the trees and then Mercy knew it was time for her bed too. Mornings had their own signs and occurrences and she familiarised herself with those too and soon began to learn from the colours tingeing the sky what kind of day it was going to be and from the feel of the air on her skin if it was going to rain.

But it was an approximate science. Often, she was not on time, late or more usually very early, and so she also learned the art of waiting patiently for things to catch up with her. By Sunday and time to go to the tent again she'd have been waking earlier and earlier all week in preparation and would get to see harsh red sunrises over black trees, the outside turning from grey to pink to yellow and the cold jelly-like air being melted by those variously coloured suns. Those mornings were glorious. She had the sense that she was discovering treasures which would always be there for the taking, that all she needed to do was to get up a little early to witness the power of them and that would be something that would always be available to her her whole life, whatever else happened.

That Sunday it was difficult to gauge the time of day because the morning dawned grey with no sun to clue her in so she decided to set off as soon as the light showed through her bedroom window.

She'd been saving a pair of purple corduroy trousers and a matching jumper all week because they were clean. Washing was an arduous business; her own things weren't so hard because they were small but when it came to Pa's jeans, they were another matter altogether. There was a plastic barrel that long ago her pa had cut off the top with the same electric meat knife that had rendered the clock on the microwave useless. He'd run a hose off of the shower and Mercy had to fill the tub up and dump in a cup of America Fresh and pound everything with an old chair leg. There was a little tap at the base of the barrel that hooked over the lip of the shower base so all the black and dirty suds could be drained away down the shower hole. Mercy did her best not to forget about the washing once it was all submerged. From experience she knew this could be a disaster because one time she came back and the water had all turned into stringy slime that near enough made her sick. On the line out back was a different matter. Once she managed to heave them up there it was out of sight, out of mind and they often got rinsed on repeat by rain. On more than one occasion she'd gone outside to find hers or Ma's panties with the black marks of some kind of mould on them that looked like snow crystals in reverse. Mercy figured that because she wore them underneath, they'd be OK, though when the girl sitting next to her in school kept asking what that funny smell was she was getting whiffs of, Mercy kept real quiet and still.

So Mercy'd kept these purple cords and jumper so careful all week because she knew what a task getting clothes clean was. She dressed then brushed her hair which was easier said than done because the curls had gone tight. Ma always said her head was like a little nest of snakes. She dragged the comb through even though it made her head sore and gave herself a ponytail with a blue rubber band. Then, mindful of what Bob had told her, paid attention to her face. She filled the bathroom sink with cold water – because hot water only ever came out of the shower – and soaped her face up and rinsed and then did it twice over again to make sure. When she looked in the mirror her face was as pink and clean as the newborn mouse she once saw nesting in a hole in the corner of their porch. She grinned into the mirror, pleased. Her pullover looked nice with the purple polo neck coming up to her chin and there was a ponytail of curls swishing on her back.

'Hey you, girl,' she said to her reflection. 'You're fit for church and no mistake!' She gave herself the thumbs up and cracked a grin and the mirror showed her where she'd lost a tooth a month ago.

She didn't bother creeping past her parents' bedroom because she knew they'd never wake anyway. They slept more than any people she ever knew, though sometimes, when they were sleeping, they did sit up and say the strangest things. They even walked right out of their room when she knew they were still asleep and would stand there, looking through the porch window at the outside and murmuring stuff about light and darkness, or their own ma and pa from long ago. Once Pa went on about the bones of some old chicken he'd had that he thought had reassembled themselves and was right now walking about the forest and making rattling sounds as it went. Mercy put her hands on them when they did this and turned them right round and steered them back to their beds 'cos the next thing would be they'd try to leave or fall down the hole in the hallway.

She set out through the trees. The forest was waking up; she'd been told by her teachers that their little corner of West Virginia was one of the most beautiful places on God's earth and on mornings like this Mercy had to believe it. The birds were singing and the ferns bobbed as if they were calling out hallelujahs with their nodding heads to her on her way. Once she reached the tent though, she realised she'd been fooled by the light that morning and in the world of men everything was still quiet. The tent was all closed up and not a soul was there. She sat down on a rock and waited. The tent had an expectant air. Dewdrops shivered on its ropes and as she watched them swinging, she imagined that the Lord was inside, ready and waiting. He was sitting on the chair on the stage in His robes with His bare feet on the blue nylon carpet knowing everyone was coming to greet Him. She wondered if He knew she was outside already and the thought made her very shy so she sat as quiet as she could on that cold rock waiting for other folk to turn up.

After the air had started to turn warm the insects in the forest at her back were the last to wake up and they began humming in the undergrowth behind and she heard voices coming down the end of the path in the distance. It sounded like two ladies talking and when they got closer she jumped up, her legs all stiff and cold from sitting so long on the rock.

'Hey there,' she said. She was a little worried they might not see her because she had begun to feel invisible on occasion.

'Well, just look who it is; it's Mercy come again. It's so good to see you make the effort, child.'

She saw it was the lady who'd given Mercy her real name. She wore white gloves and carried a ton of hymn books.

What she said was nice but there was one thing Mercy didn't like about it. It was that she sounded surprised that Mercy was there again, that it wasn't natural that she would be. She didn't seem to understand Mercy'd been straining every muscle all week to get through that tent door because she'd been saved and that wasn't a once occurrence but something she understood would need topping up by the spirit on a weekly basis. In short, there was something in what she said that made it sound like Mercy didn't belong.

But then she remembered the Almighty Himself with love and light bursting out of His heart just right beyond that canvas and it didn't matter anymore. She knew how to behave here, that she mustn't use curse words. She knew not to talk about how her ma and pa liked the needle. She also had a clean face, and last week they'd specifically said church was for everyone however mighty or humble and what a little doll she was coming by herself.

Mercy remembered the woman's name. 'Hey, Mrs Farmer. I'm sure glad to be back.'

Mrs Farmer and the thin lady in a purple dress passed looks between them. The thin lady's hands were also full of hymn books. She had gloves made of purple lace, the colour of lilacs, and looking at them Mercy didn't think she'd ever wanted anything so much in her whole life. She could actually feel what they would be like on her hands, criss-crossed and scratchy on her skin but in a nice way.

'Why, Mercy,' the lady said. She had a sort of low, serious voice that Mercy liked almost as much as her gloves. 'I noticed you here before and since then Mrs Farmer has told me all about you and I sure was hoping you'd be here today.

48

I have something for you in the car when worship is over.'

'You have?' Mercy was amazed but had a creeping hope it might be some gloves the exact same as hers except in her size.

'Sure I have. Would you like to come in with us and set the hymnals out? We could use the help.'

There was nothing Mercy would like to do better. The three of them set out all the hymnals, one on each chair, which were covered in velvety stuff and bright blue like pictures of the ocean Mercy'd seen. The blue matched in with the carpet on the stage. When that was done she sat on one right at the front next to the aisle so she wouldn't miss anything and swung her feet about in the air. The Lord wasn't sitting on the chair on the stage but she smiled to herself because she had the feeling that He'd been there right up until He heard the tent door being undone and then He'd disappeared Himself. She guessed it would be better without people trying to engage Him in their own specific concerns which you just know is what they'd do. Hey Lord, there's a hole in my roof, my back is bent, my leg is sore, the weeds in my vegetable patch are up to my knees, and a hundred other things they'd expect Him to fix for them. Mercy didn't blame Him for making Himself scarce.

People began to arrive. The Jones family were among the first – three boys and two girls – and they joined her at the front. Tina was in Mercy's class at school so she sat next to her. Mercy waved to Sheila Jackson who ran the bakery in town. She couldn't go there 'cos she didn't accept food stamps but they always waved to each other through the window and one day Miss Jackson came out with a coconut macaroon in a paper bag, and told Mercy it was for being such a good girl. That would've been a nice day if some boys from school hadn't whizzed down the street on their bikes and thrown stones at her, told her to 'git home' and called her 'junkie girl', like it was *her* taking the needle. Mercy cried all the way home and never wanted to eat coconut since. When Miss Jackson offered her a macaroon again Mercy told her that she could no longer abide the taste. Miss Jackson seemed to understand and it was blueberry cupcakes after that which Mercy couldn't get enough of.

Tina had a dress on made of fabric that looked like if it burned it would melt and stick to her flesh, real quickly. It had a stiff, frilly skirt that when she sat down rocked upwards like a bell and sat mid-air above her knees and Mercy wondered if people might be able to see her panties from the stage.

'Hey,' Tina said. 'You on your own here?'

'Uh, huh.'

'That's cool.'

Mercy nodded. 'Yah.'

'You wanna hold hands?'

'Sure.'

They held hands till they started feeling sweaty as more people arrived and began to crush in and it got so hot the air she breathed was warm in her nose and throat.

Then people gradually ceased their coughing and their stirring and everything went real quiet. Mercy felt the rush and swell of love around her as the service began. First off, the pastor got on the stage and said they were like flowers in the garden, that one day they'd all be cut down and lie on the ground all brown and dried out but that soon afterwards, probably no more than a week, would begin to come to life again. They'd rise up and their colours would come back but they'd be a thousand times more wonderful and awe-inspiring than before. They'd be like rainbows, like the colours of precious gems, but the very, very best thing of all is that no one would need soil to grow anymore and all the pain and troubles that needing dirt incurred would be done away with. They would be able to sort of hover, without any roots stuck in the dirty old earth; they'd be like that just shimmering away.

Then a hymn was sung that Mercy had trouble singing along with because the writing in the hymn book was all curly and strange, so some of it she just hummed.

The pastor held out his arms like he was about to embrace them all. 'I have an announcement to make that should set a mighty joy aflame inside you. Next week we have been blessed to welcome a visiting preacher.'

Mercy thought of Bob's warning about visiting preachers but she couldn't quite remember what it was, something confusing about snake oil and pork chops.

Pastor Frogmore carried on, 'This is no ordinary pastor, no. This man has been gifted by the Lord certain divine attributes. In short, an ability to heal. So, next week bring your sick, your lame and anyone who is in need of a cure, bring them all . . .'

A spark of an idea ignited in Mercy and she had to sit on her hands she was so excited, but her thoughts were interrupted when a woman in a blue dress that came near to her ankles scooted up to the front.

Tina whispered to Mercy, 'That's Maeve Coleman. When she walks along she farts.'

Pastor Frogmore looked slightly rattled at the interruption. 'Yes, what is it, Maeve?'

The woman said something in a low voice Mercy couldn't catch.

'No,' said Pastor Frogmore, taking out his hanky and mopping his head. 'The curing of afflictions is next week.'

'You think farting is what she wants curing of?' whispered Mercy.

'Well, I would,' whispered Tina back.

The woman murmured something again, sounding more persistent, then more in reassurance than anything Pastor Frogmore leaned down and put huge hand on Maeve's head which was so tiny it practically disappeared. Then an incredible thing happened because she fell backwards; it was like electricity had shot out of the pastor's hand and zapped her so she landed on her back. Mercy thought if she was her, she'd be grateful she didn't fart during such a manoeuvre, and she hadn't or Mercy would have heard, being right at the front.

'D'you think she's cured?' whispered Tina.

'I don't know,' Mercy whispered back. In truth, the whole thing had been a little embarrassing and Pastor Frogmore looked relieved when Maeve Coleman picked herself up and trotted back to her seat like nothing had happened.

After the service when the purple-glove lady came over Mercy's heart did a little skip because she'd been so involved with the spirit, she'd clean forgotten that there was something waiting for her in the car.

'Now then,' she said. 'Let's go fetch them. My name is Myla Joyce by the way. Mrs. Follow me.'

Mercy went with her and when Mrs Joyce took out the Walmart plastic bag from the trunk of the car and Mercy parted the handles and glimpsed what was inside her breath nearly stopped; time itself felt like it stopped for a moment or two. Inside was the most beautiful pair of shoes she'd ever seen in her whole life. They were made of pink pearly plastic with a real pink bead nestled into a little gold flower to do them up.

'They used to belong to my Carla but they're hardly worn because she only wore them to go with her princess costume. I sure hope they fit you.'

Mercy'd made her mind up to make them fit whatever happened.

'Why don't you try and see?' Mrs Joyce suggested.

Mercy slipped off a shoe with the cut-out toes and tried one shoe on and it was only a little bit too big.

'Even better. Gives you growing room,' Mrs Joyce said.

It was only on the way home, carrying those shoes in their bag because she didn't want to dirty them up on the forest path, that Mercy realised she hadn't said thank you. For a moment she got a pain in her stomach because she felt so upset at that but then she remembered she would see Mrs Joyce again next week and could thank her then.

At home everything was quiet. Ma and Pa had yet to

stir out of their beds. There was no sign of the racoon and the only sound was the peeping of a bird out in the trees somewhere.

Mercy climbed the ladder up to her room which was in the loft space of the one-storey shack and another ladder took her up to the platform bed that her pa had made a long time ago out of ply. There were two sleeping bags there; one was unzipped and laid flat as a mattress, showing the orange flowers printed on the fabric inside, and the other one was rolled up ready for her to climb into tonight.

She took out the shoes and put them on her pillow and stared at them until her eyes got fuzzy. She stroked them with her finger and touched the pink beads. Inside was stamped 'The Sylvie Shoe, Paris' in gold letters and the gold was only the teeniest bit worn off.

She swung her legs dangling from the platform bed thinking what a miraculous day it had been.

It was then she spotted something else. On the window frame was a bunch of the same little orange mushrooms that had appeared downstairs. She climbed down the ladder and knelt on the floor to examine them. Each one had a creamy white stalk that was embedded in the crumbled-up frame like it was their soil to grow in. The orange heads had a scattering of perfect white dots and the clump looked so much like a picture out of a story book at school that if an elf or a fairy popped its head out from behind them it wouldn't have surprised her.

'Jeez,' she said to herself because she couldn't think of anything else to say that fitted the bill.

Finally then, in the quietness of her room, she was able

to give her full attention to the spark of the idea she'd had in church. When she'd heard about the visiting preacher who was due to visit, she'd had a shiver of something down the back of her neck. Her idea seemed both wonderful and audacious at the same time – what if she could persuade her parents to come with her to the tent? What if this pastor could lay his hands on them? There were no two people that were more in need of healing than her ma and pa and if there was some way she could convince them to go there, and he could be persuaded to shine the light of the Lord and His healing ways on them, perhaps they could be made well and whole again. Mercy climbed back up to her bed and swung her legs back and forth and her mouth went into a thin line as she plotted how she could make this happen. After all, she only had to get them there. The Lord would see to the rest.

Carmel

2013

Mum and me communicate in layers. There's the brittle, thin crust on top of what actually makes it into words, but if you peeled that off there'd be hundreds of conversations packed below, silent, but desperate to get out.

Like this morning when we were sitting in the garden. It was a sudden hot day even though it's September and Mum had just asked me why I love the river so much. She wore a coral-coloured bikini and her scalp where her hair was parted was burning and my fingers itched to reach out and take the burn away.

In answer to her question what went through me was this: *The river is a place that, although carved through London, is as mysterious and wild as any clifftop. Every day the tides go in and the tides go out leaving a million bits of lost London on its shore. When I plunge my hands into the water an icy shock goes straight up my arms. Fog glides elegantly on the water then dissolves as quickly as it comes, blown apart by wind that chases the river's length. Small worms inhabit the rock pools and the arching backs of porpoises have been spotted playing in its waters. This, when I have experienced so many extraordinary things, is necessary for me. Did you know I once saw someone who was dying get up out of their hospital bed and walk away? Do you realise that I once han-*

dled poisonous snakes and was not afraid?

What I actually said was, 'I guess I like the mystery of it all.'

Really, I wanted to add, *That time, before summer, just after my twenty-first birthday as we stood together on the foreshore, I slipped the metal bangle I'd just found onto my wrist and I felt electrified from top to toe. I looked out at the gunmetal water and the river wind blew on me and I was changed. The river delivered me that.*

She nodded, as if she understood. 'Yes, the mystery. I get it.'

'Juice?' I asked, and on the way in I picked up her straw hat and plopped it on her head.

In the cool of the kitchen as I was mixing orange juice with soda water I remembered another river, the sight of the snaking Salkehatchie, shining. The smell of wild mint one day, bruised by our footfall and rushing up my nostrils. Smoke from the campfire.

I stopped and cooled my burning hands against the glass jug chinking with ice. Always so much change, the back doors of the truck opening and a new vista, and another, and another, the partial detail of a scene that was revealed each time, like the first clue to where we might be – a bare tree against a blue, blue sky once; snow another time, the shape of a pitched roof on the top rung of a farm gate. Always unexpected, new. A white church with a piercing steeple and a home-made cross planted in the grass in front of it, two slender tree trunks lashed together.

Mum is ignorant of all these things so it's like we're standing on opposite sides of a road, fast traffic zipping in between, looking at each other, but with no hope of getting across.

The river saved me when I came to London. I wasn't used to cities. I didn't really know what they were like. In America we were nearly always on the road, often cooking on a fire. The places we stopped at were usually small, or fields and forests. Mountains and empty roads with the smell of hot dust coming through the window.

In London there's the sight of people's sicknesses everywhere, and walking down the busy streets sometimes I have to stop and close my eyes and put my hands in my pockets, breathing in car fumes and letting the bodies all flow past me, unseen. I love them all, in a way, and it feels too much – that I'm powerless to help.

When I discovered the river here it was like finding paradise. It's a different world down there, free and open, wind-scoured, sometimes churning with boats of all sizes, sometimes eerily empty – from the marshes out at Erith, to the crumbling foreshore under the bridges with people and traffic streaming overhead, to the tiny islands that can appear or disappear according to the tides. I started to meet mudlarkers and got the bug for finding some of the millions of things that have been lost or thrown into the river. The spot where we let Alan go, for instance, is full of tiny coins the size of my fingertip with a miniscule crown standing proud from the rim. All these lost things, abandoned things. They are unseeing, unthinking, like molluscs carving a path across the ocean bed. There's always the sense that each piece I find was meant especially for me, that it sought me out.

Lost things: considering them, my hands chilled from the icy jug, I feel the chain binding me to Mercy Roberts cutting hard into me and that chain becomes brighter, more visible.

I put the jug in the sink and pull up my sleeve to look at the bangle I found that time. The two ends of it point towards each other, there's a gap just wide enough to slip a wrist through sideways. I spotted one of the tips pointing up at me out of the mud and stones and I pulled and it came up easily like it had been waiting for me. I don't know why I felt the need to hide it from Mum and Eric, first in my pocket and then on my wrist under my jumper. It's old, I think, very old. Plain, a heavy crude metal, but that or the fact it could be important or valuable didn't feature in me keeping it from them. It's rather, as soon as I held it in my hand, I felt its power. Then wearing it, looking across the water with the wind whipping at my hair, I felt a sense of urgency, of mission. The bracelet was telling me something. An energy coursed through me that I haven't had for such a long time. I knew in that moment I had a role. *You are a seeker now*, the bracelet seemed to tell me. It's taken months to accept.

All this time I've been 'home' and I didn't know why I was here or how I fit in or what I'm even for anymore, yet now I see I'm here to *find* and now I'm ready to find more than *things*. Just remembering Mercy is not enough.

Again, I puzzle the lost name they tried to give to me, Mercy Roberts, as if it didn't belong to her anymore. Again, I burn to know why she no longer needed it.

—

When the newspaper woman called I was on my way to work.

'Carmel Wakeford?' she asked.

'Yes?'

I didn't recognise the voice. Hardly anyone calls my mobile; Mum of course, Marta to ask about shifts in the café.

'My name's Kay Ward. I work for the *Gazette*. How are you?'

'Um, I'm OK?'

'Good, good. I hope you don't mind me calling. The thing is we'd love to do a piece in the *Gazette* about your mudlarking hobby. It sounds absolutely fascinating. I hope you don't mind,' she said again. 'Me just calling you like this.'

'I don't mind.' I felt a rush of something. She sounded friendly and warm. It didn't occur to me to ask how she got hold of my number.

'I'd love to meet you. How easy is that? Do you work?'

'I have a job in a café.'

The place where I work is called The Egg and Spoon and is one of those London greasy cafés that's been pasted inside a flimsy wooden shack probably for about half a century. The ceiling is still yellow from when people were allowed to smoke in there. Marta, who runs it, even stays on and plates up what's left for any homeless people that come to her back door. They eat standing up using the wheelie bins in the yard as tables although she's always particular about providing china to eat off and proper knives and forks. I have the urge to tell Kay all of this though I don't know why.

After she's rung off I realise something. How I'm often confused and how, if Kay Ward writes an article about me, about the mudlarking, perhaps my reasons for doing it will become more clear to me. She'll be able to express it in simple words and I'll be able to read the article whenever I feel lost myself and it will have shrunk down to something small and normal and understandable that I can easily talk about.

The house is quiet because I've chosen a time to meet Kay Ward when Mum is out.

I take all the junk off my bed and shove it underneath and straighten the patchwork quilt, the flowered squares that my great-granny stitched together, make it as smooth as marzipan. I scan my simple trestle shelves and make a selection from the bone section. My window is deep set and on the wide sill I arrange them. A skull the size of an egg, an eel's jawbone, a tiny spine that can be moved like a child's toy snake. I make a spiral of them all that takes their natural beauty and elevates it to something else again, an artwork.

The sound of the doorbell peals through the house.

'Hi there,' I say to the woman on the doorstep, who turns to face me as I open the door. 'You must be Kay.'

'Hey, Carmel.' The corners of her eyes crinkle up when she smiles and she flicks her hair about. 'How lovely to meet you.'

She's got brown, shiny hair, jeans, a leather bag stuffed so full of papers and books that it makes one shoulder go down lower than the other.

There's an unusual thing about her though and it's that

she's wearing really high red heels with plastic bows on the toes and I wonder how she'll manage when we go to the river to take photographs as she's suggested but I'm too shy to bring it up. I ask her to come in.

I take her up to my room and offer her tea. When I take it up I find myself standing for ages outside the door, mugs in hand, plucking up the courage to go inside because I feel so shy. I find it so hard to be with the people here. When I was with the preacher I was never shy. I had a role to fulfil. Here, every interaction is strained. I don't know what I'm supposed to say or do. If I quote scripture I'm met by blank looks. Last year I had the idea that if I could learn to dance I would be alright. I bought a CD called 'Dance Hits' though I didn't know then that it referred to a certain sort of music; I thought it just meant it was something to do with dancing. I put it on the player and started trying to move to it but it was so strange and fast with a voice that sounded like it was speeded up. When I was away I had no trouble moving with music; when devotional hymns were sung all of us swayed like we were one big field of wheat.

There wasn't much room in my bedroom so I moved out into the landing where there's more space, but I caught a glimpse of myself in the long mirror that's on the back of Mum's bedroom door. I looked like some sort of robot, my fists clenched and pumping, so I took the CD out of the player and threw it in the bin.

When I finally do pluck up the courage to go in to Kay I think I catch something on her face, a look that I'm not meant to see, like she's uncomfortable in this weird room and she's busily thinking of an exit strategy. I wonder if she realises that I was hanging about outside the door for so long.

'It's OK, Carmel,' she says. She must've read the expression on my face, seen something was wrong.

Then I feel sick because I realise in that moment that I'd had an idea in the back of my mind when I spoke to her on the phone that she could be a friend.

She's looking at the windowsill where the spiral of bones is. Bones are what I love best. I can rearrange them constantly. I love the feel of a skull cleaned up in my hand, like the finest of teacups, you can barely feel it. But now I have seen my room through her eyes and the display looks strange and shabby.

'Tell me about the bones,' she says gently, but that whole concept, the wildness of the river and the lost things moving towards me, to be *retrieved* and *found*, seems difficult to explain now.

Out of embarrassment though, out of an urge to fill the silence, I pluck up a jawbone and hold it out on the palm of my hand.

'Bird?' she asks hopefully.

I tell her no, eel.

There's an embarrassing silence.

'Carmel,' she says softly, perching on the edge of the cane chair so she doesn't displace the clean washing stacked there. 'How are you doing?'

'I'm alright,' I say. 'I'm doing well.'

Then she says so softly it's not like another voice in the room, more like a rustling in my own ears, 'Tell me how you're really doing.'

And then I finally understand with a cold, stomach-clenching certainty what is actually happening here.

I take the bone that's still in my outstretched palm and put it back with the others on the windowsill and because my hands are shaking it chinks against a bovine tooth I've set it next to.

In her car on the way to the river where she's going to take pictures of me, Kay says, 'I'm looking forward to this.'

Not for much longer, I think.

Now I know she is not friendly. She is not interested in the river. She is the deceitful worker of Corinthians; she wears the sheep's clothing that Matthew speaks of. All she wants is an exclusive story on the kidnap victim.

I checked the tide times, as I always do, before we came out. I know exactly where to go.

One of the many, many things about this situation that's making me feel sick is the thought of Mum that keeps coming back to me as we drive. Mum's always warning me not to talk to the press and here I am riding in a car with one of them.

We park up nearby and I shouldn't have worried about the shoes; she's come prepared. There's a pair of walking boots and a pair of socks in the trunk and she sits there on the open trunk and takes off the red shoes and starts putting the others on her thin, pale feet. There's red marks on her skin where the high heels have pinched and squeezed. I notice then there is something curious about the walking shoes. They are like no other walking shoes I've ever seen.

They have a kind of built-in platform sole that's at least two inches high.

She catches me looking and reddens. 'Got a bit of a thing about being short,' she laughs in an embarrassed way, and I remember how high the heels were. The thing is, she's not even short. Without her heels she would be about the same height as me. I'll never get over the stuff people worry about.

I don't answer but zip up my mac and let her follow me. The way down is granite steps but these ones are very narrow; there's no rail to hold on to. Once I'm by the water I look back. She's only got about halfway down and she's trying to hold on to the wall because she's scared. There's no purchase there though, only smooth stone that her hands slide over.

She stops. 'Carmel,' she calls over. 'Wait for me.'

I shrug and plunge on, nearer to the muddy quagmire I generally avoid.

'OK, I'll come to you,' I hear her saying behind me. Her voice is starting to sound tight around the edges.

I turn. She's coming towards me. 'If you stand over there,' I point, 'then you can take your pictures of me with the water in the background. I can pretend to be looking for something.'

Apart from the sucking mud there's something I know and she won't. This is a pinch point in the river and when the tide starts coming in you can get stuck easily, cut off. It happens faster than you could imagine.

'Ah, a director for the photo-shoot,' she says, and then grins to show there was no malice in her words, but it's obvious she really, really doesn't like being told what to do. She goes where I've pointed out but only because she's humouring me and she's worried if she doesn't, she might not get her piece about the kidnap victim.

I look down at the ground, pretending to be looking for finds, and despite everything I'm soon absorbed by what's there. I use my method of allowing things to come to me, slightly defocusing my eyes so no one rock or object is more important than another. The tide is pulled seawards and then inland twice a day. Then there's the odd piece, the odd special object, that finds its way to me. Some people like to take everything they find but I limit what I take these days. I have certain preferences, like shipbuilding nails left behind long after the boats have rotted. I have a seventeenth-century spoon with mud still stuck in the bevels in the handle and I love to wonder about the mouth it once got stuck into, the long-dead tongue it touched. There's a mystery to many pieces. There's a place where unpolished garnets with a hole drilled through the middle are constantly being found. What were they for? Theories abound – perhaps as some kind of tender in the slave trade that once flourished on this river? I have a small cache of old coins but I'm not so bothered about those. Bones and keys I love most.

Something happens down there in the water. A child's plastic necklace, worn smooth, can feel like something precious. The river is like a vast workshop devoted to transforming and embellishing every object into something rich and strange. Things, after their journey, come back made in another way.

'Hey, Carmel,' Kay calls out and I look up, startled. She's waving to me. I'd almost forgotten she was there.

I feel my eyes tighten. 'Go back a bit further,' I say.

Without thinking, she obeys. Her right leg steps back and almost instantly it's sucked into the mud up to her shin.

'Shit, Carmel.'

She tries to pull her leg out, nearly topples over and drops the small digital camera she's been using to take pictures. She has to plunge both hands into the mud to retrieve it and she starts to panic.

'Fuck,' she says. 'Help me, will you?'

I put my hands in my pockets. Beneath my wellington boots I can feel the rocks of the shoreline. The water beside us is swelling. The tide must've turned without me realising it.

I saw something before she distracted me. Underneath the foamy swirl of the tide there was something trying to show itself to me. The tide was acting like a curtain: show and hide, show and hide.

'Look, Carmel,' she says, holding herself behind the knee and pulling. 'I know you must be pissed and I'm sorry, but I'm getting really fucking scared here and you just standing and staring like that is making me even more scared. You don't want me to drown, do you? It can't be that bad.'

I realise her voice is shaking. She sounds near to tears. Perhaps she's realised how alone we are. We could be on Jupiter, just the two of us.

'Shut up,' I yell.

She goes quiet, and resorts to making little whimpering noises.

There's the thing grabbing at my attention near my feet. It's a sparkle on the edge of my vision, still starry behind my eyes even though now it's more or less concealed by the water. I have to break away from the thing shining and sparkling up at me like a dark moon, calling out and calling out for my attention, and the thread snaps as the water covers it completely.

When I look at Kay again her leg has sunk even further and the other one is up to the ankle and she's seesawing back and forth trying not to land flat on her face. My heart starts pounding. What am I doing? What on earth am I doing?

I run over to her.

'Stop trying to move,' I pant. 'You're making it worse. I'll get behind and pull you out. Struggling is the dangerous thing.'

I slosh through the water, which is up to my ankles by now, and put my arms around her from behind; she feels surprisingly thin and delicate, and that shocks me somehow. She seemed so sure of herself, so confident. It takes longer than I thought it would to get her out – perhaps I left her for too long – and I'm weak with relief when I manage to pull her from the sucking mud. She scrambles through the water until she's reached the safety of the foreshore. She's lost both of her weird shoes; they must, at this minute, be sinking down and down to the next stratum where they will eventually be sucked out by the tide to join the rest of the other million churning things in the river. One of her legs is covered in mud up to her knee and the other one up to the thigh. It's in her hair, up her arms. It gets everywhere if you let it. She stumbles and her legs buckle beneath her and she sinks to kneeling.

'Kay. I'm sorry.'

She looks up. There's a splash of mud on her face that has become very pale and in that spot of mud there are so many colours, greens, browns, even a touch of red, that it matches and even almost outshines her real green eye just above it.

'Kay,' I say it softly because I am suddenly seeing her as a tiny, fluttering bird. 'You are not short.'

She stands up and throws her camera in her bag and turns and leaves me there and crunches over the foreshore just in her socks. I know, without a doubt, she'll get into her car and cry for a long time before she's finally able to start the engine and drive off.

I think of Kay's eyes and the mud spot with its flecks of red and green and imagine right now it's mixed with tears and she's wiping it off in the driving mirror of her car. The day has left me churned and sick and shaken. I don't know what to do with it.

That night, when we've finished our meal, there's only olive oil left on our plates from the spaghetti with tiny specks of herbs in it that look like ash. Mum is reading the paper with her huge square reading glasses that make her resemble an owl. Normally, it makes me smile that she doesn't realise how she looks; her big, funny blinking eyes through the lenses are a secret joke with myself.

'Finished?' I ask.

I sweep the plates and cutlery off the table and snap on a pair of Granny's rubber Marigold gloves that she seemed to have left an inexhaustible supply of under the sink. Mum cooks and I wash up. That's how we roll in this house.

I finish quickly and sit down and take the advertising supplement but I'm not reading it. I reach under my jumper and touch the iron bracelet. I'm thinking, today was low tide so I'm going to have to wait until it's that low again. What if the tide takes her, what if she gets tugged off and floats away. I should've stayed. I should've tried to work in the water even if it was shin deep. You fool, Carmel. She'll be gone by the time the waters recede.

I remember hearing Kay's fluttering voice as I looked down at the domed object being sheathed then revealed by the incoming tide and I feel sick again. I'm hoping Kay's alright now, that she's sleeping a deep sleep where her troubles peel off her and float away.

The thing that glimmered up at me and that is right now being scoured by the salty water – I've never seen anything like it before but I know, without a doubt, even though I don't completely know what it is, it's one of those things that's been travelling towards me and its journey has been very arduous and it has gone on for a long, long time.

Mum looks up, smiles. 'Everything alright?'

I smile back. 'Sure. Ice cream?'

What I really want to say is, *I believe I've seen another of the lost girls. I believe she is trying to climb out of the river right now so I can find her. And I left her there – can you believe that?*

Beth

There's a sense of creeping danger in the house that I can't identify. It's getting into the curtains and the wallpaper. It's seeping into the carpets as surely as if the house was slowly and almost imperceptibly flooding.

Ever since I was little I've used the trick of telling myself stories about things that happen to make sense of them. I do it as I'm changing the bed, or straightening cushions or stirring pasta.

Once upon a time, a girl child was born.

That morning the light flowing through the window of the maternity ward was white and tasted of silver. There was something extraordinary about this girl, the mother knew straight away.

In this London villa I've inherited from my parents I feel the presence of Mum in the wall-to-wall carpets and fake-marble kitchen counters made of cream plastic shot through with grey veining. They'd been on the point of moving from it but health problems intervened so they ended up staying put and now I'm here.

Sometimes I talk to Mum when the house is empty. I was an only child, an imaginative and shy one, so the shock of me meeting Carmel's father – Paul – when I was eighteen, and my parents' subsequent terrible disapproval, meant that for a long time we didn't speak. I knew as soon as I met him that long ago summer as I travelled around the country with friends that I would not be leaving for my university place in far-away Edinburgh. I gave it all up in a moment. His long limbs, his country-boy way of driving, swinging the car casually round the Norfolk lanes, his curly hair and hazel eyes, his irreverence, everything. I kissed him before he kissed me, the same night we met. We were on Cromer Beach, a bonfire smouldering, my friends and his and bottles of cider and I took his face and drew it to mine. His mouth tasted of apples – the cider – and he laughed and asked if I treated all the boys like that.

'No, just you,' I said, and it was true.

The next night in his tiny room above a pub we lay twined on his narrow bed and I felt sticky and glazed by love.

My parents thought I was a fool, that he was some chancer with no money – well the 'no money' bit was true I suppose. They refused even to come to the wedding, which they wouldn't have liked anyway because our reception was out in the same pub beer garden, and afterwards we simply went upstairs for the honeymoon. The grass was brittle and yellow from the heat and people were squashing their cigarettes out with their shoes. It's amazing with the wooden fences and picnic benches dried out to tinder that we didn't burn the place down. Paper plates and kegs of beer. My parents would've hated it. They didn't speak to me for a long time. In truth I didn't mind that much; I didn't care about the lack of money, I didn't care about anything. I swam naked in the sea with Paul on the same beach where we first kissed and then we wrapped ourselves in blankets and ate hot mackerel with our fingers, cooked over a fire.

When Carmel was born I had so many names for that small being, like '*baban*' – the beautiful Welsh word for baby that I learned on a visit there, in a museum, where the word was carved into the head of a crib. Later, I called her Dandelion because when her hair grew, which it did quickly, it was curly like Paul's and it made my hand almost bounce if I rested it on her head and it stood out like a dandelion clock. So, *dandy* became another name but my favourite was always *lion*, because when I called her that she would always perform a lion's roar and there was something about the perfection of her mouth as it fashioned that roar, which was identical every time, that produced a welter of love in me strong enough it seemed to lift me up to the height of the branches of the beech tree outside the house.

Paul leaving me for another woman was a bitter fruit, but Carmel being taken was the event that broke like a dam over everything. It's as if it woke us up and left us all blinking at each other – my parents too – wondering how we could have been engrossed in anything so petty and meaningless.

The red coat Carmel wears still goes straight to a particular part of my brain. She wore a red duffel the day she was taken and I became a hawk for it when she was gone, on constant high alert for that flash of colour. Sometimes I'd even run towards it. I'd scan everything with this in mind, beaches and the waves and supermarket queues and even cinemas in the dark where I knew, because I'd taught myself, or convinced myself I had, the shade of grey that red became when the lights were off. I looked in people's cars as they drove past; I peered into them if I pulled alongside another car at the traffic lights. I looked in windows, oh God – *I looked in people's windows* for that red in case she was inside. Several times I got chased off. A woman in her own living room looked up at me shocked as I peered through her window. She had her own children about her feet, and she flicked her hands up at me in a 'get away from us' gesture and I could read her lips through the glass saying, 'Piss off.' A man storming out of his house: 'What are you doing on my property? Leave now, or I'm calling the police.'

Last night I took a book from the shelf, *The Rainmaker* – it was published in 1995, so the period I wasn't speaking to my parents. It had one of my mum's *'ex libris'* stickers she pasted into all her books with a slightly smudgy print of grapes around the edges. It makes me smile now to think of how she ran her suburban home like a tiny manor house. I opened it up and found a photograph inside of me, aged around five. The background was bright green so I guess it was a park in summer and I'm holding out a pink ice cream towards the camera and smiling, as if the ice cream should be the feature of the composition, not me. I pictured Mum tucking it inside those pages, and wondered what impulse that day compelled her to do it. I turned it over but there was nothing written on the back, no clues. I have the strong sense of the house as a puzzle, or a treasure trove, ready to give up its secrets. I'm finding myself as a child – like a little stranger – among all the books, the white china cups and plates set with silver at the rim and lip, crouching behind the concrete bird bath with the two blue painted birds supping from the edge of it.

Fay rings.

'Have you seen the *Gazette*?' she asks.

'No, haven't bought it for ages,' I say before my stomach is gripped with familiar fear. She's a good friend, Fay; she wouldn't alert me to anything that wasn't necessary.

'Why? What is it? What is it?' I hold my phone tighter.

'It's Carmel.'

'Is it bad?'

'No, Beth, in the scheme of things it's really not bad; it focuses on Carmel's interest in the river mainly but I thought you should know in case it all starts up again. I don't think there's enough information in it for her location to be given away but, you know, I thought you should be aware. I think she's been rather had.'

I close my eyes. 'Thank you,' I say softly. 'Thank you for the warning.'

'Are you OK?'

'Not really.'

'What is it?'

'I'm worried about her. She seems so lost sometimes, and angry.'

'Angry at what?'

'At everything. At me.'

'You?'

'Yes, for what happened. I think she thinks it was my fault somehow.'

'Oh, Beth.'

'I knew it would take time to readjust but sometimes I think she's settled down and it all gets smashed apart by the tiniest things.' I think of Alan, looking up from his cage. 'I think it's getting worse, not better.'

'Is there anything specific?'

I chew my lip, thinking. 'When she first came back she used to chat openly about how she could lay hands and heal and all sorts of rubbish as if it was completely bloody normal. She doesn't do that anymore, she's gone into herself. I thought it had all gone away but sometimes I get the horrible feeling she still believes in it all, she's just not saying anything. God, she didn't talk to the journalist about that, did she?'

'No, there wasn't mention of anything like that.'

'Small mercies, I suppose.'

'Beth?' The static on the line swims between us. 'Don't be too hard on her, will you? It's not her fault.'

'You don't need to say that,' I murmur.

'I know I don't. But I know how afraid you are and how it can make you feel sometimes . . .'

'I've got to go,' I say quickly, into whatever she was about to say next, to rub it out before it becomes solid words.

'Beth . . .'

'I mean I need to go before all the copies of the *Gazette* have sold out.' And very gently I take the phone from my ear and press the 'end call' button even though she's still speaking to me.

I'm in such a hurry I miss the article the first time and rip the edges of several pages. Then I find it. In the black-and-white photograph Carmel's hair is getting blown back by a gust of wind off of the river.

The headline is garish enough.

Kidnapped Teen's Trauma Helped by Unusual Hobby.

It's not even accurate. She turned twenty-one not so long ago but I suppose the fetishising of the word 'teen' was too much to resist – especially with the alliterative temptation of 'trauma'.

I read on.

'Carmel Wakeford, who at the age of eight was kidnapped by a religious cult and held against her will for five years, has taken to an unusual pastime to keep her nightmares at bay. Mudlarking is the ancient art of retrieving treasures from the Thames when the tide is low. For Carmel, it's a welcome relief in her attempt to overcome her demons. "Sometimes I wake up and think I'm back there," she says . . .'

I pause, put my index finger on the sentence and look at the wall. Does she? This is something she has never confided in me. I carry on reading.

'I spoke to her in her north-west London home where she lives with her mother.'

My stomach turns over. So, she – I scan for the name under the headline – Kay Ward, *Kay Ward* was in our home.

'"Sometimes," Carmel goes on to say, "I even get mixed up and think perhaps I'm in captivity here." She smiles a heartbreaking smile. "Though of course I know that's not true and all the time I was away I never stopped thinking about Mum and Dad."

'Carmel goes on to show me her finds, a most beautiful skull of a bird being one of the most striking. "Doing this is my saving grace," she beams. "I feel like I'm rescuing things that are lost just like I was lost."'

That last sentence just doesn't ring true. Carmel doesn't speak in such trite terms. I feel a flare of anger at the reduction of my daughter.

'I spent time chatting to Carmel then we went to her favourite stretch of water where we had a happy couple of hours looking for finds. "Not one of my lucky days," said Carmel ruefully before heading off into the afternoon.

'An extraordinary young woman with a remarkable hobby.'

In the last sentence I can sense *Kay Ward* didn't know how to end the piece, wanted to be done with it. Carmel frightens people sometimes, without meaning to. She doesn't operate in the same way as most people do.

I hear a key in the lock of the front door and quickly close the paper and shove it under the sink. I haven't decided how to deal with this, whether to pretend I haven't seen it, or to bring it up gently, although of course anything like that risks looking like a confrontation.

You and I do not need any extra confrontations, I decide. Too often we are on a knife edge; sometimes, people need to be allowed to be left alone. If I have an urge to speak,

I'll think of a button on my lip and do it up with a twist of my fingers. I hear you moving upstairs, tracking back and forth, you my daughter, who went away at eight years old and like a changeling came back at thirteen, with periods, with breasts. You came back with sharpened cheekbones, with shorn curls.

I think of my mum and that photo again and it occurs to me for the first time perhaps it's the same for everyone: we all lose our children. Perhaps not in the brutal way I did but you lose them all the same as they grow up and the grief of that is real and true for everybody.

The thing that hadn't changed was that you were still wearing a red coat. Not the one you'd gone missing in of course. Not the one done up with toggles with a brilliant crimson hood. No, the one you came back with, the one that looked like a soldier's, as if you'd been away at battle all that time. You looked like a returning Joan of Arc that day I met you again in the police facility that was nondescript and grey and that made you stand out more than ever when I saw you at the end of the corridor, through a glass wall, coming towards me. There was something of a fairy tale about it – you, spirited away at eight years old and then returned in a miraculous homecoming, crossing a threshold from one world to the next in a concrete place full of orange plastic chairs and corridors. Little Red Riding Hood turned to Joan of Arc. Later you told me you'd worn a red coat all the time you were gone, trying to hold on to your identity, I suppose. You still do today.

Your father was not calm and I was oddly so (of course, we weren't together in that sense, but we were friends, good friends by then) but I had a terrible fear that seems strange now.

It was this – I was terrified that we might not know each other, might not recognise each other when we met again. Yes, that was my main fear.

When I caught a glimpse of you, returned to me, in that red military-looking coat and that moment that I'll never forget when we both raised our hands in a kind of wave, or greeting. On my part it was something that happened instinctively, automatically, when what I expected to do was to fall on you, to cover you with kisses, to hug you until the breath nearly left your body. No, we simply held our hands up to each other and I think it was an act of recognition and my greatest fear that we would not know each other was put to bed with that simple gesture.

We have still not touched each other. I tried to hug her many times, later, but she always pushed me away. There were sharp words too about how angry she was, how Paul and I should've looked after her better – well, me mainly. Now, she doesn't seem to have a problem touching anyone – anyone but us that is.

That day though I think the biggest shock came as we were standing face to face. Neither of us cried, not then. I could hear Paul behind me gently weeping. I think, and this is a strange thing to say, I think we were too curious in that moment to cry and we only stood there examining each other. Then the biggest shock: you opened your mouth, rounded it and said,

'Mom.'

A gut punch. Your accent. As American as Donny

Osmond or The Fonz or Wednesday Addams, all things I'd grown up with, been enthralled by, and now you were part of that exotic world.

Hearing you say that word – in your strong American accent – peeled everything else away and the brute reality beneath was laid bare. You had taken on the characteristics of your captors. They had opened you up and, like a speaking doll, had taken out your voice box and replaced it with their own.

While she was gone, I'd have a recurrent dream about Carmel, that she was walking backwards towards me, towards the house, but somehow never getting any nearer. I'd wake from it crying out her name. Sometimes I'd even get up in the night and check through the window that her little figure wasn't out there in the darkness, unsuccessfully and desperately trying to walk back home across the fields against forces that were too great and that neither of us could control.

In the last few weeks, my dreams have taken a troubling turn. I dream that her hand is slipping from mine and I can feel the emptiness of my hand in my dream. I look down and see my aching, empty palm, but when I look up, it's not her at eight years old, it's Carmel as she is now, twenty-one and in her shabby clothes.

My fault, my conscience tells me all the time. It was my fault she was taken for not looking after her better. My ex-husband screamed that at me once, although he apologised afterwards. There's the missed birthdays, the shared history we would have had, the haunting trauma she's been left with, her fears, her brave attempts at rehabilitation that leave me chewed and guilt-ridden as I watch on the sidelines. *But, oh, my darling, my brave little lion, why am I dreaming of losing you again? What can it mean?*

Now I hear your feet in their Converse sneakers slap down the hallway. You come in and pour yourself a glass of water at the sink and sit opposite me at the table. You take a sip.

'It wasn't a bird.'

The accent is still there, though softened now. The language too can be odd, the Americanisms; it pains me although I don't let on.

'Mum. I said it wasn't a bird.'

She bends the word bird in an American way. That's what caught me. My mind pedals to catch up. 'Pardon?'

'The bone. It was an eel. In the paper she said it was a bird. It wasn't even a skull; it was a jawbone. I'm guessing you know about the article?'

I let out a sigh. 'Yes, but why would she do that?'

'She seemed to want it to be a bird.'

'Perhaps it sounds more romantic.'

'There's nothing romantic about bones.'

She takes another sip of water.

'Carmel. Don't worry about her, don't even think about it.'

She tenses. 'Perhaps I just for once wanted something for myself. Normal twenty-one-year-olds are at college with their friends.'

'We could do something one evening, Carmel.' As soon as it's out of my mouth I regret it. She doesn't have to say 'going out with your mother is not really the same thing'

– it's obvious and the unsaid obviousness of it crackles between us.

'Look,' she says. 'I know I'm odd.'

'Everyone's odd.'

'Not as odd as me. I am an oddment.'

'So am I,' I say loyally.

I know this is delicate territory. It's partly why she likes mudlarking, she's told me; she can be with people but they're all looking at the ground, not looking at her; they have other things they're focussing on. She told me once she tried going into a bar, buying a lemonade, sitting at a table hoping to meet people. She watched the groups chatting away for half an hour like she was looking into a fish tank; she could see them but they couldn't see her. She finished her drink and left, pulling her coat around her as she walked out, her hurry was that great. I could see her in that moment, leaving the darkness of the pub, getting tangled up with her coat in her anxiety.

The current red coat is outsize and hangs loosely down to her knees as if she could disappear inside it. I notice now that the seam just beneath her shoulder is coming undone. The hem of it at the front is rimed with mud. There is a smudge of mud by her nose too and a flick of it in her hair. Oh, daughter, I think. *Oh, daughter.*

'She was frightened that she was short.'

I startle. I'd been in a reverie. 'Who?'

'Kay, the journalist. It frightened her for some reason, the idea that she might be.' She pauses, sips water. 'Why does everyone want to think everything has to be the same?'

'I don't know, my love.'

'Neither do I.' She pushes her chair back, smells her palms. 'I'm going for a bath.'

'OK.'

She pauses on her way out of the room. 'How d'you think she found me?'

The question had occurred to me. 'I don't know. A chat in a pub. A friend of a friend. People think London's huge but it's not really, when it comes to people.'

'Sneaky way of doing it though – pretending to be interested in what I'm doing.'

I can see this has hurt her a great deal.

'Perhaps she wasn't pretending,' I say softly.

'Maybe. I liked her at first. She was a bit—'

'What?'

'Nothing. I guess I hope she's alright. I'm interested in finding people too. Perhaps I'll ask her how she does it.'

'Who do you want to find?' But she's gone and I hear her feet thumping up the stairs.

As soon as I hear the water running above me, the creak and slide of her getting into the bath, I take out the paper again and shut myself in the sitting room. I scan the piece for clues. In terms of where we live the piece says north-west London but doesn't name West Hampstead specifically so that could've been worse. It doesn't say that Carmel works part time in a café so her workplace is not named which had been my greatest fear. Perhaps Carmel didn't mention it. Anything else that could pinpoint us in time or space? I scan three times but I'm still not satisfied and I know I won't be however many times I read the piece and tell myself we're safe. I decide to look through it once again to check.

I'm looking for these clues, anything that might give us away, because I know the others will be too.

Mercy

1999

For several days now Mercy had been secretly plotting how to get her parents to the healing church service so that hands could be laid on them and they would be made well. She began with subtle hints about how much better they could feel if only they came along with her the following Sunday. Then when that didn't work resorting to all sorts of lies – saying there was a lovely surprise waiting for them there, even hinting there might be earthly rewards such as money involved.

All her pa would say, stubbornly, was, 'Never held with church, never will,' until Mercy had the urge to slap him.

But the way it turned out, her parents had been harbouring their own secret which they broke to her one morning as Mercy was eating Cheerios in the kitchen-diner.

The news was so momentous her spoon stilled mid-air.

'You're going to leave me *all alone*?' she said.

She noticed her ma was wearing her very best blouse that she kept for special occasions. It was white with intricate yellow smocking on the yoke and real lace panels that meant you could see her ma's delicate shoulders through the fabric and it made them look like budding wings. She'd done something special with her eye make-up; both lids were silver with a blob of orange, so when she blinked, it looked like two wings of a butterfly alighting briefly on her face.

She wanted to say, *Mom, you're scaring me* – but she didn't. She thought perhaps she'd misunderstood when her ma said they were leaving the house without her and they would instead tell her to get ready right away. She wondered if they'd be going out of the mountains, away from the forest. Perhaps they had different kinds of trees and birds there. She couldn't imagine it at all.

But her ma said, 'Now that's the thing of it, my lovely girl. It's something me and your pa need to do on our own. There's a sort of prospect we need to attend to and it's one that isn't right for a little girl such as yourself to be involved in. So, you see,' her ma pursed her lips, 'it's much safer if you stay here for a little while until we get back. Just for a few days. Two or three at most.'

'On my *own* in the day *and* the night.'

For the first time Mercy noticed their packed rucksacks through the open door of the hallway. No third bag for her.

'But what about you?' Mercy was crying now; a string of snot burst out of her nose. 'Who's gonna make you *eat*?' Mercy realised something else too: if they were to be gone as long as three days they'd miss church and the visiting pastor. This seemed worse than anything. 'And you won't get to come to church and be made better neither,' she wailed.

'Look, we'll get back when we can. I can't say any more than that.'

As her parents prepared to leave, Mercy stood by the door and readied herself to beg them to reconsider. She could scarcely believe that soon she would be completely alone from dawn to dusk and then through the endless night. Added to that it nearly broke her heart to think they might miss out on the blessing of the spirit that likely would run through the tent like a mighty wind when the visiting pastor came.

'Now then, petal,' her mother called from the kitchen-diner. 'You come in here so we can have a final run-through.'

Mercy flattened herself against the door. 'I ain't budging until you change your mind.'

'Come on, darling. You and I both know this is gonna happen so let's make it as easy as possible and we'll be back before you know it. If you're good I'll make your eyes up before we go. How about that?'

It was very, very tempting. Delia had painted her daughter's nails and lips before but she'd never done her eyes, and eyes were Delia's speciality. Mercy tried to stay resolute.

'You can still do my eyes if you stay.'

'That ain't gonna happen.'

Mercy could tell from her voice that no disagreement would be brooked so with a heavy heart she joined her mother in the living room to run through everything about switching the lights off at night to not going beyond the porch to what to do if anyone knocked on the door – hide behind the sofa till they went away. Absolutely no one must know she'd been left on her own and she must in no circumstances step off the front porch. It was school vacation so that was no problem – just as long as she kept her head down real well.

Her ma sat Mercy down on one of the dining chairs and fetched her palette of eye colours.

'Now then, what colour scheme would you like?'

Mercy dithered for ages between green and gold, shades of blue and a full rainbow on each eye like her ma did for herself sometimes. It was partly a genuine dilemma about what to have alongside a delaying tactic so the terrifying notion of being left completely alone could be put off even for just a little while.

She figured given the circumstances there was no point in holding back so she went for the full rainbows.

After they'd picked up their backpacks and stood on the porch and were saying goodbye to Mercy the colours of the world seemed to grow vivid and acid even as she felt her cheeks turn a hot, bright red.

She glowered at them under her rainbow lids, furious from the open door.

'Go then,' she said. 'Fuck off. Leave me on my own to die.'

And with that she slammed the door so hard it near came off its hinges.

'They've left me all on my own!' Mercy yelled out of the open front door, hoping the racoon would hear. She'd been looking for him all morning since her parents had left. Earlier on she thought she'd heard him skittering about on the broken wooden boards of the porch and she'd gone out to look. There was nothing there. He no longer seemed to want to find his way into the house. Perhaps something had scared him off. Her pa was always threatening to throw something at him; perhaps he'd fulfilled his promise. She went back in and opened a packet of saltines that she'd been saving for later but the loneliness was getting to her in a terrible way and right now she'd do anything to lure the racoon in to keep her company for an hour or two. She went outside and scattered them on the broken boards. Finally, by afternoon she was rewarded by a flash of brown fur, a skitter of claws on the porch boards. He'd come back! He snuffled into the saltines and crunched them up hungrily. Then, to her delight, he picked up a rusted-out tin cup that had been left outside and held it in his human-like hands. With his hands wrapped around it he peered into the mug and he almost looked like he was about to take a sip from it, although when she stood up in excitement the movement from the window meant he dropped the cup with a clang and he scurried back into the trees.

The first day was not so bad. As she'd watched their blue, broken-down car disappear in the dirt road cut between the trees she'd made a decision. Until they returned, she would no longer be Mercy; in fact she would not even be a human. She'd merge herself with the nature all around and become one of the trees, one of the whippoorwills that flew among them, a shy salamander that made its home under a damp stone. She practised the calls of the fly-catcher, a modest-looking little bird that threw its head back and sang a distinctive fee-bee-o note, so she did the same. As it grew dark, she climbed the ladder to her loft space, curled up inside her sleeping bag and felt she might as well be one of the gophers out in the forest, curling up into itself with a paw over its eyes in the hollow of a tree trunk. She fell into a deep, exhausted sleep.

By the next day she decided to test the boundaries her ma

had set. 'No further than the porch,' her ma had said. 'And even then, keep your ears open and your wits about you and if you hear anyone around you get back inside that house and lock the door and crawl right behind the sofa and don't come out for nothing until you're sure you're alone again. In fact, make sure the door is locked at ALL times – take your breath of air then straight back inside.'

Mercy figured that there was no way her ma was going to know if she'd stepped off that porch or not. In fact, the idea of stepping off it made her feel a whole lot better because why should her ma have a say in what she did and where she went when she'd gone and left her all on her own with only a cardboard box of food? It deserved a smidgeon of defiance.

Mercy took off her pink shoes and went out barefoot to the forest. She lay beside an ant hill and watched them for hours dragging building materials to their nest. She sat so still at the base of a tree that a moose came out right in front of her and drank from a tree stump full of water while she held her breath in awe.

That night there was a bright moon and the fungi on the window were silhouetted dark against it, their little hatted heads turning up to look at the sky. On her own now, apart from what had seemed like their unbreakable triumvirate, Mercy tried to imagine what her ma and pa were seeing through their eyes but all she came up with was a lit-up fancy café with a glass cabinet full of elaborate cakes, though she surmised it was pretty unlikely her parents were frequenting places like that and also guessed – rightly – that in all probability the vision came about because she was hungry, so she gave up on this line of thought.

She did not know, of course, that right at that moment when she decided to give up on the possibility of the fancy cakes that her parents were actually both on their knees in a motel room with a gun pointing to the back of their heads. Her mother was looking down at the green carpet, at her own knees buried in the pile of it and swearing to herself, *If we ever get out of this alive, I swear, things are gonna be different from now on. Sweet Jesus, I swear.* Their 'prospect' – the chance to become small-time dealers to fund their own habit – had turned sour. At that moment it was Mercy that flashed through Delia's mind and she wondered how she could've borne to leave her daughter like that.

In all this time there were two things like lit beacons that kept Mercy going. One was God and the thought of the tent and once again feeling the holy spirit pass through her. The other was the racoon. To Mercy they were part of the same thing, different ends of a spectrum that was a shaft of light and hope in her mind.

But the next day when she realised how long her parents had been absent, her stomach clenched painfully. She'd been keeping her own record – a corner of Pop-Tart, or cracker, or whatever she'd chosen for breakfast that morning on the counter top in front of the blinking microwave. Time had gone strange almost as soon as they'd gone, minutes seemed like hours, so she'd devised this system to keep track. Now, she counted two bits of food so today's would make that three. She'd been hanging on to the mention of two days, knowing in her heart of hearts all along if three were mentioned then they'd take that or more. Her ma was only trying to make it sound better. She counted on her fingers again to be sure. She guessed it might be easy for a 'day' to disappear – eaten by a mouse or some insect trundling across the work surface, but extra morsels of food would not get tagged on by accident. She allowed herself to think something she'd known all along; that in reality she couldn't trust a word her ma and pa said so who knew when or even *if* they'd come back, and the knowledge made her feel desolate right down to her toes. She didn't even want breakfast anymore.

It was summer but the sun had barely risen. A big hole opened up in the day. Mercy looked down at her hands. The cracks in the palms were black, full of dirt, so they looked like the forest paths. Of course! She was forgetting about washing. She knew something was missing. In the bathroom she filled the sink with cold water and looked into the mirror. It was the first time she'd seen herself since her parents had left. Mostly, she came in to use the toilet and didn't bother to even close the door now she was on her own. She'd been bypassing the mirror without even thinking to look in it. Now, the sight of her own reflection was the strangest thing. She didn't seem to know herself anymore. Her light brown curly hair shot out in all directions like fireworks. Brushing her daughter's hair was one thing her ma did often attend to, plaiting it or making cute bunches sometimes, and without that attention Mercy's hair had turned into an unmanageable, thick nest.

It was then that she noticed what had happened to the rainbows on her eyelids. The make-up was still just about there but the seven colours of the spectrum had bled together and merged into one khaki hue that was only visible now where it was sunk into the creases round her eyes. The brilliant, sharp colours had turned ugly and muddy. It reminded Mercy of going to church with a dirty face and how ashamed she had felt until she'd remembered how God wouldn't care a fig even if she was wearing rags and covered in forest dirt. Pastor Frogmore said as much in one of his sermons; in fact, he seemed to speak more slowly and look right at Mercy while he was saying it, that the fact of a person's shabby attire probably meant He loved you even more.

Mercy squeezed out the wash rag in the cold water and soaped up her face and then scrubbed and scrubbed until she could feel her skin going pink.

'You Mercy still?' she asked the reflection.

The reflection grinned back. 'Why, sure I am. Who else you thinking I might be?' She felt something float back into herself and she felt better after that.

But it didn't last for long. She'd never felt so alone. Not even when her parents had been impossible to rouse for two straight days. Not even when she was called names in town. At least then there was human noise and faces around her. She felt a burning anger towards her parents that she'd never experienced before, not even in their worst moments as addicts.

She knew from her counting of the days that it was Sunday and the image of the beautiful church tent with all the faces raised in singing came to her and she knew simply being among people would feel like a sip of water when you were dying of thirst. She had to go. Even thinking about it made her start to feel better, even a little bit excited. She wrote a curt note to her parents and left it on the kitchen counter on the off chance they came back when she was gone.

They could come and find her if they liked, in fact that was probably her best chance of getting them there. She wouldn't even care if they tried to drag her out for disobeying them about leaving the house. The Lord would surely intervene and keep them there once they'd entered His kingdom through the flaps of the tent. She dressed herself with care, cut the mould off a slice of bread, toasted it then set off.

At the tent a kind of extension had been put onto the side to accommodate extra people in anticipation of the visiting pastor. It stood out bright white against the original structure whose canvas was beginning to look a little green and mildewed with age. As usual, Myla Joyce was at the door ready to hand out leaflets.

Mercy studied the leaflet. 'Father Patron?'

It felt odd talking to another human being after all this time but Myla didn't seem to notice.

'That's him. Now you go in and get yourself a seat right at the front because you are likely to witness some miracles today.'

Inside Mercy put the Bible that had been placed on the seat on her lap, and while waiting, to take her mind off the awful feeling in her guts she let herself absorb the beautiful, godly atmosphere of the tent. Soon, it began to work its magic and the pain began to ease a little. But the knowledge that she had a big secret she had to keep covered up made her feel dizzy so she tried to concentrate on the flash of her shoes as she swung her feet back and forth. Once, she wetted her finger with spit and rubbed at some forest dirt she noticed on the toes and made the tips bright again.

By the time the tent had filled up it had become very hot. People were fanning themselves with the leaflets they'd been given at the door. Dark patches started appearing under the arms of the men's shirts and some of the ladies' pastel-coloured dresses. Pastor Frogmore came onto the low makeshift stage at the front of the tent and spoke into the microphone. He lifted his hand above his eyes and looked out. 'I have one thing and one thing only to ask of ya – are ya ready?'

The sound of 'yes' and 'sure thing' and 'hallelujah' sounded across the crowd. They were ready.

Pastor Frogmore sang 'See, What a Morning' into the microphone with his eyes closed. The service that he delivered had an electric edge to it today, but all the same the crowd were impatient. This wasn't what they came for.

Soon they became aware of a tall figure that had somehow entered without them noticing and was standing on the far aisle, by the side of the tent, waiting in the wings as it were. As he was introduced by Pastor Frogmore and moved towards the stage the light fell on his pure white hair, carefully combed backwards, and flashed off the gold rims of his round glasses. His pronounced limp as he took the side steps up onto the stage somehow had a noble aspect to it and his cream suit had just the right touch of glamour and foreign-ness – that is, not too much.

He stood behind the microphone and for a long silent moment that felt like it might split apart at any time, he stood with his arms raised and his eyes closed. Then, his eyes snapped open, revealing their intense blue colour.

'Are you here for the Lord?'

Then the moment finally gave way and the silence burst. A woman stood towards the back of the tent shouted out, 'We sure are, sir. Hallelujah.'

Mercy craned her neck back to look. Next to the woman was a young girl in a wheelchair that stood in the aisle. Mercy recognised her as one of the big girls who used to be in her school and remembered her name was Vera. Mercy had given out a hymn book to her before and Vera said 'hi' and had wanted to know her name. Now, the woman was holding up one of the girl's arms with her hand in an attitude of praise and Mercy feared for that arm. It looked like a stick that was about to break. It was like this woman was the opener for everyone else to join in and a hubbub lifted towards the ceiling that the preacher waited to die down, watching approvingly, before he spoke again.

'Know this,' said Pastor Patron 'Only those that believe will have the divine spirit descend on them today. The power visiting us will be in direct proportion to the strength of your belief. Do not doubt it for one single second. Also do not doubt the devil is stalking inside this tent today and he will take his wily chances too and seek to exploit with his sinister intent anyone who is wavering.'

A tide of moans went up, 'He's here, beware, beware.'

Mercy felt a tide of pain rising in her guts once more at the thought of the evil old devil stalking their beautiful, light church, ready to snatch up victims in his horrible long, greasy, bony fingers. She jumped to her feet and raised a fist. 'Damn him,' she shouted. 'Damn him back to hell.' Her words got sucked into the surrounding hubbub.

How she hated that devil in that moment and the words she wanted to deliver personally to the devil rose in her throat – *Get out, you dirty motherfucker, get out.* She managed to pinch the insult out just in time by squeezing her lips together.

Then the pastor's eyes fell on her and his gaze was like a blue flash and she sank back down into her seat with her cheeks burning.

'Yes, child,' he said quietly. He seemed to have been able to pick out what she'd said. 'Your words may be crude but your light shines out. He should indeed be damned.'

Then Mercy's cheeks burned harder because for a moment there it was like there was no one else in the tent because his attention was so overwhelming and focussed on herself. Mercy didn't know what she could've done to deserve it. She also was worried that perhaps the preacher could tell somehow what she'd been *about* to say and even that the dirty words might be hanging about her, written in the air above her head.

But just as she was squirming under his gaze, he turned the blue light of it away and pointed to someone in the crowd.

'You, you, boy, are you ready to be healed?'

Mercy turned to look. It was Hal who cleared tables at

The Purple Pineapple café. He might look like he worked a trifle slow when she watched him through the window as he stacked plates and glasses onto a tray but Mercy had never considered there might be anything actually wrong with him. However, he came bounding down the carpet and up on the stage where he stood, awkward and excited with his eyes shining.

Pastor Patron dragged a chair from the back of the stage to the front. 'Sit, boy,' he said.

Hal sat down and squeezed his hands between his knees. His eyes nearly bulged out of their sockets. It's clear he'd never been centre stage in this manner before and this was potentially the most exciting moment of his life.

'Now then, boy. I want you to do something for me. Can you do something for me, you think?'

Hal looked up and he nodded, his eyes bright and his hands squeezed so tight between his knees now Mercy feared he'd mangle them forever.

'What's your name, boy?'

Mercy saw his mouth open and say his name but she couldn't hear him because he was so far from the microphone and was whispering anyway.

'I want you to stay seated and stretch your legs out afore ye. You think you can do that, Hal?'

Hal nodded and stretched his legs out in front of him. Mercy was close enough to see a little hole in his black Sunday best shoes where his white sports sock poked through.

'Now then, Hal. Have you ever noticed that you have in fact one leg shorter than the other?'

Hal's eyes nearly popped out of his head as he looked

at his feet. The pastor had unhooked the microphone and brought it to Hal's lips so they could all hear him this time. 'No, sir, I did not know that.'

'Well, I did. I noticed it straight away as you were coming in.'

This caused a few of the congregation to wonder where the preacher had been concealing himself as they all arrived because none of them had seen him. They stirred uncomfortably in their seats at the thought that he'd been watching them covertly. But mostly the passing thoughts were dismissed, or at least forgotten about later.

The preacher grabbed both the boy's Sunday best shoes and started cranking them about in his hands. His bright blue eyes were raised to heaven.

'In the name of the Lord, heal, heal this boy of all his afflictions. Oh Lord, take them, take them and let him be whole again.'

The preacher gave Hal's feet a final jiggle. 'Now stand, Hal, stand and show everyone what the Lord is capable of.'

Hal jumped up and looked down at his feet in amazement. He walked across the stage, then overcome with enthusiasm, zipped back and forth in a run before skipping off the stage. Even though Mercy hadn't known there was anything wrong with Hal, she sure had never seen him move this fast.

Then the blue-eyed, white-haired pastor, who still had the air of a man in strong middle age, turned to the congregation and held his arms out and said, 'Come, come all of you, those who are afflicted, those who believe enough to be healed.'

This whole performance was so sure, so slick and professional, it seemed a world away from the hick gathering of last week with Maeve Coleman and her farting cure. This felt like being part of something extraordinary.

Mercy didn't know it at the time but this performance would be one that she'd witness many, many times.

People surged towards Pastor Patron and he descended the front steps of the stage like a film star knowing himself to be at the height of his powers of attraction. Somehow Mercy found herself pushed forward. She gazed upwards and could just about see the preacher, who stood a little taller than the crowd because he hadn't descended down to their level and was standing on the lowest step of the stage. She could see his hands hovering above the heads, choosing which one to alight upon, then when he'd chosen, his hand descended and it was as if he kept electricity in his palm, because inevitably the person touched fell backwards as if pushed, as if jolted by an unseen current, and fell right into the uplifted arms of the crowd, who carried them off.

Nearly right by the stage now, something banged painfully on Mercy's foot and she spun to see Vera, the girl from the wheelchair, who was now on crutches and being dangerously jostled by the crowd so she swayed round like a toy, only just managing to keep herself upright. The rubber plug at the bottom of the crutch had accidentally thumped on top of Mercy's pink shoe.

'Careful, girl,' Mercy shouted, but her voice got swallowed up by the crowd.

Vera, several heads taller than Mercy, with long wispy blonde hair and a summery green and white dress that hung nearly to the ground, swayed towards Mercy.

'Careful,' Mercy shouted again, but the girl appeared to fold sideways and crashed into Mercy's outstretched arms. Mercy felt the force of her body and was almost knocked off her own feet. She did a trick she kept for when she needed strength for performing any difficult domestic tasks, or even for lifting one of her parents when the need arose, if they were about to crumple and fall. She tightened all her muscles and made herself into a tree, like one of the trees right outside her front door, an oak perhaps hung with moss and ready to withstand any force, so when the girl fell against her and Mercy put out her arms, she didn't topple but held her there, upright with both of them locked in a gaze. And then the really extraordinary thing happened, the thing that Mercy couldn't understand or explain: the girl dropped the crutches that had become entangled under her arms, pushing them away like they were abhorrent to her.

'Look,' Vera said. Then when nobody heard her, she raised her voice. 'Look, everyone, look. Spirit's gone through me.'

Then gradually everyone did look and a silence began to fall and the people that had been crushed and sweating and almost on top of them both began to move away until it was just the two of them – Mercy and Vera – both panting a little and standing face to face.

'I can stand up,' said Vera, her voice almost worried and perplexed. Her hands hovered over her hips, pointing down at her legs. She raised her head to look at Mercy. 'Look, see? It was Mercy. Mercy did it.'

Then Mercy turned to look behind her. Everyone was

silent. She saw Lena who worked in the Piggly Wiggly store. Miss Forbouys who'd taught her two years back, and Myla Joyce who was dressed entirely in lilac again. There was Hal from The Purple Pineapple who'd skipped around the stage so lightly earlier. There was Brad Barnard, who collected the town's garbage in a growling truck every Friday morning and who always wore cologne to church as if he wanted to make doubly sure the smell of garbage had not followed him, even though it was unusual, even slightly suspect for a man to wear fragrance amongst the menfolk there. There was Mrs Baker, who only had one eye because of a botched cataract operation, and Doug Finchdale, who was one of the boys that had thrown stones at her in main street, all silently staring at her.

The one who stared the most though, whose bright blue eyes seemed to laser through the congregation, seemingly with the ability to cut through bodies and chairs and hymn books held aloft, was Pastor Patron.

Carmel

2013

Between the ages of eight and thirteen, in the period I was *gone*, I would often become muddled about the day, the month, the year. Sometimes birthdays were missed and I wouldn't even know what age I was so I developed a specific habit to mark time because this ignorance of it made me feel seasick, or like I was falling through the air with nothing to grab on to.

I began giving names to stretches of time leading from a day that had been especially significant for one reason or another. So there was the Day of the Holy Nails for example, that was completely distinct and in no way to be mixed up with the Day of the Tree and Snake. These days coloured the periods that came after them – whether it was weeks or months, it did not change until a new significant day occurred. The Small Blue Gate only lasted a couple of days as I recall, unlike Arriving at the Shore of Galilee, which went on for months – although I believe now that it was some kind of National Park we were in and nothing to do with Galilee at all.

The Day of the Tree and Snake often itches at me, like there's something in it that needs to be uncovered but that would take time and there's low tides to think about now. That little lost girl that was me and untangling the mysteries of what happened to her will have to wait.

I wonder what would *this* time could be called.

Low tide. It's time to go back to see if I can retrieve what I saw the day I was with Kay Ward. I wake up to a strange cast of light. It's violet, like purple cellophane has been put over a lens and it floods the room because I never close the curtains at night. Even the air seems faintly mauve; there's something violent, urgent about it. I automatically reach for the iron bracelet around my left wrist. Today it seems charged with electricity. I jump out of bed and scramble into my clothes left out the night before on the wicker chair. A storm is coming.

The light before a storm has a quality to it like nothing else and if I can get to the foreshore before the storm breaks it will help me, because everything is delineated in this light, like a pin-sharp photo lit by arc lights on one side.

I grab my rucksack and run downstairs. Mum's coming out of the living room with an empty mug in her hand. She's got a few days off because her friend Ellie is coming to stay from Norfolk.

'Storm is coming,' I say, dragging my coat off the peg and pulling it on.

'You're going out in this?' She's laughing as she says it because she's used to me being out in all weathers.

'Yep.' I zip myself up and tighten the cord round my hood. 'Got to go.'

But Mum's looking the other way, at the weird light

coming from the kitchen. 'I think I'll go and get Ellie in the car. She'll get soaked otherwise.'

By the time I reach the granite steps to the foreshore the light has intensified. The violet is brighter, like a white light is now behind it. I nearly stumble down the steps I'm going so fast and I tell myself to slow down. I'll never find her if I end up with broken legs.

To save time I take the direct route to the water and I wade through a patch of plants that come up to my knees. Things that grow down here tend to be either slimy or springy and these are the springy kind. They look like rough thistles and must be strong enough that they can survive being drowned twice a day. They must dry out quickly too because as I push through them they rasp and scratch against each other.

There's not another soul around. It can be a dangerous place down here in a storm, and like birds that hide themselves when they sense a change in the air the people have all left, and it occurs to me how like animals we really are. Even the insects that are usually hopping around my feet appear to have gone. Only the little holes they make can be seen, like they've buried themselves away where it's safe.

I think this is the right spot. I measured it with my eyes to the position of the steps against the embankment wall but the river is a force that won't stay the same for anyone. It churns and changes and expecting things to be the same twice over is folly, I know that. Down here matter is unreliable and even stuff that's big and heavy can get tossed aside like a toy. It's all shifted around by the animals and the tides and the boats and even the other mudlarkers, although on the whole I would say they are the most respectful people you would hope to meet.

I begin pacing along the water's edge. A large drop of rain falls onto the back of my hand. I try not to entertain one sliver of the idea of not finding her today.

The tide laps, retreating another inch, and I walk the few yards again and double back and then there she is, lit clearly from the side – a perfect circle, a graceful dome. I fall on my knees, not caring about the mud and the water, and cup the little thing in my hands. My hands turn numb as I push them into the cold, wet mud to get underneath her and my fingers find the edges of the little dome quickly, easily. They graze my fingertips and I pull and she comes away so cleanly, like she was waiting for me so she could spring free, and it's so quick I land backwards and I look up at the top half of the skull in my wet hands, which drips thick drops of mud onto my knees, the bracelet dark and freezing on my wrist. I don't know how but I know she is a girl. Her bottom jaw is missing and because of the angle I'm holding her I can see through her eye sockets the tower blocks on the bank opposite with bruise-coloured clouds swirling across their glinting frames.

Then the rain comes, slanting from one side and powerful, like something's trying to drive me out of this place.

When I take the skull out of my rucksack at home the smell of the river is strong. The pile of clothes on the floor makes a damp patch on the carpet and the fleecy tracksuit I changed into feels like a balm against cold, wet skin.

I unwrap the light package of bubble wrap and it shocks me how small she is in my hands. I rub my thumb along the curve of the upper eye sockets. I cradle the bone and think about all the million little thoughts that must've happened inside of it. Now it's a scooped-out, empty thing, where have they all gone? They've fizzed away in the air and I feel so tender towards this thing that once used to be inside a human head, protecting the owner's thoughts like armour.

I fetch a wet flannel from the bathroom and gently wipe at the mud, and there, suddenly, startlingly, is the tracery of the zigzagging lines that cross a skull.

'What happened to you?' I ask the skull, but the bone stays quiet in my hands.

I had the impression that it was going to sing to me, to tell me its secrets, but it stays silent.

I want to do something for this girl, something to mark her passing from this world into the next, because the way she's been tossed aside it looks like no one else ever did that. I pluck the spiral of bones from my windowsill and return them to their shelf and put her in their place. The skull is a deep caramel colour and gleams quietly. Outside, through the window, I see the rain has stopped. Over the bottom fence I can see into our neighbour's garden. There's a woman's figure in a tartan dressing gown and wellingtons inspecting the plants in the border that runs along one side for storm damage.

I pull on some boots and in the kitchen look for a sharp knife in the overstuffed cutlery drawer. Outside, I can't see our neighbour anymore; she's shielded by the fence. A flock of sparrows in the tree at the end of the garden bursts into song.

I have the idea of making the girl a little crown woven of flowers but everything looks tattered from the storm and the cold weather. There's a few big purple dahlias, their petals as complicated as tucks in a child's dress, but they're huge, nearly the size of the skull itself, and would dwarf her. They droop and weep rainwater from the curled funnels of petals. The leaves of the ferns have sagged from the weight of the water and the orange lilies in the border have been battered to one side so their long, pale green leaves are muddy.

I remember a toy gardening set I bought a while ago. I'd only wanted the rake. It looked sturdy in its box in the newsagent with red metal and a wooden handle, ideal to use on the foreshore with its wide-set teeth that would be easily wiped clean of the mud from the Thames. But it was in a set with a watering can and a trowel, both red, and real packets of seeds, so I had to buy it all. I open the shed door to see if the trowel and the watering can's still there. There's a strong smell of soil and wood inside. They're both on the window ledge covered in dust. On the back wall of the shed Mum has hung to dry bunches of seed heads from honesty plants from a row of nails.

Mum's always grown this plant. She loves it, and told me how it's also called 'moonwort' because of the way the seed heads look when they're stripped of their rough casings, luminous, like an elongated full moon. There was a big stand of it in the flower bed in our garden in Norfolk when I was growing up. I used to help her shed the casings of the seeds by rubbing them between finger and thumb and the bright moon would appear, transparent so you could see the three or four seeds trapped inside. I unhook a bunch from one of the nails by the string that it's tied with and take it inside.

In my room the casings come away easily and flutter to the floor, making a little rustling pile at my feet. As they emerge they're as bright as something polished, as bright as the moon that they're named for. I hold a single stem up to the light at the window and twirl it between my fingers. There's something about it that reminds me of looking down a microscope, the luminous disc, the five seeds encased inside the papery cover like mysterious little dark organisms magnified by the lens.

The wreath I make is so light, it weighs nothing in my hand and when I put it on her head the moons glow against the pale brown bone in the last of the afternoon light.

I sit cross-legged in front of her on the floor. I kiss her forehead and the seed heads tickle my face.

I want to tell her my story, to communicate to her how I was lost too once, that I know what it is to feel abandoned in this world. I remember Mum used to tell me how, if something was troubling me when I was little and it was difficult to talk about, to make it into a story, to start it with 'Once upon a time', and that way you could look at it more easily.

Once upon a time, I begin.

The eye holes in the skull seem to darken. She has an expectant air and it encourages me to continue.

Once upon a time a girl lived in a house made of smoke and wind but that was still a safe place, or so she thought. She lived with her mother and always wore a coat with a hood as red as a heart, as red as the reddest rose. But the mother did not watch her child as she should. She did not take the care that she should have done because a wolf with exceptionally blue and bright eyes tracked the girl down and took her away.

I want to go back home, the girl cried, I want to go back now. Ho, the wolf replied, but you cannot because your house was made only of smoke and air and the wind has blown it clean away and your mother too is dust. But now you have me, beautiful red hood, you have me and that is a very good thing and I shall tell you why. It's because you are a very special girl. And only I know how special so you would be worthless to anyone else. Certainly wasted on your mother, who, like I've told you, no longer exists anyway so is even more useless than she ever was . . .

I stop.

'I'm wondering if the same wolf got you,' I whisper.

Mercy Roberts: the preacher tried to make me take her name, but I wouldn't. All across America I wrote my real name on the walls of toilets and in the dust on the back of vans and in glitter glue on diner tables, because I was trying to leave a trail of breadcrumbs to be picked up.

Then one day I saw Mercy's tiny face in a passport with an eagle on the cover that had been hidden. The pastor was gone and there were ducks quacking and calling on the water outside as I snooped inside the truck, searching places I was not allowed to look. The face in the photo looked like my own; the same curls, the same heart shape. When I read her name I went cold because I remembered the baptism, and even then I wondered what he'd done with her for her not to need her name anymore.

Would he do the same to me?

That's when I started thinking of her as my secret sister and she would keep me company in the churches where I was called to lay on hands, in the darkened hospitals I was sneaked into in the dead of night, my hands in front of me, floating like a ghost's, the feel on the backs of them from the breath of the person whose afflictions were being cast out. Mercy Roberts; did she like wearing her socks round her ankles so they didn't itch where the elastic was tight? I was sure, just like me, she would. Did she always wonder if there would be cinnamon buns when she stopped in her travels? What about the crispy feeling of sunburn on her shoulders – did she secretly like it too until it began to itch? Her little ghost was ever-present, following our truck like a balloon bouncing behind it on the road.

I take the skull in my palms. *Mercy, do you have this same hollow-eyed look now?*

Of course, this can't possibly be Mercy. She could not have floated to me across the Atlantic all the way from America. But I can't shake the idea that if this face wore flesh again it would look like that little girl in the passport. It would sprout curls and grow a heart-shaped chin.

So I decide to name them, the lost girls, like I once did with periods of time, so I can keep track of them all. This one, the skull, I'll call 'The Mermaid' because of where I found her. Mercy will be known as 'The Secret Sister.'

This period of time: 'The Reckoning of Mercy Roberts.'

Downstairs I hear Mum and Ellie coming back, chattering in high voices like they always do when they haven't seen each other for a long time. The light outside has nearly gone, the skull's face has darkened a little more. I hang the wreath of honesty on an empty picture hook above the desk and place the skull on a folded towel in the bottom drawer and whisper to it, 'Goodnight.'

When I go downstairs I feel more serene than I have for ages. The kitchen door is half open and electric light spills along the hallway. I can hear Mum and Ellie laughing inside. Mum says, 'You're joking?' and Ellie replies, 'Can you believe it? It was ten to midnight,' and they both laugh again. As I push open the door Ellie is saying, 'So what you were telling me earlier . . .' then she breaks off abruptly so I'm guessing she was about to talk about me.

Inside the kitchen is warm. The oven is gently pumping out heat and something that smells like vegetable lasagne. Mum and Ellie are taking alcohol. There's tiny glasses on the table and a bottle of vodka that's so cold from the freezer it smokes. One of Granny's glass dishes is full of peanuts and Mum is biting one in half with her front teeth when I walk in.

Ellie looks up. 'Hey, Carmel, how lovely to see you.' We give each other a hug while Mum watches.

She's not changed much since the last time I saw her, over a year ago. She wears denim dungarees and pink Doc Martens, the sort of clothes she's always worn, but she looks a bit heavier around the middle perhaps, her face altered in a way I wouldn't have noticed if I'd been seeing her every day. She looks at me curiously, like she does since I've come back. I know she's avaricious to know, to ask me about what happened, but she never does because she's too kind. I sit next to her.

The things I could tell her if she did! How I sometimes

laid down and slept on the ground, even on the earth. How I saw not only snakes but deserts. Gold telephones. Twins. Iron beds. Gas station after gas station. That when the crowd parted I knew more sick and lame were on their way. Sometimes there were too many and when that happened the blood would drain out of me and I'd crouch down and curl into myself because there was no more left to give that day. There were people about to die who stood right up again and walked. I made them walk again.

'Will you have a drink, Carmel?' Ellie asks.

'I do not imbibe,' I say and at the same time Mum says, 'Carmel doesn't drink alcohol,' so we're talking over each other.

It's true. I still think of it as sinful. These things have gone deep into my bones.

Then because the moment is slightly awkward Ellie rushes to fill it. 'Hey, Carmel, remember how you used to give us all head massages? Oh my God, the feel of your fingers, it could take a whole sea of troubles away.' She flexes her neck. 'I'd give anything . . .'

I stand up and plunge my hands into her thick brown hair and we both start laughing.

Later, after dinner, as I'm going up the stairs my hands start itching. I wonder if it was touching Ellie's warm scalp, the feel of the skin pliant under my fingers, that started it off. I scratch the backs of them just like I used to do and I have a rush of familiarity that leaves me breathless at my bedroom door. Perhaps it was brought on by the human touch, but it's the exact same feeling I used to get in my hands before a healing.

By the time I go to bed the itch is gone but the red marks on the back of my hands where I've scratched them are still there.

Over the next days my room becomes a little repository of bones. There are the lovingly cleaned bones on my trestle shelves from the river: the eel's jawbone, a turtle's rib, the piercing fangs of fish, the knobbly vertebrae from a sheep, the tip of a tail I think to be a monkey's, and some I haven't been able to identify.

It's the ones in the drawer that I keep as carefully as those in a reliquary the preacher took me to see in a cold stone church. I recall how he pressed his hands up against the glass, leaving fingerprints, how he put his forehead to the box and stayed there, his lips moving. When I asked what he was doing he said, 'I've come seeking healing as it's something you've withheld from me.' I could only hang my head in shame, because however many times I tried to cure him, he limped on. The Saint's bones – in three small, grubby pieces from who knows what part of the body on a piece of rotting red silk – didn't have the magical effect he was hoping for either. If anything his limp got worse.

The skull in my drawer has been joined by a fingertip from The Mermaid and three little ribs that remind me of the story the preacher loved to tell of Adam and how he forged a woman from one of his own ribs.

I returned to the site where I'd found The Mermaid's little skull again and again although the crime scene wasn't mine. When I found the tiny finger bone I held it in my palm like a charm from a bracelet. I washed it in the Thames and took it home. I had an inkling as to what it was but needed it confirming so I fetched one of my mother's anatomy textbooks from downstairs to make sure. I leafed through the section on the hand and there, there it was, the distal phalanx, and when I laid the real bone next to the minutely detailed drawing, the real thing and the illustration were almost exactly the same size because my bone was so small. How crude and real the bone looked next to the intricately etched drawing. How powerful and pulsing with life despite the fact of having come from something that is dead.

But even after that The Mermaid wasn't satisfied and the fingertip seemed to be calling from the drawer, tapping on my shoulder and wanting my attention.

I searched for a long while after that and found nothing. In that spot motorboats often powered by and the wake sloshed water over my knees as I knelt there searching with my bare hands or raking at the mud with the red-toothed toy. I dug and dug in that spot for weeks, feeling like a criminal for I was becoming obsessed with finding her. I started to wonder if I should call the police – after all, I'd found a body; somebody who was not me might be looking for her, and I was taking her, helping myself like the preacher did with me. Perhaps he was like I am now, afraid, obsessed, and something about that fear makes me keep the secret.

I needed to retrieve The Mermaid so I could stick her back together with glue and tape, with pins, to make her whole again. 'Is that all there is, a fingertip?' I cried out one day. Shortly after that I found the ribs, two together and then a third. I washed them in the water and marvelled at their construction.

The ribs were so perfect they could've been carved. Skull, fingertip, three ribs. The Mermaid was reconstructing bit by bit before my eyes. Then she went quiet and I knew I'd found everything of her there was to find.

My attention turns back to Mercy, The Secret Sister, and my questions about her multiply and form a toppling pile. They change from the simple, childish ones such as does she have a liking for strawberry jelly, if she found it as hard to put a comb through her curly hair as I did and still do.

For example, I now want to ask, could she lay on hands and cure sicknesses with a light that burned inside her? Did she get that itch inside her hands? Did the preacher make her lay hands on him too, like he did with me, to try and cure him of his limp, his sickness and his pain? Did she, like me, fail every single time she tried? Was it the same for her? Is that why she had to go?

I remember then, shortly after I was returned, they showed me the same picture of her I'd seen in the passport. 'Do you know this girl?' they asked, and I nodded. 'When did you meet?' they asked. How could I explain? 'I have not gazed upon her true face,' I said, as I still spoke a certain way then, the way of roads and churches and the readings of the Bible. Sometimes I still do, though I try and catch myself and stop when I hear it in my ears. 'Then how do you know her?' they asked. Perhaps I shook my head, perhaps I told them she was my secret sister, I can't remember. But

I do recall their murmurs to each other: 'It doesn't seem like she's seen her. It doesn't seem like she knows anything.' That was not right either but when I tried to speak it was like my mouth was full of river stones and I found I could not.

I have a novel idea. I don't know why it's not occurred to me before. I go into Mum's study where there's a computer that we share and type 'Mercy Roberts' into the internet. I'm still unfamiliar with computers. I was not raised with them like other people my age. I could have applied myself more to learning about them since I got back I suppose but somehow I couldn't shake the feeling of them not being part of my world and I still approach them warily. I pick out the letters on the keyboard with two fingers.

I learn about Mercy Roberts who in her freshman year played Maria in *West Side Story* in Ohio but when I check it out that was the year just gone. There's a Mercy Roberts that runs a sunbed centre in Illinois and looks about forty-five with crispy, straight black hair and orange skin and another one that posts her poetry from Louisiana. The latter one had me excited for a moment but I look further into it and she's eighty-three. I type simply 'Mercy' and that's hopeless; there's 'the quality of mercy is not strained', and the definition of mercy in the Bible: 'love that responds to human need in an unexpected or unmerited way'.

Then I do something I've never done before – perhaps I've been avoiding it, I don't know – I type my own name into the internet. Instantly feel sick. There's hundreds of references, one on top of the other, and I want to throw up. I slam the lid down on the laptop and run out of the room.

I look out of the window in my room and see how the sharp east wind has smashed through the last of the honesty seed cases and I realise something that seems to drain away every last drop of blood from my face.

There is only one person alive that knows what really happened to Mercy Roberts. I know he began to make some garbled confession or other the day I was found in Texas at a gathering of the faithful in tents. 'I lost her,' was apparently what he kept saying. Rambling, confused, it wasn't me he was talking about yet it was only me that he was charged with, me that makes him languish still in a prison cell far away.

Who knew that Texas could be so cold? The ice storm blew that day and sang through the canvas tents and decorated the guy lines with tinkling icicles. The preacher stopped his own singing once he was taken into custody. He went as hushed as those bones we saw in the reliquary. Not another word would he say about the girl who came before me.

When I came back to Mum I thought all this was over, that the wolf was slain.

But looking through the window at the windblown winter garden, I realise I haven't killed the wolf at all. He's still alive in a state penitentiary in Texas. He's been waiting for me all this time, not a wolf at all – a trapped spider.

It's to him I'll have to turn in this. I've known it all along deep down.

I take a pen and write 'Dear Pastor' on a piece of paper and just doing that makes my hands shake so the writing spikes up and down. I wonder what to say to him after all this time, how I can word it. I don't even know if I'm allowed to write to him so I'll have to make up a name that only he will recognise as really being me.

I have to use the internet again to research how you do it and I learn I have to look him up on a list and I find out he's not in Texas at all. I only thought he was there because that's where I last saw him at a revival meeting with tents spread out like sailing ships across the grass. He's not there but in Wisconsin and when I find his listing I cry out at the sight of it flashing on the screen because even just the shape of the name – Dennis Patron – seems too real.

I scribble the letter quickly, telling him my phone number before I have a chance to change my mind, and run to the post office through the icy streets.

It's only when I'm back, sitting on my bed and shaking uncontrollably, that I remember something about the preacher that makes me go so cold it even stops the shakes. During our days of healing there was one specific thing he used to do. He'd invite a member of the congregation or someone in the crowd to come up and seat them on a chair, and instruct them to stretch out both their legs before them. Then he'd ask them if they knew they had legs of differing lengths, to which the answer was always, 'No.'

'I thought not,' he'd reply. 'Just look.' And they would look and their eyes would pop out because from above it always looks as if legs are different lengths. Then he'd grab one of their feet in his hands and crank it about, twisting this way and that, until with a flourish he'd fling out his arms and say, 'Look, now they are the exact same size. Walk, walk now without impediment,' and the person would almost jump off the stage, happy they had been cured, and likely as not would put dollars in the velvet bag at the end.

It took me a long time to realise it was a con. Now I remember how I must be careful because I can't rely on anything he says. If I can even get to him, whatever he tells me will likely have a grain of truth wrapped up in a bundle of mystery and Bible words because he is a trickster, a shape-shifter, a con man who claims the way, the truth and pure, golden light stream out of his cracked black heart.

And again I go cold with fear because I feel I've set something in motion that won't be stopped when I wrote, *I need to speak with you.*

Then after a few days I almost forget about it. I think, it'll never reach him, or did I ever really send it, and that way it becomes like a message in a bottle that you sometimes find in the river that has been floating round and round for decades, half a century even, without ever finding its true recipient. I think, it'll be out there like that forever.

Beth

What is healing?

Is it the pulsing bursts from the radiotherapy machine that bombard cancerous tumours? Is it medications administered, so powerful they suppress the immune system, in an attempt to stop the body eating away at its own joints and organs as if they were intruders? Is it the surgeon's knife digging deep inside the cloistered parts of the body?

Or is it something else? Or rather, is it something else *as well*? Once, I washed a man from the top of his head right to his big toes. It was a quiet night. It took over an hour. Afterwards, he cried and said he hadn't been touched by another human being for twenty-five years.

In this house I see myself as a child, my footfalls swallowed by the thick carpet as I went upstairs, library books tucked under my arm. I remember one day the birthday gift of an Olympus Trip camera I had, how I'd used it to catalogue all the flowers in the garden, carefully winding the film up after like Dad taught me. Later I'd neatly stuck the photos of flowers into scrapbooks made of sugar paper. Perhaps after all she came with me, this girl, tiptoeing into my marriage. Her solitary and meticulous nature casting her eye over it all, wondering at the recklessness of what her adult self had done.

Today I lift the lid of the piano stool. Inside there's a stack of old *Good Housekeeping* magazines in date order, so looking through them is like an archaeological excavation through the rock strata of the recent past. Then underneath all of those I find five thick pamphlets titled 'Teach Yourself Piano'.

I flick through them, smiling. It begins with 'first mastering your notes'. I remember now I studied this for hours, made little stickers to attach to the keys to identify them. I open the lid of the piano and peer inside. The greyish patches of their gummy backs are just about visible. I sit on the piano stool upholstered in green velvet, the fake kind made of nylon that can crackle with static if you're wearing the wrong thing, and open one of the books at random. I nearly laugh out loud. At the top of the exercise, the tune 'As the Deer', I've graded myself 6/10 in a firm pencil line. I'd forgotten how I did that, how assiduous I was. I would never have cheated, given myself a ten that I didn't deserve. No wonder how shocked my parents were when I ran off with Paul, how they couldn't believe this careful child could be so careless with her future. I start to sound out the notes of the tune.

Behind me I hear the door open and I turn to see Carmel leaning in, grinning.

'Hey, I've never heard you playing that piano before.'

I wrinkle my nose. 'I think playing might be the wrong word.'

She comes over and I scoot across the piano stool so she

can sit next to me and I resist the urge to put my arm round her.

She picks up one of the books and flicks through it. 'Look, there's a duet here. Wanna try it?'

'OK.'

She props the book up on the stand and makes the piano trill with her fingers.

'Ready?'

We begin playing. She's much faster than me; she only has to glance at the book. 'C'mon, Mum, it's "Chopsticks",' she laughs, and her arms cross over mine and we're playing together, me slow and stumbling, and we're both breathless, laughing.

'Again,' she says, and we play faster this time and the notes fly upwards. The room fills with sunshine, with music; it moves through the house, turning walls into bright dust, opening up spaces long closed up, dancing from room to room.

'Come on, faster,' says Carmel and we start again and the roof feels like it could blow off from the light and dancing notes and I swear if I turned round right now, Mum would be there with her head around the door, one hand in a yellow rubber Marigold glove holding the door open, and there'd be a huge smile on her face as she watched us both.

We play to the end again, her finishing before me, and we turn to each other, cheeks flushed. The music takes a moment to die away. The piano still hums.

'That was cool,' she says.

Where did you learn to play the piano, Carmel?

'How about something else?' I ask, flicking through the pages on the stand.

'Another time – got to get ready for work.' And she's gone, leaving me dizzy, the musical notes on the page cavorting before my eyes.

A package arrives, addressed to Carmel. It bears the stamp of the *Gazette* on the envelope, the paper that interviewed Carmel, that sought her out and found her and printed her photograph and her name in their pages. I weigh it in my hand; it feels heavy.

I prop the envelope up on the empty fruit bowl on the kitchen table and make some coffee. I'll do it all properly, I think, slowly and with attention. I take coffee beans from the freezer, grind them up in the little Moulinex grinder I bought when I first got together with Paul. It had seemed to cost a fortune then.

I sit with my cup of coffee in front of the envelope. I take a sip but today it's nasty in my mouth. I feel like it's going to choke me, make me throw up bitter black stuff that looks like stagnant, rotten water so I get up and chuck it into the sink.

I'm kidding myself with this ritual, of course. I'm putting off what I'm fully aware I'm going to do because I know it's wrong. I pick up the envelope and it feels smooth and bulging under my fingers. I weigh it by balancing it on my fingertips: quite heavy. My heart's pounding, not from the effects of the coffee, I only had a sip, but from what I am about to do. I make quick calculations. Carmel is out, she's only been gone an hour and her shift is usually for five. I have plenty of time alone. As I dig my fingers behind the flap of the envelope it only occurs to me then I could've steamed it, that quaint method of intercepting other people's correspondence I've read about in novels. Too late. The envelope is open with a jagged gash at the top. I shake out the contents. More envelopes containing letters inside, some opened and some not, and a single typed page folded in half. When I unfold it, I see a large squiggle of signature with the name Kay Ward typed neatly below it. I read.

She was sorry. She would've emailed as well but she'd neglected to take an email address. She hoped Carmel was well. The article she'd written had attracted a surprising amount of interest. They'd had correspondence about it sent to the newspaper, some even from overseas.

I fight the urge to really vomit this time. I force it down and continue reading.

If Carmel no longer wants to receive anything else that comes their way could she please be in touch and communicate that fact. Until then, she wishes my daughter well.

I stare at the envelopes for a long time before I pick up the one on top of the pile. The pages inside are thin and the writing is scratchy, done in blue ballpoint pen.

Dear Carmel Wakeford, it begins.

I blink rapidly, as if there's grit in my eyes. I feel hot and angry, like hands are reaching out to snatch Carmel.

I read the article in the Gazette *with interest. Of course, I remember you from the trial, you are famous! Famous too in our little faith community. There are a few people who are known to be true spirits and you are one of them – the genuine article, just think of that! How blessed you must feel. For some years now I've suffered terribly with rheumatoid arthritis, it's very hard to get up out of the chair and of course that is difficult because I live alone. I have been to Lourdes on more than one occasion . . .*

I stop reading. I can picture her, this – I scan the bottom of the page for her name – this Esther Martin. She sits with her knobbly hands on one of those chairs – covered in floral brocade – where you can release a lever and the seat tips up to lift you to a semi-standing position so you have a fighting chance of getting up onto your own two feet. I know the effect of rheumatoid arthritis. Even a simple manoeuvre like that can be a protracted and painful ordeal. Esther Martin sits next to the window, I can see her; the breeze stirs the net curtains, making them billow and cover her face. If she could she would stand and close the window, or even more impossibly move the chair away from the draught, but she can't. The lever is stuck. She's been trying to get up for over two hours.

Stop it, I tell myself. Stop imagining things. Neither you nor Carmel owe her anything. Not even the time of day.

I drop Esther's letter to one side and pluck another from an already open envelope.

Hi Carmel.
I'm so happy to have tracked you down, yay! We've heard of you but Mum and me reckon you must've been

in hiding all these years so welcome back.

I look at the address at the top of the letter. It's a place by the sea on the east coast that we had a day out to once, me and Paul, when I was pregnant. I lumbered around the streets with both Paul and I laughing for me having to move so slowly. I carry on reading.

I'm what's known as a 'life-limited' teenager. Yeah, I know it sucks doesn't it. But I thought you being young you might relate. Actually, I have a pretty full life. I love my music and listen to it until I drive my mum crazy! I'm really into fashion too and Mum's friends with the manicurist in town and she comes and does mad things on my nails every couple of weeks. I'm in contact with people all over the world on the internet. We're in one of the houses near the beach which is great because it's all on one level but what's even better is that I can hear the sea at night.

I picture this girl too; I look for the name – Charmaine Taylor. I remember these houses. They're shabby bungalows, obviously housing people that couldn't afford to regularly paint them or upkeep the windows. I remember seeing a dreamcatcher on the porch of one, swinging back and forth, and at the time I wondered what dreams it was catching. Charmaine wouldn't have been born then, but could this be the one where she lives now?

I'd love to meet you. You don't need to perform a healing or anything (though it would be great if you could, hahaha) but maybe we could just hang out. It would be difficult for me to make it up to London (hey, that mudlarking sounds really cool by the way) but maybe you could come down here one day? I can look up all the train times and Mum says she'll reimburse your ticket for you. We could arrange for Sue – that's the manicurist – to come perhaps and we could both get our nails done . . .

I stop reading. I can't bear it. She sounds so bloody lovely and desperate and sweet. It's not fair, just not fair.

I move on without finishing. Charmaine has touched me in a way I didn't want to be touched.

The next unopened envelope makes me stop breathing. It's from the States.

Carmel Wakeford,

You were in our town once and Betty came back and said you'd cured someone of the cancer. Well, my daughter has cancer too – of the larynx. I have powers of my own. If you don't come you will die in pain of the same thing that's killing my daughter now . . .

I feel the coffee rising up in my throat and I run to the sink and retch. I bring up nothing and stand, breathing deeply. These fucking people. Who do they think they are? I grip the edge of the sink feeling pale and shaky and knowing what I need to do.

I gather the letters together. I can see by date order that it's the later ones that are unopened. Didn't the paper owe Carmel some duty of care about correspondence they received?

It's like Kay Ward had stopped being able to stand reading them. Perhaps like me she couldn't stand all the lies they've obviously lapped up, the same lies that were fed to Carmel.

Their voices – vulnerable, sick, needy, threatening, hopeful – are already chattering far too loud in our home. They need cutting off at the root.

I take the fistful of letters and envelopes upstairs, being careful to gather up the original envelope with the *Gazette* stamp that has fallen on the floor.

This is a sizable four-bedroomed family house. Carmel and I have our own bedrooms, there's a spare and also a small box room Mum used as a study and I've kept it like that. I detest the sight of files and paperwork so I keep it all in one room with the door firmly shut. It also houses a paper shredder for getting rid of old bank statements and bills. It's a good-quality one. I splashed out on it like I did with the coffee grinder so when I feed the letters still in their envelopes into its teeth it makes short work of them, shredding them into unreadable strips and dropping them into the bin below.

There's so many the bin gets jammed full at one point and I tear the lid off and tip the vile spewing mass of paper into a plastic recycling bag and start again until every inch of paper has been shredded except for Kay Ward's covering letter.

I open the window. There's dust now in the air in the small room from the paper shredding. I sit sideways on the swivel chair and look around me. Everything about the room looks tired. I pick at the green plastic that's beginning to peel from the arm and gently swivel side to side. The dark green curtains with a shiny stripe in the same colour I remember from when I was a kid, except they were new and clean then. On the desk is a reading lamp with a gold column and the classic rectangular green shade. It strikes me suddenly what my mum was going for in here. It's like a set of a study she might've seen in a film or in a magazine. It was always her room, Dad wasn't interested. For the first time in my life, I wonder: what did she do in here?

I always felt she led a circumscribed life, my mother. Now I burn to know how she spent those secret hours in this room that at the time I cared nothing about. Suddenly, the knowledge of no longer being able to ask questions of the dead passes through me like an electrical storm. She often came up here and firmly closed the door. Was she writing stories? Completing household paperwork? Or was she simply getting away from me and my father, finding room to breathe?

'Hey, Mum,' I say. 'How about helping me on this one? You're listening, right?'

I feel her smiling at the acknowledgement and I take some deep breaths and pick up the sheet of paper in front of me – Kay's letter – and look for her number.

She answers the call from my mobile straight away, breaking off from saying something like she's in the middle of a conversation.

'Hi, it's Beth Wakeford.'

'Beth . . .?'

'Carmel Wakeford's mother.'

There's a pause and when she speaks again it's clearer and more intimate, like she's brought the phone closer to her face and moved away from whoever she was having a conversation with. 'Ahh, hello. What . . . what can I do for you?'

'Carmel's received a pile of your letters,' I eye the coils of shredded paper even as I plan my lies, 'following the article you wrote.'

'Yes, that's right.'

'Well, she's not happy.'

'I'm sorry to hear that.'

Anger flares. How pat. I bet she can't wait to get me off the line; she's regretting pressing answer as we speak.

'Yes. She feels the article has compromised her safety.'

There's a short pause.

'Oh dear, but being featured in the article is something she chose to do herself. She must've realised it meant going public to a certain extent. I mean, she must've thought about it.'

'She is very young,' I say quietly. 'And she has gone through a great deal. I'd appreciate it if you didn't contact us again and if you receive any more letters for her please do not send them on. We can do without all this.'

'And she told you to call me? She told you all that herself?'

'Yes.'

I'm about to say goodbye and ring off but Kay interrupts me, sounding breathless now.

'Mrs Wakeford.'

'Yes?'

'Your daughter . . .'

'What about her?'

'I don't know. She's . . . she's quite strange, isn't she?'

'What?' I'm suddenly furious. 'What on earth do you expect? Really?'

I've stood up at the desk, sending the chair behind me spinning to face the other way.

'No, sorry. I didn't mean like that. I didn't mean to upset or offend you.'

'I do remember her saying that you had a problem with your height or something.' I'm being mean on purpose, wanting to wound.

'No, I haven't. I mean, I haven't anymore.'

'Pardon?'

'It's hard to explain.'

'You really don't have to. I need to go now.'

But she carries on anyway. 'I've chucked all my high heels away.'

There's a short silence. She still sounds breathless on the other end of the line.

'Goodbye,' I say coldly, and after the call has ended I stay for a long time, still standing, looking out at the tops of the leafless lime trees that line the street.

By the end of that night's shift I'm exhausted. I'm thinking of bringing the car in now winter's coming so I can go straight home but the parking here is rotten so for now it's a walk to the Tube. In the locker room I take out my wicker basket and pack up my empty lunchbox, the inside creamy from leftover pasta bake, and my book, which is a strange Japanese novel about a man whose dead parents return. The thing that's strange about it is they are not spooky ghost-like beings, the parents, they are exactly as they used to be when they were alive. They camp out in his apartment, make him noodles, bicker between themselves. For some reason reading it is really unsettling me. I take off my uniform and stuff it in a plastic bag to be washed and change back into my jeans and trainers.

Downstairs I get that old familiar feeling I have on finishing my shift. I'm tired, I'm looking forward to a bath but at the same time I'm reluctant to leave. Despite all the sickness here this place is so blindingly, near the bone, dizzyingly alive. I miss it when I'm not here, I really do.

In the foyer there is the buzz of voices. People are sitting in the café drinking out of paper cups, stripping the wrappers off chocolate bars as they wait for appointments or visiting hours. There's a sprinkling of shops selling nighties and newspapers and sweets, a chemist for shower gel and aspirin. The light filters down from the high-up windows and I catch a glimpse of something, and in one pin-sharp moment something jolts through me because I see Carmel amongst the crowd. I still get it when I see her. It was all those years of looking and not finding.

'Calm down,' I tell myself and raise my hand in greeting.

Carmel lifts her hand in recognition across all the milling people, some with bandaged arms and crutches and wheeling drips beside them but most in normal clothes because they are visitors or staff or patients about to be admitted.

We've walked towards each other so we're close enough to speak. She has her hands shoved in her pockets.

'What are you doing here?' I ask.

'Hey, um, hi . . .' she answers, in mild reproach because I

haven't even said hello before blurting this out.

I put my basket down and slide my arms down my coat sleeves, putting it on to give myself a minute's grace. 'Hey, yes. Sorry – hi. I just didn't expect to see you here. Got a bit confused.'

'You're easily confused,' she says drily and rubs her nose with the back of her hand like it's started to itch. 'I just thought it might be nice to meet you for once but I can go again if you like.'

'No, of course not. Don't be silly. It's a lovely surprise.' I'm going too far the other way now.

I notice for the first time she looks strained, even like she might've been crying, and with monumental effort I stop myself from asking what's wrong.

'Hey, d'you fancy a hot chocolate before we head home? The café here doesn't do a bad one.'

She looks around, slightly bemused. 'Sure, why not?'

'I'll get it, you find a seat.'

I weave through the milling people to the counter. It's not much of a treat, I think, hot chocolate with squirty cream sitting amongst the sick and afflicted and worried, but it's the best I could come up with on the spur of the moment.

As the woman behind the counter makes the hot chocolate at the shiny machine I glance over to where Carmel is sitting. She looks scruffy, it strikes me; her coat is creased, her hair looks unbrushed and on one foot the strip of her Converse shoes is coming away from the rest of it. She looks like she isn't taking care of herself properly. I wish she'd let me take her clothes shopping. I would love that. She could have whatever she wanted. I long to be one of those mums sitting outside a cubicle giving an expert opinion on a stream of outfits coming through the curtain. Asking, 'So what are we having?' at the end of the session and taking an armful of clothes to pay on a credit card and not even baulking at the price they all add up to.

When the woman says something, I realise she's spoken to me already but I was too far away thinking. 'Anything else?' she asks and I shake my head and count out coins.

What happens next is like watching a car accident from afar.

I'm carrying a tray with the cups carefully because they are so full of hot chocolate and elaborate tufted hats of cream and flaky chocolate sticks and the whole lot is in danger of sliding off the edge of the cups in a gooey mess and I don't realise for a minute Carmel's focussing on something across the aisle from her. I'm at a distance so it's hard to see where her eyes are directed, but there is a tightening aura of tension around her, in her body and the angle of her head, which is peculiar. It's off somehow and I know instinctively something wrong is happening.

I have to stop because in my peripheral vision I've seen something on the floor blocking my path. I look down. Someone has dumped their bags there. A tapestried overnight bag and another see-through plastic one full of towels and newspapers.

'Can you move your bags please?' I'm trying to sound polite because I don't want to get involved in anything that holds me up but the couple at the table take their time in swivelling their eyes up towards me.

'The bags,' I say again. 'I can't get through.'

Now I've spotted what has absorbed Carmel. It's the man at the table across the aisle from her. His head is bent over his cup of tea and I think I see what she sees; there's something not right about him but it seems we are the only two in the room that's aware of this.

Now the pair at the table, in deliberate slowness, turn their eyes down to look at the bags and seem mildly surprised to find them there.

'No need to be rude, love,' says the man, who has fat, pink cheeks and stubby fingers wrapped around his mug. 'It's only a few bags, nothing to get irate over.'

I know my voice can come out sharp when I'm panicky but all the same they're enjoying this, enjoying stretching it out, wielding their little bit of power by not acting too swiftly. It would be pathetic in normal circumstances but now it's becoming a big and dangerous part of what's happening because I see Carmel is tensing, is rising out of her seat and is falling to her knees in front of the man opposite her like she's about to pray. And the man himself, his head is toppling forward, it's threatening to land on the table, but he stops himself at the last minute and it kind of swings there, as if it's in mid-air.

With reluctant slowness the pink-cheeked man is leaning forward and pulling at the handles of the bags but he's doing it far, far too slowly, muttering something to himself and the woman is soothing him, saying, 'Take no notice, Don. Don't let her get to you. Just let her pass.' And something in the back of my brain reminds me that everyone here is fragile in some way, every single person, but I haven't got time to attend to that or to them because my every sinew is straining towards Carmel and I can see from this distance even in profile that her eyes have closed and her face has become a sort of pale vision of ecstasy. Her skin takes on the colour of marble. From her kneeling position she unfurls herself and stands, and not caring who is looking on, which is practically everyone now, she puts her hands either side of the man's head and she stands there, a tremor passing through from her head to her feet and with her face going whiter and whiter.

The slow motion ends like a ribbon being cut. The tray tilts in my hand as my grip loosens and as I look down there's a vision of spraying hot chocolate, flying cream, but I let it go, I let the whole lot clatter to the ground and I leap over their bags, which are covered in the whole mess now anyway. I race towards Carmel and it seems to take an age to get there. I don't think there's a single person in the whole foyer that hasn't turned and is right now staring at us.

When I reach Carmel, her face is so white there's almost a tinge of blue to it. Her closed eyelids twitch. Her fingers which are slightly splayed at the ends hold the man's head either side and her lips move as if she's silently muttering to herself.

'Carmel, stop it,' I hiss.

I can see from his face that he's having a stroke. There's the telltale turning down of the corner of the mouth, the droop of his eye, the sheeny waxiness of his skin.

Carmel doesn't respond; I don't know if she's even heard me.

I put my hand on her wrist. 'Carmel,' I say louder. 'This man is sick; you have to let him go.'

I look round desperately. 'Please, someone. Call the crash team.'

She still hasn't responded and I grip her wrist harder, too hard. 'Get off him,' I say. I begin to pull savagely at her. 'What d'you think you're doing? For Christ's sake just get off him and let him get some real help.'

The whole room has turned silent and is watching. 'Carmel, stop with this. Stop it now, please.'

The idea that she is so deluded, that she clearly thinks she can lay hands on the sick and make them better, is chilling. That she actually believes it to the extent she'll make this gut-wrenching display of herself in a busy hospital foyer is beyond anything I'd feared. I yank again and finally she lets go of him and looks at her hands, then at me, her eyes wide.

My heart's beating so fast I can feel it in my neck. I want to cry, desperately and noisily right there. Despite all our best efforts, all our best intentions – this. There is only one thing worse than the knowledge that there is something wrong – really wrong – with one of your children and that is if you don't know where they are. Now I know both.

She's been hiding her delusion well, cleverly, but it's just burst right out into the open here, so violently and so publicly. It was there all the time and I want to weep for both of us. The crash team have arrived and they are leaning over the man next to us, efficiently loosening his collar, asking his name.

'Carmel,' despite the adrenalin coursing through me I try and make my voice even and conciliatory. 'Please, let's just go home.'

Mercy

1999

When Mercy heard singing outside the shack she froze.

She cut a strange-looking little figure now. Her face was blotched with make-up and her body festooned in gaudy scarves pinned to her T-shirt with cheap, glittery brooches. The shack was upside down. The kitchen cupboards open and ransacked. Raw pasta and Cheerios crunched underfoot. In her parents' bedroom the contents of her ma's jewellery box was spread across the bed and the palette of eye makeup that used to resemble a shining treasure chest was half gouged out and trailing colours from one little dish to another. She thought it might be five or even six days she'd been on her own now but she'd given up on using bits of her breakfast to mark the days – it started to seem pointless – so she couldn't know for sure.

The voice outside was melodic and assured. The singing seemed to reach the tips of the trees and wrap itself around the shack.

'Amazing Grace, how sweet the sound, who saved a wretch like me.'

That morning Mercy had not known how much longer she could hold on for. She'd pushed open her parents' bedroom door, her ma's red bandana hung on the bottom bedpost, already knotted, and Mercy had slid it over her head and rubbed the rough cotton of its tail between finger and thumb.

Her eyes had lit on the row of CDs on the mantlepiece. All her ma's CDs were Madonna. Delia had seen *Desperately Seeking Susan* shortly before she met Colm and was smitten. Her fandom was set in stone when 'Get into the Groove' played as she first laid eyes on Colm at the little mountain hop with a glitter ball lashed to the ceiling by electrical flex. She danced in Madonna's style with her arms above her head, flashing her armpits, and Colm was smitten too.

Mercy had dived under the dressing table and plugged the trailing flex of the CD player in. Behind the bedside table she had spotted something wedged behind it, a flash of yellow. She slid her fingers in and worked it free. It was a yellow silk scarf wrapped around something square. She wriggled out from under the bed and unwrapped it. It was another Madonna CD, but this one was unopened, still in its plastic. Mercy traced the words on the cover: *Ray of Light*. There was something so sensitive and private about how the CD had been hidden Mercy rewrapped it and slid it back. She selected another one from where they were lined up on the mantelpiece and fed the silver disc into the hole in the top of the player and pressed the play button and skipped straight to her favourite track, 'Holiday'.

Madonna's voice sang out into the empty space of the room.

Mercy grabbed a narrow scarf patterned with purple and orange flowers that trailed over her parents' bedhead and wound it round her neck over the bandana.

She'd danced, shimmying into the hallway sideways through the open door, then again into the kitchen-diner, scarf flying as she spun.

She'd whirled around, giddy, singing, the music belting out from the bedroom. She flung open the front door and let the music sing out across the porch, into the trees beyond.

'Look at me, Racooneey,' she'd shouted. 'Just look at me. We're having a holidaaaaayy.'

She'd started the CD again and worked her way through every track, donning a different adornment of her mother's for each one. 'Lucky Star' was paired with a diamanté brooch in the shape of a cornet full of flowers pinned to her T-shirt. 'Burning Up' went with clip-on dangly earrings with green beads that touched her shoulders and rattled and flew out in ninety-degree angles as she twirled. By 'Everybody' twelve costumes were layered onto each other. She'd fallen into the music, using her whole body, her whole mind in the dance, which became more than a movement of limbs, the mouthing of lyrics. It had become a psychic expression of the will to live.

The afternoon light was falling over the shack when Mercy heard the melodious tenor singing outside. After being glued to the spot in shock for long moments at the sound of another human voice, Mercy forced herself to move. She sank to the floor and crept over to the window on her knees. When she peeped out she saw a flash of white amongst the trees and it took her a moment to identify the pale suit of the pastor from the service.

She watched, her eyes rounding, as he stood still and smiled to himself. 'I once was lost, but now I'm found,' he sang up to the sky, 'Was blind but now I see.'

He started walking again, faster this time, towards the shack. Mercy remembered her ma's exhortation just in time and dived behind the sofa as she heard him put his foot on the first step of the porch. Then his singing came so close it made the front door reverberate,

''Twas grace that taught my heart to fear.

And grace my fears relieved,

How precious did that grace appear,

The hour I first believed.'

Mercy cowered behind the sofa and a terrible thought crossed her mind. She couldn't remember for the life of her if she'd locked the door as her mother had strictly instructed her to do every time she came back inside the house. She held her breath. Had she pushed the bolt back last time she came back in? Things had got hazy; she didn't know.

She heard rapping on the door. 'Mrs Roberts? Anyone home?'

She screwed her eyes shut as if that could make her invisible.

'Mercy? Mercy Roberts?'

Quiet descended for a moment and Mercy could hear the blood pulsing in her ears. Then there was a rattling and a creak as the front door opened. She dug her nails into her palm as if in punishment. Fool! She'd left it open.

'Mrs Roberts.'

She guessed the pastor was stood at the open front door listening.

'Mrs Roberts. Mercy,' he called again.

After an age seemed to pass she heard his feet in the hallway. Mercy closed her eyes again and prayed he wouldn't fall down the hole. Lord knows what would happen if he got stuck there. Then she heard his footsteps enter the kitchen-diner and come to a standstill yards away from her.

'Uh, huh,' said the preacher, as if he was understanding something. She heard him move round the room, cereal and pasta crunching underfoot. He seemed to be tapping things as he went past. She listened as he creaked cupboard doors and then what sounded like her food box being picked up and rattled about. 'Uh, huh,' he said again.

The sound of her own blood being pushed around her body was so loud in her ears it was a hiss. He *must* be able to hear it.

Then he began to sing again, only this time his voice had a different tone, a quieter one, and the song was different.

'Are you washed in the blood,

In the cleansing blood of the lamb?

Are your garments spotless? Are they white as snow?

Are you washed in the blood of the lamb?'

Silence. Mercy put her hands over her ears. Something about the song had made her mouth dry out.

More creaking, this time as if the pastor was swaying back and forth on his heels, then a commotion that nearly made her heart stop until she realised it was him spinning on his heel and leaving and the front door slamming shut.

Mercy felt like she was bursting out of water where she'd been held down underneath.

It took her an hour to emerge from behind the sofa. What had he been doing here? She put one hand inside the other, both of them trembling like skeleton leaves on the ground in autumn.

By the time it was starting to get dark outside Mercy almost wished the pastor would come back. If he did she wouldn't hide this time; she'd cling on to him and beg him to take her with him. She flicked on all the lights to make the house blaze, opened the door and went to retrieve the hidden CD wrapped in silk. There seemed little point keeping its secrets now.

Mercy couldn't know the reason that the *Ray of Light* CD was still unopened in its plastic was because Delia couldn't bear to find out what the music might do to her, that the title alone near killed her. By the time this CD came out, Delia – who'd managed to stay clean for her pregnancy – was many years into addiction again. She bought it, though kept it unplayed, wrapped and hidden, because it also represented a shimmering line into the future, one that Delia one day hoped to grasp on to and follow. Not yet. One day when she was ready. Until that day Delia couldn't open up all that hope and longing listening to it would entail.

Mercy slid one thumb nail under the plastic flap and pulled. It came away easily and soon lay like a discarded insect husk on the floor. Then, with a painfully throbbing heart she inserted the disc and pressed play and words and music filled the house. When it came to the song about a ray of light she played it three times, the third singing right from her guts. She felt a real ray of light beaming down, bathing her, God's love holding her in its spotlight.

Then mid-sentence the music chopped off. The house fell half dark and silent. Mercy stopped, arms still outstretched in her dance. For a moment she wondered if she'd just died and this was part of the process, the silence, something that happened when your heart ceased beating. But then the sounds from outside, coming through the open door in the hall, began to filter through. The whoop and cheep of birdsong. The distant buzz of a power tool. It was then she realised what had happened. The generator must've cut out. Now she was left with no food and no power either.

She clenched her fists. 'Mean bastards,' she yelled. 'Mean bastards leaving me like this.'

'Mercy?' A voice fluted from outside the open door.

The silhouette of a feathered fascinator hat bobbed in the open doorway.

'Mercy, child. What're you hollering out profanities for? Where are your folks, child?' The figure stepped further in and Mercy recognised the face of Miss Forbouys in the gloom.

'Are you all alone here? What happened to the lights?' Miss Forbouys stepped into the kitchen-diner and by the fading light looked round with sharp eyes: dirty boards, the springs pinging out of the sofa, rotting window frames. 'Where're your folks, Mercy?' Her voice was sharp too now, matching her eyes.

Mercy stayed silent and Miss Forbouys took the opportunity to move in on her, pink feathers bobbing in her hair. 'Come on, girl, where are they?'

Mercy stared mutely. The fact that it was all so nearly over gave her no sense of relief; she felt more like she was a leaf frozen in ice. She felt beyond thought, beyond speech, just seeped with the knowledge that the world was about to change forever.

Little red spots had appeared on Miss Forbouys' cheeks. 'Child, you are all on your own in this pit of despond, aren't you?'

The moment seemed to stretch into infinity when shockingly the lights burst back on, leaving them both blinking at each other.

Then, like a miracle, there were her mother's legs in the kitchen doorway, wearing jeans and the black loafers Mercy recognised. However, by some weird turn of events the top half of her mother seemed to have turned into a small house. Wary of giving herself away to Miss Forbouys by commenting on this disturbing phenomenon too soon, Mercy decided to keep her own counsel. It was something she had learned to do over time and had found often paid off.

'My, what a remarkable doll's house,' said Miss Forbouys.

Her mother's knees abruptly forked outwards as she lowered the doll's house to the ground. And here was another miracle. She looked well, entirely well. The grey pallor was replaced with rosy cheeks. Her hair gleamed.

Mercy couldn't help breaking out in a huge grin at the sight of her.

If her ma was taken aback by the presence of Miss Forbouys in the room, she didn't show it. Mercy guessed she was deploying the same tactic as she had done herself only moments beforehand and felt relief. Her head even nodded in a small, private approval at her mother for taking this tack.

Miss Forbouys was now clearly flustered. Her eyes darted between mother and daughter and then alighted again on the doll's house on the floor.

'Mrs Roberts,' she said. 'When I came by just now your daughter was *totally alone.*'

Mercy could see this confrontation was difficult for Miss Forbouys, who was always kind but in a vague way – she was grabbing the collar of her lemon-yellow linen blouse and twisting it between her fingers.

'And why were you dropping in on her?' asked Delia.

Truth was, this was difficult to answer. Was it what happened at the church last week? Whatever it was, Mercy, the solitary girl with such an open heart, came into her thoughts as she drove past from a nephew's christening and on instinct she decided to call in. She chose not to answer the question.

'Mrs Roberts. Mercy is only eight years old; that is not a fit age to leave a child alone like that. She seemed in a state of distress and looking unkempt, I don't mind saying.' She obviously did mind because she gave her collar an extra-hard yank when she said that, nearly pulling it off. 'Really, it's quite unacceptable and as her former teacher . . .'

Mercy's mother held up one hand to silence the other woman. To Mercy's surprise her ma was not looking cross, or worried at all. In fact, she had quite a beatific smile on her face.

'But Mercy, you see, Miss Forbouys, was not on her own at all.'

'She wasn't?'

'See,' her ma carried on, 'I just popped out to pick up this doll's house, that's all. Colm's been right outside fixing the generator.' She slipped off her coat and pushed up her sweater sleeves. 'We've been having some fun and games in here and now's time to set everything straight, eh, Mercy?'

Mercy nodded but kept her mouth tight shut. She didn't know how they'd done it; it appeared they'd pulled off a magic trick somehow but she sure wasn't going to give the game away when they'd been so sly and clever, no siree.

In fact, Delia and Colm had arrived to hear Miss Forbouys talking about the lack of light, and Colm cleverly understood it must be the generator playing up again. 'Get in there and cover,' he'd whispered, 'while I go fix it.'

Now, Delia's expression was unmistakable. It said 'back off'.

Miss Forbouys smoothed down her skirt. 'Well, if that's the case I apologise for the intrusion. Mercy, perhaps we'll see you in church again on Sunday?'

'We'll see,' her ma said, like she was telling Miss Forbouys who was really in charge of things in her own household and it certainly wasn't Miss Forbouys.

After Miss Forbouys left, Delia got down on her knees, for all the world looking like she was begging her daughter's forgiveness, which is how she felt inside.

'Baby girl. Sweetpea. I'm so, so sorry. We never meant to be away for so long, I promise you that. Things happened that we weren't expecting and we couldn't make it home when we should've done but there wasn't a moment I wasn't thinking about you, sweetpea.' Her ma brushed her thumb back and forth over Mercy's cheek and Mercy thought that she'd never felt anything so nice. 'I promise to be a better mother here on in, and this present is just the start of it.'

Mercy wiped her tears away with the back of her hand.

'Go on, take a look inside the doll's house,' said Delia, as if she was enticing a small animal to eat.

Delia unhooked the front wall of the house and let it swing open to reveal the inside. Each room was papered with a different exquisite wallpaper: checks in the kitchen, roses in one bedroom, candy stripes in another and the hallway even had hummingbirds.

Mercy was speechless.

'I'll go get the furniture. It's in the car,' said Delia. 'The doll family too.'

Mercy would not let go of her hand. She insisted on holding it and coming out into the night and waiting, not taking her eyes off Delia, while she rooted in the trunk of the car for the boxes of miniature people.

Carmel

2013

Since the hospital things have come into sharp focus. They are lit in a way similar to that day on the foreshore before the storm but now it's the same with people, on the Tube, in the café, walking the streets. I can see right into them. The scale of sickness is unimaginable. Every few yards I see another one. There's a tumour riding like a barnacle deep inside the lung, there's a cataract pooling over an eyeball as frost forms on a pond. From two feet away I can see the plaques in the tubes of the brain of the man ahead of me in the grocery store.

In some ways it would be a relief that my vision has been fully restored like this from childhood if it wasn't for one thing. Now I can see with complete lucidity the hole left inside my mother that opened up when I was taken. It's her bound, damaged, hollowed heart I see and for once I cannot help because the past has been written and there's nothing to be done that can fix or alter that.

The man in the hospital was fragmenting before me, his body going off in different directions like rockets.

'Hold on,' I whispered to him. 'I'm coming. I can help you. They've tried to make me forget but I haven't and I can help you.'

I barely heard Mum in the background screaming, 'For

Christ's sake get off him, Carmel. Get off him *now*.'

On my way to work it's there, on the doormat. The light seems to catch it a certain way so the whiteness of the envelope shines out.

A letter with a postmark from the United States. I turn it over and stamped on the back it says, 'This was mailed by an Incarcerated Individual Confined . . .' but I'm too scared to read any more. I run upstairs with it crumpling in my hand. I want to scream like I did the day when I saw his name on the computer. I shove the letter under the rug and stamp on it three times.

Later, after work, I decide I'm never going to read the letter. It can stay where it is, rotting.

When I try to make sense of everything these days it becomes like pictures and information on the glossy page of a magazine that I am trying to decipher even as it burns, bubbles up and flakes away. The letter sits there under my rug and I try to forget about it for days, weeks. Then the preacher calls when I'm at work. I'd almost forgotten about what I'd done by then. Things were returning to a steady pace but when I see the unfamiliar number ice runs down my back and I realise I haven't forgotten about any of it at all, it was all lying just below the surface ready to burst out. I go to the place where we hang up our coats and answer and then put my face into the coats with the phone clamped to my ear. There is a lot of clicking, an American accent saying, 'Ready, go ahead,' then silence.

'Gramps?' I whisper. I know somehow I have to be the one to speak first.

'Peter Shadow,' he answers, the name I made up for myself.

That voice. I fall backwards through time to mists and fields and roads and tiny gatherings of houses. To diners with broken neon signs and smoke rising from distant cities.

'Child, it's so good to hear your voice,' he says. 'I've been so long without it.'

I close my eyes. There's crushed rosemary by the side of the road, candle grease, stagnant water, cooking on an open fire, sweat, his sweat. I smell his sweat from over three thousand miles away.

'Child, did you get my letter?'

'I never opened it.'

'Why, child?'

'I've been so scared, Gramps.' I whisper. 'I'm so confused.'

'Tell me.'

'I don't know what to believe anymore.'

'Our time here is limited. What are they telling you, child?'

'That none of it was real. That everything you taught me was lies.'

'I see. I feared they would do this.'

'But I remember that woman with MS, I remember people getting up and walking. They're trying to tell me none of it was real.'

'You know the truth, child.'

We are both quiet for a moment, listening to each other's

breathing. Then I remember what I really need from him.

I say, 'I don't know the truth though, do I? I've been thinking and thinking about *her* . . .'

'Who?'

It suddenly occurs to me that someone might be listening in and that I need to speak in a kind of code. I press my mouth close to the phone as if that might keep our secrets.

'You know, *her*.'

'Child, what are you talking about? You're speaking in riddles. Stop it.'

This makes me so angry I forget the possibility of someone listening in.

'No, it's you that talks in riddles. Always confusing me, telling me one thing, then another. You know who we're talking about. The one you referred to as "John the Baptist". I need to know if you . . . if you . . .'

There's a long silence. Then into that comes a snuffling sound. It starts off quiet and gains gradually in volume until it's ringing in my ear.

I can't tell if he's laughing or crying. The sound chills my blood.

'You think this is *funny*?'

The sound continues.

I put the phone in front of my face and hiss into it. 'Leave me alone. If you're not going to tell me leave me alone forever. I'm becoming as mad as you are and it's all your fault.'

Then I cut the call.

Now, a doll joins these bones in the drawer, a cheap thing

with a face worn down from being kissed. The human bones are straightforward, stripped clean of flesh. They are the pearls The Mermaid left behind.

The human likeness – the doll – is more problematic. Why I took it. Why I'm keeping it. It happened today just after I heard from *him*. After that the world seemed to bend and warp. I guess the doll was part of it.

I brought her home with me from the café, hidden in the bottom of my duffel bag.

It was well after the lunchtime crowd had thinned and I was wiping empty tables down that I heard the bell on the front door tinkle. The tremors of speaking to *him* were still passing through me. I couldn't believe people were still talking to me normally, that they couldn't see the fear I was feeling inside.

It was a mother and daughter I recognised and who were always holding hands. That day there was a doll dangling from the little girl's free hand.

They chose a table near the corner. The mother was wearing jeans, a cheap stripy top and a thin khaki jacket. Nothing really enough to keep out the cold on a chilly day. The little girl climbed up on her chair. Small, but judging by her face I guessed her to be about seven or eight. Her face was plain, with serious eyes, a quiet expression. She, in contrast, was dressed rather lavishly and I made the assumption her mother made sacrifices for her to be that way. She wore a blue velvet hat that was slightly too big and that partially covered one eye. Her matching blue coat looked old-fashioned, but well made, likely from wool, with a velvet collar that buttoned up against the weather.

Her feet in patent leather shoes swung back and forth, a way off from the ground. Her mother smiled, picked up the laminated menu off its wooden holder and said something to her then tucked a lock of stray dark blond hair behind her daughter's ear. She looked round for someone to take their order and despite the fact that she caught Janice's eye I went over to them as if pulled on a string.

'Hey,' I said, taking my pen and miniature waiter's pad from my apron pocket. 'What'll it be?' I tapped my pen on the paper.

'A tea and a chocolate ice cream.' The woman smiled at the little girl again, love dropping out of her like melting snow. I noticed the doll sitting up on the girl's lap, looking over the table like she was expecting to be served too. She looked like a much-loved toy, her face worn down, the red of her lips practically gone and only flakes of paint left of her blue eyes. Her hair was curly brown but in places had gone straight or come out in clumps. For some reason I couldn't fathom the sight annoyed me, the expectation of the doll, the pretence that she was sitting up like she was alive. Also, the girl herself playing the part of mother – I didn't like that either.

I shook my head. 'Pardon?' I'd heard perfectly but I couldn't remember what had been said.

'Tea and chocolate ice cream.'

'No,' the little girl piped up; she'd had a chance to reconsider, change her mind from what was probably her mother's suggestion. 'Can I have a Coke float?'

'Sure,' I said, even though she was asking her mother, not me. Then I turned away abruptly because I had an overwhelming urge to flick that doll off the girl's lap and send it falling to the floor.

Drinks and desserts, we do ourselves. Marta was busy at the six-burner stainless steel stove with her back to me. I poured out the Coke from a can and let the fizz subside before I got the vanilla ice cream from the freezer and put a curled scoop of it on top. The ice cream made the Coke fizz up again and I jabbed a couple of plastic straws into it. The tray was ready to take out with the tea poured but I stayed, my head bent over. I had a terrible urge to gather spit in my mouth and let it drop into the glass of Coke, for it to sink to the bottom of the glass like molten lava. I glanced at Marta. Her back was still facing me; she wouldn't see. The spit would end up mixing with the Coke, invisible. Then I felt suddenly dizzy and grabbed the tray and took it out.

The customers are generally more relaxed when the café begins to empty. It's quieter and they can take their time over their tea and cake. I kept glancing over to mother and daughter as I loaded crockery onto a tray and wiped tables. The doll was now poking out of the large patch pocket of the girl's coat and the girl was pretend feeding her tiny teaspoonfuls of ice cream, then bending the straw down to the doll's lips to drink. All this the mother watched with an enchanted expression on her face, as if her daughter was doing the most charming thing in the world. I imagined her as one of those women with extravagant claims for her daughter's intelligence, who bored people with repeating the supposedly extraordinary and insightful things the little girl had said. When I returned through the yellow plastic strips that hang down from the open kitchen door, having loaded up the dishwasher, I was strangely relieved to see them leaving, the bell tinkling over their heads.

By the time I got to the table where the girl and her mother had sat, only a couple of tables were still full. There was a sticky mix of ice cream turned brown in the bottom of the Coke float glass. When I stooped to pick a crumpled napkin up from the floor I saw the doll had fallen and landed face down. The skirt of her dress was over her head and I could see the cheap white knickers on her plastic bottom. A brown plastic shoe had come off and lay beside her. Without thinking I dipped down and scooped up the doll, the shoe, and opened up the roomy pocket of my apron and dropped them in there. I used the tray as a shield on my way back to the kitchen to disguise the lump the doll made at my stomach.

I dumped the tray and went and stood in the little dark cloakroom, breathing hard, putting both hands to my stomach, cradling the bump there. Then I opened up my duffel bag, dropped the doll inside and pulled the rope so it was shut tight. I emerged back into the kitchen, back into the light and Marta there. I startled; there was a slightly puzzled expression on her face and instantly I assumed she knew what I'd just done and felt my cheeks redden.

But she just said, 'There you are. I wanted to ask you about the rota next week. I wondered if you'd be available for an extra shift. Janice has got a dentist's appointment on Tuesday.'

In that moment I thought she looked beautiful in her blouse with yellow flowers against an umber background and I felt moved by her, the way she feeds the hungry after a long day's work, but I wanted to get out quickly because of the doll.

'Yes, Tuesday's fine,' I said and grabbed my bag to go.

As I opened the front door to leave, a big wave of cool fresh air speckled with drizzle hit me in the face. I glanced up at the sky and took deep breaths. The sky was whorled grey, tempestuous. I locked the door behind me.

When I turned again the mother and daughter from earlier were there, standing on the pavement in front of me. The little girl's face was pale, tear-stained.

'Oh, I'm so glad to catch you,' the woman said. 'Lydia has lost her doll. We think she might be still inside.'

I hitched my duffel bag further up my shoulder and shook my head. 'No,' I said. 'I've just cleaned everything up. There was nothing there.'

Lydia looked like she was about to start crying again. She gripped her mother's hand tighter.

'But can we just check?' the mother persisted. 'Can we just look under the table where we were sitting? It'll only take two minutes. She's so upset. She loves that doll.'

I had been about to refuse, say I had to run and catch a bus, be somewhere, but her last sentence made that difficult. It was obvious it wouldn't even take the two minutes she'd suggested to look.

When I opened my bag to take out my keys, I glimpsed the doll's face looking up from the bottom of my bag. I fished out my keys and my own hand knocked against her plastic one.

The three of us went over to the table and I pulled out the chair where Lydia had been sitting.

'Look,' I gestured to the floor theatrically. 'Look, there's nothing.'

The little girl's lips started trembling. They both stayed standing there as if they were having trouble accepting what their eyes were telling them and that shortly the doll would materialise on the ground in front of them.

Marta's head popped through the plastic-strip curtain. 'Oh, I thought I heard the bell. Everything alright?'

I exhaled sharply.

'It's OK. They thought they might've left something here but there's nothing.'

She pushed through the curtain. 'Oh dear. What was it?'

'It was Lydia's doll,' the woman said quietly, like there'd been a family bereavement. 'She had a flowered dress and a home-knitted red cloak on. I made it myself.'

Lydia pulled on her mum's sleeve. 'She had brown plastic shoes with straps but the straps don't undo, you have to pull the whole shoe off.' Lydia's cheeks had turned pink with emotion.

'Oh, sweetie,' said Marta. 'I'm so sorry.'

Don't encourage her, I thought, but it was too late. Lydia's lips pursed up and she really did start crying then, big tears sliding down her face and dripping off her stupid little chin.

Marta knelt down in front of her. 'Oh, sweetie,' she said again. 'You might still find her. Perhaps you dropped her outside somewhere.'

The mother shook her head, slowly, sadly. 'No, we traced our exact same steps back. You were our last hope.'

Marta tutted and looked up at me. 'You didn't find anything at all?'

She only wanted to help but it was such an obviously pointless question, prolonging everyone's agony.

'I didn't find anything.'

Lydia took off her hat and started wiping it all over her face. I could see it was going to get covered in snot. Nobody seemed to be moving, or to want to move, and I wasn't sure how to break away without betraying myself. The mother hunched down on bended knee to Lydia so there were now two adults kneeling either side of her like supplicants and I felt like screaming.

'We'll get you a new doll, darling. We'll go to that toy shop on the corner and look now if you like. D'you want to do that?'

But Lydia was overwhelmed now. She shook her head sharply side to side. 'I don't want another one. I just want her.'

Marta stood, finally, and dusted off her knees. 'If you leave a number and we find anything we'll let you know, won't we, Carmel?'

Did she look at me sharply then, or was it my guilty conscience?

There was another age while the mother looked for a pen in her bag and when none could be found, with relief, I darted into the kitchen for one of my waiter's pads and a pen and she laboriously wrote her name and mobile number down.

Marta said, 'I do hope you find her. I remember losing my favourite toy rabbit when I was a girl and I know what it feels like. Carmel will let you out.' Then she ripped off the page with the number and gave the girl the miniature pad and pen because she'd noticed, like I had, that the girl had looked at it acquisitively. Hey, I wanted to say, childishly, hey, that's mine. But of course, I didn't. I let them out and followed behind them and locked up again.

'Bye,' I said and turned away to walk down the street, feeling shambolic, all over the place, with the burdensome weight of the doll in my duffel bag against my shoulder. I wouldn't have been surprised if she'd started crying out. If I heard a high little voice from inside my bag calling out, 'Help, help, help. She's taking me away. Help me, Lydia. Please help. Rescue me from the monster.'

So now there are three lost girls: The Mermaid; The Secret Sister and The Well-Kissed Doll. I couldn't even tell myself why, but I had to have that doll. It was like my life depended on it.

It's weeks and weeks before I hear from him again. This time he sounds different. I'm in the kitchen at home when the phone rings. When I hear his voice again it has the same effect as before. Things seem to change, elongate; the kettle stretches upwards, the plastic surface I place my hand on to steady myself turns to mush.

'You've got me remembering things I don't want to be remembering,' he says. 'It pains me to think about them. I think it's making my affliction worse.'

'You need to tell me about *her*. I'm not interested in you. I know you well enough.'

He is silent for a long time.

'If I tell you, will you come to me?'

My heart starts pounding. 'What, you mean face to face?'

'How else would you heal me?'

'I fear I can't.'

'Don't you want to know?'

I bite on my lips. 'You mean that is your price?'

'You put it too crudely. I was the one person you refused to heal.'

'How could I heal you? My body must've known what you'd done underneath and stopped it working when it came to you.'

There is another long silence. 'I require healing.'

'Then you must tell me.'

'I can't,' he whispers.

'Well start by telling me something. What sort of clothes did she wear?'

'She used to wear a funny little grey suit. I used to think it made her look like a monkey.' He sounds like he's about to start crying.

I put my mouth close to the phone. 'I need to know where, and what and how. You have to tell me or this is all over.'

There is silence again. We breathe together. 'I am breathing life for you,' I say. The words come out of nowhere and surprise me. I carry on because they feel true. 'I am a life for you and if you don't tell me what I need to know I will switch you off. I'm the only thing keeping you going. I am breath.'

'I know.' His voice sounds strangled.

'Then you need to tell me. Did she speak to you about herself?'

'That angel I told you about.'

'What angel?'

'I told you in my letter. It haunts me.'

'I already said. I never read your letter. I ripped it into tiny bits.' The second bit of this isn't true, but I want him to know how small he is to me.

The line stills between us.

'Just something, any little thing that you remember, to start you off,' I wheedle.

'She was a talkative little thing.'

I screw my eyes shut and see the skull on the folded towel in my drawer in my mind's eye. 'Please,' I whisper, so he can't hear, 'I can only think of one rescue at a time.'

'What was that?'

'Nothing. Tell me what happened, Pastor. Tell me where she is now.'

'Such long years I've been in this place but I do not regret a single minute of our time together.'

'How can you say that? How can you even say that?'

'Child . . .'

'Envy is a terrible sin. You carried envy of me in your heart didn't you, *Gramps*?' I make the name I used to use for him thick with sarcasm. 'You couldn't do what I could do so you thought you'd help yourself to what I held in my hands so you could live through me. I hope you're as well and happy now as Rachel was when she was weeping for her children.'

'Stop.'

'I'll stop when you tell me what happened to her.'

'If I do. Would you really find a way of healing me, child? Finally.'

Silence.

'Child . . .?'

'I would.' There is another long silence, an age. 'Now tell me,' I order him.

'It will come by messenger,' he says. 'It will come on a wing. Inside the belly of a whale like in the tale of Jonah.' And the phone goes dead.

I know what that means, of course. It means he's going to send it inside an aeroplane by airmail. I am better than anyone in interpreting his language. I became an expert in it between the ages of eight and thirteen.

I make some tea and try to calm down. Then I start wondering if perhaps Mum was right about the preacher, about him being sick, a monster. I keep changing my mind about him. Sometimes I think of him as being made of animal bones, or glass – a strange being. Other times I miss him. I remember his habit of bowing his head when he was thinking, his deliberate way of talking. He was always so certain of things. The way he understood the restless energy in my hands. 'Go on, Carmel,' he'd say, 'lay your hands on that poor, afflicted soul. You know you have the power to make her well. You know it deep within yourself and your gift is heaven sent, it is not human.' When I remember him like that, it's not a cracked black heart I picture; I see him like he's a messiah with a wind blowing on him that makes his hair flow back and a light shining all around him like his whole being is inside a halo. These two different ways of remembering, I'm never sure which one is real.

Beth

The dread and the feeling that there's something wrong grows and invades the house like a supernatural damp. It's so slow it's almost imperceptible. The brackishness of autumn turns into steely winter and the house has a chill to it that's nothing to do with the weather. Carmel and I, we don't talk about what happened in the hospital.

In the shower this morning I catch a real strange, damp smell clinging to the back of the shower curtain though when I put my nose to the folds it's gone and I think perhaps it was only in my imagination.

Today, before I leave my shift I go up to the stroke ward and ask the sister in charge there about the man in the foyer that Carmel tried to lay hands on, but she doesn't know anything about it.

'I must've made a mistake,' I mutter, embarrassed both for myself and for Carmel. What happened caused a bit of gossip here, mainly among the receptionists who were on the scene. As in any big place, people like to talk and normally I ignore it, but when it comes to Carmel I'm sensitive.

As I pack away my things at the end of my shift my locker smells sharply of apple. I find it at the back of the locker, yellow and withered, and I take a deep bite. It still tastes good despite its wrinkled skin; it has retained its sweetness and firmness and I crunch it to the core.

At home I stop in the hallway and listen to the house. I'm guessing Carmel and I both do this, listening, assessing, creeping round each other. I don't want to call up the stairs today. I have the dislocating sense there's stuff going on she's not telling me about and that petrifies me. Perhaps that's why I'm having my old dream of empty hands dished up to me, reinvented for the present.

Perhaps I'll get my head down later then take her out tonight, whatever she fancies. Then my heart sinks and I know I'm not up to it. Not the stilted conversation across the table, the silences. There's something about doing stuff like that together that often brings out the worst in us despite both of our best intentions. I think it's something to do with the fact it always feels like it's some weird date, that it's a 'get to know you' session after the long-enforced absence that has left us as partial strangers. Added to that Carmel always avoids looking at the couples, or the young friends crowded seven to a table and laughing and joshing noisily with each other. 'Out with old Mum again,' I joked once, stupidly, clumsily, and her eyes turned down to her plate and she spent the next ten minutes minutely cutting up her pizza into quarter-inch squares.

As usual I try to plan ahead what to make for dinner. It's too much of a scramble to leave it till just before work. I don't hear her enter the kitchen as I'm staring into the fridge, bathed in its light, trying to decide what I can do with a tomato, a bunch of basil that's become nearly mulch and half a dozen jars full of various sauces and pickles. I spot one with an inch of capers in the bottom.

'Some kind of pasta sauce,' I declare, expecting her to say, 'Again?' But she doesn't. When she first got back she got really excited when she saw the shops here stocking stuff like Oreo cookies and I hadn't anticipated that, that even her tastes in food had changed. But then she turned vegetarian and it got easier somehow and I mainly follow along with that now.

'Carmel . . .?'

'OK. Whatever,' she says.

Her voice sounds funny, enough to spin me around.

'What's wrong?' I ask before I have time to stop myself. I'm not supposed to do this. We've talked about it. She discussed it with the therapist she used to see. I'm not supposed to come out with the, *Is something wrong, are you sure, no it's just you look a bit pale, you sure, never mind then, sure something isn't bothering you? No sorry. Never mind, never mind, never mind.*

Again, she doesn't react to this so I really do know something's wrong. I become very still and close the fridge door quietly.

'Honey, about supper . . .' I ask. I realise I've still got my trench coat on. It's dripping wet from the rain outside. I look down and see I've made a small puddle on the kitchen tiles. I slip it off and hang it behind the kitchen door.

'What a day,' I say, and when she doesn't answer, 'How was work this week?'

'Mmmm?'

'The café?'

'Oh . . . yes.'

'Anything interesting happen recently?'

Her lips stretch across her teeth; the corners of her mouth turn down in an expression I don't recognise. It frightens me, her face.

'Some kid lost its doll, came back to the café to look but it wasn't there.'

'That's a shame.' I keep my voice neutral, reaching out for an onion from the little metal basket hanging from a hook underneath the kitchen cabinet.

'Yeah well. Maybe she should've paid more attention to it.'

Suddenly my hand with the onion in it appears disconnected from the rest of me. I put the onion on the chopping board and look at it, trying to breathe lightly. Did she really just say that? Of course, it's directed at me, for losing her. I know that even if she doesn't fully realise it. Something really strange is happening; it crackles around the kitchen, it lifts the hairs on the back of my neck.

I twirl round; for the first time I register *she's* got her coat on still. 'Going out?' I ask in a neutral voice.

She opens up both hands in front of her and stares at them. Then her face sinks into them, covering her eyes. 'I don't know.'

I sit abruptly opposite her.

'Carmel, my darling. Please tell me what's going on.'

I'm breaking all the rules here but I don't care. I have to get to the bottom of this. My heart's beating double time. The sleeve on her jumper has ridden up. For the first time I look properly at the heavy metal bangle she wears these days. There's something overly dense about it and for some reason it strikes me as a grey, inert snake coiling around her wrist that's got her in its grip.

She sweeps her arms to her sides like she's opening a pair of curtains; her nose is pinched she's breathed in so sharply, her eyes are wild.

'What if I tell you?'

'Tell me what?'

'Please, please, please don't freak out, but I've got to tell someone and I haven't really got anyone else.'

I try to ignore the twisting effect her last words have on me.

'Carmel, you can tell me anything, my love.'

'I have to speak with someone. There's a mighty storm inside me.'

'Of course, of course. Tell me anything. I promise, I *absolutely promise* I won't freak.'

'I've been in touch with him.'

'Who?'

'*Him.*'

I'm instantly dizzy. No she can't possibly mean . . . I'm jumping to ridiculous conclusions here and I'll alienate her.

'Who exactly are we talking about?'

She breathes heavily, not answering but keeping her eyes on my face.

'Carmel?'

'Mum, don't make me, please. You know who I mean. The man that took me, the man that's in prison for taking me – that man. Gramps.'

Hearing the name she called him makes me feel sick right to the core. I unglue my tongue from the roof of my mouth. I can't make any sense of what she's saying, but what I do know is that we are in terrible, terrible danger. I know that.

'But, Carmel, he couldn't possibly know where you are. There's no way, unless . . .' something dawns on me and I press my palms down hard on the table, 'unless it was that bloody article in the newspaper. Is that how he found you?'

She looks calmer for a moment, surveying me almost speculatively. 'Mum, it was me that contacted him.'

I realise I'm touching my mouth with my fingers. Is it an unconscious attempt to stop the words coming out? I think it might be because my impulse was to grab her across the table, to grab her violently and shout, you stupid fucking kid, what do you think you're doing, don't you know he's a lunatic. He'll smash our fragile peace into bits.

But then she is gone. The chair opposite is empty. I hear her feet slapping up the stairs. My hand trembles on my lips.

She's violated absolutely everything that's between us. I don't know what to do with this, how to react, how to pretend I'm not angry and afraid.

She arrives back in the kitchen holding two thin sheets of paper and an envelope in her hand.

'See,' she explains to me, almost eagerly. 'It's that there's certain things that need to fall in place before I can do anything at all and until I know them, I'm going to be stuck forever. I need to *reconstruct* everything.'

'Like what?' I manage.

'The one that came before me. I need to know what happened to her.'

'Who?'

'Mercy, the other girl he took before me. I have to know what happened to her.'

'Why, Carmel? What good would it do?'

'I only know that I have to and only *he* can help me with that. Until I find her or find out what happened to her, I'm never going to get better. I don't know how to explain it; it's like she's part of me, like I was her for a while. I could've been her. It's something I know I have to do before I'll ever be able to feel any peace.'

'Darling, it's survivor's guilt. It's a common thing.'

She shakes her head to silence me and hands me the letter.

I worry that my hands are shaking too hard to hold it but somehow, I manage. The handwriting is bold, sloping, particular in style and it feels like the hand that wrote it is reaching out and grabbing me by the throat.

'Carmel, this is dated weeks ago. How long have you had it?'

She shrugs. 'A while. I've only just opened it though; I hid it under my rug. I read it just now upstairs. I thought it might help explain things to you.'

I start to read.

Dearest Peter Shadow—

'Why on earth is he calling you that?' In my confused

brain I'm thinking it's something about Peter Pan and Wendy. I look at the envelope. That's addressed to Peter Shadow too.

'Who's Peter Shadow?'

'I didn't know if he would be allowed to write to me so I didn't use my own name. I used a reference he'd understand instead. I knew he'd know it was me.'

'What's the reference?'

'It's the piece in the Bible about healing the sick he often used to quote in his sermonising before a healing about the power of Peter's shadow.'

'And that was always about you?'

'Yes.'

She pauses for a moment then her face goes rigid, like there's a wind blowing on it, and Carmel begins to speak in a voice I barely recognise.

'So that they even carried out the sick into the streets and laid them on beds and pallets, that as Peter came by at least his shadow might fall on some of them. The people also gathered from the towns around Jerusalem, bringing the sick and those afflicted with unclean spirits, and they were all healed.'

I listen, speechless. It's like listening to a recording.

She pauses. 'I thought about signing it in glitter glue too as that would've been another clue. Turns out I didn't need to. He knew exactly who the real Peter Shadow was.'

'Glitter glue?' My head's spinning with all this.

'I was always writing my name all over the place, in glitter glue when I could get a hold of it. On tables in diners and stuff.'

I've never heard about this before. 'Why did you do that?'

'I dunno. I guess it was to remind me who I was. Or maybe I thought someone would see it and come and find me. Didn't work, obviously.'

I look at the letter. I'm still deeply shaken at her transformation when she quoted from scripture, and her rapid change back. But I have seen her look like that, of course. It was the day in the hospital with the man who looked like he was having a stroke.

'Read it then.'

I look down. I'd almost forgotten the pages were in my hand.

Dearest Peter Shadow,

I have been waiting and waiting for some kind of communication from you.

Let me tell you there were times when I almost gave up hearing from you. Somehow though, I managed to retain my fortitude, my strength, despite being so sorely tested.

You arrogant bastard, I want to scream. You are ticking my daughter off, the child that you kidnapped, for not getting in touch sooner? I feel soiled by having to read this letter. It's like I now have a relationship with him, whereas before I managed to keep him behind the locked door of a prison. Now, he's reached out of that cell, reached across the ocean, into this city, into my home.

So, my darling. You are asking questions about John the Baptist . . .

I look up. 'My *darling?* Christ.'

She stays silent.

'OK. What does it mean?'

'He means Mercy, the girl that came before me. He sometimes referred to her as John the Baptist because he came before Jesus.'

All these mad allusions, I'm getting dizzy with them. I take a deep breath. 'Right . . . why?'

'I told you. It was how he referred to her sometimes. I suppose it meant she was a kind of precursor to the real thing – me.'

'So let me get it. He related her to John the Baptist and you – to Jesus?'

'Yes.'

I laugh, I can't help it, and she looks at me as if disgusted.

I bend my head over the letter so she can't see my expression.

These are things that need to be answered gradually, a piecing together if you will. But first, I want to know if you are using your gift wisely, child. This is a truly serious question that is of the utmost importance. You have been gifted by the Almighty with an incredible power in those hands. All I wished to do was to harness, to direct, to enable but . . . We do not need to go into the obstacles and the blocks along the path of righteousness that have befallen me. I have tried with every fiber of my being not to succumb to the forces that work against us both.

My dearest, I have taken to reading here. There's a library that I've been making great use of. A while ago I found the strangest thing, something that's come to haunt me in my dreams, in my days too often. It's the drawing of an angel – a most unbecoming angel you might think, but it has something in its lines that I return to over and over again, that takes me back to that book for one more sight of it. That's the last time of looking, I tell myself – gazing upon it causes a kind of pain that is unendurable. Then I say, once more, it will not be so bad this time, it's a collection of lines clumsily drawn. So I look and it seems to burst from the page at me. The first time I saw it I began to pray out loud, right there and then between the stacks of books.

There's something there – I can't name what – that reminds me of myself as a boy. In the simple lines of that angel, in the way it stares. Paradise for me now is a cratered, wind-blown planet, empty of all but that angel standing on its dust.

Here, the writing becomes thin. I get the impression he's left off it for a while because below that the writing returns stronger.

Dearest, these things are hard to communicate by letter. I have added your telephone number – under the name of Peter Shadow – to the small list of numbers I'm entitled to call. To think, we will speak in person soon!

I remain yours in faith and humble belief,
Father Patron.

'Oh, no, no, no.'

'What?'

'No, you cannot possibly contemplate talking to him on the phone.'

Her face turns closed, mutinous. She's hiding something from me.

'Can't you see what he's doing? He's trapping you, inveigling himself into your life for a bit of information he'll probably dangle forever without telling you the truth. I can't believe you're falling for it.'

'You make me sound stupid.'

'No, of course not, Carmel. You're just confused, very, very confused, and that's understandable after everything that happened.'

'I need to find her, Mum. She's lost out there.'

'But even so, you cannot, you really cannot begin any sort of relationship with this man.'

'I already have a relationship with him,' she yells unexpectedly. 'It's not beginning one at all. I was with him for years and years and we know each other inside out. You can't just disappear all those years because you want to pretend they didn't happen.'

I'm shocked into silence but she's right. I hate the idea she formed any sort of relationship while she was gone, that she has boatloads of memories I know nothing about. That she celebrated Christmas with other people. She's yelling so loudly now I have to put my hands over my ears.

'You can't tell me what to do. You're not even a believer. You're godless. You don't believe in what I can do, you've always trashed it, made me think I was brainwashed.' She stops, gasping. 'I'm sorry. I don't know what I'm saying.'

'Carmel. I'm not trashing you, it's just that I can't join in with what he's told you.' I take my hands from my ears and clasp them together. I am actually pleading. 'They are delusions, Carmel. You must realise that somewhere inside you.'

Her face turns flinty. 'I have seen things that you couldn't possibly comprehend. I have experienced things that are beyond your understanding, and all you do is tell me they aren't possible. Who are you? A false idol pretending to be my mother?'

I feel like she's just hit me. She carries on.

'You don't really know me, do you? You don't know what I like or even who I am. You make me doubt myself all the time. He never doubted me for one minute. That's why he took me, to show me how, to educate me. All you do is make me think I live in a fantasy world.'

'You can't possibly believe that that man knows you better than I do. That it was a good thing he kidnapped you. Christ, Carmel.'

My eyes alight on the envelope, on *our* address in *that* writing. A sickening anger begins to bubble through my system.

'Carmel, you've told him where we are. Where we live. You've invited him into our home. How could you possibly do that? And all that mumbo-jumbo – he's sick, Carmel. Really sick.'

She stands, her face white, her eyes fiery. 'I can't do this anymore.'

'What?'

'You need to leave me alone. I need a place I can live in on my own away from you.'

'Please . . .'

But she's gone, her feet pounding on the stairs. Let her get over it, I tell myself, she'll simmer down, but I know deep down that this is different, that we've touched on something we've only crept round up till now. Him and that letter has cracked it all open wide, it's made us ask the question – the one fraught with peril that we both knew should never be asked because it would break our fragile lives into pieces. The question: *What happens when a person goes away and when they come back, they are not the same person at all?*

I've been avoiding the answer for eight years.

I hear her racing down the stairs and I come out of the kitchen.

'Carmel.'

'I'm not staying here. Leave me alone. He knew who I was, accepted me. I'm not living under the same roof as someone who doesn't believe me. I'm going.'

'Carmel, please . . .'

'No, just leave me alone.'

She slams the front door on her way out and I run upstairs and look out of the window where there's a good view of the street. The storm's burned itself out but it's still raining. There, there she is, a bright slant of red against the grey pavement, the grey drizzle, her head down.

I dash into her room. Her mudlarking finds have been

swept from the shelves and litter the floor.

I run downstairs, outside into the rain, leaving the front door wide open but the street is empty, no indication of where she might've gone, so I make a choice and run left, to the end of the street, and that's empty too, just the rain filling it. It's the void of my dream, my empty hand.

The thing that happened the day the police came to my house and told me they'd found her happens again. That day it was relief that made me collapse to the ground but now, as my legs give way and I find myself kneeling alone on the wet street, it's because in that moment I realise that I have lost her once again.

Sound the klaxons, I want to yell. I open my arms wide but no sounds come out of my mouth. Set off the sirens. Unfurl the flags that say DANGER in vast red letters. Let people take to the streets calling out Carmel's name, saying, she's gone, she's gone, she's gone until people can stand it no more, are driven mad by it and will tear up the very earth beneath their feet to find her.

I unpeel my knees off the wet, silent street and walk home.

I try her number three times. No answer.

I sit at the kitchen table, shaking. The knees of my jeans are soaking. The skin on the back of my hands is wet and white. I make myself go through to the hall and retrieve my phone and I try her number. It clicks over to answerphone and I leave a message. 'Carmel, it's Mum. I'm really worried, my love. If you could just ring me and let me know you're OK, that would be enough, I promise. Please take care, my lovely.'

Then I phone the police.

'My daughter has gone missing,' I say. My voice sounds cracked and strange to my own ears.

'Right, madam. How old is she?'

'Twenty-one. She's twenty-one years old.'

'And where does she live?'

'She lives with me.'

'How long has she been gone?'

I scrunch my eyes up trying to gauge. 'About an hour.'

There's a sigh, I'm sure it's a sigh. 'I'll take her name and details but don't you think you might wait a little bit longer to think she's missing? She might've popped out somewhere.'

Something thick and dark and raw rises up in me. My vision begins turning black. I yell into the phone, 'Don't you realise? She's done this before! It's happened before!'

I punch the end call as I slide sideways, nearly blacking out, clinging on to the spindly little hall table which comes down on my head, the landline telephone we rarely use now following it and bouncing off my forehead. I crawl along the hallway, the carpet soft and unfamiliar being in such close proximity, into the kitchen and haul myself up to the sink where I take long, lapping gulps of water straight from the tap.

She's been taken from me again.

The blackness fades and I sit at the kitchen table thinking what to do. Of course, she was about to do a shift at the café. She's probably just gone there. I run back into the hallway and put the table back on its legs, the receiver back on the phone and look up The Egg and Spoon in the Yellow

Pages with shaking hands. I'd asked Carmel at least three times to write the number in the address book but each time she didn't and somehow evaded my asking about it until I finally understood what she was doing – marking that territory as private.

The number rings and rings, then I ring off and call it again, at the same time trying to remember where it is. I went there with her for her interview because she was so nervous. I didn't go inside. She turned decisively at the last minute and said, 'Thanks. I'll meet you back at home. I'll be OK now.' I wanted to convey to her that it wasn't a big deal, that they would be lucky to have her, a tatty little café in a run-down street, but of course it was a big deal to her so I said nothing, except, 'Good luck.' When she came home, she was beaming all over her face because she'd been given the job.

A woman answers, sounding harassed. 'Hello.'

'Hi, it's Beth Wakeford here, Carmel's mum. I'm just checking if she came into work just now.'

'Well, she did . . . briefly.'

'Briefly?'

'I hope she's OK.'

'Why, what d'you mean?'

There's a pause. 'She kind of ran out on me.'

'What happened?'

'It's a bit complicated. A while ago we had a little girl and her mum and they were convinced they'd lost a doll in here.'

'Yes, she mentioned that, but what's it got to do with today?'

'Well, I think it's possible that Carmel stole it.'

My heart winds up a little tighter.

'What makes you think that?' I ask quietly.

'On the day it happened Carmel was acting a bit oddly. She was a bit mean to the child, truthfully. I can only say that because it was such a contrast to how she usually is and wasn't like Carmel. She's really good and kind with the customers, that's one reason why I value her.'

'But what makes you think she actually stole it?'

'It seemed to disappear into thin air and then this morning I put the apron on that Carmel was wearing that day and I found the doll's shoe in the pocket. When Carmel came in, I confronted her about it and she got really upset, really quickly and ran out. The thing is, after she left, I realised the shoe had gone from the place where I'd put it. She'd taken it.'

I look into the gilt-framed mirror above the hall table and notice for the first time there's a cut above my eye. I look down at the blood on the edge of the table and put my finger up to the cut.

'I see.'

'Look, I have to go – I'm short-staffed now but I hope she's OK and tell her she can just come back to her job. It doesn't matter about before, about what happened. She can come back and start again any time she likes.'

'Thank you,' I say again.

I sit on the stairs with my head in my hands. I do not know if I can do this again – to not know physically where she is.

I climb the stairs to her room and stand breathing deeply in and out as if by doing that I can channel her whereabouts.

184

Nothing, the line's gone dead. I'm buzzing from anxiety and lack of sleep. There's a tiny wreath of honesty seed heads hanging from the wall that surprises me because I've never seen it before and I remember how when she was little she loved to help me when I was drying them out. I sit on the end of the bed; the room's quite small so my knees almost meet the desk that's against the wall opposite. She could've had a bigger room. This is cluttered from all her finds. The spare room's twice this size but she liked this one. I think it gave her a feeling of security at first, its small size and the fact it faces the garden rather than the street. Then, I see her phone on the floor. I pick it up, knowing my message is trapped inside.

'Oh, Mum,' I sigh. 'Tell me what to do.' There's nothing I'd like more than to sink my head on my own mother's shoulder and have her stroke my hair, to give up a little of the pain and responsibility for her to bear.

I start opening drawers to see what she's taken. It doesn't seem much but I know that doesn't mean anything. I could hear in her voice that she was breaking something permanently. I rifle through her wardrobe, faded jeans and tracksuit bottoms on hangers, then open the top drawer of her desk, then the second. There's her tools, a magnifying glass. I open the third without much expectation.

My breath freezes.

Very, very gently I take out the object nestled there on a towel. I put it in one palm and hold it out in front of me. With my other hand I trace the twin arches of the eye sockets. I know exactly what I'm looking at. It's a child's skull.

The feeling from earlier, of knowing something behind

the scenes is terribly wrong, crystallises. Then that twists again and I feel almost joyful because I've just thought of something.

Maybe the police will start listening now.

Mercy

1999

Over the coming days and weeks Mercy struggled to come to terms with her new reality. Most days, Delia was up and dressed and at the stove making breakfast by the time Mercy climbed down the ladder from her bedroom.

'Scrambled, fried or poached,' Delia asked. 'Muffins, toast or cornbread. Bacon and maple syrup on the side?'

'Sure,' said Mercy in a small voice, climbing on the chair at the table.

'But which then?' asked Delia.

In some ways Delia felt truly born again, although not in the way her exceptional and unusual daughter, who had a heart like no other she had ever known, would mean it. This chance of a new life that had presented itself was so unexpected and unlooked for that it made everything seem to shine like it was being reflected in a silvered mirror.

From the point that Delia was on her knees with a gun sticking in the back of her head things had taken a turn that was, she now reflected with wonder, mundane and extraordinary at the same time. They'd gone down to Roanoke in the hope of buying enough stuff to set themselves up and do a little dealing, mainly in support of their own habits, which were getting difficult to manage. Delia had a small bequest left to her by an uncle who knew nothing of the turn her life had taken and they decided to use it to get them started.

In the event their contact, it transpired pretty quickly, had only summoned them there to rob them, but even as he was doing it in their motel room he was strung out, twitchy and paranoid. He yelled at them both that they'd informed on him, that they'd been having him followed, and Delia knew deep within herself he was only a hair's breadth away from blasting both their brains out. Just at that point there was a knock at the door. The three inside, one standing, two kneeling, held their breaths in the semi-darkness of the room with its curtains drawn. Delia considered crying out but the certainty that doing that would lead quickly and directly to her death stopped her. This awful play that she seemed to be starring in was nothing, absolutely nothing like the one she'd envisaged when she was growing up, a teenager who fan-worshipped Madonna and who lived for a new episode of *Friends* coming out. Who wore bright scrunchies in her hair and sewed similar ones out of scraps of colourful fabric for all her girlfriends.

However their contact was so spooked by the knocking he fled through the bathroom window, taking all their money, and soon they fell into a terrible withdrawal that stranded them for days. They never found out who was knocking at their motel room door. Sometimes, Delia wondered if it could've been an angel.

—

The truth of it for Mercy was that her life had become partly hollowed out. The fierce resistance she'd held on to before was sapped away. She had nothing to do, no overarching purpose in a way that was sudden and overwhelming. Added to that there was something off about Delia's performance. Her lipstick was too thickly applied, her face shiny with strain and her hands often shook as she handled the skillet and the wooden spoon.

Mercy usually went back upstairs to play with her doll's house after breakfast. The racoon had long disappeared, chased off by all the new people in the house where his alliance had been forged only with Mercy and in the quietness of the forest clearing.

More gifts followed: like the doll's house, all purchased on credit. A gingham dress with a white collar. A book of Russian fairy tales. A Barbie doll with her own plastic horse. A toy disco set with five plastic records that played real music. New shoes with patent leather bows on the front.

As she sat in front of the magnificent doll's palace with the doors opened on all the rooms, somehow the irony of its luxury inside this crumbling shack was lost on her. She moved the gilded furniture around, walked the dolls dressed in fancy clothes from room to room and flicked the overhead lights on and off – in the living room there was a real crystal miniature chandelier – which were all powered by a battery in the attic, and found herself bored by it all. Where was the life in all this? The sleek pelt of the racoon, the call of the whippoorwill, the unfurling of the forest and the clouds speeding across the sky were what she had thrived on before. Ever-changing things that were alive with promise.

When Delia acquired a washing machine things got slightly better. Mercy instantly fell in love with the machine, its little red and green lights, its beeping and the whooshing sound as it started up and the water began flowing into its belly. She loved how clean and sweet-smelling the clothes were after being washed in it, not like the old musty smell when she used to do them all by hand. She marvelled at the hours of drudgery it curtailed. After some persuasion Delia allowed her to take charge of it. When the washing programme began Mercy would often settle cross-legged in front of it and watch their clothes as they tumbled round in beautiful white suds.

It was the small things in the house that began to disappear first. Mercy understood what was happening completely and instantly. She realised she had been sort of waiting for it, the expectation and tension an ache at the top of her belly that came and went. She wandered through the house doing an inventory. Some of their smaller new belongings had gone, the expensive skillets and the new electric knife. Later the electric iron went too, along with the new microwave, whose clock, unlike the old one, kept up its unblinking stare through the whole twenty-four hours, and the ache of tension in her stomach stayed as a permanent guest now. So, it began again, the days spent in bed by her parents, the relentless drive to make them eat by leaving Pop-Tarts by the bed, the small subterfuges at the grocery store. This time, there was a weariness to it that she hadn't experienced before that the break seemed to have imposed on her. The one bright spot was the return of the racoon, lured by the peace of the dreaming addicts and the corners of sliced bread left out for him.

Strangely, when she saw the empty space where the doll's house had been that ache disappeared. It was one of the very last possessions to go, but the only one that caused Mercy real loss was when she went into the bathroom and saw the rubber hose dangling down that once used to be attached to the back of the washing machine.

One bright Sunday morning Mercy put on her pink shoes and left for church. While her parents were well it had been sort of forbidden. Now, Mercy knew they would no longer care. To her surprise the visiting pastor was still there. She was even more surprised when he spoke to her before the service.

'So you came back?' he said. There was a flushed expression on his face she couldn't quite read.

'Uh, huh.'

'I came to call on your folks last week but they weren't there.'

So, he'd come back again. It must've been while she was in school. Mercy was reminded of the time he'd called when she'd been alone and how scared she'd been, but that whole period had the feeling of a fever dream and none of it she could properly understand. She couldn't remember now quite *why* she'd been so scared.

Mercy kept her lips buttoned tight. This time, chances were her parents had been there but they were not answering the door.

'I'm sure glad you came again,' he said.

'You are?'

'Yes, I think you are a real special girl. Remember what happened with Vera?'

She nodded. She did. 'Mrs Farmer told me the Lord acts in mysterious ways.' Mercy squinted up at him. She wasn't *entirely* sure what Mrs Farmer had meant about the incident with Vera but it seemed Mrs Farmer did and who was Mercy to argue?

'He sure does, child. That He surely does.'

Carmel

2013

After running out on Mum this morning, when I arrived at the café, Marta didn't smile. I'd tied my hair back and rubbed at my face to try and clear away the terrible argument with Mum etched there. I hoped perhaps I could do my shift as usual.

'I thought I heard the bell. You're early,' she said.

'Yes, I . . .'

'Carmel, can you come through? There's something I want to talk to you about.'

Not smiling, Marta confirmed everything had gone bad. The kitchen was steamy. The smell of the herbs was strong and my eyes started stinging.

'What's the matter?' I asked.

'There's something I need to discuss with you.'

She reached behind her and to my horror – my utmost horror – I saw the doll's shoe in her hand. For some reason it had become misshapen – big on one side and twisted – and that fact somehow made sense, like we were all being dipped into another universe and being warped by it. I had to open my mouth to breathe.

'I sent the aprons to the laundry as usual and when I put this one on this morning, I found this in the pocket. Carmel, it's exactly like the one that poor little girl and her Mum described the doll wearing that they lost. Why wouldn't you mention it if you'd found it when they were here? They were so upset.'

Of course, that's why it was a funny shape. It had been through the laundry.

'Maybe it was Janice that found it,' I said.

'No, it was the apron you were wearing that day. I know because it's the one with red ties and there's only two like that and I was wearing the other one.'

'I remember now. I found it when I was clearing the table and I must've put it in my pocket and forgotten about it.'

The doll was one thing I grabbed before I left this morning. She was at the bottom of my bag. If she could speak she would've been squeaking right now, *Marta, Marta, ignore her. She's lying. She's a child-snatcher. A monster. Marta, help me, help me, help me.*

'Well, alright. Seems strange though.' Marta clearly didn't believe me. The conversation we had that day about the lost doll was so exhaustive I would have been bound to say something about the found shoe. It wouldn't have been something so easily forgotten.

She put the shoe back on the windowsill and turned back to her saucepan. I felt her back – cold, disapproving. I couldn't bear it, not after this morning. Marta has always, always been kind to me. On impulse I went up and put my arms around her. She felt thin under her cotton dress. I laid my cheek against her shoulder blade.

'Carmel,' she said softly into her bubbling saucepan. 'What's the matter?'

I couldn't answer. My throat had closed up too much. I

really didn't know if she knew what had happened to me as a kid or not. I'd never told her. I didn't know if she'd seen reports at the time or that piece in the *Gazette*.

She put her hands over mine and peeled them off her ribcage where I was hugging her. At first, I thought she was pushing me off but I realised she wanted to turn so she could see my face. She stroked my cheek with one hand and hugged me with the other.

'The sauce will burn if you don't keep stirring it,' I said.

'Come on, you can tell me.'

I shook my head. Her eyes were such a beautiful brown, and kind. Marta's the sort of person who pretends there's too much apple pie left so the pensioner who looks threadbare gets a free slice. Injustice makes red spots come up on her cheeks. She'd help anyone if she could. But I couldn't speak.

'Carmel, did you take that doll? Honestly, I won't be cross but I want to try and understand.'

I couldn't stand her asking this, just couldn't stand it. I pushed her hands away and her eyes rounded in surprise.

'Leave me alone.'

'Carmel . . .'

But I was gone, and as I ran out of the kitchen, I grabbed the doll's shoe in my fist. Outside, the rain had gotten heavier. I felt it trickling down my back.

I had no idea where to go and the realisation struck me that I was homeless. It had happened as quickly as that, in the space of a few hours. I was like one of the people that have to sleep in shop doorways, like the ones that Marta feeds on the wheelie bins out the back of the café. I stood for a minute, too scared by the idea to move, but my head started getting wetter and wetter until I could feel water dripping off my forehead. My feet seemed to decide what to do. They took me to the Tube station. I put my pre-fed Oyster card onto the card reader.

When I emerged out the other end, I could barely remember how I got there. It seemed natural that I came here on instinct, where I let Alan go, the place familiar to me from mudlarking. This part of London looks like something out of the olden days, the quay, the dark narrow streets, the medieval pubs. There's underground places too, I expect. Hollow walls. Places that have been built over and rooms bricked up.

I've practically read the pages off Granny's set of Dickens with gold lettering on brown cardboard spines meant to look like leather that have their own little special shelf on the landing. Here it looks like something straight out of one of those books if it wasn't for the cars and people walking past talking on their mobile phones, and the office tower blocks across the water.

I leaned over the wall and breathed in the smell of river water. The shoreline below was a thick brown smear. There was nobody there and I wanted to go down, to lose myself there, but I doubted whether I'd ever want to come back up and that felt dangerous so I didn't. I walked past the Globe theatre and stood under the porch of a pub for a while to keep out of the rain, watching people with umbrellas or newspapers over their heads go by.

I knew I couldn't go back to the house. It was destroying me, us being together.

I wondered briefly what Mum would say if she saw me now and I felt terribly ashamed, like she was never going to be without the problem of me. Mum's always giving money to people on the streets. Once, we passed a girl who was sitting on the pavement crying and Mum gave her loads of pound coins. Then about half an hour later we came back the same way and the girl was sitting with someone else cooking up drugs in a teaspoon over a lighter. When I pointed this out to Mum – where her hard-earned money had gone – she just shrugged and sighed and said, 'Maybe she needs them. I'd need drugs if I was sleeping on the pavement at night.'

My hand was hurting and I looked down and saw how tight my fist was. It was so locked up I had to use my other hand to open up the fingers. The shoe was still there, in my palm that had red crescents cut into it from my fingernails.

Now I've been wandering about all day and it's starting to get dark. Over the other side of the river I can see the flashlights and headtorches of mudlarkers taking advantage of the low tide but it feels even the river is lost to me. It's stopped raining at last so I hunker down into myself in a doorway, onto the ground, and build a little wall with my duffel bag. Suddenly I'm on the level of people's knees, their feet. Faces float far above. Two young men in bright white T-shirts and smart jackets start laughing at me as they pass.

'Get a fucking job,' one of them says. His lips are very red stretched out across his teeth, in contrast to his white skin and dark hair.

'I have got one,' I say, but so quietly he doesn't hear me.

It feels so unjust him saying that but then I realise I don't actually have a job anymore. I've just run out on it and my throat tightens up in shame and fear.

I squeeze a bit more into myself like a tortoise into its shell, not even wondering what I'm going to do anymore, hoping I might just disappear into nothing.

Those things that Mum said about the preacher, I have to admit that they're not entirely untrue. After all, he did take me and tell me Mum was dead, even though I know he thinks the ends justified the means. At the bottom of my letter I scribbled, *I know you are a damn liar so don't think I've forgotten that.*

I'm pleased I said that now I think about it.

I still haven't heard anything about Mercy from him like he promised. I've begun to fear he was lying about that too though I mustn't lose heart or I'll be finished. I have to keep believing that there's a letter coming towards me mile by mile, inch by inch.

Slowly, the air becomes darker as it's tinged by twilight. I feel the other city emerging around me from its sleep, the violent, terrible one. Usually London is lumpy, soft with rain. This other place is always ready to come through. It's the one where people are slashed with knives, where they fall from buildings, get struck on the back of the head, are electrocuted on Tube lines, where bodies are thrown into the river. I shiver violently in my coat. My back is still damp from the rain that trickled down my neck earlier. One of my ears throbs inside the eardrum.

Two women squat down by me; *come home with us,*

come home with us, they say. I don't like the feeling from them.

'You're really pretty,' says the one in the long green coat.

The other is literally licking her lips as she looks at me. 'I've had experience of wolves,' I yell at them. 'I've had interactions with your kind.'

They stand up, straighten up. 'Please yourself,' says the lip-licking one and they stalk off, but I notice they look around them to see what people have seen.

There's a girl about to start peeling an orange as she walks along. She stops stock-still and plops the orange in my lap and walks off without a word. I stare at the brightness of it. It's like she was giving an offering to the gods to make sure the same fate as mine never happens to her, and she hoped the sacrifice of bright fruit would protect her from that destiny.

I need to move; I'm too visible here. The two men that called out about getting a job have long gone but I bet everyone's thinking that. They either glance at me and look away quickly or you can see they're really purposely trying not to look. A woman and a man walk along and I hear her say, 'Wait, I won't be a minute,' to him and she gets her purse out of her bag and fumbles with it.

Oh no, no, I think, but she comes over and lays a pound coin in front of me like it's an offering to a saint.

'I've got money,' I say, but again my voice is so quiet she doesn't hear me.

'Bless you, child,' she says. Her breath smells of wine. 'You take care of yourself now.' Then she's gone.

I stare at the pound coin winking in the street light. I get up and my legs have gone all stiff from sitting on the ground for so long and I take my bag but I leave the coin where it is.

I need to be more hidden away. There's a church round here, I remember that. Maybe that'll be quieter.

It takes me a while to find because I'm disorientated. I'm starting to feel glazed over, like if I move too much I'll crack. The building looms up unexpectedly, a dark shape against the night sky. I use my fingers to reach out and touch the wall. It feels rough like it's covered in the oyster shells I find so often on the foreshore, remnants of long-ago meals, although this is more likely to be flint or some stone like that.

I move round to the gate but it's locked. I put my forehead on the bars and stare inside and try to think. I had the idea I could curl up in the churchyard somewhere but I'll have to think again. I skirt the perimeter of the building, down an alley, and find myself in a narrow courtyard full of wheelie bins. There's the rumble of trains overhead and nearby the chatter from a restaurant or pub garden. I curl up in the corner and hug my knees. I remember about the doll and rummage at the bottom of my duffel bag until I feel a spiky plastic arm and I pull her out. In the artificial light her face looks vague, like she's thinking about something else.

Her little knitted red cloak feels damp under my fingers. The red has turned grey in the light. I unzip my mac and drop her in there, just above my stomach, and I zip my coat back up and I hug her tightly and that's how I go to sleep, the cut of her plastic body in my stomach.

When I wake there's a man standing over me. I can see him clearly because it's early dawn and a pale blue light illuminates it all, somehow making everything appear thin, brittle.

'I haven't seen you here before,' he says.

I know I should be afraid but I'm too numb for that, too stiff and disorientated. His face appears to be coated in wax, gleaming slightly. There's a brown blanket over one of his shoulders. I begin to shiver violently.

'Hey,' he says. 'Don't worry. I won't hurt you or anything. I came over to see if you were still alive. You were really still.'

I blink up at him. 'What are you doing here?'

'Same as you, I guess. Trying to get some shut-eye.'

He uses one of his legs as a lever to lower himself next to me. He holds his left arm across his body like a shield. As he sits a strongly sour smell puffs out of his coat and I resist the urge to put my hand over my face so I don't have to smell it.

'I'm Cyril,' he says. 'I know, it's a weird name, but it is what it is.'

'You don't like it?'

'Would you?'

'I think it's OK, but you could always change it.'

'No, I don't want to do that.'

'Your family wouldn't like you doing that?'

'I haven't got any family,' he says. 'Or friends.'

I'm about to point out in that case, if there's no one to mind, then it would be an ideal opportunity to give himself a brand-new name like a present, one he really likes. But then I stop. Who am I to talk about changing names? I clung on to mine so hard my knuckles could've turned white.

I start shivering again.

'Here,' he says. 'D'you want to have my blanket for a while?'

In one way I really don't. When he sat down the blanket stayed stiff on his shoulder and I'm wondering if that's because it's so dirty. On the other hand, the idea of being a bit warmer is very tempting, and I don't want to hurt his feelings. He looks happy to have the opportunity to share something of his, to reach out a helping hand. I realise then that as I'm breathing it's hurting a little, like it's cracking my ribs.

'Yes please,' I say.

He arranges the blanket around me and I do my best to keep it away from my nose without seeming to. Whatever it smells like it's lovely and thick and it soon starts warming me through.

I noticed as he was tucking the blanket around me, he was only using one arm to do it – his right. I look again at his pale skin, the pale blue fire like a gas flame that seems to be passing over him, running down like water. It becomes clearer the more I look.

'Is there something wrong?' I ask.

'What?'

'With your arm?'

He touches it lightly. 'Yeah, I thought it was just a scratch but it got bigger. It's turned into a sore now. I keep meaning to go back to the hospital. They dressed it once and gave me antibiotics and they told me I needed to come back but I don't seem to get round to it. Things get a bit complicated.'

I'm more awake now, more observant. For the first time I notice how his teeth chatter if he doesn't clench them together.

'Let me have a look.'

He looks surprised. 'What?'

'My mum's a nurse. I might be able to help.'

He thinks for a moment, then shrugs. 'OK.'

He has difficulty shedding his coat so I help him, peeling the sleeve down over his arm so he can shrug it off his shoulders. Without his coat I can see his skin puckering in shivers under his thin T-shirt. Something in me becomes still, like the sudden ceasing of the action of a storm on the surface of a lake.

'Haven't you got a sweater?' I murmur, because he looks so suddenly thin, so frightened and exposed to the cold, to the early dawn.

He shakes his head. 'Nah, I did have one but I lost it. Or maybe it was stolen, I'm not sure.'

I take his arm in both hands and lift it up.

It's much, much worse than I expected. The colours are a butcher's counter, deep reds to meaty blue. Pus drips off it.

My hands start up like there's bees inside of them and I have to fight the urge to scratch the backs of them.

'It's poisoning your blood,' I say.

'What?' He twists his arm to have a look. 'Why would you say that? How would you know?'

The muscles in the corners of his jaw clench and unclench. I see, with an eye that's not on the front of my face, but somehow inside, the poison yellowing his blood and flowing freely.

A trapdoor opens. It's the same one that got slammed shut the day in the hospital when Mum grabbed me and dragged me out. It swings open wide now, with force, because what's behind it has been damming up so much. My hands become a cup in front of me and the blue light streaming off his body tumbles into it. I reach out.

'Hey, get off. What are you doing?' he says and tries to push my hands away. But he's too weak and he's no match for the power that is now streaming freely out of me, a tidal wave.

I hold his arm tight with both hands and at first he jerks to get free and then he has to stop because we are locked together and we're vibrating. But it's not only our bodies that are vibrating; it's everything around us, the ground, the walls above. He becomes still then, his brown eyes turned up towards mine, and in them I read fear but incomprehension too and a sort of resignation to me, that this overwhelming force of mine is impossible not to succumb to. That I am a holy warrior with a power like lightning or electricity in my fingertips.

Then, as it began, it stops, suddenly and without warning.

I gasp, sit back.

Both of us watch as he turns his arm to look, twists it this way and that.

'What did you just do?' he asks quietly.

'I don't know.'

He brings the fingertips of his other hand to touch the skin. It's just the same, the bloody butcher colours, the wet gleam of pus. He's shaking from the pain.

'How dare you touch me,' he says. 'How dare you do that.'

He scrambles to his feet and I reach out my hand to calm

him, to appease, but he knocks it away.

'No, don't you fucking go touching me again. You're evil. That's why you were hiding out in here. You've come out of one of those graves from that church over there. Don't come near me. I never want to see you again.'

Then he's gone and I am alone in the dawn. I stand and the blanket he's forgotten to take falls from my shoulders. There's a clunking sound. I look down. The doll has fallen out of the bottom of my coat and lies with an arm pointing upwards. I crouch next to her and stay there, rigid, until my legs are cramping over.

'Fierce' – that's what Mum said when I asked once how other people saw me on the outside. It was one thing I didn't have a clue about and needed to know. If I was ever to find my way back into society, I needed something to work with.

I didn't expect her reply so I took some time to answer. I said, 'Fierce – but that's not nice, is it?'

'Yes, it can be,' she said. 'It is with you. Fierce like Joan of Arc, fierce in a good way.'

'Who's Joan of Arc?' I really had no idea.

'She was a warrior girl. She had a heart that could burst into flames if she wasn't careful, it had such power. In the end she was consumed by real flames but they couldn't take that heart. Be ever careful of yours, my darling. Don't let them try and destroy your heart.'

I'm not a warrior girl now, that's for sure. She was wrong. I'm an empty husk.

I stay crouched over and hugging myself for ages but then my stomach growls and I straighten up, forced to move by something as ordinary as hunger pangs. I fold up the blanket and leave it there for Cyril in case he comes back. Nothing fierce about me now as I walk, head down, along the embankment, gulls crying above me. No heart of flames. I buy a fried egg roll from a van parked by the river and sit on the wall to eat and pick off bits of bread to share with the gulls.

I can't stop looking at my hands. Once I've eaten my sandwich I fold them in my lap and stare at the emptiness of them. They seem as hollow as a bone. There's nothing there. Mum is right. There are no healing energies trapped within. It was a delusion.

A girl walks up the embankment towards me. Her padded blue coat is tightly zipped up and her short hair combed and teased up into spikes. She carries a rolled-up sleeping bag strapped to her back. When her eye meets mine just for a millisecond I nod to her, but she looks away quickly, out across the water.

She is about to walk past, but maybe it was the nod that encourages her; she comes and sits next to me on the wall. I notice she is careful to sit at least five feet away. I don't know if that's to protect herself, or showing me she's not invading my space. There's something about her, oh, I don't know. She looks so cold.

'Are you hungry?' I ask.

'You're alright,' she says, her almond-shaped pale blue eyes skimming mine. Her cheeks are pink, wind-whipped. She wears a denim skirt and her skinny legs are in thick black tights.

'Don't go away.' I scrunch up the wrapper that my roll came in and go to the van and buy another and two coffees.

'Here,' I hand the cardboard cup and the warm roll wrapped in greaseproof paper over. My hand brushes hers; her skin is freezing.

'You didn't have to . . .'

'I know. It's OK. I slept near that church last night. It was so cold – a bit of something to eat helps you warm up.'

'Thank you.'

She looks for a moment like she's going to cry, but she doesn't, she wolfs down her egg roll then slurps her coffee until there's only a drip left in the bottom that she tips her head right back to get.

She shoves her hands in her pockets. 'Thanks again. I feel better now. I'm Rosie.'

'Carmel.'

'OK, I guess I need to go now, but thanks again. Perhaps I'll see you around.'

'You don't need to keep saying thank you.'

She gives an ironic salute with one finger above her eyebrow, still not looking directly at me, and is off. I wonder how long it is on the streets until you lose your embarrassment, your shame. It was radiating off her. A tender soul, I think, and then with a feeling that's like panic I realise now there's another lost girl – The Tender Soul – and I've gone and named her already without even thinking about it.

What now? I still have the keys to the café. Marta won't be there yet and I remember there's a stockroom upstairs with a red painted floor that is hardly ever used. I touch my ribs. They feel tender inside and I know if I have too many nights like this I'm going to get ill. Perhaps I can go there for a while and hole up; at least it'll be warm.

Upstairs in the café, I sit on a pile of coffee-scented hessian sacks and wind the iron bangle round and round my wrist. Along the side wall are trestle shelves, the kind I use at home for my finds from the river. Here, they're used to store kitchen equipment that's outlived its use. Everything is coated in a fine layer of dust. The light coming through the window brightens and makes the red-painted floor look like lacquer as I hear Marta arriving downstairs. There are the sounds of the kettle being filled. Thumps that are probably shopping being unpacked and put on the counter. The dragging of a chair. Then someone starts singing and I don't realise at first it's Marta. I've never heard her singing before and her voice is so pure and sweet and assured. As quietly as possible I lie on the floor and put my ear to the red-painted boards and close my eyes. It's not English she's singing, not a tune I recognise. It's a kind of folk song and I wonder if it's her native Hungarian. I put my hands flat on the floor as if I could reach down and touch her and close my eyes. I realise I'm crying then, the tears splashing down and running into the gap between the floorboards and I imagine them raining down on Marta below and I have the thought that she only ever sings when she thinks there is no one to hear her and the reason I'm crying is that the idea of that is breaking me into little pieces.

Beth

Two policemen stood quiet and erect on my doorstep. They arrived an hour after my call telling them about the skull, the fingertip and the three ribs. They introduced themselves but I didn't catch their titles properly. Their names, Fletcher and Greenaway, I gripped on to though, and I asked them to come in.

They sat on my mum's three-piece suite and rested their hands on their knees. Fletcher was dark-haired with pale skin that looked very freshly shaven. Greenaway was smaller, dark blond with a suit that looked too big for his shoulders. I don't know what it is about the police, we have a fair few dealings with them at work and I got to know them well for other reasons, of course, but to me they seem to be made of heavier matter than everyone else. I've always found you can spot them a mile off. Perhaps it's all the sinning they have to absorb.

Fletcher said, 'Please can you tell us what you said on the phone. I know you must be a bit agitated but just take your time.' He'd taken a notebook out of his pocket and held it in his palm, a tiny pencil in the fingers of his other hand.

I unplaited my fingers and laid them on my lap.

'My daughter went missing.'

'Right, sorry, forgive me – I thought it was something

about you finding a skull and some other remains?'

'Yes, yes, it was but it's all mixed up with my daughter going missing.'

'When did she go missing?' His voice was reasonable, not like he was dealing with someone crazy but like he wanted to get to the bottom of it all, and that gave me confidence to take a deep breath, calm down slightly and carry on.

'Well, this time it was this morning. The first time was when she was eight.'

His pen paused. 'She's gone missing twice?'

'Yes. Her name's Carmel Wakeford. She was abducted when she was a child and didn't come home until she was thirteen. The case was known in the papers as "The Girl in the Red Coat".' I swallowed.

'Yes, yes – I remember that. That was your daughter?'

'That's right, and I'm terribly, terribly worried about her. She ran off this morning and I've no idea where she is. She's not some usual twenty-one-year-old who's gone storming off and will be back when she's simmered down. She's been through some terrible things.'

I had their attention now and was triumphant at that so I described everything – her leaving with her things, Marta and the doll, the finding of the skull. Oh, I left out her mud-larking hobby though. I wasn't having people looking for simple explanations. I wanted them to be more alert than that.

'Perhaps we'd better go and take a look at what you believe are human remains,' said Greenaway when I'd finished.

'I'm a nurse. It's a skull.'

Greenaway bobbed his head in apology. 'Sorry, of course you do know then. Can we see it?'

I nodded. 'I've left everything out on her desk. I'll take you up.'

Somehow, they got ahead of me on the stairs even though I was supposed to be showing the way. I looked at Fletcher's back as I climbed the stairs behind him. It was a wide strong back in a good-quality dark grey wool jacket. I felt a flash of something unexpected, a sudden warming. No, surely not that, and in this situation, really? I remembered there was a thick burnished gold band on Fletcher's left hand. I'd noticed it downstairs, so I guessed I must've been looking even then.

At the top of the stairs, Greenaway asked, 'Which room?' I pointed and realised they intended, for whatever reason, to go into the room alone because they pulled the door to when they entered Carmel's room and spoke to each other in murmurs that I couldn't catch.

When they emerged, I looked down at the carpet because I was ashamed. I didn't want Fletcher to glimpse the drowned desire on my face.

'Yes, certainly looks like a skull to me. A small one,' he said. 'And other body parts.'

'Three ribs and a finger bone.'

'I see.'

Greenaway was on his mobile phone talking to some kind of forensics team.

Fletcher said, 'Let's wait downstairs.'

In the sitting room we were alone. Greenaway was still talking upstairs. 'It's not every day you find a child's skull in your daughter's bedroom,' I burst out.

'Indeed.'

I noticed how he sat very, very quietly and still.

He cleared his throat. 'Do you think it's something to do with a mudlarking hobby?'

My head shot up. 'How did you know about that?'

He smiled. 'All the stuff in her room, it's obvious. I used to be with the river police and we'd see them from the boat, out in all weathers.'

I'd tidied everything up, picked it up off the floor before they came. 'I guess so, but she never mentioned anything about finding it.' My pathetic little strategy had easily been found out.

'Finding human bones is obviously an unusual occurrence; you'd imagine that she'd mention it.'

'I'd like to say "yes" but the reality is I think she's been keeping a lot back from me recently. Things have never really returned to normal – I was foolish to expect them to I suppose. Now, she has some strange ideas that she can't seem to shake. I've had a bad feeling recently too, like there's stuff going on she's not telling me. I worry about her mental health a lot . . .'

When the doorbell interrupted me, I realised I was running on, spilling all my fears out to this handsome man, as if with his darkly protective presence he'd magic them all away. I was tempted to mention the fact she'd been in touch with the man that stole her but something stopped me – the knowledge that she'd probably never speak to me again if I did.

'That'll be the forensics team,' he said and went to answer

the door. I heard him talking to people on the doorstep, a man and a woman from the sounds of it. I heard Fletcher say, 'Up there. Up the stairs. He's waiting for you.' There was movement, sound in the hallway, and the two in pale blue suits passed the open door of the living room and nodded to me. How easily they'd all inserted themselves into my home. How expertly they glided about and did what they had to, almost as if I wasn't there.

Fletcher returned and sat back down. 'They won't be long.'

'What happens now?'

'I'll take a statement and the bones will be sent off for analysis.'

By the time everything was finished up the light was beginning to fade. Night-time with Carmel out there, God knows where. The forensics pair left quietly, their rubber soles respectful and muted on the stairs. I'd glimpsed something that resembled a cool box that they must've been carrying the little skull, the ribs and the fingertip in. An immense sadness went through me like a chill wind from the river, bringing on its wings the mess of human life, with its extremes and cruelties. I pulled my raspberry-coloured cardigan closer around my shoulders as I said goodbye to Fletcher on the doorstep. It felt like long-ago cries and laughter echoed on that wind too; it whisked them up the street, past my front door.

'Will you stay in touch?' I asked. 'Let me know what's happening?'

I looked out behind him into the evening. I desperately needed to get my head down for a few hours before my next shift. 'Of course. I'll put a call out about Carmel. She's a vulnerable adult and I'm sure a lot will remember the case. She needs to tell us exactly where this came from because we don't know what we're looking at here. Please try not to worry too much about her. Most people end up coming back, as you know.'

'Yes. Yes, I know.'

I'm back to looking. It seems I was born for it.

The next day I take the car and drive round, scanning the streets, the shop doorways. I park up at the place we let Alan go and walk up and down the foreshore and when there's no sign of her get back into the car again. Twice I nearly crash the car because I think I might've glimpsed her. I stop and ask questions of a group of homeless people in a shop doorway. I offer my rolling tobacco round and they dutifully take it, roll up two or three cigarettes and melt away, except for one young man in a dirty beanie hat who stays for whatever unknown reason.

'Have you seen a girl, a young woman. Curly hair, called Carmel?'

'Your daughter?' he asks.

I squat down next to him eagerly. 'Yes, yes. Have you seen her?'

He shakes his head sadly. 'Got to be off,' he says.

It's in that moment I realise. They wouldn't tell me even if they had. How many people are here fleeing from home, from family? They are not about to break that code, the one they all understand. They know that to survive some things need to be left behind forever. So I continue driving, looking.

Her father still doesn't know of this Act Two of her going missing again. I've done enough to ensure – through trite phone conversations – that she's not there. I can't bear to tell him just yet. It's wrong, I know, yet still I keep it from him.

Day three it occurs to me to look for Eric, in case he's seen or heard anything. I climb down granite steps and stumble over the grimy stones slippery with green.

I find him at last.

He's a long way below so I put my hands around my mouth and call down to him. It's not quite fully light – a murky winter morning – and his headlamp beams up at me as he looks up.

He points to something on the wall and to my horror I see a rusty, rickety-looking ladder screwed there and realise he's expecting me to climb down that.

I move to the head of it and peer over. It's horribly vertiginous and doesn't look properly attached at the bottom but despite that I take a deep breath and throw one leg over the wall. I waggle my foot about in thin air and find the next rung, then the next, then stop. The granite-like stone of the wall is right in front of my face and I can see the granulations of different colours in the dim light, some hard and shining like glass, packed together. A tiny dried-out snail shell is tucked in a crevice between stones. I grit my teeth and move down another couple of rungs. The stone that the ladder is affixed to is no longer bare at this level. There's a greenish long-haired plant growth on it, the ends dried out, smelling of salt that denotes I'm passing the high tide mark. It feels like a descent into a watery grave-like world. I become acutely aware that I am between two worlds, clinging on, and if I fall I'm likely to be killed. I give out an involuntary whimper that is swallowed by the cries of the gulls behind me and I freeze for I don't know how long before I force myself to get moving again. Somewhere upriver a boat's horn toots, the noise travelling towards me across the water. By the time I make it to the bottom it's light enough for Eric to have turned his headlamp off.

I've never really noticed the colours down here before. These are hues you don't see on dry land. The colour of the river today is like a paintbrush has swept a line of grey across the page and the foreshore fans around it with shades as complex as a mottled owl's wing.

'Have you found anything yet?' I ask.

'Yes, don't move. Look to your left.'

Wedged up against a stone is a vicious-looking knife. The sky is almost completely light now and the chinks of sun coming through the clouds light up its tip which is pointing over the river to the huge office blocks on the other side.

'That doesn't look old,' I say.

'No, it's not. There's a lot of knife crime in London and where better to hide a weapon than a river?' Eric takes some bubble wrap and picks up the knife by its handle to wrap and chuckles. 'But either they don't know or they forget that the tide goes out.'

'You'll take it to the police?'

He nods. 'They know me of old.'

'I'm looking for Carmel. She's . . .' I bite my lip. 'She's gone.'

'Oh dear, I'm sorry to hear that,' he says. 'I haven't seen her for days.' He shakes his head sadly and takes his filthy hanky out of his pocket and with his filthy fingers uses it to blow his nose. It almost makes me smile because I realise how not so long ago it would've made me wince.

'If you leave your number I'll call you if I do see her,' he says. 'She's a gem, Carmel.'

On day four I can't look anymore. I'm tired to the bone. Later in the day I make myself some proper food, salmon and peas from the freezer with new potatoes. I catch the reflection of myself in the window opposite, the fork moving from plate to mouth. I have the impression of myself as someone knobbly and fractured, as if all the traumas of the last years are contained inside my body and a thick skin has grown over all the breakages, rendering me lumpy and broken-looking. The battle for survival will do all sorts of things to you if you let it. I stand up and firmly let the roller blind half down and go and finish my meal.

When I'm done I stack the knife and fork to one side and lean back and close my eyes because there's something itching away at me. It has been ever since I came home and filled the kettle. I mentally scan through the house, searching for what it can be and toss the idea around; it could be simply the flake of a feeling, something brought home from the hospital. No – I turn to look – it's that, it's that book out on the countertop. It wasn't there before.

I go and pick it up. It's an old cookery book of my mother's that's been wedged in the cupboard above forever. *New England Cookery.* There's a print of coloured ink drawings of a woman and her daughter on the cover. They wear long dresses and frilly aprons and a cornucopia of lobster, turkey, oysters and a tureen of soup is on their kitchen worktop among the working tools of their industry – the flour shaker, a wooden spoon, a hand whisk. The little girl in her yellow apron grinds a spice box. The illustration provokes a jolt of recognition. I used to examine it for ages when I was a kid, entranced by the vision of domestic bliss, but it's lain in the cupboard untouched since I've been here.

I'd almost forgotten my mother spent time in America. Always a competent cook and domestic planner, she'd somehow secured a job as a housekeeper there long before she married. On rare occasions she'd talk about it wistfully.

The pages are spattered with long-ago meals but when I pick a spot off with my thumbnail it's impossible to identify what food it was.

I turn the pages. Sugar cookies, apple pandowdy, Indian pudding flavoured with cinnamon – the memories of the meals she cooked are conjured straight up out of the pages and I can almost taste them, smell them. Why did she stop cooking these American foods? Perhaps my dad didn't really like them, perhaps he wanted to go back to familiar British fare and let it slip one day. Perhaps she tired of them, or maybe as the years went on the memories they conjured were too wistful and painful.

Mum is there on every page, in the cocktail sauce for seafood and in the griddlecakes and the mustard pickles. Under 'Cakes, Cookies and Frostings' I find something that makes me cover my mouth, half smiling, half gasping. It's a recipe for marble cake and I remember making it with Mum in this very kitchen, her standing and me kneeling on a chair: *A sort of personalised cake that's a joy to make, to behold, and to eat at teatime.* What homely magic it had seemed, the layer of white batter in the cake pan, then the layer of chocolate on top, and all of it perfumed with the slightly cosmetic scent of vanilla that would grow warmer and fuller once the baking began. But while the mix was still in the pan Mum showed me how, with a spoon, to gently lift the white batter through the brown and make swirls so it resembled veins through marble once it was baked.

With a blue biro I sketch a cross-hatched heart next to the recipe.

But why was the book out on the counter? I run my fingers over the cover, thinking. I've sensed it all along, that's why the dam of anguish has somehow stayed poised over my head without breaking too hard – she's been here, Carmel. I've known it subconsciously in the shivering drip of water falling from the showerhead, in the minutely altered angle of the blind in her room. I saw it illuminated in a shaft of sunlight through the bathroom window that lit up the floor as if it was trying to show me something and there in the powder-fine dust of the polished boards was her footprint, nakedly new. She's been here, she's OK, just avoiding me.

And this, this cornucopia of America, did she leave it out on purpose, some kind of message or sign to me? Either way, she comes here, she goes, we come and go around each other. Her bed is untouched; she's not sleeping here and we continue our relationship barely touching at the edges of each other, but it is enough.

I find an index card upstairs and scribble on it, 'Carmel, my love. Please don't worry about anything but stay safe and this is for you.' I prop it up against the mirror in the hall and slide a twenty-pound note behind it.

Mercy

1999

On Sundays it was now Mercy up on the stage with the pastor in her pink shoes or the black ones with patent leather bows on the toes. Several of the congregation even clubbed together and bought her new dresses because even the new ones Delia bought her ended up having a beating from all the chores she once more performed.

A lot of times Mercy felt confused. She said to Pastor Patron 'When I heal these folk, I don't feel anything. You sure it's not them doing it to themselves and not me?'

Solemnly he would shake his head. 'No, child, you must not doubt yourself. You have powers that are heaven-sent and it's a grave sin to question them.'

Mercy sure didn't want to commit a grave sin so she stopped asking these questions.

Even Bob at the grocery store became different with her, almost as if he was a little scared of her. His eyes narrowed like he was looking at her through fog, as if he couldn't figure out who she truly was.

'I bin hearing things about you, Mercy.'

'Oh yeah?' She didn't quite like the fact that people were talking about her, and thought from Bob's wary gaze perhaps they weren't saying things that were good. He'd always been such a kind friend to her and now she didn't know what had happened to that friendship.

'Sure. I hear things about that old tent down there and the stuff that goes on.' He made it sound like it was bad things going on. 'Vera got sick again you know.'

Mercy put her shopping bags down on the floor in front of the counter. 'Well, I'm sure sorry to hear that, I really am.' She felt tears pricking in the back of her eyes at the news. 'I haven't seen her lately.'

'No, she's real sick this time.'

'That's real sad. It sure is.'

They both looked at the floor for a long time, waiting for Mercy's tears to dry up in her eyes.

She so desperately wanted to get their old friendship back that seemed to have disappeared into the wind since the advent of her healing powers. When her eyes were finally dry, she racked her brains for something that might rekindle it. Finally, she thought of something.

'Hey, Bob, Racoon is back.'

Bob knew all about her racoon and she thought the news might get some of the old spark going. They always talked about him like he was a cartoon.

'Oh boy, you be careful now. He'll be up to tricks,' Bob said, but listlessly.

It grieved Mercy's heart that Bob now seemed so far apart from her. She loved him with a love that flowed through her stomach and whooshed out. It was as if the people around her that she cared for were part of the same web as her, they were woven into each other, and when a spider's legs tickled on them, she felt it too.

There was something else that pained her about Bob, that

he continued to live without the love of the Lord. There was nothing she wanted for him more than for him to be saved and feel that joy it bestowed upon a person, but he never appeared on Sundays at the tent however many times she'd asked him. It occurred to her now it was perhaps because he wasn't saved that he was doubting her so much now.

'You look kind of sad, Bob.'

'Yeah, well. Trudy's sick, you know. She has cancer.'

'No, I did not know that.'

'She's real sick.' For a moment Bob looked like he was going to cry.

'You wanna let me try and heal her?'

He shook his head. 'No, you're OK on that one. Thanks for thinking of it though.'

'That's OK, Bob.'

'Hey, Mercy, you be careful,' he said, looking down at his hands.

'Careful about what, Bob?'

'Everything. Things people tell you.'

'Sure I will. I'm always careful. High five, Bob,' she said, holding up her small hand, though when it came, with Bob leaning over the counter to smack her palm, it seemed without enthusiasm.

Later, Mercy began to worry on the news about Vera. She remembered on the day how sure everyone had been that it was the light from her own small hands that had healed the other girl, but what Bob had told her troubled her. She was frightened of saying anything but the worry gnawed at her so much she managed to tell Pastor Patron about her concerns before the service one Sunday. It seemed he liked their little community because he'd decided to stay on even longer. A clear light filtered through the canvas and with its blue carpet and display of sweet-smelling flowers near the entrance that Mrs Miller had arranged earlier in the day the church seemed the most beautiful place in the world to Mercy. It pained her to question one morsel of anything about it.

'See, perhaps that means there's nothing in my hands when I lay them on a person,' she said. 'Vera is sicker 'n ever.' Then something else occurred to her. 'Perhaps I even made her worse,' she said, alarmed.

Although she felt great love for the people around her, for Vera, for Bob, for Miss Forbouys, for the baby with a cleft palate they brought her once, deep down she could never shake the feeling that nothing happened when she laid on her hands. The act was often accompanied by whoops and moaning and speaking in tongues by the congregation and the noise added to her confusion.

When Pastor Patron turned to her his blue gaze seemed to be both burning and freezing.

'No doubt Vera's plight has been caused by a lack of conviction on her part.'

'I don't understand,' she said, miserable and frightened by his sudden change in demeanour.

'I mean she does not love the Lord enough and that's why she has become sick again. I've told you before not to doubt yourself, child.'

There was a silence for a while, then Mercy asked in a small voice, 'Would you like to be healed, Pastor Patron? That leg of yours sure looks bad sometimes.'

For a second he looked outraged, then he blinked and the outrage was folded away.

'Perhaps one day. For the moment I do not think it's a good idea that the congregation see me being in thrall to you in this way. This is a joint enterprise where we are on equal footing and to have it any other way would be a mistake at the moment.'

Mercy again didn't know what he meant but felt sufficiently slapped down to stay quiet until the congregation began arriving, casting glances up at her sitting quietly on her chair on the stage wearing her pink shoes.

In truth a few of the congregation, mostly the ones who'd speculated on Pastor Patron's whereabouts as he spied on them entering the tent that first time, had asked themselves the same question. Given access to all this miraculous healing, why did the good pastor choose not to present himself to be rid of his painful-looking limp? For most though, they accepted it as an ingrained part of his persona, along with his bright blue eyes, the pale suit that he always wore, and the little gold-rimmed glasses he hooked over his ears whenever he read from the Bible. It even gave him a glamorous, slightly dangerous air; it hinted of a history of struggles, of dark happenings, potentially even some bravery involved. Could the injury have something to do with time spent in the military? Who knew?

Quite how the proposition occurred that Mercy be taken away to spread her talents far and wide was hard to stitch together once the suggestion took root. Most assumed it came from the pastor although nothing definite he'd said could be recalled. It quickly went from a few chance remarks amongst the congregation after the service to being openly discussed over teacups in the drowsy heat of the afternoon in people's homes. There was a sense of rescue too – surely Mercy should have a chance to get out from that awful shack; nothing good for her could come of the way things were there.

That the pastor had taken on the most humble member of their community was heart-warming. Most people who knew Mercy had a soft spot for her. Even one of the boys involved had cycled after her that day he'd thrown stones with his friends, found her walking by the side of the road and split his candy bar with her. Now, it was wonderful to see her in fresh clothes, her light brown curls shining around her head up on the stage with the pastor on Sundays. She always waited so quietly, her legs crossed at the ankles, until the end where she would be called on to lay on hands.

Taking her talents into the wider world seemed a natural extension of what was happening, because it was something so pure and blessed it would feel sinful to keep it to themselves. That's what the pastor hinted at anyway. For Mercy to tour around other churches would not only be the right thing to do, an act of overwhelming generosity on the congregation's part, it also felt like they would be taking a tiny part in something that was extraordinary, that lifted them far above the everyday to a different plane altogether. They were all so proud of her and of what had taken place in their forest tent.

Soon there were bake-offs and yard sales. There was a coffee morning at The Purple Pineapple with Hal putting all the money collected into a canvas apron bag and counting it out assiduously afterwards, pencilling the sum on an envelope then biking it down to the pastor. A collection was held after every service. Lena Butterworth at the Piggly Wiggly store even kept a plastic money box on the counter with a picture of Mercy's face taped to the front of it. It seemed unstoppable, gathering pace at breakneck speed.

At first Mercy was excited but it was all happening so fast that underneath there was an increasing unease building.

'But I will be able to come back to Ma and Pa?' she kept asking Pastor Patron.

'Sure you will, child,' he said. 'No doubt about it.'

'How long before I can come back?'

At that point he looked over his glasses at her. He was reading from the scriptures after a service, sitting on the chair where Hal had had his legs cured. The pastor had one leg crossed over the other and one hip lifted painfully up. He looked enormous from down below the stage. 'That is a question for the Almighty and not for us; it depends on the quality of need. It is not our decision to make,' he said simply, and there seemed little answer to that.

Her parents were febrile ghosts, the part of them still alive only focussed on one thing, and Mercy's imminent departure didn't trouble them as much as it ought to have done. Mercy felt a helplessness about them she hadn't experienced before. So it came down to a small band of women, which included Lena Butterworth from the store but not Miss Forbouys, to get everything ready. Where would they be going, they asked the pastor, what sort of climate might Mercy encounter, what might her needs be? They wanted to send her off with decent clothes, fit for purpose and that would bring credit to their community. It wasn't certain. The Bible Belt states for sure but Asia, Australia, Europe were mentioned so a passport needed to be obtained. Of course, everyone knew you could get frazzled alive in Australia so Mrs Tyler whose husband ran the auto repair shop offered three sundresses, each one a different sweet pastel colour and with a little matching jacket to go with it. Mercy couldn't speak when she brought them to the service one morning to show her, the largesse and beauty of the gift was overwhelming. The one thing that everyone agreed on was that Mercy's hair needed to be cut. There was no way a man like the pastor could be expected to take charge of *that* bird's nest.

'But what will she need?' asked Thelma Nightingale of the visiting pastor. She was the boldest of the group but even she quailed when he stripped off his gold-rimmed spectacles and fixed her with that blue gaze. It was no use asking Pastor Frogmore; he just said, 'Ask Pastor Patron. He has it all in hand. He knows exactly what he's doing.' Their local pastor seemed in awe of him, in truth.

Now, Pastor Patron replied to Thelma, 'These things are just trifles, Mrs Nightingale. Cannot they be sorted out at the last minute?'

Inwardly, she burned at this. All their stitching, their fundraising, their cake baking and preparations being reduced to trifles. The feeling of being a valuable part of a great enterprise cooled a little. She realised she'd always felt that the pastor was somewhat supercilious with her group of ladies. He made it sound that what Mercy took with her in her suitcase to see her through the coming days and months was something that he shouldn't be bothered by. In that moment she felt wary; she wanted to express some unnamed worry but found all she could do was bite her lip. He seemed so self-assured, like he really must know what he was doing so much better than any of them. She decided the least she could do was to make Mercy a sharp-looking grey pant suit out of a warm wool that she could wear on stage with a white blouse to go underneath – though in the end the leaving was so abrupt the seams were only held together by temporary basting stitches.

It was only after Mercy had gone with Pastor Patron that Mrs Nightingale and Miss Butterworth both lay awake on separate nights, thinking for the first time – do we actually know who this man is? Do we even really know *anything* about him?

They never communicated these thoughts to each other though. They were both far too complicit in the whole enterprise to give voice to those concerns.

When her bag was packed and ready Mercy changed her mind. She realised firmly and conclusively that she didn't want to go. In fact, the thought of being separated from her parents was unbearable. So, with tears in her eyes she confessed to her mother that she didn't want to leave. She wanted to stay right here in the little shack with her parents and the window mushrooms and the racoon with its human-like hands, for it to be like it had always been.

Delia was feeling particularly unwell. Her usual hit was taking time to spread through her and she was beginning to panic that perhaps it wouldn't. She sat with bare feet on the beat-up old sofa, her legs in their ripped jeans pulled up to her chest, and watched her baby girl plead not to let her go. She felt utterly unequal to motherhood. In truth, there was even a tiny part of her that had been growing steadily and surely that felt the need for a break in the awful responsibility that it entailed, just a while so she could dive fully into the arms of blissful morphia and hopefully emerge from it again like she had once before. The feeling was so strong in her that day that Mercy's pronouncement that she didn't want to leave was – and she hated herself for feeling this so much she pushed the realisation deep down inside – a disappointment.

'I think you should definitely go,' she said quickly before her heart had a chance to melt. 'You'll get to see all sorts of places you'd never have a chance to see if you stay stuck on this old mountain.' This last part she really meant. She'd been excited for Mercy about this and together they studied a world map as well as one of the United States in an old encyclopaedia she had and speculated on all the places Mercy might visit.

'But, Ma, I don't want to leave you and Pa. I don't want to leave the mountain. Please don't make me.'

Delia held up her hand. 'Mercy, you're going. No arguments, you hear?' And the way her teeth were gritted together made the words come out harshly.

Then as Mercy was about to indeed argue back the hit flooded through Delia like a tidal wave and her eyes uplifted in their sockets and she slumped backwards and Mercy knew there was no point saying another word to her. Something in Mercy at that point gave up. All the struggles to keep her parents alive, the chores, the confusion when they seemed well and now weren't again. She bent her head sadly and went outside to see if the racoon was there to say goodbye to. The whole forest seemed to be shining and alive in a way that made her heart ache. She could beg no more, she realised that, and something that she'd kept within her, as hard and pure as a diamond, crumbled into dust. That time spent all alone had weakened the links in the three-part chain that bound her to her parents. The link between the two of them was just as strong but hers had grown loose, so it became possible to break away, though that in no way stopped the sadness she felt at the breakage – it seemed she might get smashed to pieces in the process.

Before she left Mercy sneaked into her parents' bedroom. She picked up the Madonna *Ray of Light* CD and slid it into her bag. She had the sense she needed to safeguard it somehow.

Afterwards, a phrase occurred to Delia about her daughter's departure that she quickly squashed down in the usual way.

It was this: *Her feet didn't even touch the ground.*

The trip began in the States in a sort of campervan. Once they were on the road the pastor appeared to relax. His cream-coloured suit was swapped for a black one with a collarless white shirt underneath that gave him the appearance of being in uniform.

Mercy had her own little bedroom in the camper with flowered nylon sheets, brand-new blue honeycomb blankets and a blue padded sateen bedcover. The slippery fabric of the bedcover meant it was always sliding off when they drove round corners because the pastor often drove late at night to their next destination, but she loved it so much she didn't mind constantly retrieving it off the floor. These things made up somewhat for the pink shoes, which somehow had been left behind in the rush to go. There was a narrow built-in wardrobe at the foot of the bed where all her new clothes were hung up or folded away. She loved the neatness, the cleanliness of it all. The pop of the gas on the two-ringed cooker in the kitchen area, the overhead cupboards with mugs and plates stowed in them, the tiny humming fridge that was restocked in whatever town they alighted on.

The pastor seemed energised through this time, almost happy, and this made her feel more at ease. The people that they met in the churches were pleased to see them. The healing services became less of a worry now they weren't people she might see day in, day out. Being the centre of attention, up on stage, letting her hands float down to touch the tops of heads was much easier when it was not in front of people who might throw stones at her or talk behind their hands about her ma and pa. They even spent time with people like them – devotional people who also lived in trucks like it was the most normal thing in the world.

After the services, people from the congregation were always telling Mercy how adorable she was, how special. The churches themselves seemed often full of light and peace and the afflictions people brought before Mercy made her heart fill up like a balloon with love and empathy for her fellow humans. The women of the community would press johnnycakes into their hands before they left, oatmeal biscuits, or a perfectly crisped peach pie still cooling in its blue and white enamel tin. The pastor and Mercy would eat these offerings at the fold-out table in the camper while they studied a spread-out map to see where they were going next. Then the pastor would get into the cab to drive and Mercy cleaned her teeth then shut herself in her little room and went to sleep to the swing and sway of the vehicle.

The pastor pencilled their progress on the map and it reminded Mercy of a serpent snaking its way through the bottom of the country, through the Shenandoah Valley, southward into Southside Virginia, the Carolinas, skirting the top of Georgia and Alabama then the snake's head sweeping upwards to Missouri. When Mercy touched the pencil tip to the finger-like protrusion that was Florida the pastor informed her that that state was not on the itinerary, that it was a godless place full of false palaces and where crocodiles used the swimming pools and they would not be going there. Mercy at once longed to see the creatures swimming through the clear blue water and skittering their claws on the tiles as they climbed in and out.

The memory of her parents she tried to keep to one image only for it was safer that way. They were forever seated at the table, her pa in his best jeans and her ma with the red bandana blazing in her ash-blond curly hair. They held hands across the blue and white check of the plastic tablecloth, and were guarded by the racoon on the porch outside.

The attendance at these healing services could be sparse and as the winter drew on people seemed less willing to leave their homes. Sometimes there were only eight or nine in the congregation of the smaller churches or hired halls. The pastor grew discontented at their lack of success. The cakes and biscuits gifted by the ladies of whatever tiny community they visited were pushed across the table towards Mercy with a disgusted look, without him taking a bite. The shabbiness of the hall where they'd been performing their healings was mentioned, the unsavoury appearance of the participants; the paucity of the contents of the collecting bag was of particular concern. It was in the run-up to Christmas – Mercy spotted the glitter of it in the shop windows of the towns they passed through – that one day he returned from using the telephone kiosk, which he did from time to time along the way, and he selected a fat raisin cookie from the plate and took a big bite.

'I have made a contact,' he said through the crumbs, 'with people who will truly appreciate us. I think great things await.'

It wasn't until several weeks later that Mercy realised this meant they were going away on an aeroplane – which she was truly excited about despite everything – and several days after that the pastor told her the contact was with a kind of spiritualist church member in England. More calls were made along the road and Mercy was told to pack her bags.

She was sorry to leave the pale blue sateen coverlet and wanted to take it with her but the pastor told her that was ridiculous and you could only take one bag to go into the hold of the plane and one bag to take on board with you. Mercy chose her Bible along with the *Ray of Light* CD, her two most precious possessions, to have with her in the plane. She never did find out what happened to the sateen coverlet.

During the plane journey Mercy felt that she was riding with the angels and kept expecting to see one through the window, flying close by like dolphins tailing a boat. A lady in a beautiful little red hat pushed a trolley along and gave her Coca-Cola and peanuts. Looking down on the cloud and up at the blue sky and the sun sparkling on the silver wing tip, Mercy felt she would only have to reach up to touch the hem of God's mantle.

Carmel

2013

I found the old cookbook in the cupboard while I was looking for some tea. It was wedged up behind the mugs and tins
of herbal tea and I stood at the kitchen counter turning the
pages. I've been coming back to check the post, to have a
shower, safe in the knowledge Mum's on nights and there's
no chance of us running in to each other.

The book gave you instructions on how to flute pastry,
and hard-cook eggs and beat egg whites, and some of the
recipes were familiar from eating American food but when
I got to the method for steaming clams the memory came at
me like a tidal flood. We ate those once.

*The oldest eating tradition along New England's rocky
shoreline is the clambake, a legacy from the Indian tribes
who greeted the white man. Basically it consists of green
corn, clams and fish closely covered and steamed in seaweed over white-hot stones to a medley of goodness that
has not its equal this side of paradise.*

The salt taste of New England floods into my mouth.
A time we'd done well at a healing service and there were

plenty of dollars in the black velvet pouch, we came across a roadside clambake, a fire in a half-barrel sunk into a sandy pit. The owner of the little shack restaurant was just stripping off the canvas from the pit and the smell that came from it near made my stomach fold in two I was so hungry. The preacher bought us both a paper bag packed full of clams and a basket full of bread and butter and little paper cups of clam broth and we sat on the rocks that bordered the parking lot and ate right there, with our hands, the paper bags hot to the touch, the sea air whipping at our cheeks. The broth tasted as if an entire ocean had been boiled down to this one essence in my paper cup and the smell of wood smoke mingled with that seaweed and cooking clams and *that* mingled with the ache in my hands, a good ache – the ache they got after doing much work healing.

At night the lost girls join hands and form a ring around me. They circle round, chanting songs, reciting rhymes, then they change direction and go the other way. The Mermaid. The Well-Kissed Doll. The Tender Soul. The Secret Sister.

I wait for the preacher's letter about the last one, but nothing comes.

Each morning I go back home to shower and check the post to see if anything has arrived. The sound of the post plopping on the mat makes my stomach tense into a knot. The Mermaid is missing from the drawer and I worried that Mum found her and put her in the trash but then a note appeared in the drawer, the same day the money in the hallway did. The note said, 'Don't worry, she's being taken good care of,' and I was glad that Mum seemed to realise that it was a *she* too, even if it was a shock knowing that she realised I was letting myself in and out. I felt bad for ever thinking she'd do something like throwing the skull away.

I began the hunt for Rosie in the wait for the preacher's letter because like I knew she would, she began to haunt me in my waking hours. The Tender Soul: there was something about Rosie that made me think she'd end up like The Mermaid if I didn't seek her out and rescue her. The more I thought about it, the more sure I became that that would be her fate.

Like the objects in the river I had the powerful sense of things travelling towards me: letters; young women who inhabit the embankment; girls tossed aside as false prophets.

Firstly, I patrolled the place on the embankment where I'd met her and bought her the egg roll. Gradually I widened my search, peeling off to cross London Bridge, Tower Bridge and to look down dark alleys and peer in shop doorways. She'd melted away into the masses. The cacophony of crowds of people confused me. Their sicknesses were clear, painted in vivid reds and blues and seeing them and knowing there was nothing I could do about it made the hollow ache in my crabbed and empty hands become almost painful.

Nothing, I couldn't find her. I spent days walking up and down peering into shops and at the lumpen sleeping bags in doorways. At one point it occurred to me that this is what Mum was like while I was away and knowing that and feeling a pinch of what it must've been like for her was a revelation and made me stop stock-still on the road as people passed, bumping my shoulders.

Then I realised the way I was searching for Rosie was all wrong. I needed to look like I did on the foreshore, to defocus my eyes to find her. So the crowds of people became rocks and rivulets of water. Their exhalations of breath were the same as the sharp pop an insect hole expels as it closes up. The gleam of an eye the shimmer on a discarded oyster shell. That's how I found her. I saw only the trembling drop of water on a wet spike of hair, the cold, red end of a narrow nose and I knew it was her. I held her cold hand and told her about the room with the red-painted floor and now she's here.

I bring us back carrier bags of food that we can eat with our fingers or a plastic spoon – potato chips and crackers with sliced cheese, bananas. She always tries to take as little as she can, I've noticed that.

Mostly we're out by the time Marta opens up the café but if we're not we both put our ears to the red floor and listen to her singing. Sometimes, in the evening I borrow the radio from the kitchen and we listen to that, music stations or the shipping forecast that Rosie likes because she says it sounds like a poem. Some nights, if anyone looks up they'll see a light blazing and our shadows thrown against the walls and ceiling as we dance. I can do it with Rosie in the room and somehow I no longer care if I look like a robot or not. I make sure the radio goes back to its exact same spot before we climb into bed – Rosie in her sleeping bag and me on the coffee sacks. Then we sleep, all aboard the good ship *Egg and Spoon*, safe and warm for now at least.

There is no post for me again today and I make it back just in time before Marta arrives. Her movements sound sharp and angry and I wonder what all that is about. Rosie and I listen as she bangs pots around, jabs the radio on then off again and slams the back door.

With Rosie found and made safe, no word from the preacher about Mercy and the note from Mum telling me The Mermaid was being taken care of, I have time to think of other things. The Day of the Tree and Snake has been worrying at me again and I turn my mind to it and seem to remember that was about a letter too.

I'm sitting on a bench overlooking the river that has been turned into a ribbon of liquid mercy by the setting sun when I remember. My hand rises up, seemingly of its own accord, and alights on my collarbone.

There was a tree with no leaves that I used to climb and sit in. Below, there was sand on the ground where I used to write my name – Carmel Wakeford – in the hope that an aeroplane might see it from above and come and get me and the writing looked like it had been done by a writhing snake. Then one day I was sitting in the tree and a real black snake went across the writing, scrubbing it out. That day I was hiding. My shoes were sparkling in the sun so they must've been made of something shiny.

Just before there'd been a letter from my dad, then I'd written my name and climbed the tree because I was upset.

'Dear Carmel,' the letter began.

I can't of course remember the exact words written from Dad on the cheap, thin paper but they ran along the lines of: you are my lovely daughter but I have a new family now and I love them better, so you must stay with the people who are kindly looking after you and you must treat them with respect. It would be easier if you no longer contacted me because that way we can both get on with our lives which will be better in the long run . . .

'You read the letter?' the preacher asked.

I stuck my chin out and lifted up my face towards him, because as I remember, he was tall and often seemed to black out the sky. 'I read it and wept,' I said. 'Just like you said I would.' But he didn't laugh or look pleased that his prediction had come true. Instead, a thoughtful and slightly puzzled expression came over his face and I could see he was trying to figure my newfound attitude out, and had decided he probably didn't like it. It was a new development and potentially a troubling one.

The Day of the Tree and Snake had ushered me into a new stage when I was a child. It was one of defiance and I tended to that like it was a tiny fire that needed to be kept burning with slivers of kindling.

My hands grip on to the lip of the bench.

The river burns into my eyes. *Now* I understand the reason why I've not wanted to communicate with Dad ever since I got back; that poison seeps through me every time I hear Dad's voice.

Then logic kicks in hard. Dad didn't write it, of course. The preacher faked it to evade my questions and my entreaties to go and live with my dad. I couldn't live with Mum because *he* told me that she was dead but then to find out Dad didn't want me – it was lies, all lies and his lies are still working me like I'm a puppet. The lie about Mum works in a different way because I spent so many years believing that she was dead that now sometimes I have trouble thinking Mum really is my mum while my real mum, the young, tender one from before I was eight, truly was killed in a car crash like *he* told me and is right now mouldering in her grave by the sea.

The wind blows up from the river, bringing with it the achingly familiar smell as I press Dad's number with shaking fingers.

'Carmel!' He sounds pleased and taken aback I've called him. 'How lovely to hear from you.'

I guess from his tone Mum hasn't told him anything about me leaving home and hiding out like this. I guess I can't blame her. He told me once that he'd been angry at Mum for losing me and that it was unjust and he was sorry about it now. I didn't tell him that I understood, that I was angry at her too.

'I'm OK,' I blunder, before he's even asked me how I am because I want to get this bit of the conversation out of the way and ask him what I need to know. 'Dad.' I stop, clear my throat, start again. 'Dad while I was . . . *away*, did you ever write to me?'

'Oh, Carmel.' His voice sounds tight, squeezed up in his throat. 'How would that be possible? Nobody knew where you were. If we'd had an address for you, we'd have come after you like an avenging army and scooped you up and taken you back home again. What on earth makes you think I wrote you a *letter*?'

'It's OK. I've just realised. *He* must've wrote it. He wrote that you had a new family now. That you didn't want anything to do with me. I'd been asking about you, see.'

There's a silence that practically throbs. It's always the same round Dad when there's any mention of the preacher.

'Dad?' I whisper.

When he answers I can hear in his voice that he's crying. 'You were asking about me?'

'Yes, Dad. I asked about you all the time.'

'Not only about your mum? You thought about me too?'

I can see why he would think that, the way I've been with him ever since I've been back.

'It was the letter, Dad. I didn't remember until just now. I'm sorry. It's like my brain has been all scrambled up and it's going to take years and years for me to sort out all the wires.'

'You must take the time you need. You are my darling, darling girl, you know.'

Then neither of us can speak and we just stay on the phone for a while breathing. Then his voice comes back strong in my ear.

'Carmel, let me take you out one day. You know, I'd love to take you for a proper London day out. A cheesy musical, and buying you something silly in Oxford Street and dinner at a pizza place.'

'Really? You'd want to do that for me?'

'Oh, Carmel.'

'You really would?'

'Yes, would you come?'

And I said yes and don't even mention that I've never been shopping in Oxford Street, I wouldn't know how to begin there so could we skip that bit?

Marta arrives again to open up the café and Rosie's face lights up and she says, 'She's here.'

It's as if Rosie feels close to her even though they've never met and I get the feeling she loves too easily and that's why my name for her – The Tender Soul – seems right. Today Marta doesn't sing again. There's more banging of pots and pans. The phone rings and she says something that sounds like a curse and lets it ring.

Then there's footsteps on the stairs. Rosie and me turn rigid and stare at each other, Rosie's eyes wide over her bunched fists she's pushing into her cheeks. Marta never comes up here.

Outside, on the landing, Marta pauses. There's a snuffling sound and it takes me a minute to realise she's crying. She must be looking out over the back window onto the yard. How I long to step outside, put my arms around her like she did with me, but we both sit yards away from her through the wall and the closed door, with our breath frozen. Rosie keeps turning her blue almond eyes towards the sound as if she's longing to go and comfort her too. Silently, I shake my head at her. The quiet snuffling carries on. I think of love, think of pushing it under the door, through the keyhole, but if she feels some invisible stirring warming her cheek it's impossible to know. Rosie and me silently stare at each other and then, to show her what I'm thinking, I make a heart shape with my hands and hold it against my chest and Rosie does the same.

Eventually, Marta's crying stops and her feet thump so hard on the way back downstairs it makes us jump.

'I hate to hear her sad,' says Rosie. 'It breaks my heart.'

We settle down to sleep early. Sometimes we talk into the night but tonight we keep our thoughts to ourselves. Later, I'm only half dozing when Rosie gets up. She goes to use the toilet out on the landing and in the open door she is a silhouette in the moonlight streaming from the window on the landing. I don't know what it is but there's something about that silhouette that makes me unsure if Rosie's a girl or a boy. I turn over and close my eyes and pretend to be asleep as I hear the toilet flush and she returns and climbs into her sleeping bag.

All the lost girls, I think; whether we have pearls in our ears, or sleepy, blinking eyes, charm bracelets or leather straps on our wrists, or fingers smelling of cigarettes, or waft the scent of berries or vanilla, or have cars or bikes or false names, and grieving mothers and grieving fathers who divert their attention to the grass growing outside that must be cut, and only occasionally devote themselves to the bright sharpening of a blade they fantasise may one day be used in revenge. We all have something in common that binds us together so tight it's hard to breathe sometimes.

The preacher wants to extract a price for telling me of my secret sister that I don't think I can pay with my empty, hollow hands. He craves a cure, of his sin and his pain, and his hunger for it is as ferocious as a wolf's.

At The Egg and Spoon a card has been stuck in the window. It says,

Dear Loyal Customers. My landlord has sold these premises to be developed. I'm trying to find new premises but so far have been unsuccessful. I can't tell you how much I've valued your custom over the years, Marta x

Poor Marta. Everything's coming to an end. I can feel it.

Rosie senses the ending too. She says, 'You're going away aren't you?'

'I don't know,' I answer truthfully and she turns over in her sleeping bag and cries.

'Look, is there someone who you can call?' I say to her prone back.

'Ghostbusters,' she says into her sleeping bag, but neither of us laugh.

Below, Marta begins to sing but there's a plaintive note to it now that wasn't there before. It's only an old café, some might say, hardly the most salubrious one at that, but I know that's not what matters. It's the work she's poured in, all the smells of cooking that have wafted in the air day after day, every fat red tomato and oily caraway seed that's landed in her pot. It's the customers with their frayed collars and their love of golden potato chips and perfectly fried eggs who come seeking warmth and light and a good full belly. It's all of that, it's Marta's creation, and it's about to be blown away as if it was nothing more than paper and I wonder at how easily everything can be destroyed.

Beth

The money I leave on the hallway table for Carmel
disappeared, as I thought it would. She left a scribbled
'thanks x' on the same postcard I'd written to her and
since then the card has amassed many more 'thanks x' as I
continue to leave money for her. The first time I brought it
to my lips and kissed it. Now it's beginning to remind me of
the library cards inside books I remember from when I was
a kid, each twenty-pound note and the 'thanks x' is a kind
of check-in and -out we've devised. She's still not sleeping
here, I know that, her bed remains undisturbed, but our
little system has allowed me to breathe again.

Fletcher calls. He of the good shoes and nice wool suit and
broad hands. He wants to meet me to talk about the skull.
I'm burning with curiosity and something like terror about
what he has to tell me. Now in that way when something
is on your mind you see it everywhere, there seem to be
skulls marking my way all the walk home. On the back
of a man's biker jacket in crude white paint. Glittering in
the window of a shop, decorated with gems Damien Hirst
style. Grinning among flowers on a poster, as in a Mexi-
can day of the dead. Amongst life we are in death, they tell

me through their jagged smiles.

Fletcher is already there when I get home. He's waiting on the Victorian path, the red and blue tiles glazed by the rain that must've fallen when I was inside the hospital. We're often marooned from the weather inside that environment. It can be like being inside a spaceship.

'Hold on,' I say, digging for my keys in my bag. 'They're in here somewhere.'

I'm slightly surprised when he accepts my offer of tea and he takes the mug and politely uses the coaster on the little table next to him to put it on.

I'd already let him know about Carmel coming back for clean clothes and such. 'I still haven't seen her in person though,' I tell him now.

'Well, we will have to talk to her at some point.'

Again, I have the urge to confide in him about Carmel's communication with the man that took her. My relationship with her is on too much of a knife edge for that but the urge gets me thinking.

'Carmel always manages to make me feel like she's going to cut off contact with me if I do the wrong thing, put a foot wrong,' I say slowly. 'It's quite . . .' I sit up straight because this thought is new, and somewhat revolutionary '. . . quite controlling actually.'

He nods as if he understands. 'About the skull,' he says.

My throat tightens. The whole thing seems suddenly so horribly sinister.

'We've had it carbon tested and it's around three hundred and fifty years old. Looks like it's been floating around the river for a long time. A child of around seven, they think.'

'Do they, do they have any idea of how she died?'

'We're not able to identify whether it's a little girl or boy, or how they met their end. Children's remains have been found in that area before. There was a chapel and a gallows nearby so it's possible . . .'

'What, that she was executed?' My hand flies to my mouth.

'It's just speculation. Children were executed for relatively minor offences in that era but who knows. It could have been an accident, a drowning, a murder. The child might have been a mudlarker itself and got caught by the tide. It's a dangerous place down there and traditionally people have foraged a living with what they can find in the mud. Carmel must have found it while she was doing the same thing – there were traces of river mud on it, but we need to confirm that. Human remains are human remains.'

'She should've said something.'

'It's probably quite an important find. I don't know why she would've kept that to herself.'

'She's been pretty secretive recently.'

'Yes.' He nods again like he understands.

'What will happen to her . . . I mean the skull?' I want to see it again. To mark that child's passing in some way.

'I expect we'll be in touch with museums, see if they're interested.' He drains his cup. 'I'll let you know what happens.'

I'm caught by a sudden impulse. 'Another?'

His answer surprises me too. 'Why not?'

I make the tea and hand the second cup over. He starts to chat and tell me about his time in the river police. It's a unique place to patrol, as you'd suspect. One of the busiest stretches of water in the world and no day ever the same; he loved it, he says, although he saw some awful things. He was there as a young policeman the night the pleasure boat *The Marchioness* sank, when fifty-one people died. Some things like that are hard to forget but there's always the changing tide, the wind that's never the same, the colour of the water that can magically transform from one minute to the next. He understands Carmel's draw to it; he himself once found a trader's token, those little coins used when small denominations were not available that were stamped with a picture that placed them directly to a street, a tavern, or a family. His one has a picture of a bull on it that he's been told is directly linked to The Bull Inn which used to stand not two hundred yards above where it was found. The river, he says, holds so many secrets. Only a fraction of them will ever be found.

'You miss it!' I say.

He nods and finishes his tea again. There's a short silence before he bursts out, 'Listen, would you like to go for a walk some time?'

My surprise makes me sound ungracious. 'What?'

'You don't have to. It was just a thought.'

'But, what about that?' I nod towards his wedding ring and then I blush slightly because it shows that I've noticed.

He looks down and smiles. 'My wife died four years ago and I haven't quite been able to take it off. Besides, sometimes it's useful. It can act as a . . . as a . . .' he stops, embarrassed.

I burst out laughing. 'Were you going to say a deflection?'

'Well, I suppose, something like that.'

'A deflection against women like me.' I smile and lean forward and cradle the mug in my palms.

'No, not like you. I had two cups of tea before I came out and in all honesty I didn't really want that first one you offered let alone the second; it was an excuse to talk to you, so not a deflection. But I am going to have to ask to use your loo before I go.'

'Yes,' I say, amazed once again. 'I'd love to go for a walk some time.'

After he's gone, I look out at the darkening afternoon. I'm convinced the skull belonged to a girl despite what Fletcher said. What happened to her? Her little life quivers in the darkness through the window, a tiny flare in that history that churns around us.

'Please come back to me, Carmel,' I say to the night, which ignores me and chooses to roll on regardless.

'Goodnight, sweetheart,' I say, and I realise I'm talking as much to the girl that's been lost to the river all those years as much as I'm speaking to Carmel.

Time for another shift – the first day shift for a long while. I do a handover with my double Aanya in a small office we find empty and I find out that an old lady, who I've become stupidly fond of in the last weeks, has died.

My legs feel instantly shaky. 'Oh,' I say. 'Oh dear.' I sit down abruptly on the swivel chair in front of the desk. Someone has written 'collect shoes' on a yellow Post-it note there.

'Was she one of those?' asks Aanya sympathetically. We all know who 'one of those' are. They are the ones that get to you.

'Yes, I do believe she was.'

'I think she's still there if you want to say goodbye. It happened not very long ago and the mortuary have been run off their feet today.'

The pink and white spotted curtain is still around her bed. I slip inside and her body lies there, tiny and frail as a husk with her grey bob fanning out across the pillow.

The veins in her wrists seem a very bright blue. Her hands look old and worn. Last time I saw her she used the left one to grab me by the arm. 'Love,' she said. 'Never deny it. There is nothing else. There can be only love.'

As I stand and say a quiet 'goodbye' to the old lady's body I feel an overwhelming, surging tide of love for Carmel. My girl. My only child. The feeling reaches out like it's growing branches. It wraps itself round this hospital, all the people in it. We pride ourselves on our professionalism here, on science, yet how much is truly done through love? It's never talked about but I know without hesitation how many of us would say 'it's the patients' if we were asked what keeps us here. The patients in all their mess and pain and bravery and humour. Even the bitter, selfish ones, even those.

The branches that have burst out of my chest grow, out into the street, out into London with its mass of people, and reach up to the sky. They curl round the dead body in front of me lying under the sheet.

—

Because of my shift change I find myself in my own bed at night for the first time in a long time; I sleep a deep, dreamless sleep. I wake just once and the pattern of the suburban tree reflected in the street lights onto the wall above me is so familiar for a moment I think I'm a child again.

When I wake again in the morning I turn over in bed feeling ancient, hips bashing against mattress, joints creaking.

I hear keys in the door, footsteps in the hall. I lie, fully awake now, listening to Carmel moving around. I listen intently to the sounds of her in the house. There's the kettle being filled then not long after a thump, thump, thump up the stairs and the shower being turned on. It's switched off abruptly then she goes into her room. She's not trying to be quiet. Of course, she won't know about my shift change. She thinks the house is empty.

I lie silent, breathing quietly. I've already decided what to do. The money is there in the hallway waiting for her. I will wait until she's gone.

'Carmel,' I mouth silently, just stopping myself in time from calling out. The love I felt yesterday reaching out like branches, snakes down the stairs and tries to follow her but there's the slam of the front door and the house shivers for a moment and then grows quiet.

Mercy

2000

In the time that followed Mercy often thought of the doll's house that her mother had briefly given to her. It seemed to relate to the experiences she had after she left her mountain-top home, because after that it seemed she was living through a series of collapsing and expanding worlds. Sometimes, the world shrank small enough so it had to be crawled into, other times it ballooned so she felt like one of those tiny dolls that she used to move around from room to room.

London was overwhelming – the dirt, the noise, the movement, the strange clothes. There were purple puffer jackets and orange sneakers. Sky-blue fingernails and faces skewered by piercings. Confusingly, she spotted green hair like the girl who sported it had draped seaweed on her head.

In contrast, Mercy, in her little grey pant suit and black lace-up Oxfords, cut a very peculiar figure. With her very slightly bowed legs – a result of sporadic bouts of poor nutrition – she resembled more a little old man than a young girl. This place seemed such a dirty and chaotic contrast to her cloud land. The fact that her head was often bowed in sadness – missing her forest, her pool where she fished with Tony, her mother, her father and her church tent – added to the effect. The pastor had grumbled at how nearly all of her clothes involved pants because the ladies at home had been concerned about her keeping warm, and his dismissive attitude to involving himself in questions of her wardrobe and their quick departure had ended the discussion. Now he wished he'd paid more attention. He didn't want to pay out for more clothes and the glittering windows of the clothes shops secretly intimidated him, so her little old man outfit was the one that she wore in the small, crowded living rooms of people's houses, to the churches made of tin or clapboard, or on makeshift stages like the one she was on today in the back room of a pub during the services that the pastor called 'carrying out the glorious and urgent work of the Lord'.

At first Pastor Patron had been incensed by the idea of a healing service in a bar. His contact, a bespectacled man in his thirties who wore a greasy-looking black suit, explained that British bars were nothing at all like the ones in the US.

'Pubs often have many different rooms,' he explained. 'It means you can hire a separate room for a function. We won't be anywhere near the customers or alcohol of any kind.'

'I very occasionally imbibe,' the pastor explained. 'But I do not think alcohol should be freely available to the general population.'

As it turned out the back room of The Butcher's Arms turned out to be more suitable than the pastor could've hoped for. Its dark wood floor, gloomy light and stained-glass window had a distinctly churchy air, although the window did not depict a religious scene but a woman with an improbably curved neck holding a huge sheaf of arum lilies. Mercy was desperate to examine this but couldn't; she was seated on a hard wooden chair underneath it as soon as they entered the room. The pastor sat quietly, reading from his Bible as people began shuffling in, but she knew one movement from her if she tried to twist round and look upwards would have him alert and placing his large hand on her head to make her face the same way again.

Mercy was feeling particularly disconsolate that day. Missing home was like a sickness. She seemed to be losing all her pep and vim, as Bob in the grocery store might've said. The pastor, she had begun to realise, was not always a kind man. As time went by on this trip, he seemed to lose his temper with her with more and more regularity. This morning, just the sight of her at breakfast in the cheap hotel where they were staying seemed to infuriate him.

'For goodness' sakes will you try and look less miserable,' he snapped. 'Who would put faith in a face like that to do anything but make them feel downcast to the bottom of their hearts? You are doing the Lord's work and that fact should make you more cheerful and light of spirit than anything.'

He smashed the top of his hard-boiled egg with violence. 'Sit up and smile right now,' he ordered.

She did, but the sight of her false, pasted-on smile, coupled with her wan face, the dark rings under her eyes and the horrible little grey suit she was wearing nearly sickened him. He couldn't bear to look at her and instead looked furiously out of the window, spooning egg into his mouth. When Mercy realised he was no longer looking at her she gave up and slumped forward again and stayed like that until he had finished eating and he told her tersely to, 'get up'.

The difference between here and home was so vast Mercy struggled to comprehend it and today was one of the worst. In the dingy corridor on their way into the back room of the pub they passed a gambling machine blinking its fruits and bells on and off in the gloom. The coloured lights reflected off the pastor's round glasses and his face turned hard at the sight of it.

It must've started raining outside because the people that shuffled in made the air turn fetid. There was a smell of damp wool, damp hair and slightly unwashed bodies. One old woman in an ancient purple coat had shoes with no laces because her ankles were so swollen, they would have been impossible to do up. The tongues of the shoes lolled over her toes and she sat in the gap between two chairs, taking half of each up without seeming to realise it. There was a lot of coughing as people adjusted themselves and someone strenuously sucking on a sweet somewhere. Outside the noise of a radio and the power drills of the workmen who were listening to it filtered through. Then just before the pastor was verging on standing and beginning the service – she sensed the coiled energy gathering in him – the swing doors at the back opened. There was an uncomfortable scraping of metal on wood.

'No, no, no,' Mercy whispered under her breath. She put one hand inside the other and realised she was shaking. A woman with harsh yellow hair was pushing a wheelchair that was catching on the swing doors. The occupant of the wheelchair was twisted to one side like a tree trying to grow towards the light. His chin was resting on his chest and his jumper was darkened at the front by a large patch of drool. He was the sickest Mercy had seen so far.

And she knew that she was going to be expected to heal him.

The pastor was standing now and she was so transfixed by the figure in the wheelchair that she'd forgotten to stand herself. He reached out and gripped her by the shoulder of her jacket and yanked her upwards.

He began by welcoming everyone to the service but he seemed nervous and agitated, out of rhythm with himself. Although, after several fervent prayers, he fell into the comfort of his well-known routine.

'Please, sir,' he smiled at one of the few men in the room, a young man bundled up in a coat whose face flushed when he was singled out. 'Would you join us up here.'

The man hesitantly came to the low dais and stepped up. 'Please sit,' said the pastor, with his large hand indicating the empty chair. 'Please sit and if you could stretch both of your legs out in front of you.'

The man stretched out his legs, showing his scuffed soles to the congregation and crossing his arms tightly across his body.

'Did you know, sir,' said the pastor with a flourish of his arms, 'did you know that you have legs of differing lengths?'

That's where the familiarity ended though. There was something different in the air today. Mercy could sense that it came as much from the pastor as it did from the people shifting about on their wooden chairs in the gloomy room. When a man at the back began the contorted sounds of clicks and calls that she knew were a prelude to speaking in tongues, the feeling doubled. Several people near him joined in and formed what seemed like a horrible barnyard chorus.

She had become familiar with the fact that people were much less demonstrative here, less inclined to show their emotions, but that made when they did start speaking in tongues more frightening. At home, it had seemed natural, and something she herself hoped to master one day. Here she had to fight the urge to put her hands over her ears to stop the noise. Goodness knows what the pastor would do to her if she did that, he was just beginning to get into his stride.

'Yes, the God-given gift this child has, this innocent and uncomplicated child, from a simple, wholesome mountain family, is here at your disposal today.' He smiled a big, flashy smile that showed lots of his teeth. 'Only those with true faith need apply.'

Then he closed his eyes and spread out his hands and his lips moved in urgent, silent prayer while his face glistened with sweat. Then his eyes popped open, quickly swivelling to one side to check Mercy's whereabouts next to him as if she might've run away while his eyes were closed.

'Come, come, the afflicted. Come to this innocent child and feel the lifeblood of the lamb, the living, tender, fierce spirit that courses through her veins and washes away those afflictions like she is a torrent of God's strength.'

People began shuffling forward. The desperation was clear on some of their faces. Mercy began to feel like she was in a nightmare. Hands reached out for her, fingers thrusting forward and even the pastor seemed knocked off balance by the blatant, hollow need that boomed around the room.

Mercy felt hands tapping on her head, tentative at first, then less so, batting at her like she was caught in a flock of birds. She tried to push them off but her own hands were too small, too weak to counter their adult strength.

'Leave me be,' she said, but nobody heard her and the crush they formed began to feel dangerous, as if it might take the breath right out of her body. The pastor seemed to realise it was getting out of hand.

'Hey,' he said. 'Let's keep it peaceful here. Let's manage ourselves in a dignified fashion.'

The old woman in the purple coat Mercy had spotted earlier was using her bulk to force her way to the front of the crush, but at the pastor's words she fell back a little.

'Let Bobby through first,' someone who Mercy couldn't see cried out.

'Yes, yes,' there were various cries in the room. 'Let him up first, it's only fair.'

Alongside the others the woman in the purple coat fell back further, but her hands clamped on to the handle of her black bag in frustration.

Then just as she'd known and dreaded would happen, the young man in the wheelchair was pushed forward. To her left the pastor had tight hold of her shoulder like he knew she had an urgent desire to escape. He wasn't looking at her though, he was reading from the open Bible that was balanced on his large palm. Drops of sweat fell from his forehead and onto the page. To Mercy, it seemed a blasphemy, dirty sweat dropping onto God's word. Miss Forbouys or Myla Joyce would never have tolerated anything like that.

'This young man has presented himself today to this girl with extraordinary talent, except the talent is not hers, no, it belongs to God, and it's God, working through her, who will untangle those limbs, who will reach deep inside this body and make good all the unclean components that he has to suffer.'

Mercy was nearly crying now. If she could just be back home she wouldn't even mind being in main street while the boys rained stones down on her; it would feel like a bene-diction compared to this.

'Heal him, child, heal him.'

Mercy glanced at the woman who had wheeled him for-ward, she guessed it was his mother. Her bleach-blonde hair was the only thing shining in the room. Her mouth was half open and her eyes wide, covered in a kind of dew and bulging. She too was sweating, a glistening moustache of it above her top lip.

'Yes,' she was saying. 'Please, please heal my boy. I can't take it anymore, it's killing me. Do it, do it.'

Mercy tried to shake her head but the pastor was grip-ping her neck now and it made it difficult.

'I can't,' she whispered.

The spirit wasn't here, Mercy thought, not the Lord's spirit anyway. There was *something* in here; it occurred to her that the devil really had slipped in the door like she was warned about back in her lovely, airy, flower-scented church tent at home. Yes, surely the devil was here. He was responsible for the yellow light, for the horrible stink in the room, for the way people were looking crazy and pushing each other around.

She gathered as much breath as possible into her little lungs. 'I can't,' she yelled at the top of her voice. 'I can't. I can't. I can't. I can't do it.'

There was an absolute silence until a voice at the back piped up, hot with resentment. 'Then what are we doing here?'

The pastor's head turned so slowly it seemed to be making its excruciating journey on some kind of mechanical device, like it was attached to a turntable in his neck. When finally his bright blue eyes fixed on her, she could see little veins of blood in them threading through the white like red worms.

She expected him to blast at her, to grab her by the shoulders, to shake her, but all he did was take a deep breath and turn back to the crowd and begin addressing them in a reasonable voice.

'The child is tired today. Up and down the country she's been, mending bodies, healing minds.' That was news to Mercy, who hadn't set foot out of this city, but the pastor continued. 'We must not expect too much of her. The Lord might be working through her but He is having to work through a child's brittle body. Like anything else that is overused it will break eventually, like a car that has been driven far too fast or a household implement that has received too much electricity. She needs time to recover. Now let us pray.'

He lowered his head and his lips began moving in prayer. After a few moments most of the people before him did the same, although some took their time, standing, with their eyes shifting from side to side as if they were having trouble catching up with the pace of events. The man who'd asked why they were there didn't take part in the prayers though, he banged out of the room leaving the swing door trembling on its hinges. Mercy noticed the pastor's own eyes cracking open for an instant to locate who it was in the crowd who'd left and to check nobody was following behind. Then the flash of blue disappeared as he again closed his eyes and resumed his prayer, out loud this time, his words urgent and fervent.

Then gradually people left. There was muttering and murmuring outside of the swing doors where Mercy could see through the frosted glass they'd gathered in a knot. She had no doubt that they were talking about her and what had just happened. The woman with her son Bobby in the wheelchair didn't say anything as she left but she gave Mercy a look that made her quail down to the soles of her shoes. It was a look of such hot spite and disappointment that Mercy hadn't seen the like of before. Finally, they were all gone except for the man in the greasy black suit that had arranged the venue for them. He began tidying up the chairs, making the rubber tips of their legs squeak against the floor.

'There,' he said at last. 'All done. I think we better leave going ahead with next week's scheduled event if you don't mind for now. I'm not sure it's working out so well.' He rubbed his hands together nervously. 'Shall we adjourn? I need to lock up the room and return the key to the landlord.' Mercy had noticed often how the pastor made people nervous, but like earlier, she was surprised again by his reaction.

'Of course,' he said in a mild voice. 'That's no problem at all. In fact, I've been making enquiries elsewhere. There is much need of the Lord's work and London, I've found, is a rather godless place. I will not miss it.'

They were walked out of the room, over the stone floor of the saloon bar and out of the ornate main door in what felt very much like an ejection. She trailed behind the pastor, who stopped abruptly on the pavement. Then she found herself lifted off her feet and dumped back down in a narrow alley between two high brick walls dripping with damp and dotted here and there with a glistening moss. She supposed he must've whisked her there by picking her up but she couldn't be sure, it had happened in a flash.

He leaned over and skewered her to the wall with one hand which was so large it could fit round her tiny neck like a metal vice. Though it wasn't large enough not to squeeze her throat and hurt.

'Now then,' he leaned down so his face was right in front of hers. 'Do you want to tell me exactly what happened in there today?'

'You're hurting me.' She tried to prise his hand away with both of hers but she didn't stand a chance.

'I took you on. I put all my faith in you, now this. You know, I'm beginning to question you, beginning to question everything I've done for you. Why are you doing this to me?'

Snot ran out of her nose that she couldn't reach up and wipe away. 'I can't mend them,' she sobbed. 'I know they are broke but I can't fix them.'

He appeared not to hear her. Drops of spittle fell on her cheeks as he spoke. 'I am giving you one last chance, child. One last chance to prove yourself. You had better not let me down again, I swear to the Almighty.'

The only bit of resistance left to Mercy was to switch her eyes sideways so they didn't have to look straight into his face. She concentrated on the dripping brick wall behind the pastor, and truly felt like what she'd left behind, her mountain top – which might not even exist anymore as far as she was concerned – had in fact been some kind of paradise that had been lost forever. Time dissolved in that moment. All that was left was a jumble of memories. She tried to cling on to them – the smell of flowers in the church, her ma's beads on the bureau, Bob behind the counter in The Full Cart; warm, everyday familiar things that she loved – but they fell away even as she tried to make them solid. The most persistent one was eyelids coloured like rainbows, and even that disintegrated and broke apart as she tried to conjure it, became gasoline in a puddle.

All the way on the train from London to Norfolk there were trumpets playing in Mercy's head.

Cymbals too, clashing metal on metal, sparks flying. Music in praise of the Lord. She could hear it despite the silent carriage. Miss Forbouys used to put music on a record player sometimes at the end of the school day when she was tired and needed five minutes to herself. Sometimes it was Buddy Holly. Sometimes it was opera. Mercy's favourite was the devotional music though, it stirred her blood.

When she eventually came to be saved she remembered the tunes and they seemed like they could've been a voice from the future that had been showing her the way forward even before she'd encountered the tent and was saved forever.

The music was so loud that when Pastor Patron leaned forward and said something, she couldn't hear his words.

She shook her head in incomprehension and, clearly annoyed, he repeated himself.

She tried to pick out his words from the shapes his mouth made and wondered if she'd have to learn to read lips. There was a deaf boy in school who could do that and he was brilliant at it. He could tell what you were saying from right across the schoolyard and it seemed to Mercy that it was some kind of superpower she'd love to possess though if she'd ever be able to master it herself, alongside speaking in tongues, was another thing.

She shook her head and stuck her fingers in her ears like they were full of water and the music stopped dead. Silence roared in. Under that the train tracks running like a sewing machine.

'Did you hear me?' Pastor Patron's voice came in loud and clear. He had his hands on his knees and seemed like some colossal statue carved out in front of her.

She nodded yes even though she hadn't. Over the last few months she'd learned what the taste of fear was like in her mouth and acted accordingly.

'I'm counting on you this time,' said the pastor. 'This community we're staying with does not appreciate little fakes and liars. I know I was not mistaken in you when I witnessed that girl rising out of her wheelchair and walking in the tent that first time. Now you have to prove that I was indeed right.'

Then the air darkened as he leaned over her. 'You will not betray me again. Many years ago, I thought I might have the talent such as yours and it was taken away from me, cruelly. Now though, I have the gift to divine it in others. These people who have invited us in are serious people, and we must not debase ourselves in front of them by appearing to be charlatans. By the end of our stay there they will be firmly convinced of everything I say.'

He settled back in his seat and folded his hands in his lap. Mercy was tired of moving around from place to place. In the camper it hadn't been so bad because she'd had her own bed, with the same blue covers, all the time. Here she never knew where they were going to end up. Increasingly, the pastor left her on her own while he went off on mysterious business for what seemed like an age. In the cheap guest houses she often put a chair against her door at night because it was so scary to be alone. Once, a long bedspring had popped out of her mattress and pierced her side. She'd had to unhook herself from it in the night.

Mercy looked out of the window at the dull, flat landscape as it moved along and pined for mountains. She wondered what Racoon was up to. She pictured her parents but this time they'd moved from the kitchen-diner table and they were two lumps under their quilt in bed and even though it felt her survival could depend upon it, try as hard as she might, she could not get her imagination to make them get up or even stir. In her heart she felt they were finally gone.

By the end of their stay, he said.

By then everything will have changed again. The train chugging through the flat landscape is taking Mercy to a destiny her mother could never have dreamed of in this old country of grey skies and thin rain.

By the end of their stay Mercy will, in fact, be lying in a large earthen hole in a field. Its corners are crumbled and roots thread in and out of its walls. By then the pastor is already long obsessed with another miracle girl. This time, he firmly believes it's the real thing and he is jubilant. He will be making plans to extract the new girl, who is called Carmel, from her mother so artfully, so completely this time, in a way the Lord would approve of, that he is on fire. The healing that Mercy is so profoundly and obviously incapable of he will see as merely a test, a dry run. The journey he believes he will fulfil in his life will begin anew. Mercy has become redundant to his plans.

Then a beetle will scuttle across Mercy's cheek in her hole in the ground, across her closed eyelid and disappear unharmed into her curly hair. The rain falling from stones will drip water into her open palms, the skin as pale and delicate as the insides of shells, as if they are the silent and only mourners weeping at her burial.

Carmel

2013

I decide to make the marble cake for Mum. She drew a heart next to the recipe for it so I guess that means she must really love it.

It's a thank-you, for the money, and it's a sorry too, and perhaps even a going-away present because I sense some sort of departure won't be long, though to where and what I might find is still a mystery.

I've never made a cake before but how hard can it be?

I copy down the ingredients so I can go shopping.

1 ½ sq. (1½ oz.) chocolate
2 cups sifted cake flour
2 teaspoons baking powder
½ teaspoon salt
½ cup butter
2 teaspoons vanilla extract
1 cup sugar + 1 tablespoon sugar
¾ cup milk
3 egg whites

The thin winter sun is shading London a pale lemon as I let

myself into the house this morning.

I take out the ingredients one by one and lay them out on the kitchen table in a row and root in the cupboard for mixing bowls, cake pans and the set of scales still in its frayed cardboard box with the photo of a woman with 1970s hair, smiling delightedly with pearly pink lips at the flour she's just weighed out. I tie my hair back with an elastic and put on Mum's apron and open the recipe book and flex my fingers ready to go to work.

The recipe book is pockmarked with specks of food. I know it was one of Gran's because her name is written inside the front cover. I met my gran after I got back from being away because her and Mum were talking again by then. I'd been desperate to know her and Grandpa as a child but I tried not to let on because I knew it would upset Mum. Funny how you can know these things when you're little without a word ever being said. When I finally met them they seemed thin, withered even, lines crossing and recrossing Grandpa's face. Shortly afterwards Grandpa died and Gran followed a few years after. I overheard Mum say she thought it was the strain of what happened that did it and I felt guilty then, as if it had been my fault.

This cookbook in my hands, with its marked and fragile pages, it's a historical document as much as anything in a glass case in a museum is. It's splattered and worn out by its journey through time just like my finds from the river. Why are these things that hold so much tossed aside so easily? Gran and her life are in those pages, maybe even Mum's, now mine.

I flick through it until I find the marble cake recipe.

I set the chocolate to melt in a metal bowl over hot water on the stove and cream the butter and vanilla essence together then add the sugar gradually, beating with an electric whisk until it's fluffy like the recipe book tells me to. I pause, bowl held in my arms like a baby. Cake batter and the lemon-coloured light pouring through the window merge and I'm remembering something, not from when I was *away* but from *before*, a time that is so lost and long ago it's like an out-of-focus film. It's Mum mixing cake batter in the kitchen in Norfolk and she's telling me how she used to have the bowl and the wooden spoon to lick the sweet mixture out of once the cake was in the oven and she was so greedy for it she'd put her face right inside the bowl and it got onto her nose, into her hair. *Can I do that?* I ask, and she pushes her hair away from her face with the back of her hand so I can see the tail of her blue eye from where it was hidden beneath her fringe but she tells me no, that people think maybe raw eggs are bad for you now and they didn't know that then but she spoons out some butter and sugar mixture before the eggs go in and forms it into a cone that I eat in little pinches.

I stir the mixture slowly. All that care, all that attention she gave me. How little I think about it compared to the mountains of America, lightning forking over plains, roads and roads and roads. The world with Mum from before I was eight was so small. I had a china lamp in the shape of a mushroom with badger figures inside in their tiny mushroom house and I think of it like that. I remember how Mum used to warm my slippers in front of the fire before I put them on. She'd sit up into the night and make doll's dresses out of scraps of fabric for me and in the morning say, ta da, Carmel look, look, look what I made you last night. She'd dance with me in the kitchen with the radio turned right up and we'd pretend we were pop stars and use spoons as microphones.

I feel something slide down my face and it splashes into the cake mix. All that care, that attention – smashed apart in a moment like it wasn't worth a thing when he took me, and then for me to just forget about it all. Don't think about it now, I tell myself, there's too much going on. Pour it all into the cake. Beat egg whites into peaks. Grease the pan. Turn one half of the batter into the pan. Mix the chocolate with the remaining half then spread that on top and swirl them together. Do not cry and salt the mixture. Do not think about what is lost; you'll never take breath again. Besides, it'll make the cake taste bitter.

I slide the cake into the warm oven and lick the spoon clean. Raw egg seems such a puny danger now. I wash up and leave everything on the drainer to dry and as the kitchen smells sweeter and sweeter I hear the mail landing on the mat.

I go through to the hallway and lean over the mail fanning across the jute doormat and nearly stop breathing. It's here, the preacher's letter, his writing looping over the envelope. I take it through to the kitchen and put it on the table. The cooker timer beeps and I take the cake out. It's cooked lopsided; one half has risen more than the other. I put it to cool next to the letter.

In this moment I can't open it.

I need to know too much; what she liked for breakfast

and who she played with. What was her favourite dress and did she rhyme words together just to see how they sounded? Did she make bracelets for herself out of grasses? Did she kick the ground when she was upset or angry? I need her to know that she did not go unnoticed. That in one way she saved me.

I stuff the unopened letter in my rucksack. I have to have time before I face it.

In the hallway as I'm about to leave, I hear a small noise from above. I look up and there's Mum, sitting on the top stair in her pyjamas and watching me. Her feet curl over the lip of the stair. They look so bare and bony, her face floating above so raw. I try to say sorry, that I'm starting to understand now, but no words come out and I flee.

Beth

Today I was already awake when I heard the door opening downstairs. She was early. There was the sound of the shower being turned on, then abruptly off – as usual – then she moved through to the bedroom and I was listening so hard I could hear the *whick*, *whick* as she pulled on her trousers leg by leg.

I heard her going through to the kitchen; there was the sound of cupboard doors opening, then, unexpectedly, the noise of the food processor. I sat up and hugged my knees to my chest then swung my legs out of the bed and gently put them on the floor, listening furiously. I must've chucked off my plaid pyjama bottoms in the night because they were in a tangle by my feet.

Soon something started to float up, a sweet smell that was at once unexpected but something in it was so familiar I wanted to take great gulps of it. I didn't stir; the smell grew stronger and stronger. I was bursting with curiosity. There was the sound of taps being turned on and more thumping around and I held my breath as the post arrived and she went to collect it. She was slower after that, her footsteps almost dragging.

Like being drawn by a string I stood and pulled on my pyjama bottoms and crept like a burglar in my own home to the landing. Downstairs I could hear her coming out of the kitchen, pushing the door closed. Those branches of love that wrapped round an old, dead body in the hospital felt like they were rammed inside my chest, battering to get out.

I crept along the hallway. By the top of the stairs I could see clear to the front door. The sweet smell was even stronger now, floating up. She had her back to me. Slowly, I lowered myself to sitting on the top step. I wanted to watch her for as long as I could before she left. I wanted to stuff the sight of her in her red coat as greedily as the sweet smell before it was gone. My Joan of Arc, my Joan of Arc. The branches of love burst out of my chest and rushed down the stairs towards her.

She turned and looked up as if she'd felt them too, snaking round her ankles, trying to pull her back into the house.

'Mum, I'm sorry,' she mouthed. There was no sound but I could read the words. Then she opened the front door and turned to bolt, leaving just the red of her singing behind my eyes.

We all know, of course, how tastes and smells can evoke the people and places of the past. But this is more than that. When I pad, barefoot, into the kitchen and see the marble cake on the table it's like my mother has conjured it out of the air, from the past, from my childhood and made it materialise before me.

The cake is still steaming slightly and the air in the kitchen is butter sweet.

I sit down. The surface of the cake is slightly wonky and

has been carved off to try and make it flat and that fact alone makes me push my fists into my cheeks because it gives me that swimmy sensation at the back of my nose as if I'm going to cry.

But this is a cake that should be celebrated. Like my mother used to do, I fetch a side plate and a fork that I place on a folded triangle of a paper napkin next to it. I cut into the cake and the brown and white swirls inside are revealed and it looks moist and perfect and the perfumes of sugar, of vanilla, of warm butter grow ten times stronger. It's like once again Mum is in the house, standing at the sink clattering dishes while I eat a slice of cake. It's like she and Carmel have joined forces somehow and are holding hands across the generations, across the divide of this world and the next.

As I eat the warm cake, forkful by forkful, slowly and with reverence, I have the powerful sense of how the threads of my story are mixed in with all the others, so there's three-hundred-and-fifty-year-old bones and a cake and my mother's warm hand on my head and the beak of an old lady's nose pointing at the ceiling and Carmel's quick smile and we're all woven inextricably together like one multi-coloured piece of cloth that in one way is a domestic homespun thing and in another spreads out as infinitely as space.

Mercy

2000

The place the pastor takes Mercy to in Norfolk is known as 'The Centre'. It's a large house in the middle of trees and that fact alone made Mercy feel like she had at last reached some kind of ship that she could climb aboard.

They were greeted by a woman who offered tea and wore a long, flowing dress rippling with green leaves whenever she moved. It reminded Mercy of her beloved forest on a windy day and the way the canopy undulated.

The forest-dress lady said her name was Betty and explained that they were all encouraged not to have too many personal possessions here. Mercy instantly worried that her suitcase might be too much but like she could read her mind Betty said that what Mercy had would be fine. In the morning there was prayer which they were welcome to join. Volunteers were needed in the vegetable garden and there was a book by the back door where they could put their name down for a slot. She was interested to know what pathway to healing the pastor practised.

Then she sipped her tea and said 'uh, huh; uh, huh' as the pastor spoke, and he did his particular smile that involved a great many of his teeth in between speaking. All the while Mercy was silently asking, 'Will you be my mom, will you be my mom, will you be my mom?' of Betty. When Betty absentmindedly reached out and patted Mercy's curly hair, Mercy's cheeks pinked so hard she felt they were on fire. Later, she heard the pastor murmur to Betty that there were 'no parents to speak of'. Mercy was a 'sad case' that he was struggling to cope with, despite her natural gift. He'd been coming to the realisation that a man of his age was not a right and appropriate person to be keeping her in tow.

'Poor, poor child,' said Betty. 'We will have to give her extra love.'

'The Centre' seemed an odd name because outside by the front gate there was a sign with the words 'Oakfield House' painted on it. When Mercy pointed this out to Betty she just laughed and said, 'But we're at the centre of everything here.'

Mercy had a bed in her own little room in the attic and couldn't believe her luck when that first day she looked out of her window and saw trees. She loved everything about this place. She loved being back amongst trees again. She loved the wide wooden floorboards in the hallway, worn dark and shiny from feet. She loved the picture of Jesus Christ looking so young and handsome in His white robe but with beautiful, sad blue eyes that hung above a glass-fronted cabinet of books in the same hallway. She loved the quietness and how everyone took care of everyone else. How everything was shared. She loved Betty. The pastor came and went, she didn't know where or why, and often the absences seemed to go on for some while and she particularly loved this and the fact he was no longer keeping watch on her. It wasn't like before in London when she was left on her own. Here, it was humming with life.

The only thing she didn't love about the place were the outside toilets where you sat over a hole and let your poop drop down into the earth and you couldn't flush it away but that seemed a small thing to put up with compared with everything else.

There were often people arriving at The Centre. They arrived with a suitcase and were assigned rooms just like Mercy herself had been. On their day of arrival everyone was called to the big room in the middle of the house (the centre of The Centre, as Betty joked) and they were introduced and everyone else had to introduce themselves in turn. Then the guest was taken off – sometimes there were even four or five guests at a time – to benefit from the quietness and the various therapies on offer aside from devotional practices.

The pastor seemed out of place, uncomfortable here. It was at dinner where she sensed his discomfort most. Everyone took part in preparing it (which the pastor hated, Mercy could tell – he looked at the vegetable peeler put in his hand as if he didn't know what it was and had never seen one before) and it was eaten all together around a long table. Whoever was sitting next to him engaged him in conversation, about God or what it takes for a body to heal and the pastor would nod sagely and cast his eyes down and stroke his chin like he had all the answers. Except Mercy knew him well enough by now to realise it was only because he didn't have a clue what to say. *You think children don't notice things, buster,* she said to herself. But Mercy noticed a great

many things about him, one of which was that he was beginning to get really anxious about something. Pretty soon she
found out what. Soon, she learned, there was to be a special
healing session carried out by the pastor and herself.

When she heard this, she felt sick to her guts. Not again,
not again! These people were so lovely and kind it made it
even worse than that time in The Butcher's Arms. Then the
pastor vanished.

'He's on urgent business,' said Betty when Mercy asked
where he was. 'Again.' Sometimes it seemed he was barely
there but in fact, Mercy had only asked because she was
hoping he'd bolted to avoid 'the session'. But Betty said, 'He
told me he was going on some urgent business for a few
days but he'll be back in time for the healing session.'

Mercy was sorely disappointed when she came downstairs the next morning and spotted his familiar bulky
shape in the hallway. She knew it was him just from his silhouette, which was outlined against the bright light coming
through the open door.

Straight away she knew something about him had
changed. There was new purpose and energy about him.

'You have a rival,' he told her, although the way he said
it was like he was speaking to himself, not her. She had no
idea what he meant but she knew it was in some way significant from his renewed verve and way of speaking.

She looked at him. There was something about
him, about his head specifically that reminded her of a
building she'd seen somewhere that was being worked
on, men climbing up and down ladders, buckets being
pulled on pulleys, a hammer chipping roof tiles off;

the pastor's mind was a hive of activity.

'What do you mean?' she asked.

'There is another girl . . .' The pastor had to stop for a moment because he was so overcome with emotion that his nostrils pinched together. He stared out of the door like he was in another world. 'She is a true light. She is a holy place, a mount that from time long gone holy things come forth. The name is significant, it must be.'

'What is it?'

The pastor flashed his blue eyes quickly down. 'Her name is Carmel,' he said quietly, as if there was a whole world of meaning in this.

The pastor had been following this new girl called Carmel for some time secretly in a borrowed car but there was a very big problem. Already, he'd witnessed her gifts. A friend of her mother, a weak, thin-looking woman as the pastor thought of her, took the child to a church with a tin roof down a side street in a town nearby. The pastor had been attending a service there looking to pick up more contacts. At first, the pastor thought this woman – with her wide woven bracelets on each wrist no doubt hiding some godless injury – was the child's mother. After he witnessed this child's miraculous interventions he discovered from the woman that she wasn't the child's relative, and that the child came from a single-parent family. He covertly followed the pair, stuck with them fast and found the girl lived in a small cottage in the country with her mother. This was, to the pastor, a good and a bad thing. Good, because he had not lost sight of the child and now knew where she lived. Bad because he could see this girl was never going to be extracted as easily as Mercy had been. The pastor had spent time outside the cottage – no husband appeared to be around – and knew he had to have her if he was ever going to fulfil his calling of taking true succour out into the world. He began to put detailed plans into place.

But there was a problem: her mother watched the girl like a hawk, her face softening every now and again then back to being a hawk. Even though he was parked behind trees he noted her watchfulness and wondered if he'd been spotted. He knew what had to happen was something drastic, something to rend the two apart, that meant the girl could be his apostle definitively and completely. Unlike Delia, that particular mother was never going to agree to anything. He'd be chased off should he so much as look at her precious daughter.

The Centre became busier than ever; every room was full. When Mercy realised this was partly because they were coming for a special healing session, she felt like dying, remembering all the hands stretching out to her, suffocating her, in London. Yet in another way she was resigned. There was nothing she could do. She felt part of something, a wave that was pushing her inexorably forward and that would one day inevitably break although not yet, not yet. Until it did, she would be forced to ride it and when it came crashing down, she just had to hope that it didn't break her legs.

The air turned crisp and clear. A cold, hard spring but beautiful, the skies a pure, washed blue, the smell of leaf mould in the air.

The service was held on a Sunday, the pastor insisted on that, and began to coach Mercy on her responsibilities. He'd felt the whole enterprise shifting inch by inch away from the Lord to people believing they held the potential for healing within themselves and he didn't like it. It stank of witchcraft.

'It doesn't come from you,' he told Mercy. 'It comes from Him, remember that. This is your last chance to impress these people. You never know, they might let you stay.'

Somehow, she divined in this she was about to be offloaded. She fervently hoped so.

The pastor seemed to have gained a calmness. So much so that Mercy was surprised when the day arrived and he actually reached out and took her hand as they were waiting outside the big room to make their entrance. He was nervous, she realised. His hand shook a little and his face was drawn tight. Behind the closed doors was the unmistakable noise of a crowd – like the sound of wind blowing through wheat as they stirred and shuffled and murmured. Someone laughed out loud, a jarring sound, and Mercy felt the pastor stiffen beside her.

Inside, they sat on the hard-backed chairs arranged for them at the front. The pastor seemed on edge. Strangely, that made her *less* nervous. It was his certainty she found frightening. He stood and read out a piece from the Bible about Peter's shadow and how it only needed to fall on a body to heal it.

The Bible words loosened something in Mercy. It was such a relief and a joy to hear them again in this lovely place she began to remember how she felt that first morning after she'd been saved. She forgot her worries in the beautiful sound of the familiar poetry of the King James Bible which Miss Forbouys once told her was the only true one. For the first time since coming away she felt pure and full. She sat bolt upright in the chair and kept her eyes fixed on his mouth so she wouldn't miss a word.

When he finished he paused slightly and bowed his head and she couldn't help herself, she jumped up and punched the air. 'Amen to that,' she cried out. 'Amen to that.'

The congregation stirred approvingly. 'Amen, little sister,' someone said.

'You read us something,' called another one, a man, with a hint of humour in his voice. 'Show us that fire in your belly.' There were calls of agreement all round. The pastor paused then nodded to Mercy.

'Go ahead, child,' he said quietly.

She began with St Luke 5, Chapter 5, which she loved because of its message of abundance, the empty boat, then the fish caught that broke the net after Jesus's intervention and Jesus's promise to Simon that henceforth he would be a fisher of men. It made her think of Tony and the river pool. There were several approving murmurs from the crowd. Her face cracked into a brief, joyful smile then she straightened it. These passages were too serious for that. She continued, the words surging through her and realised that the verse led into another one which indeed contained a healing, of palsy. 'And they were all amazed, and they glorified God, and were filled with fear, saying, "We have seen strange things today."'

By the time she came to the end of the passage which was

about putting old wine into new bottles she felt winded with the powerful emotion. Even the pastor seemed infected with it; his eyes were shining and he nodded along approvingly like he was tapping out a rhythm. The faces in the crowd were becoming flushed and sweaty and the enthusiasm of a congregation was a delight she hadn't experienced since they'd left America. She finally felt on the verge of speaking in tongues.

She paused for breath and the pastor took the opportunity to pick up the baton.

'Take the devil, cast him out,' he thundered. 'He stalks amongst us, every day, every hour. He must be given no truck, no harbour. Cast him out of this place.'

Mercy felt as if she could be lifted right off the floor. The power of the old church she'd loved so much back in the new world came bursting out into this new church of the old world. She raised her little fist at the devil.

'Yes, leave this place,' she shouted.

'He's here,' the pastor said. 'He is amongst us – he has slipped through the door and is amongst us. Do you reject him?'

'Yes, yes,' people yelled. 'We reject him.'

'Do you reject all his pomp and works?' shouted the pastor, punching the air. 'Do you reject it all?'

'We do, we do,' they called back.

Mercy could feel the devil's presence, feel him stalking down the aisle towards her. She pulled as much air into her lungs as possible and puffed out her chest and the words she'd forced back in in their beautiful tent back home came surging out of her before she could check them.

'Do you reject him forever?' the pastor bellowed.

'Yes, fuck him to hell,' Mercy screamed. 'Be gone with you, you dirty, bad old motherfucker. Leave this place forever and die.'

Like dust settling, the sound in the room ceased. There was a nervous, suppressed laugh. Feet shuffling.

Mercy turned and saw the pastor's face, contorted as if there were wires pulling it from the inside.

'Come out,' he hissed. 'Come outside.'

Then everything went black because the pastor had put his arm around her and her face was in the scratchy black wool of his suit sleeves. She knew instinctively he was making it look like a caring arm, but he was hurting her and she could feel the Bible clamped under her own arm. Her feet hardly touched the ground as he whisked her out of the room and then outside onto the steps, down the path, like a single monstrous, scuttling spider until they were on the forest path that ended in a field gate.

Here he grabbed on to her and lifted her up so her feet were dangling and pointing downwards, the Bible still under her arm. When he let go she ran from him and climbed up a gate. The Bible fell into the mud on the other side and she stooped to pick it up. She lost vital seconds doing this; she could see the pastor's long leg in its black cloth already over her side. She tried to run again, Bible safely in hand, but he was twice as tall as her, his stride quickly catching up with her. He grabbed on to the tail of her grey jacket and spun her around.

They stood, facing each other by the grey stone wall.

His forehead seemed to have grown. It was bulging

outwards like his brain was inflamed above his eyes.

'You have failed. You have failed me and led me down the wrong path,' he said. 'You are just a precursor. I see that now. But now I have found the true one and she is a light to your darkness. Your despicable darkness. Your filth and your mess.'

Mercy felt a warm patch travelling down her leg and knew immediately what it was. She'd never wet herself before, not even when she was little, and it seemed in that moment the worst thing that had ever happened.

His face was so twisted it didn't even look human. 'What did I expect from those filthy parents of yours. They'll be dead and gone by now, you know that . . .'

He went to grab at her and she dodged away. '*You're* the motherfucking devil,' she cried. 'You are. You are.'

Then his big hand was on her chest and pushed her with such a force her feet flew up in the air and her head cracked against the wall and her small body was tossed aside and she lay immobile on the grass.

If Mercy had been able to open her eyes she would've seen him peering over, wiping his face. She would've seen the terrible expression in his eyes as he witnessed her twisted little body. Then that face withdrawing then returning with a spade in his hands and beginning to dig. She would've felt herself being rolled into a hole and seen his face above her contort with fear at the sound of voices over the wall nearby, and she would've heard the sound of the spade being thrown aside and then his footsteps thudding on the earth, running.

Then nothing else until it began to rain and the drops of

water dripped from a stone jutting from the drystone wall onto her closed eyelids and the open cups of her hands, the Bible flung open on Deuteronomy.

Carmel

It is the year of our Lord two thousand and thirteen. London is lit by the sun and is as radiant as the golden city of New Jerusalem; it glows the exact pale yellow of a wisp of straw floating through the air in a barn in Pennsylvania that the faithful have kicked up by their heels.

Today is the day to be washed clean of all the mess, this filth, these rags I've been clothed in since that one moment at eight years old when I was taken from a storytelling festival in rural England.

The preacher's letter makes my rucksack heavy. It's a door I'm about to walk through that will finally set me free. My secret sister, the last lost girl to be rescued, will be finally restored to her rightful place and perhaps I will once again be able to breathe freely, which I have not done since I got into his car in that parking lot all those years ago. We've tried forgetting about it, Mum and me, but it doesn't work. I need another way.

I have the urge to walk until my shoes wear through. To run until some of the electricity coursing through my body is released into the air. Instead, I go underground because the Tube is a relief, the ever-moving mass of people and trains a balm of Gilead.

On the train people jog gently in their seats as we worm

through the dark tunnels. Two men – boys almost – wearing city suits and fresh shirts strap-hang and talk about bank bonds, their dark hair gleaming under the artificial lights.

Open it now, Carmel. Or you might never have the courage. Open it now and let the light pierce the tomb.

I unzip my rucksack and take out the letter and hold it for a long time. We turn a corner and the two strap-hanging men brace without thinking. They ride the Tube every day and their bodies are attuned to its movements as if they are animals.

I dig my thumb under the flap of the envelope and tear at it. The paper inside is crisp and delicate, only one sheet. The light flickers and dies for a few long moments and I wait, patiently, for it to come back on. When it does I see the lines are sparse, scratched deep into a single sheet of thin paper as if the author of them has tried to carve them there.

A large house. Perhaps twenty bedrooms. I cannot recall its name. Norfolk.

It has a path leading from door to gate. There are trees beside the house, a short walk through them and there's a wall made of stone. In that wall is a fence. Climb over the fence and turn left. John the Baptist is by the wall.

Please, by anything that is scared and holy, when will you come? The wind is blowing in paradise and even the angel's wings are broken.

At first I can't take the implications of what it says there. Then I can.

I have the urge to vomit. I knead my fingers into the seams of my jeans on my thighs, trying to hold on. The windows opposite, the black tunnel wall speeding behind them warps. I'm certain the next lurch will be the tipping point and I'll be sick straight into my lap. Then the nausea fades and instead a noise comes out of me that seems to come from somewhere right in my middle; it's a low kind of keening noise growling in my throat and I appear to have no control over it. The two strap-hangers, the woman opposite in a striped uniform with a rooster with a bright red comb stitched to her left breast advertising a chicken shop, the two girls carrying cello cases between their legs all turn their eyes towards me and then away. Then the woman next to me, who because I am looking at the grimy floor of the train I can see is wearing navy court shoes with a thick heel and white linen slacks, very gently puts her hand on my arm and leaves it there. She does not speak; she pats my arm three times then lets her hand rest there and in the warmth of her skin radiating through my coat I feel the shy kindness of London but all the while my thoughts still keep rhythm with the train: *she is by the wall, she is by the wall, she is in a field by the wall.*

In the middle of the night I awake on my coffee sacks in The Egg and Spoon. I lie there and imagine dirt on my face, in my mouth, the feel of cold earth on my skin.

My bladder forces me to rise from the coffee sacks and something from inside my coat that's been half zipped up at the chest rustles to the floor, light and white like a falling bird. I poke it with my toe. It's the letter, illuminated in street light that has turned the red floorboards almost black. I must've crumpled it to my chest after I'd read it and it got caught there. I go sit on the toilet across the hall with the old-fashioned chain pull then back to the coffee sacks and curl into a ball, the weft of the hessian biting into my cheek.

When I wake in the morning the floor has become a hard enamel red again. Rosie kneels on it at an angle to me. The letter is smoothed out in front of her and she studies it intently, like she's studying for an exam.

She looks up. 'What is this place?'

I lick my lips. They feel cracked under my tongue. 'I can't tell you but I need to find it. I don't know how.'

'Are you going to leave?'

'I have to, for a while.'

She nods again. 'Is there a computer here?'

I give her a blank look. 'What for?'

'Google Maps. You don't know about them?'

I shake my head and take her to the computer tucked into an alcove downstairs. Rosie powers it up and I can see the back of her shorn head and the dip in the middle of her neck going into her hair where a tiny pulse moves, and the sight of it is so fragile I want to reach out and place my fingertip on it. Then, in a few short minutes we're flying over Norfolk like a bird. We scan the county, zooming down on all the large houses that stand on their own near woods, looking for ones that have a gate in a wall nearby that leads to a field and we move through the map as if it were a living land. I'm looking for the detail, the specifics, as we glide. It reminds me how mudlarkers love to say, 'Can you see it?' showing their photographs of the foreshore and what looks like a jumble of mud and stones. Then they'll chuckle and point out the flask, the pin, the crown, the lid of a tobacco tin, the turtle shell that was so obvious to them and that to you looked no different to everything else.

As we go along I make a list of all the places that seem possible and in the end it's more than two dozen long and I determine I'll walk the walls and scan the ground of each one and I will not stop until I find her. Because even though I know now why she did not need her name anymore when he tried to make me a gift of it, no girl deserves to just get erased like that. I will rescue whatever is left.

I reach my finger to the pulse on Rosie's neck but my finger hovers, mid-air, an inch from her skin.

'Marta will be here soon. I need to leave but I'll come back,' I say. 'But I don't know how long it'll take or what I'll need to do.'

She nods, then gets up and climbs the stairs and I think she's gone but I hear her feet coming back down again and she's carrying my rucksack and her sleeping bag which is rolled up neatly again and tied with rope as it was the day I first saw her carrying it on her back.

'This might be useful for you. I'll take the coffee sacks,' she says, not looking me in the eye. She sits, elbows on knees on the stairs, her head down. In exchange I slide the keys to The Egg and Spoon and two of Mum's twenty-pound notes next to her and bend down and kiss the top of her head and her hair feels soft and spiky beneath my lips, like a newborn chick.

'Take care of your tender soul,' I murmur and she runs up the stairs and I try to close my ears to the stifled sobs from the red-painted room that has been our refuge. 'Later,' I say, 'I'll come back for you later,' although I know she can't hear me. Then I step through to the café and unzip my rucksack and take out the doll. I bend her plastic legs and sit her on the table that she was lost underneath.

I pick up one of the waiter's pads and a pen from by the till.

Dear Marta, sorry I took the doll. I can't really explain why I did it but could you give her back to Lydia now? Also, there is someone in the storeroom with the red-painted floor upstairs. Her name is Rosie and she's very fragile. Would you be able to look out for her for a little while? I'm sorry to ask but I can't do it myself right now. She's no trouble – we've been staying in that room for a while now and you didn't even know so that's how little trouble she is, right? Sorry about that too.

I hesitate, then write: *I love you, Carmel.*

As I let myself out I glance back and the doll is waving at me, spurring me on.

I board a train back to this land of my birth with only the vaguest idea of what I might do when I get there and a terrible fear in my heart. I have the list in my pocket, and tied to my rucksack – packed with clothes, a map and tools – is a shovel, newly bought, with a pan that dips into a point so it looks like a shiny metal heart.

'Lord,' I say, because I am on my own in the train carriage and there's nothing to stop me speaking prayers out loud, even though these days I don't think there is really anyone listening to them, 'you need to really help me now.' Then I can't think of anything else to say to Him so I stay quiet.

I watch the flat winter fields pass, one after the other; sometimes there's a farmhouse or a black-painted Norfolk cottage with a white window frame like an eye in the side. And I'm thinking maybe I'm wrong to go back into this cursed and mystical land from where I was taken so long ago, that only bad things happen there, but it's where *she* lies so I have no choice.

Norfolk in winter. Fields crisped by frost. Low, grey skies that are broken by rooks that take to the air, calling.

By day I tramp the narrow lanes and the coast paths fringeing a sea so wide it feels that to fly above it would be entering the ends of the earth. By night I find a secluded spot, beneath a bush or in a wood, and I don all my jumpers at once and slide into Rosie's sleeping bag. I wake with frost on my lashes, my breath fogging. I wake and look at the blue-washed sky. It is the year of our Lord two thousand and thirteen and finally I feel something melting that was set glass-like many years ago; it's becoming warm and runny and changing shape like hot taffy.

An old man stops me on the road. He has rheumy eyes and gnarled hands.

'That there a bow and arrow you're carrying?' he asks, nodding at the shovel that rides on my back, higher than my head.

I smile and shake my head and ask for directions to Mayfield Farm.

I explore the farm but the ground by the gate shows no sign of being disturbed so I buy some milk from there and sit by the roadside and drink it down in one go.

I buy fingerless mittens in one village, a green woollen beanie in another that I pull down right to my eyes to keep warm. I buy hot pizza and wait till I'm back on the road to eat, sitting alone on the verge burning my fingers. Afterwards I fold the box into my rucksack for when I find a garbage can. Then I put my boots to the road once more.

Cheaney Farm. Whiteford End. Ashcourt Place. I tick them off my list one by one after I have surveyed the place that lies to the left of the gate by the wall. A farmer asks me what I'm doing and I stay mute. 'Are you one of Hardy's Poles?' he asks and I nod and climb back over the fence and walk straight past him because I have already satisfied myself that it is not in his fields that *she* lies.

In another place there's a bull in the field that I have to survey and before I climb the gate I take off my red coat and hide it on the other side of the wall because I've heard what the sight of red can do to a bull. Despite the danger I look here properly, running my fingers over the ground, looking for minute anomalies in colour and texture and I am relieved this time instead of disappointed that there are none and I scramble quickly over the fence as the bull eyes me from the other side of the field.

—

Now nearly all the places on my list have ticks next to their names.

Today, the country lane I'm on is bordered by stone walls that are velvety with yellow lichen. The only sound is my footsteps on the ground and crows cawing in the field nearby. Everything is winter hushed.

It seems I'm in a pop-up book illustrating my childhood.

Vistas like pages open up. I remember once in that misty, out-of-focus time of *before,* seeing geese flying low in formation over fields like this, their necks straining out as they flew. Perhaps I came down this very lane with Mum, I could swear I did. We were always walking everywhere because she couldn't afford a car.

There, another scene, its pop-up picture sliding across the lane: Mum in her old blue coat and big boots and with carrier bags on each hand that are so heavy they leave red stripes across her palms.

'Mum,' I breathe into the cold morning air even though I am alone and the words turn into smoke. The sight of her fills me with a kind of longing and love that I haven't felt for years, that I didn't want to feel.

'Oh, Mum, it wasn't your fault was it?' I say out loud and I could almost swear the figure in the blue coat ahead turns and smiles at me, a rueful smile.

I thought all these years it was that you weren't watching me close enough, that you didn't care. But you were always watching me weren't you, and I was cross and childish and looking for escape.

In her old blue coat, she turns to look, to check I'm still there behind her then those pages close and I'm again alone, silent and shaking.

A horse surprises me by popping its head over the wall and staring, frosted breath gushing from its nostrils.

As I explore every place on my list, I search over the ground as I would the foreshore. Everything falls away and I become footsteps, a heartbeat, no different to the cows munching grass in the fields beside me, the buzzard circling overhead, the light chasing across a cold field.

One morning, I awake in my sleeping bag to a ceiling of criss-crossed twigs and branches above. I crawled under bushes last night in these woods when it was already dark because I'd spent so many hours looking yesterday.

When I peep between the bare branches there's a tiny hut on wheels in a clearing in the trees. A woman with a long grey braid sits on the steps and warms her hands on a small fire at her feet. She sips something from a bowl that has steam rising from it. Then she stands and looks into the trees with alert, bright eyes and extinguishes the fire with the remains of the liquid in the bowl. There's a bang and a plume of steam like she's performed a magic trick. Then she unties her hair so it's a grey river over one shoulder and she brushes it slowly and thoughtfully then rebraids it with deft fingers until it looks like a rope of shining clam shells.

I think, *I could live like that.* I could have a tiny house on wheels that I can move from place to place and Mum could drive out to see me sometimes and I'd cook something for us both on the fire. Yes, I want to live like that woman on her own, so poised and quiet amongst the wild things.

I crawl out from the bushes when she goes inside her hut and silently I thank her for being a guide.

Three places left. I check my map and set off.

This place is off a winding lane that runs steeply into a wooded area at the bottom. In the woods the light dims and it's hushed and potent with expectation. I don't want to stray off the path into the darkness of those trees but if I have to I will. The soil here smells of twigs and acorns, of soft, rotting wood.

There's not a soul about, just birds I can hear hopping about in the undergrowth, the stirring of the canopy above me.

Then through the trees I see a large grey stone building surrounded by a wall, and as I get closer there's a painted sign mounted on two wooden battens by the gate: 'Oakfield House, Therapy Centre'.

This gate to the field is not padlocked so I open it, then close it behind me. A crow lands, pecks at the earth and watches me as I walk the wall. I defocus my eyes as usual but I do not have to walk far, five feet maybe, and I can see straight away the ground has been disturbed: the grass grows differently, and there's a scattering of stones on a surface that is roughly rectangular and shaped like a mounded grave.

I fall on the mound and trace it with my hands. If I am in the right place what would be left of her down there – were parts of her carried away by animals, did foxes gnaw on her bones?

Then chills run up and down my neck because I can almost see it, Mercy running out and climbing up that gate in her little grey suit, the preacher chasing after her, catching up with her.

It's so quiet and I'm so intent and a noise startles me out of that because it sounds like the distant howling of a wolf and it dawns on me *he* was here once, the wolf, snuffling around. He was in this exact spot digging. I lift my nose. He's left his scent behind; I swear it. The hairs on the back of my neck prickle. Did I have a narrow escape? If I'd never been rescued what would've happened? I'm momentarily breathless and I have to sit back and put my head between my legs because all the blood in there seems to have drained away into my boots.

'Courage, Carmel, courage,' I say to a crow who is watching me. 'It's just an old farm dog.' Then I begin doing what I need to do.

I unstrap the spade and begin to dig into the grass, down into the brown earth, sifting the soil between my fingers. Stones, roots – nothing else. I excavate deeper, digging my fingers into the soft earth, looking for her bones, for her little skull. I dig as deep as I can but all that comes up is deep loamy soil, soft and yielding, small stones, bits of bark. I start moving earth with my hands. Has she gone to the earth so soon? I dig until I feel my fingernails break.

'You left her here,' I ask out loud. 'Is this the place?'

I stand up to reach for the shovel again to dig deeper, deeper and it scrapes against the stone wall as I pick it up but then I freeze because the front door of the big grey house opens and a young woman walks down the path, bucket in hand. At first, I think it's myself I'm seeing because she has the same head of curly hair, she is around the same age. I want to shout out but no sound will come out of my mouth so I lift up my hand to wave and she spots me. She walks over to where I am and we stand opposite sides of the wall, she with her bucket and me with my shovel.

Then we stay and observe each other in silence because it's like twin planets have just aligned.

Later, she will tell me how she saw the figure with soil-streaked face and hands standing on the other side of the wall at the exact same spot where she lay in the ground all those years before. How a shock went through her because it was like she'd really been down there, underground, all these years waiting to emerge in a rebirth.

Now, as she observes me quietly over the wall she finally says, 'You better come with me. I'm just going to feed the chickens.'

I follow behind the young woman with the clanking tin bucket and I watch as she unbolts the gate and steps inside the enclosure of chicken wire and empties the pail on the ground and the bustling brown and black creatures speed over and peck greedily at her feet. I put my hand against the wire, as if reaching out to touch her.

Do you like strawberry jelly? I want to ask. Did you twirl your ringlets round your index finger when you were little because you liked the feel of it? Instead I say, 'You are Mercy, aren't you?' and she looks up and nods.

'How do you know?' she asks.

'Because,' my chest hurts as I speak, 'I believe I was taken by the same person that took you.'

302

'The pastor?' she asks.

'The preacher,' I reply.

Then she takes me inside and shows me a bathroom and gives me a towel that is well worn but soft and clean and some soap that smells of rosemary and has nubbly dots of the leaf and the occasional starry purple flower embedded in it.

'My room is there,' she says, pointing. 'Take your time.'

When I do emerge, cleaned up as best I can, trailing the smell of rosemary with only a hint of mud, there's tea and seed cake waiting in her room. She sits in the deep windowsill with the teapot pluming steam next to her and she indicates for me to sit opposite.

We study each other again, for the resemblance, but up close it's more superficial. The same age, the thick head of curly hair, the hazel eyes.

I say, 'I thought you were dead.'

She sips her tea and nods. 'I know who you are. You're the one he called the "real deal". I was a disappointment to him. A burning disappointment. Is your name Carmel?'

'Yes.'

She smiles. 'The "real deal" then.'

'Except I'm not.'

'He believed you had a God-given gift.'

'He's a liar and a thief. He took what was not his and tried to make it his own.'

She shakes her head, sighs. 'I didn't know anyone would think or know about me. I didn't think anyone would ever come looking.'

She glances at my coat. I think it's perhaps because it's

such a mess but Mercy says, 'I used to like wearing red when I was little.'

'Yes, girls do. It makes them feel brave.'

I'm quiet for a moment, then say, 'He tried to make me take your name. You were always there in my childhood. I used to think of you like a fish. You'd swim past me and I'd try and grab on to you but you were gone. I used to think,' I feel shy saying this, 'that you were my secret sister.'

She smiles, then she begins to tell me what happened to her, what happened after the preacher left.

She'd already been saved once, but the day that Mercy lay in her field grave was one that she came to regard as the time that she was truly born again. So much so that it reminded her of a chicken that her pa used to talk about in his fugue, because as she walked under the trees, she sometimes felt that she'd been split into pieces and reconstituted in a different form.

This form was full of light. It spilt out onto its surroundings sometimes, it burned so bright.

That night Mercy had been awakened by the dripping of rain on her eyelids.

'Oh Lord,' she said to herself. She looked down at herself and she was covered with earth. Above her were prison walls of roots and brown earth. 'Where in the world am I now?'

She sat up and a shower of earth and stones fell from her small body.

The memory of how she got there was fuzzy. Her knees hurt and she understood she must've fallen on them. Her trousers were ripped on the left knee and she could feel small stones embedded there when she searched the bare skin with her fingers. It took a long time for her to come properly to. As she did it, the sky darkened and she lay back down and fell asleep. By the time she awoke a huge yellow moon shone from above and lit up the earthen hole like a basin full of glowing liquid.

'Oh Lord, you always do give me what I need,' she said fervently. On the ground was her Bible lying open. She must've still been clutching it when the shove and the bang to her head knocked her unconscious. The moon was bright enough to read from the random opened page. It was from Deuteronomy. '22 And if a man have committed a sin worthy of death, and he be put to death, and thou hang him on a tree:

23 His body shall not remain all night upon the tree, but thou shalt in any wise bury him that day.'

She shuddered and slammed the Bible shut, thinking the Lord had really got it wrong this time offering up those words. That's about the last thing she wanted to read.

Then she remembered what happened before she woke and the memory made her crouch down in the hole and cry out: the pastor's long leg in black hooking over the gate, his breath in her face, how she screamed curses at him, terrified, his bulk looming over her. White-hot pain and then nothing. Tenderly she felt the back of her head. A large painful egg had grown there.

By the light of the moon, she did up both her shoelaces. The hole was only shallow but she was so bruised it was too painful to climb out of. She put her Bible on the edge and sat next to it, lifting her legs by holding on to the fabric of her pants. She stood painfully, filthy, looking like a little person made of mud, in the field lit so brightly by the moon it was like lamplight.

Returning to The Centre, she went straight to her room. Many of her things were gone as if packed in haste, drawers left open in the chest by the window. He'd taken her suitcase, her warm wool coat and the two cable-knit sweaters. He'd forgotten the drawer of underwear, and the laundry hamper at the bottom of the wardrobe was still full even if the hangers above were empty of her blouses and clanged together as she opened the wardrobe door. Hurriedly she cast about for her cross-body handbag and let out a shaky sigh of relief as she drew out the *Ray of Light* CD from within.

She sat on her bed, soil-streaked and trembling, wondering what to do.

In the end it was something unexpected that rescued her. Unexpected because it had seemed so terrible at the time – something that needed to be forgotten – it was that period spent alone in her mountain-top house. Not only had it hardened something within her, she now knew what she had to do to survive. All she had to do was hold on for as long as it took, and in this instance that meant staying. It meant clinging on to this place of safety like her life depended on it – which in a way it did.

When in the morning she went down to breakfast, cleaned up, pale, her hands trembling as she shook out wheat flakes into her breakfast bowl, she already had it all planned out. When Betty said, surprised: 'I thought you'd both left?' she shook her head firmly. 'He told me to stay,' she said.

She stuck to this line through thick and thin, sometimes varying it cleverly into, 'He told me to stay. He said he'd be back for me,' if the question seemed in any way searching. This time she'd been saved only by the skin of her teeth, from a dark and dangerous place that tasted like cold soil that often still haunted her dreams. She clung to the place like a life raft. Her cheeks burned every time she remembered the curse words she'd used in front of everyone and she just hoped fervently they would be forgotten.

At first she attached herself to Betty, but Betty expressed concerns that the pastor had gone and left her and when would he be back to collect his charge? So she tried to move away from her a little and towards an elderly couple with otherworldly smiles called Jennifer and Augustus. Mercy was relieved when Betty and her big questions about her rightfulness to stay left with many flowered fabric holdalls for Scotland one day.

After that she became subsumed in the life of The Centre naturally. People came and went and over the years the emphasis of what they did there changed. People with more urgent problems began to arrive. Then when Mercy was fifteen a couple came who wanted to rehab. Mercy instantly understood what needed to be done. Despite the fact that she still assiduously read her Bible every day she knew that prayer alone would not fix what was wrong with them. She took food to their rooms and quietly left it by their beds. She fetched bowls of warm water sweetened by geranium and lavender oils and sponged the sweat off their backs. She listened to them quietly, without interruption.

'You're an angel,' they murmured. 'You must be truly a real angel come to earth.'

Over the years Mercy evolved her own complex and self-taught system to aid recoveries. Plants and oils played their part, as did massage. From books and her own observations she learned those foods that heal and those that harm. Walking in the forest, sometimes in the early morning to witness the magnificence of the sunrise, sometimes by the light of the moon, played its role. Listening was the major part though. The pure and simple act of listening to another person and completely hearing what they were saying.

After that first couple it became known that Mercy worked with addictions, that she had an understanding of it, people seemingly felt able to tell her anything and this unburdening seemed to help them greatly. It was a talent that became called upon more and more as the years passed.

Now, as they sit on the windowsill Mercy wonders how many times a person can be born again and saved in one lifetime. She reaches out and takes one of Carmel's hands and feels that Carmel coming here today will save her somehow once again.

They are silent for a long time.

'What if you are the real deal? What if you are?'

'He was always trying to make me heal him but I never could and now I don't know what's true and what's not anymore.'

'But you thought you could with others?'

'I don't know. I thought I could.'

'Perhaps you were angry with him. Maybe deep down you knew he'd done something wrong?'

'Sometimes I hate him. Other times, and this seems a terrible thing, I kind of miss him. Right now I hate him though, leaving you for dead like that. But I've promised to see him one last time. It was an exchange for your story, that was the price.'

We are quiet for a long time watching the winter afternoon darken through the window. 'If you go, will you help me with something?' Mercy asks.

'Yes, anything.'

'I've wanted for a long time to know what happened to my ma and pa. I could've found out if I'd really wanted to, I guess, but I didn't. Something's always stopped me. I guess I didn't want to know because . . . because, well, I doubt they survived. Not knowing seemed better, more hopeful, but now you're here, maybe it's a sign . . .' Mercy bites her lip and goes to her chest of drawers and squats in front of it. She opens the bottom drawer and takes out something wrapped in a threadbare yellow silk scarf.

'What's that?'

Mercy sits back down and hands me a CD case. 'I've played it about a million times,' she says, 'but it still works.'

The plastic is so worn and scratched the cover inside is hard to see. I can just about make out the name of it.

'*Ray of Light*,' I read out loud.

Later I call Dad. 'Daddy.' I can't believe I called him that. I'm panting with emotion. 'Daddy, I am nearby and I've got something to ask. The thing is would it be at all, I mean would it be possible that I could come and stay with you for a while? Will you come and get me please, Daddy? Come and get me.'

Beth

Children slip through the cracks easily. So easily. I know.

We think they're all precious, coddled to their eyebrows, but it happens all the time. Look at Carmel, what happened to her. Look at the children that slip out of the care system, to reappear sporadically perhaps, or not. Look at the little girl that fell, or was pushed or perhaps dumped into the Thames and not seen again for three hundred and fifty years.

On the phone Carmel tells me about another one, the Mercy that she's been seeking. Now she's found her, her voice sounds different; there's something stronger and healthier about it.

'Mum, will you come and get me from Dad's?'

'You want to come home?'

'For a little while, but there's something I need to do. I need to talk to you about it.'

I haven't been to Paul and Lucy's new house yet. They've only just managed to move to somewhere bigger to stow their three kids in. I pull up and peer through the trees to the big brand-new brick house surrounded by its own garden. It's more her than him. My Paul was wilder than that, our house old and ramshackle. Or, I reflect now, perhaps that wasn't him either, maybe it was all my choice. Perhaps he just wants to please. I always used to feel dusty and untidy next to Lucy. God, how I hated her when he left me for her. How bitter my rivalry was. The little gym pig, I used to call her to my friends. The woman that likes nothing more than spending her Saturday cleaning out her nifty little car. The amount of make-up she wears, her face'd crack if she dared to have an expression. What a bitch I was. How kind she was to me. Then Carmel was taken and the unthinkable happened: we all became friends. They asked me to be godmother to their youngest and I was unbearably moved.

I manoeuvre the car up the drive and climb out. I spot Paul over the other side of the garden and raise my hand in a wave. He doesn't see me at first and I get to glimpse the thing that's the person when they don't know they're being looked at. I feel a rush of warmth for him; there's something about the angle of his shoulder going into his back that is suddenly old.

'Hey,' I shout, pulling off my bobble hat, static crackling round my head. 'Hey, Paul, over here.'

He looks up and smiles and leans on his rake and we regard each other for a moment. Old, old friends. Then Lucy is out and the kids surrounding her looking like they're on springs they're so exuberant and Carmel trails behind.

Carmel and I face each other across the lawn. The red of her coat almost hurts my eyes against the dull winter green of the grass.

'Hi, Mum.'

'Hello, Carmel.' I can't help sounding cold. Seeing her

now hunched in her red baggy zip-up with her hands deep in her pockets I feel fury at what she's put me through that I'm finding hard to repress. 'Are you still coming back with me?'

She smiles, looking contrite. 'If you'll have me.' And at that my fury dissolves.

After the cups of tea and looking at the kids' drawings and the gift of windfall apples from the garden we set off. I was so glad to see the huge hug she gave her father before we left even though in all this time there's never been one like that for me. Perhaps it's a sign that the barriers are finally starting to come down? It's been a horribly prickly relationship between them and I know Paul has been upset about it. As ever with Carmel, you don't give any indication of being pleased or not pleased about anything though in case it frightens her off.

It's beginning to get dark already and I hate driving in the fading light so I clutch the steering wheel and focus doggedly out of the window.

We're well out of town and in the silent lanes of Norfolk by the time she speaks.

'Mum, I want to say I'm sorry.'

'What for?'

I expect her to say, 'For putting you through all this worry again,' but instead there's a long silence before she says in a cracked voice, 'You know, for blaming you about what happened to me. I know it wasn't your fault now.'

I want to cry very hard now so I don't reply. I think, I need to stop the car – focus on that, Beth. The road ahead is blurring dangerously. I start driving at a crawl.

'The thing is . . .' she continues.

'Yes?'

I have the impression of her next to me, biting on her lip, frowning out into the fading light.

'The thing is I have to see him one more time. I've promised.'

'Who?'

'You *know*.'

The response of my muscles in my chest, in my shoulders, is as if tight-fitting armour has just been put on me. I slow down even more, aware of the way my hands might jerk at the steering wheel. Finally, there's a layby and I gently roll the car into it. I wipe my eyes and turn to face Carmel. Behind her, beyond the window, is an ancient hand-built stone wall. She doesn't turn to look at me. Her profile against the stone wall is carved, fierce.

'Carmel, you can't. Not after what he did to us, did to our family, to me, to *you*.'

'I have to.'

I hold on to the steering wheel and sink my face onto the backs of my hands. 'Please, please, this is impossible.' I'm whispering and I don't think she's heard me.

'Mum. I need your blessing. I need to know you'll still be OK with me if I do this.'

I lift my head up and we sit in silence for a long while. There's the sound of high-pitched shrieks somewhere in the field next to us, probably an owl snatching up some prey. I flinch. The sound is too prescient. Now only a sliver of yellowish light shows in the far horizon.

'Please,' says Carmel. Her voice is small and breathless

in the dark. 'I can't do it without your blessing but I have to do it.'

I switch the interior light on. She sits, her head slumped, looking at her open hands in her lap. I've made a decision.

'I will give you my blessing, but *you* have to promise me one thing.'

'Yes.'

'You have to promise me that I can come with you. I don't want to meet him but I want to come with you, to look after you. To make sure you're safe.'

'OK. There's another thing too.'

'What?'

'I'll need your help.'

'What d'you mean?'

'With, you know, organising it. You know I don't know how things work. I wouldn't know where to begin.'

I turn my face to the road.

'Mum, please?'

I grit my teeth and restart the car. 'Alright then. I guess so, yes.'

Of course, I know what she wants to do is impossible; they'll never let her in on a prison visit. But I make a promise that night as we drive through the dark roads back to London that I'll help her all I can. Systems and laws and computers still confound Carmel so I agree I'll start looking into it right away, knowing that what she proposes will never happen.

At home we have something else to do together. Fletcher – whose first name turned out to be Laurie, which is what I call him since we've begun to see each other a bit – has been in touch to say the Museum of London are putting the little skull on display for a few months and would we like to visit her? I find myself dressing carefully for the occasion – my best black shoes, my good coat – as if this visit is to honour her. Somehow her story feels as if it's become so wrapped up with ours, with Carmel's.

I notice Carmel's done the same. Unusually she's tied back her hair, which is generally a riot around her head. My heart – or the strange knotted thing that's in its place – turns over – again, yet again – at the sight of the haphazard ponytail.

'Ready?' I ask.

She nods. 'I guess.'

We ride in silence on the underground, sitting next to each other on the itchy nylon seating, the reflections of both our faces sliding and blinking on and off with the movement of the train.

At Barbican Station I say, 'We're here.'

It's a part of London I hardly ever come to, where all the bankers and financiers weave money from flashing screens into the night. But it's also home to the Brutalist development of the Barbican: a utopian vision containing flats, a theatre, walkways for rest and exercise in the open air, and the Museum of London.

It's very hard to find your way round and we get lost before we find the museum, which is almost tucked away.

I give our names at the desk and, as arranged, the deputy curator comes down to meet us.

'How lovely to meet you,' he says. 'I've been really

looking forward to it. I hope you think she'll be happy in her new home.'

I notice he calls the skull 'she' too. He's a gentle-looking man with intelligent brown eyes and a dark grey speckly suit that manages to look both serious and comfortable. I follow behind them as they chat and I hear him asking Carmel about the discovery, exactly where and in what conditions, although I can't catch her murmured responses.

The room that he takes us to is darkened save for a lit glass case in the middle. Beside me I hear Carmel gasp.

'I'll leave you to it,' says the curator tactfully. I suppose he above all others will know the power that objects can exert. 'I'm afraid we don't name individual mudlarkers in the museum display but we all know it as "Carmel's Skull". Um, if you know what I mean.' He disappears through the door.

We approach the glass case. 'There she is,' I say. Her skull is on black velvet. It's a rich caramel colour and has the lustrous gleam of a pearl. The graceful arch of her eye sockets show in stark contrast to the black. Next to it lies the fingertip and three small ribs.

'She's beautiful,' I say.

For a moment I think we're going to hold hands as we stand before the glass. But we don't, we don't. I put my hands in my coat pockets.

Carmel twists her shoulder up and rubs her cheekbone with it. 'I can't believe I thought it was Mercy's skull. Why would I think that? It makes no sense.'

'The brain tries to make connections. I guess it was just doing that. Mercy must have been very much on your mind to think it.'

She's silent for a second. 'Mum, I don't know what's been happening to me these last months.'

Very cautiously I ask, 'And where are you with it now?'

It takes her a long time to answer. 'I think I'm getting through it, bit by bit. I mean things are getting clearer, like when you're in a fog and start being able to see things again.'

Immediately, the dense fog on the day she was taken comes back to me but I stay silent.

Back on night shifts. Deep into winter now and it is always nearly black outside the hospital windows. I carry out my promise to help with the crazy idea of the visit and in my breaks begin researching. To my utmost horror I learn that it's not out of the question at all. It's up to the discretion of the prison governor. I resolve to write to him and tell him what a bad idea it is, why it should never happen, that my daughter needs protecting.

Carmel asks me all the time how it's going, what's happening and over cups of tea – she having just risen and me back from work – I say, 'It's up to the governor. I'll write to him today.'

She narrows her eyes at me. 'Give me the address. I'll write.'

So it goes on. Permission is granted and I find myself now having to look into all the details, checking and rechecking the paperwork, which is considerable. Filling in forms, organising our visas, studying the rules and regulations, and my fury mounts at every turn. I made a promise, I know, but having to actually facilitate this feels far too much.

I find out there is a strict dress code for prison visits: no hats or scarves can be worn, a skirt must not be wrap-around, sleeves must cover the arms. It terrifies her that she'll go all that way and at the last minute get turned back because of something she's forgotten or hasn't thought of so she asks me about it all the time. We agree that her mobile phone or anything else that might be in any way problematic will be left in the glove box of the hire car that I will be waiting in outside. All this I do through gritted teeth just as when I agreed to help, and all the time inside I'm screaming, *We should not be doing this.*

I insist that she visits the therapist she saw after she came back, and again when she was about fifteen and experiencing a difficult blip. She comes home after the session looking clearer, more focussed, and I'm glad about that and resist the urge to ask what they talked about under the guise of 'How did it go?'. Christmas comes and goes with us barely noticing, a few gaudy crackers, a nut roast and cranberry sauce. I give her a plain silver bangle that I think she will like because something in its surface has an appearance of an object that has spent time underwater. The heavy iron one she used to wear has gone who knows where but she says her wrist feels naked without it. She gifts me chopsticks because I've bought a Korean cook-book that I'm experimenting with. The chopsticks come with tiny carved wooden cats for them to rest on between mouthfuls.

I call Laurie and tell him what's happening and that we'll be back soon and he's worried about the both of us and I have to admit to myself that part of me finds that nice.

—

Then we are flying through the clouds, she and I.

I swore never to set foot in that land, that country that swallowed my daughter for all those years, but here I am, next to Carmel, who seems to have bought a new red coat for the occasion. Her shabby parka mac has disappeared and now she wears one that has a slight military air to it that reminds me a little bit of the one that she returned dressed in when she was thirteen years old. Perhaps she chose it because she feels she's going into battle.

She's gone back to work in the café for now. Sometimes she mentions someone called Rosie and there is a protective note to her voice when she does. I hear more about her life now than since she was a child, but I still don't know where she gets her clothes. This is not fashionable; it has an almost 1980s ring to it with its extravagant gold buttons. My guess is that she uses Army and Navy stores, second-hand places, old lady shops, nowhere that is too big or glittering or confusing. Nowhere where she'll feel lost and inadequate next to her contemporaries.

I smile at her. 'D'you want anything? The trolley will be coming back soon.'

'Are you going to have anything?'

'You know what? I'm going to have a glass of champagne if they've got it.'

'I'll have a Coke.'

We get our drinks and sit side by side sipping them, then I don't know if it's the fizzy white wine because they didn't have proper champagne, or the gentle bumping of the flight or the strain of these past months, but my eyelids begin to slip and I have the sensation I experienced before, eating marble cake in my kitchen. I have a strong sense of time as a woven piece, like a blanket. It's made of multicoloured threads: one is Carmel as a baby; another is my mum and dad waving at me as I learn to ride a bike; another is Paul and me walking in a wood, before she was born even, our feet pressing into the soft earth. All these threads are as one, woven together. They are happening at once so my hand is reaching out for Carmel's on the day she went missing and I'm cooking dinner for Paul and humming, waiting for him to come home, and I'm talking to the old lady's body on its hospital bed and again Carmel is gone, then she is gone and she is gone again.

I'm not quite asleep, although I can sense my head lolling to one side. A shower of sparks hails through the darkness and I startle before I realise it's a long-ago Bonfire Night and Paul sending rockets up into the air. The smooth leatherette of the arm rest under my fingers is the same one as the hairdresser's chair where I sat to have an expensive cut I couldn't afford before my wedding.

Then another one, that all the rest have been leading up to.

I'm on the pathway of our cottage in Norfolk. Paul is out, Carmel is a little girl. She's wearing a corduroy skirt that hangs unevenly around her knees and a hand-knitted jumper with blue stars across the chest.

I'm carrying the shopping. I'm flustered and holding too much. The path is wet. It's started raining again. I look up at the sky – is it beginning to get dark? I think, my shoes are stupid for this weather, thin leather soles, will I ever become a country girl? The path is wet. I'm on my back. There's sickening pain. I look down at my own body and it's a strange shape, in a kind of puzzle, knees at unnatural angles, something showing through the skin. The shopping is flung across the ground, bright oranges on the stone, getting wet. Carmel kneels next to me. Stupidly I say, 'Your tights!' but she ignores me and kneels anyway and I feel her hands on me, her whispered breath. The path is wet. Long moments pass then I get up. I feel shaky, but there is no pain, there is no bone sticking out where it shouldn't be, piercing through the skin like the metal in a car through the interior leather after a crash. I am intact; there is nothing. I think, I've had a hallucination, a waking fever dream; perhaps it was the shock of falling, the mind showing me something that wasn't there. There is still the shopping on the ground but before I pick it up, I turn to the little Carmel and say the exact same thing as I do now, to the grown-up one sitting next to me in the plane seat. I say:

'What happened?'

Carmel

2014

I was a set of Russian dolls for the longest time.

Deep inside there was the littlest doll who was solid all the way through. It wasn't me. It was something the preacher put there. He operated on me in the night and put a doll of himself in its place. I often saw phantasm surgery taking place in the churches, cutting into the body and operating on internal organs using only hands and without making a single incision. I used to suppose he'd done it like that.

When I came back from being away that doll gradually dissolved inside me. In its place was only emptiness, but the real Carmel doll is back. It might be only the size of a kernel right now, but I sense it growing.

The last thing I did before we left was throw the iron bangle back into the water. It gave me the strength to be a seeker perhaps but it's done its job and I don't want to be looking for the rest of my life. I stood on London Bridge with the crowds surging past me and flung it over the side for it to resume its journey, knowing it may never be found again.

Wisconsin is as flat as Norfolk but unlike the place of my birth it is vast. The fields go on and on and the roads and the telegraph wires stretch ahead into the horizon. We're parked up on a dirt track just off the road and the sky is a strange, solid white.

Mum is looking at the prison with terror on her face. The building looks like a huge animal, a grey beast with frills of razor wire. I used to growl at things she was afraid of when I was a child but I too am afraid now and the growl won't come.

'Don't you worry about me,' I say, but we're both transfixed by the sight and I can't move.

'It goes without saying, you don't have to do this.'

I reply by stowing my phone in the glove box. Then I take off my new silver bangle and put that in there too. I don't know if wearing it matters but I'm erring on the safe side.

Mum starts tucking her hair behind her ears like she always does when she's nervous. 'Listen. I will be right here the whole time. I'm not going to move a muscle. The *whole time*, you hear me?'

I open the door and the cold hits me. It's bitter. I get out and start walking. Just put one foot in front of the other, I tell myself.

Then the beast opens up and swallows me.

My paperwork is minutely checked and rechecked, alongside five other visitors. None of us look at each other. Then the building takes me deeper and deeper inside itself through clanging metal doors and concrete-floored corridors, until I feel I'm entering its heart, its belly. The smell of its guts claws to the back of my throat and makes me want to gag. I guess it must be the smell of people caged up together.

I've been led through so many doors I've lost count and I start to panic. He must be close. I can feel him nearby, tuning to me, waiting, muscles and sinews straining in anticipation. I'm panting under my breath, *I can't, I can't, I can't*, but no sound comes and no one can hear me.

I turn to tell the prison guard I've changed my mind, I can't go through with it, but already I'm being ushered into another room with the other visitors, each one – like I'm sure I have – with a shuttered-up face.

Inside is a row of booths with plastic screens.

I see him through the plastic.

He's mouthing something, his face red and furious. Moments pass and I realise he is shouting, but the plastic means I cannot hear the words.

My legs are trembling as I walk over, draw out the metal chair and sit.

I point to the phone on the table in front of him and pick up the receiver of the one in front of me. He speaks and it comes at me like the snap and crackle of electricity.

'You're late.'

His voice.

So familiar yet tuned to a different frequency now some-how. I close my eyes so I can't see him and press the receiver against the side of my face. What I see instead is the thin, crispy pages of a Bible. Water, parting in front of me as I wade in, my white dress rising around me like a cloud. I hear the rumble of our truck.

Then right in my ear, like a sharp metal object is being inserted there: 'Well, say something, child. Do not sit in stone-cold silence like that after being late.'

I open my eyes. His blue ones bulge outwards. His forehead is mottled red and white like marbled meat.

'Calm down,' I say.

I hear his urgent breathing through the phone.

'Calm down right now or I'm walking out of here.'

He wipes his mouth with the back of his hand, nods.

I focus on slowing my breathing. In through the nose, out through the mouth, like I've been taught. The churning waters gradually still, become ripples. I realise my gaze has been blurred when it suddenly sharpens, the edges of his face hardening. Something reminds me of a painting, a portrait of a face that has become cracked and dusty. What comes out of my mouth next surprises me.

'I need to look at you,' I say.

I find I want to study him. Through the plastic it's strange, but it means I can look as long as I want, observe like looking into an aquarium. I take my time. And it's a shock to me, because even through the plastic I can see he is not made of animal bones, or pins or glass. He is not a sea beast or a river worm. He does not have light spilling out of him, or even darkness; he is only cracked flesh stretched out over human bones.

He's older, of course, and his skin has coarsened. His hair is thinner and meticulously brushed back from his face, like he's spent careful time getting ready to see me. His eyes are the same bright, bright blue but thick threads of red are criss-crossing the white bits all over now.

For a second I catch something else. There is something trying to slip off of him. It's like a layer of skin, or a shell. What's inside is loose and working to break free.

He stays quiet, his eyelids half down, as if he's allowing me to look, waiting.

I sit back in my chair and the curly wire of the phone extends.

'You are the same, but different,' I say finally, quietly.

He nods. 'Time spent here will of course wreak its havoc.'

I shrug. I want it to mean, *what do I care?*

I think he understands this because his jaw sets a fraction harder. He never did like being defied or dismissed, and for a moment my legs start trembling again and I feel panicky. I lay the phone down and put my hands on my knees to still them. When I look up again, he has his head tilted to one side. I pick up the receiver.

'Alright. We can speak now.'

He leans forward. 'Your gift, child. Your gift. Are you using it wisely?' He says it slowly but he cannot keep the urgency out of his voice, the greed.

'Is that all you're interested in?'

'No, but—'

'It was nothing to do with you, you know. You didn't *cultivate* me like I was in a Petri dish, if that's what you think.'

He wipes his mouth with the back of his hand again. I'm not behaving like he expected.

'I don't want to talk about that yet. Firstly, I want to talk about something else. I want to talk about the terrible thing you wrought on my life and my mum and my dad's lives.'

He blinks rapidly. 'Child, we are short of time . . .'

'You left our lives in ribbons and for what?'

'Is that all you came here to say?' This isn't going to plan for him.

327

I catch that thing that is trying to come away from him again. I close my eyes; it's confusing me, interfering in what I wanted to say. I think of all the oyster shells I've found in the river; the insides and outsides were once a piece, the shell growing layer by layer around the creature until the thing inside was picked out by the tip of a knife and the two parted company. I shake my head. I need to focus.

'We made a pact, child. You came here with a promise.'

I look down at the empty hollow of my left hand on the fake wood plastic it rests on. I think of what Mum told me on the plane. 'It's something that was strong in me when I was a child. Now, I don't know. I think it comes and goes but I don't know.'

'See, I was right . . .'

My hands ball into fists. I hiss at him, 'Who knows, perhaps you destroyed it just like you did my parents' life.'

He was about to say something, but he closes his mouth.

'I decided on something on my journey here. It's something I only came to understand after I left.'

'Our time . . .'

'Please,' I say, closing my eyes again to blot him out; I've rehearsed all this. 'When you talk you make me forget what I have to say.'

I open my eyes again. He's listening. 'See, I thought of something on the plane. Travelling is good like that. It shakes things out of your head that could've got stuck.'

I spread my free hand wide on the counter in front and flex my fingers.

'For a long time I haven't known what to do, who to be. I tried to forget about everything that happened, about you. I tried to make it like a strange dream I'd woken up from that I could forget about. But it didn't work; the dream has gone through and through me.'

He nods like he understands.

'When I was little, my mum used to tell me that if I wanted to look at something, something that maybe frightened me, I should see it like a snow globe or a story, and I could hold it in my hand and tip it one way or the other and be able to look inside without it ever being able to touch me.'

I can see him blinking through the screen; he may be behind plastic but I'm not sure if he's really in that snow globe yet. I shiver slightly and plough on.

'So I've decided I'm going to put it all in the snow globe. Everything. The hospitals. The sick people. The roads. The . . . the . . .'

There's tears dripping off my face now. I let them splash onto the fake wood.

'Everything. I'm going to write it all down so it's all there, inside the globe. And I know that means it won't be gone, but I think other people might be interested in knowing about it too.'

Finally, I scrub my face with my palm.

The phone has dropped away from his mouth and he moves it back. 'You're going to write about *me* . . .'

'Yes. I will write every day and in the evening I will cook over a fire.'

'As simple as that?'

'Yes, as simple as that.'

Silence, then: 'Why are you telling me this? You shouldn't

go saying things about me, writing things about me. That's not why you're here.'

'You see, I think it is, although I didn't realise when I came. A woman called Kay tried to tell my story once, but it wasn't her story to tell. Or rather, she didn't tell it very well and got frightened by it because it was too much.'

I smile, but not at him. I'm closing my eyes and smiling because for the first time since I was eight years old I feel something clearing.

When I open my eyes and look at him again the preacher has his head in his hand. I can see the pink scalp beneath the strands of white hair. I see the thing loose in him again, the oyster shell. I see it's slipping off. It's tacked on loosely but it's persistent. I realise then what it is. It's his life.

I lean forward as close as I can to the plastic screen. I'm so close my breath mists onto it as I speak. 'I believe, if I try to lay hands on you, that truly something will happen in the night. I do not think you will wake.'

He stays silent for long moments then almost imperceptibly nods, a tiny gesture, and I hold my hand up and it seems to hover for a moment like a bird. He puts his against the dirty plastic. I can see his lifelines pressed up there, the callus on the base of his thumb. I press my own against it and I do not move my gaze and I do not for one second waver.

Beth

Was that the hardest thing I've ever done?

As I watched her walk down the asphalt road towards the main prison gates, she was a tiny figure in red, dwarfed against the grey monolith of the prison. She became smaller and smaller and then was swallowed by the building. I looked down and saw I was holding the steering wheel so hard my knuckles had turned white.

When she reappears I can breathe again.

She walks much slower as she makes the return to the car. Her feet drag behind her. I swear she looks thinner inside her coat than she did when she went in.

She climbs in the car. I look at her profile. She looks awful, sunken and hollowed out. Something is over and it's exhausted her, drained every last drop.

She says, 'Could we just drive in the car for a bit?'

I start the engine and we roll off without a word. We've also come to the end of something, she and I although I don't yet understand what it is.

I drive with no destination in mind. There's a bluish tinge to the sky. Soon, the roads narrow and we find ourselves in country lanes, flat fields as far as the eye can see. Barns made of corrugated iron present their flat angles to the fading light so the gable end stands out dramatically. There seems a hush over the land. Not a soul in sight.

'Can we stop for a bit?' she asks.

I find a farm entrance and pull into it. The scale of this place is so vast the farmhouse is nowhere to be seen. I press the button to make the electric window go down. In our insulated bubble a miraculous gust of country air enters, earth-sweetened, speckled with needles of ice that feel like a balm on the skin of my face.

'Good Lord,' I murmur. 'I'd no idea it was so beautiful here.'

My mind's grasping back for something, a poem.

I recite the verse that I remember, for the distraction as much as anything else.

'Sometimes, riding in a car, in Wisconsin
Or Illinois, you notice those dark telephone poles
One by one lift themselves out of the fence line
And slowly leap on the gray sky –
And past them the snowy fields.'

We're staying on for a while, travelling around the States for a bit. I'm glad we decided that now with the enchantment of this place. She's keen to show me something of her former home that I know nothing about and I know enough to realise this is another big step for us too.

I stop, glance at her. 'You look tired.' It's an understatement. She looks on the brink of collapse.

She doesn't answer and I have the sense of her protecting

me from things. I've never realised she did that before.

'You don't have to . . . you don't have to keep things from me to protect me. I mean, do it if you want to, but not to protect me.'

'Maybe.'

The ice seems to intensify in the air.

'Let's get out,' she says.

We climb out and stand side by side on the road. A country road, with dark telephone poles stretching into the distance. Cold twilight settling round us, the light tinged a greyish pink. Flakes of snow begin to fall. They land on her hair, on her red coat. She flexes her hands and looks into them.

'It was so strange seeing him like that, his face behind plastic.' She stops and almost smiles to herself. 'I'd always thought of him as not being like anyone else, being made of glass or metal or something, but seeing him just now it was like that bit in *The Wizard of Oz* when the screen is taken down.'

'And there's only a funny little man behind it?'

She looks up and scans the darkening sky. 'No, not even that. I can't even explain; more like something human, made of flesh, and old, so much older.'

Her face looks like bone in the fading light.

'Mum,' she cries out.

'What is it?'

'Hold me, Mum, hold me.'

She falls into my arms. We do not move; we hold each other and I feel something happen to my heart. The tightly wound bobbin catches and it's painful; it's like a fish being tugged on a nylon line, a barb in its mouth. Then a hatch opens in my chest and the thread pokes out like a tongue; it looks out into the world and starts unspooling.

I feel drops of something cold on my hands and look down and see the snow on them.

Once upon a time, a girl child was born.

That morning the light flowing through the window of the maternity ward was white and tasted of silver. There was something extraordinary about this girl, the mother knew straight away. Oh, every mother thinks that, she told herself, but in her heart she knew her first thought was the true one, that this child had something exceptional about her. The mother counted all the baby's arms and legs, her belly button and her vagina and anus, her eyes and nose, her ears, then her fingers and toes, her nails on the ends of those toes and fingers, and then counted them all again.

On that day with that strange and particular light, that sometimes appeared to have sparkles in it, a deep and pervasive worry began inside the mother that started to grow like she'd swallowed an apple pip and a tree had taken root in her stomach and was now slowly pushing up its slender branches into her diaphragm, her chest, her throat. 'I will never let anything bad happen to you,' she whispered to the wrapped bundle. And she meant it.

The girl child seemed to know something she didn't because after the mother lowered her back into her plastic cot, the baby continued to watch her mother through the clear plastic side as if she had a question to ask, but would need to grow up and gain language before she could articulate it. The mother lay on her side, her belly loose and empty from the recent pregnancy and told herself she was imagining things.

After she took her child home the worry tree inside her grew faster. Time and again she put her fingers in front of the little mouth to check her baby's breathing. As the girl child grew, she seemed to be always tumbling away from her mother. The mother tried not to show it but she was only really happy when the girl child was in her sights, very close by. The sense that something bad was going to happen got bigger and bigger as time went on and the worry tree grew until its branches finally reached her brain. Sometimes the mother told herself, if her daughter was an ordinary little girl, she wouldn't fret so much. But she wasn't ordinary. Everyone felt it, not just the mother. Some people said she was simply wise beyond her years or perhaps she was an old soul that had walked the earth before, all sorts of nonsense. But almost everyone felt there was something special about her, even if they kept quiet about it.

As time went on the nagging, needling concerns of the mother began to have a malign effect. The child was always being told to stay where she was, or in sight, or being asked not to run in case she ran and ran and didn't stop running until she was a red dot on the horizon. The girl naturally began to resent it and feel her mother was spying on her. Sometimes, the girl purposely gave her mother the slip.

Then one day the thing happened that the mother thought about all the time and dreaded most in the world – when she was only eight years old, her little girl disappeared. In her grief, and because the mother had thought about this exact scenario so frequently, had even woven scenes in her head where such a bad thing occurred, the mother began to ask herself certain questions over and over again. These questions included: Was the fact that my daughter vanished really my fault? Did I make it happen by the way I behaved with her? Did I in actual fact make what happened come true by imagining it so often – did I will it into existence? These things, of course, were very painful ideas to think about.

Five long years the girl was away. The mother became thin and mourned her daughter every hour of every day. Her dreams were full of the presence of her child and she had to wake every morning and learn over again that she was gone. The house was haunted with memories of the girl but the mother was compelled to stay within its walls in case the little girl somehow found her way home. After all, what would happen if she returned and the house was empty? She may become lost again.

Then, like some miracle, her daughter was returned from a distant land where she'd been kept. The mother rejoiced. But it soon became clear that this girl who had come back to her was not the same girl who had been ripped from her bosom. It wasn't only that the girl had grown and was on the cusp of womanhood now, and all this happened in a twinkling of an eye. No, it's that the girl seemed another person altogether; the mother barely recognised her at all and they lived as strangers. The mother even sometimes wondered if a changeling had landed on her doorstep, that

*she'd been replaced by someone else and her daughter was
still out there somewhere, lost.*

*It made the woman realise how change can happen all
the time, often quickly, and when your back is turned. The
apple in the bowl suddenly has stippled white rot on its
underside. A stone in an old ring the colour of a raincloud
is polished up and turns into a razor-bright diamond. A
friend, who you thought you knew, does something inex-
plicable, wounding, and to you they become a different
person. Where there was a boy alone, a girl alone, now
there are clasped hands and already – so soon! – the bud of
a baby pressing into the world.*

*A red hood is pulled back and there are furry ears being
ruffled by the wind where once a human head was. The being
inside changed when you turned your back for a moment.*

After a long time, my daughter and I gradually unfurl. Her
face is a little less pale now, slightly more healthy-looking.

'I want to give,' she says. 'I want to help but I no longer
know how to.'

'There are many ways of doing that,' I murmur.

She looks again up at the sky. 'Perhaps I should get rid of
this red coat.'

'Really?'

'Look, I could throw it up onto the power lines like the
gangs do with their shoes.' She points up.

We both contemplate the idea. It would look so dramatic
hanging there, like a battle flag in this luminous landscape,
like the rag held out to the bull.

'Perhaps you really should.'

She shoves her hands in her pockets. 'I think I'll keep it for a bit. Besides, it's freezing. I'll be OK now, Mum.' She tips her face to the sky and lets the snow fall onto it 'It's so beautiful here, so, so beautiful.' She laughs. 'Perhaps we should stay in this spot forever!'

But the night is racing towards us and the snow is falling and she takes my hand which is freezing now. 'Come on,' she says. 'Let's get you warmed up.'

Oh, my darling, I think; my dandy, my lion, my Joan of Arc. I knew so much about you, that you were somehow different, you were special, but what I don't know, my little lion, and want to ask is – how you came to be so brave?

Epilogue

No one ever knew what happened to Mercy Roberts.

Although after she left her Appalachian home and had been gone a good while she still sometimes drifted through people's thoughts like a trail of smoke from a bonfire.

Sheila from 'The Cherry on the Cake' bakery store would insert her tongue delicately but precisely in the mauve buttercream of one of her own blueberry cupcakes, making a perfect triangular groove. She would look out through the window onto their single main street as the sweet gloop dissolved in her mouth and remember how Mercy was also particularly partial to blueberry cupcakes.

Tony, a man now, thought of her as he threaded bait on his fishing line because he'd shown her how to do the exact same thing down at the pond. The image of her thin, little arms as she threw the line and it wicking across the surface of the water was a stamp in his memory. She'd turned to him, beaming, because she'd done it perfect first time.

Bob, in the grocery store, would occasionally shift on his feet uncomfortably as he stood behind the counter, and remember her high five, her funny little eyebrows like window arches rising up as she performed it. He should've paid closer attention, he rebuked himself. He shouldn't have been so worried about interfering. But his wife had been sick with cancer at the time and although she'd now made a full recovery, he'd been too distracted to pay much attention. Besides, the town had changed so much. New people had come, old people had gone, everything shifting into fresh patterns so the place that Mercy had filled became smaller and smaller, less significant.

Miss Forbouys, with her rows of little ones in the classroom, would sometimes think of Mercy when she carried out her customary practice of putting some music on the old-fashioned record player at the end of each day when she was tired to the bone. She remembered how Mercy always did love the devotional music in particular, even though Miss Forbouys wasn't sure if she was really allowed to play it in school. But heck, music was music and her children should be introduced to all the good things in the world, wherever they sprang from. How Mercy had loved it, her little feet in their shoes with cut-off toes tapping away under her desk in time to the rhythm.

Miss Forbouys would at this point give a shake of her head. At least she'd had nothing to do with it all, she told herself. Something had stopped her becoming part of the whole enterprise and she was glad of it now. *That* she couldn't have lived with.

Of course, the one person who never forgot Mercy is her mother. Delia is now clean but suffers from the complications of over two decades of heroin addiction. First one of her veins collapsed, then another; this led to smaller veins trying to take over the same function and this in turn affected her heart alongside causing numbness in her limbs. She is often slow and breathless and walks with the aid of crutches.

Her husband, Colm, has been dead for three years now. In the end heroin killed him but in a roundabout way. He liked to take night-time rambles when he was high and the country roads he frequented were often not lit. The sight of a four-by-four with extra lights and bull bars transfixed him for a moment too long and he didn't get out of the way in time. Inside the vehicle, the driver hardly felt the bump but to his credit still stopped to investigate and found Colm's body flung into the bushes like a rag doll.

Delia has left Broke Moon House. It's empty and now slowly crumbles into the ground. If anyone climbed the ladder to what used to be Mercy's bedroom, they would still find her bed roll on the platform bed and her pink shoes on the floor with the toes pointing towards the window although everything is covered in a thin layer of green mould. The toadstools on the window ledge now riot across the skirting board.

Delia lives in a tiny flat in an assisted-living building made of breeze blocks on the outskirts of town. Slowly, her emotions have returned to her which were once numbed by morphia. They seem to arrive one at a time, distinct from each other. One day it is anger at her mother: she never wanted any of her girls to make anything of themselves, only the boys; she wanted her girls to stay right where they were so they could look after her. Delia may have not escaped very far but the very fact that she had exerted a high price. She'd been far too young and at sea to handle it, and had nowhere, really, to go. Then another day the power of first love came to Delia, the day she'd met Colm, and the full pleasure and pain of it rang through her as if she was living through it again before subsiding, leaving only the memory of their lives together, their love, like the tolling of a bell that continues ringing in the ears after it's silent.

The one thing that is always there and does not come and go is Mercy, Mercy, Mercy. Sometimes it's a background drip and other times it rages through her and she knows there is nothing she can do but give herself up to it. One day, she resolves, she will try and find out what happened. All avenues seem closed to her; the town, the law appear disinterested. Who was she anyway? An ex-junkie with a boyfriend who'd turned himself into roadkill. People – if they considered it at all – thought Mercy had got away, that she was using her talents to wow people in the rest of the world and perhaps one day she would return triumphant.

There is something Delia is so ashamed of she's pushed it to the back of her mind every time it bobs to the surface. It was back when she and Colm had been really high one day some cops had come to talk to her. They'd told them that Mercy's passport had been used in the case of a kidnapping but the perpetrator had shut as tight as a clamshell about it, said he didn't know, couldn't remember anything.

Delia and Colm couldn't wait to get the cops out of there. The effort of talking to them as if they weren't out of their minds was exhausting and when they'd gone they both heaved a sigh of relief and took out the tinfoil from where they'd hidden it under the sofa. But Delia didn't forget and often wonders if they were special police, like the FBI or something, a fact she might have blanked out because it scared her so much. Now somewhere deep inside herself Delia has resolved, when she doesn't feel quite so sick and so hopeless, that she will find out. When she has the where-withal, she will take after Mercy like an avenging angel and find her. One day, she tells herself, one day soon I'm gonna feel strong enough.

It's Thursday morning when she takes her crutches and goes to buy bread and tinned spaghetti at the Piggly Wiggly store in the high street. The crutches press painfully into her armpits; her whole body is tender like this, as if a single, light touch would leave a bruise the size of a dinner plate. She has her rucksack strapped to her back for her purchases. Today, she is feeling a little stronger, harder around the edges; her heart is ticking at a steadier rate than it does normally. That's until she sees the figure ahead of her. Then it begins racing at double time.

The high street ends in an upward slope more or less where the two rows of opposite facing shops end, so the figure in the distance almost appears to be looking down from a height. Delia's eyesight has also been affected by the years of substance abuse and she squints to try and see better and puts her hand over her chest to stop the feeling that her heart is going to burst out onto the pitted road in front of her and flop around her feet. It's a woman, a young woman, the age Mercy would be. There is a head of thick curls outlined against the chilly blue sky.

'Oh my God,' she whispers, and one of her crutches falls to the floor.

—

Almost exactly three minutes beforehand Carmel had been inside Laura's diner.

'I'm looking for Delia Roberts,' she'd said to the woman behind the counter in a pink and white nylon uniform.

Laura's natural instinct was to tell her nothing. This woman was a stranger and therefore suspect but there was something about the girl's hazel eyes, something so inherently humble and good about her, that all of those natural instincts fell out of the door.

'Who's asking, honey?'

'My name's Carmel Wakeford.'

Laura happened to glance out of the window. 'Why, you're in luck,' she said. 'She's coming right up this road. Look there's Delia, God bless her poor soul.'

Carmel followed Laura's gaze and saw a woman with a red kerchief tied around her head hobbling along the high street.

'Thanks,' she said to the woman in the diner. 'Have a great day.'

As Carmel approaches Delia she takes her in in all her bravery and brokenness. There are the crutches, yes, there are the thin legs that look like they might snap with every step, but there's also the red kerchief around the head. There's the turquoise shine on her eyelids the colour of a mermaid's tail.

Carmel bends and retrieves the crutch and gently slides it back under Delia's armpit. Delia is pale with emotion.

'Mercy?' she asks. 'Is that you?'

Carmel shakes her head. 'My name's Carmel. Carmel Wakeford, but I have something for you.'

Inside her bag is a piece of folded paper. Carmel knows what is written inside it because she helped Mercy pen it that day at The Centre. It says:

Dear Ma and Pa
If this finds you at all I hope it finds you well. I want you to know I'm alright. It's been such a very long time, hasn't it? Yet I think of you near every day and hope the old racoon is keeping up his visits. If he's still around he must have a white pelt by now.
Well, I have included my address and my number at the top and would sure love to hear your voices again or get a letter from you.
Your dearest Mercy.

That's not what Carmel gives Delia first though. She delves into the satchel on her hip and draws out the *Ray of Light* CD and holds it out to the other woman who takes it in her long fingers, standing on one leg and propped up by her crutches. For a long time Delia turns the plastic case over and over in her hands, as if it is a relic that has been lost at sea, tossed and turned and has finally jumped out of the turmoil of the waves right into her hands, scratched and worn from its journey.

Acknowledgements

My huge thanks go to my editor Louisa Joyner and also to the wonderful Libby Marshall and Sara Helen Binney for their dedicated, creative and inspired work on the book. As ever huge thanks to my lovely agent, the talented Alice Lutyens, and everyone at Curtis Brown. To the publicity director Sophie Portas, the whole sales team and everyone beyond at Faber & Faber – thank you! Many thanks also to Hayley Shepherd for her brilliant copy-editing, likewise Jodi Gray for her proofreading and Joanna Harwood, Faber's project editor extraordinaire!

Thanks also to Penny, Hugh and Patrick Brown for their gift of real pipe stems mudlarked from the river Thames to be sent as gifts to first readers, very much appreciated!

I want to take this opportunity to send special and heartfelt thanks to readers – I honestly believe a book is reborn every time it is read and this one, like the others, will take on a new life.

Thank you to my husband for your unfailing support.

Read on for the first three chapters of

The Girl in the Red Coat

The bestseller that began Carmel and Beth's story

1

I dream about Carmel often. In my dreams she's always walking backwards.

The day she was born there was snow on the ground. A silvery light arced through the window as I held her in my arms.

As she grew up I nicknamed her 'my little hedge child'. I couldn't imagine her living anywhere but the countryside. Her thick curly hair stood out like a spray of breaking glass, or a dandelion head.

'You look like you've been dragged through a hedge backwards,' I'd say to her.

And she would smile. Her eyes would close and flutter. The pale purple-veined lids like butterflies sealing each eye.

'I can imagine that,' she'd say finally, licking her lips.

I'm looking out of the window and I can almost see her – in those tights that made cherry liquorice of her legs – walking up the lane to school. The missing her feels like my throat has been removed.

Tonight I'll dream of her again, I can feel it. I can feel her in the twilight, sitting up on the skeined branches of the beech tree and calling out. But at night in my sleep she'll be walking backwards towards the house – or is it away? – so she never gets closer.

Her clothes were often an untidy riot. The crotch of her winter tights bowed down between her knees so she'd walk like a penguin. Her school collar would stick up on one side and be buried in her jumper on the other. But her mind was a different matter – she knew what people were feeling. When Sally's husband left her, Sally sat in my kitchen drinking tequila as I tried to console her. Salt and lime and liquor for a husband. Carmel came past and made her fingers into little sticks that she stuck into Sally's thick brown hair and massaged her scalp. Sally moaned and dropped her head backwards.

'Oh my God, Carmel, where did you learn to do that?'

'Hush, nowhere,' she whispered, kneading away.

That was just before she disappeared into the fog.

Christmas 1999. The children's cheeks blotched pink with cold and excitement as they hurried through the school gates. To me, they all looked like little trolls compared to Carmel. I wondered then if every parent had such thoughts. We had to walk home through the country lanes and already it was nearly dark.

It was cold as we started off and snow edged the road. It glowed in the twilight and marked our way. I realised I was balling my hands in tight fists inside my pockets with worries about Christmas and no money. As I drew my hands out into the cold air and uncurled them Carmel fell back and I could hear her grumbling behind me.

'Do hurry up,' I said, anxious to get home out of the freezing night.

'You realise, Mum, that I won't always be with you,' she

said, her voice small and breathy in the fading light.

Maybe my heart should have frozen then. Maybe I should have turned and gathered her up and taken her home. Kept her shut away in a fortress or a tower. Locked with a golden key that I would swallow, so my stomach would have to be cut open before she could be found. But of course I thought it meant nothing, nothing at all.

'Well, you're with me for now.'

I turned. She seemed far behind me. The shape of her head was the same as the tussocky tops of the hedges that closed in on either side.

'Carmel?'

A long plume of delicate ice breath brushed past my coat sleeve.

'I'm here.'

Sometimes I wonder if when I'm dead I'm destined to be looking still. Turned into an owl and flying over the fields at night, swooping over crouching hedges and dark lanes. The smoke from chimneys billowing and swaying from the movement of my wings as I pass through. Or will I sit with her, high up in the beech tree, playing games? Spying on the people who live in our house and watching their comings and goings. Maybe we'll call out to them and make them jump.

We were single mothers, almost to a man – as one of the group once joked. We clustered together in solidarity of our status. I think now maybe it was not good for Carmel, this band of women with bitter fire glinting from their eyes and rings. Many evenings we'd be round the kitchen table and it would be *then he, then he, then he*. We were all hurt in some way, bruised inside. Except for Alice who had real bruises. After Carmel had gone – oh, a few months or so – Alice came to the house.

'I had to speak to you,' she said. 'I need to tell you something.'

Still I imagined anything could be a clue to the puzzle.

'What is it? What is it?' I asked, frantically clutching at the neck of my dressing gown. What she told me disappointed me so much I turned my face away and looked at the empty shell of the egg I'd eaten yesterday on the kitchen drainer. But when she started to tell me my daughter had a channel to God and could be now at His right hand – how I hated her then. Her false clues and her finding of Jesus, those wrists in identical braided bracelets turning as she spoke. I could stay silent no longer.

'Stop it!' I yelled. 'Get out of here. I thought you had something real to tell me. Get out of this house and leave me alone, you stupid cow. You crazy stupid cow. Take your God with you and don't ever come back.'

Sometimes, just before I fall asleep, I imagine crawling inside the shell of Carmel's skull and finding her memories there. Peering through her eye sockets and watching the film of her life unfold through *her* eyes. Look, look: there's me and her father, when we were together. Carmel's still small so to her we seem like giants, growing up into the sky. I lean down to pick her up and empty nursery rhymes into her ear.

And there's that day out to the circus.

We have a picnic by the big top before we go in. I spread

out the blanket on the grass, so I don't notice Carmel turn her head and see the clown peering from between the tent flaps. His face has thick white make-up with a big red mouth shape drawn on. She puzzles why his head is so high up because his stilts are hidden by the striped tent flap. He looks briefly up at the sky to check the weather, then his red-and-white face disappears back inside.

What else? Starting school, me breaking up with Paul and throwing his clothes out of the bedroom window. She must have seen them from where she was in the kitchen – his shirts and trousers sailing down. Other things, how many memories even in a short life: seeing the sea, a day paddling in the river, Christmas, a full moon, snow.

Always I stop at her eighth birthday and can go no further. Her eighth birthday, when we went to the maze.

2

For my eighth birthday I want to go and see a maze.

'Carmel. What do you know about mazes?' Mum says.

If I think hard I can see a folded puzzle in my mind that looks like a brain.

'I've heard things,' I say. And Mum laughs and says OK.

We don't have a car so we go on the bus, just the two of us. The windows are steamed up so I can't see where we're going. Mum's got on her favourite earrings which are like bits of glass except colours sparkle on them when she moves.

I'm thinking about my birthday, which was last Thursday, and now it's Saturday and I'm thinking about how my friend gets cards and presents from her nan but Mum doesn't talk to her mum and dad even though they're still alive. I don't mind so much about the cards and presents but I'd like to know what they look like.

'Mum, have you got a photo of your mum and dad?'

Her head shoots round and the earrings flash pink and yellow lights. 'I'm not sure. Maybe, why?'

'I just wonder what they look like sometimes and if they look like me.' It's more than sometimes.

'You look like your dad, sweetheart.'

'But I'd like to know.'

She smiles. 'I'll see what I can do.'

When we get off the bus the sky is white and I'm so excited to see a real maze I run ahead. We're in this big park and mist is rolling around in ghost shapes. There's a huge grey house with hundreds of windows that are all looking at us. I can tell Mum's scared of the house so I growl at it. Sometimes she's scared of everything, Mum – rivers, roads, cars, planes, what's going to happen and what's not going to happen.

But then she laughs and says, 'I'm such a silly old thing.'

Now we're at the top of this hill and I can see the maze below and it *does* look like a brain. I think it's really funny I've thought about a brain inside my brain and try to explain but I don't do it very well and I don't think Mum really gets it. But she's nodding and listening anyway and standing there with her long blue coat all wet from the grass at the bottom. She says, 'That's very interesting, Carmel.' Though I'm not sure she really understood, but Mum always tries to. She doesn't just ignore you like you're just a mouse or a bat.

So we go in.

And I know all of a sudden it's a place I love more than anywhere I've ever been. The green walls are so high the sky's in a slice above me and it's like being in a puzzle but in a forest at the same time. Mum says the trees are called yew, and spells it out because I laugh and ask, you? I run on ahead down the path in the middle where the grass is squashed into a brown strip and Mum's far behind me now. But it doesn't matter because I know how mazes work and that even if I lose her, we'll find each other sooner or later.

I carry on round corners and each place looks the same. Bright red berries pop out of the green walls and birds fly over my head. Except I don't see them fly from one side of the sky to the other – they're above the high green walls so I only see them for a second and then they're gone.

I hear someone on the other side of the wall.

'Carmel, is that you?'

And I say no even though I know it's my mum – it doesn't sound quite like her.

She says, 'Yes it is, I know it's you because I can see your red tights through the tree.'

But I don't want to go so I just slip away quietly. It starts getting dark, but I still feel at home in this place. Now, it's more like a forest than a maze. The tops of the trees stretch up, up and away, and get higher, like the dark's making them grow. There's some white flowers gleaming and once I see a piece of rope hanging from a branch, I think maybe a child like me used it as a swing. It's in the middle of a path and I go right up to it so my nose is nearly touching the frayed bit at the end and it twists and turns in the breeze like a worm. Dark green smells are all around and birds are singing from the middle of the walls.

I decide to lie under a tree to rest on the soft brown earth because I feel tired and dreamy now. The smell of the earth comes up where I'm squashing it and it smells dark and sweet. Something brushes across my face and I think it's an old leaf because it feels dead and scrapy.

The birds don't sound like they're singing now, more like chatting, and the breeze is making the trees rustle. And I hear my mother calling me but she sounds just like the rustling and the birds and I know I should answer her but I don't.

3

I ran down hallways of yew. Each one looked the same and at the end, every time, I turned a corner to see another endless green corridor in front of me. As I ran I shouted, 'Carmel, Carmel – where are you?'

Eventually, when there was only enough light to just about see I stumbled on the entrance. I could see the big grey house through the gap and the front door looked like a mouth that was laughing at me.

Across the field was the man who had taken our money, leaving. He was walking towards the brow of the hill and already a long way from the house.

'Please, come back.' My ragged shout didn't feel like it had come from me.

He hadn't heard. The sound was swept up by the wind and carried away in the other direction. Only crows answered me with their caws.

I began running towards him, shouting. He seemed to be walking very fast and his figure was disappearing into the last of the light.

Finally he must have caught my cries and I saw him stop and turn his head. I waved my arms about and even from such a distance I could see his body stiffen, sensing danger. I must have looked crazy, though I didn't think about that then. When I caught up with him he waited for me to get my breath back as I rested my hands on my knees. His face under his old-fashioned cloth cap was watchful.

'My little girl. I can't find her,' I managed to say after a minute.

He took his cap off and smoothed his hair. 'The one with red legs?'

'Yes, yes – the little girl with red tights.'

We set off towards the maze. He switched on his torch to show the way.

'People don't just go into mazes and never come out,' he said reasonably.

'Has anyone else been here today?' I asked. My throat closed up waiting for his answer.

'No. At least, there was a couple here this morning. But they'd gone by the time you arrived.'

'Are you sure? Are you sure?'

He stopped and turned. 'I'm sure. Don't worry, we'll find her. I know this maze like the back of my hand.' I felt so grateful then to be with this man who had the plan of the puzzle imprinted on him.

As we approached the maze he switched his torch off. We didn't need it any more. A big moon had risen and lit up the place like a floodlight at a football match. We went in through the arched entrance cut into the woven trees. In the moonlight the foliage and the red berries had turned to black.

'What's the little girl's name again? Karen?'

'No, no. Carmel.'

'Carmel.' His voice boomed out.

We walked fast, shouting all the way. He turned the torch back on and pointed it under the hedges. There were rustlings around us and once he pointed the light straight into the eyes of a rabbit that froze for a moment before bolting across our path. I could tell he was working through the maze methodically from the plan.

'I think we should call the police,' I said, after about twenty minutes. I was becoming frantic again.

'Maybe. We're nearly at the centre now though.'

We turned another corner and there she was, in the crook of the hedge. The torchlight flashed over her red legs poking out from underneath the black wall. I put both hands into the gap and dragged her out. Her body felt pliant and warm and I could tell at once she was asleep. I lifted her into my lap and rocked her back and forth and kept saying to the man smiling down at us, 'Thank you. Thank you. Thank you. Thank you.' I smiled back at him and held her lovely solid warmth.

How many times I was back in that place that night. Even after we were home and safely tucked into bed, I kept dreaming I was there again. Walking round and round in circles and looking. Sometimes the rabbit bolted away – but sometimes it stopped right in the middle of the path and stared at me, its nose twitching.